P9-EMH-452

# INCORRUPTIBLE

*By Barbara Nadel*

*The Inspector İkmen Series*
Belshazzar's Daughter
A Chemical Prison
Arabesk
Deep Waters
Harem
Petrified
Deadly Web
Dance with Death
A Passion for Killing
Pretty Dead Things
River of the Dead
Death by Design
A Noble Killing
Dead of Night
Deadline
Body Count
Land of the Blind
On the Bone
The House of Four
Incorruptible

*The Hancock Series*
Last Rights
After the Mourning
Ashes to Ashes
Sure and Certain Death

*The Hakim and Arnold Series*
A Private Business
An Act of Kindness
Poisoned Ground
Enough Rope
Bright Shiny Things

# BARBARA NADEL

# INCORRUPTIBLE

HEADLINE

Copyright © 2018 Barbara Nadel

The right of Barbara Nadel to be identified as the Author of
the Work has been asserted by her in accordance with the
Copyright, Designs and Patents Act 1988.

First published in Great Britain in 2018 by
HEADLINE PUBLISHING GROUP

1

Apart from any use permitted under UK copyright law, this
publication may only be reproduced, stored, or transmitted, in
any form, or by any means, with prior permission in writing of
the publishers or, in the case of reprographic production, in
accordance with the terms of licences issued by the
Copyright Licensing Agency.

All characters in this publication are fictitious
and any resemblance to real persons, living or dead,
is purely coincidental.

Cataloguing in Publication Data is available from the British Library

ISBN 978 1 4722 3467 4 (Hardback)
ISBN 978 1 4722 3468 1 (Trade Paperback)

Typeset in Times New Roman by Palimpsest Book Production Limited,
Falkirk, Stirlingshire

Printed and bound by CPI Group (UK) Ltd, Croydon CR0 4YY

Headline's policy is to use papers that are natural, renewable and recyclable products
and made from wood grown in well-managed forests and other controlled sources.
The logging and manufacturing processes are expected to conform to the
environmental regulations of the country of origin.

HEADLINE PUBLISHING GROUP
An Hachette UK Company
Carmelite House
50 Victoria Embankment
London EC4Y 0DZ

www.headline.co.uk
www.hachette.co.uk

To Pat, Ruth, Jeyda, Earl, Virginia, Senay,
Sirma, Elsie and Lutfu.

# Cast List

---

**Inspector Çetin İkmen** – late-middle-aged Istanbul detective

**Inspector Mehmet Süleyman** – forty-something Istanbul detective, İkmen's protégé

**Sergeant Kerim Gürsel** – İkmen's sergeant

**Sergeant Omer Mungun** – Süleyman's sergeant

**Commissioner Hürrem Teker** – İkmen and Süleyman's superior

**Melis Bila** – Commissioner Teker's secretary

**Dr Arto Sarkissian** – police pathologist, an ethnic Armenian

**Technical Officer Turgut Zana** – electronics expert, an ethnic Kurd

**Sergeant Yıldız** – middle-aged uniformed officer

**Acting Commissioner Selahattin Ozer** – senior officer from Anatolia


*Other characters:*

**Fatma İkmen** – Çetin's wife

**Gonca Şekeroğlu** – Süleyman's mistress, a gypsy

**Sinem Gürsel** – Kerim Gürsel's wife

**Pembe** – Kerim Gürsel's lover, a transsexual

**Sheikh Abdullah** – Commissioner Teker's cousin

**Peri Mungun** – Omer's sister, a nurse

**Asra** – the Munguns' neighbour

**Silvio de Mango** – a Levantine translator

**Ayşegül de Mango** – Silvio's Muslim wife

**Maryam de Mango** – Silvio and Ayşegül's elder daughter

**İbrahim de Mango** – Silvio and Ayşegül's elder son

**Mevlüt de Mango** – Silvio and Ayşegül's younger son

**Sara de Mango** – Silvio and Ayşegül's younger daughter

**Angelo de Mango** – Silvio's brother

**Francesca de Mango** – Angelo de Mango's wife

**Fabrizio Leon** – a Levantine, Silvio's best friend

**Lobna Amara** – a Levantine, Fabrizio's ex-wife

**Mina Amara** – Lobna's sister

**İrini Mavroyeni** – a prostitute, an ethnic Greek

**Yiannis Livadanios** – an undertaker, an ethnic Greek

**Father Mesrob Kalajian** – an Armenian priest

**Dr Rizzi** – Italian oncologist

**Bishop Juan-Maria Montoya** – Catholic Bishop of Istanbul, a Mexican

**Father Benito Esposito** – priest at the Church of St Anthony of Padua

**Father Colombo** – priest at the Church of St Anthony of Padua

**Father da Mosto** – priest at the Church of St Anthony of Padua

**Father Marek Wojtulewicz** – priest at the Church of St Anthony of Padua

**Katerina Marmara** – housekeeper to the priests of the Church of St Anthony of Padua

**Büket Teyze** – a fortune-teller

**Sevgin Balcı** – cemetery caretaker's wife

**Mr Demirköz** – a lawyer

**Sultan al-Khoury** – a Syrian refugee

**Layal al-Khoury** – Sultan's elder daughter

**Nour al-Khoury** – Sultan's younger daughter

**Kemal Öneş** – a barber

**Erdal Çelik** – a protester

**Burhan** – a gypsy coffee shop owner

**Erol Hasefe** – a fundamentalist

**Ata Goner** – grave robber

# Chapter 1

If it hadn't been for the blood, he would have thought she was asleep. She was smiling. The contents of her abdomen lay beside her amongst the tea leaves and the cigarette butts on the ground, and she was smiling.

There weren't many places that Inspector Çetin İkmen could go to drink coffee and smoke in peace these days, but Burhan the gypsy's coffee house was one of them. In the ancient Roma quarter of Sulukule, Burhan's was one of the few traditional businesses that remained. Pressed tight up against the Byzantine walls of what had once been Constantinople, the gypsy's tiny business struggled on in spite of the mass construction of new houses that had mushroomed around it. That so many of the new properties were either empty or being rented by refugees with money from Syria made İkmen angry. In a city whose population had grown from two to fourteen million in thirty years, people needed housing more desperately than ever. But much of what had been built in Sulukule was so expensive, nobody wanted to move in. And the gypsies whose hand-built homes had been demolished to make way for the new development were too poor to even consider returning. Rehoused in flats many kilometres from the city, they mourned the demise of their old way of life in silence.

And now, here in Sulukule, death had come.

İkmen, a weary, skinny individual in his late fifties, had been policing the city of İstanbul all his adult life. A product of the heyday of Atatürk's secular republic, he'd watched his country change over the years, sometimes with delight, sometimes with dismay. That morning he'd felt in need of comfort, which to İkmen meant things he remembered from his youth – like run-down coffee joints, too many cigarettes and gossipy old gypsies like Burhan Bey.

As soon as he'd arrived, the gypsy had buttonholed him.

'Ah, Çetin Bey,' he'd said. 'Before you sit and relax, could you call the municipality for me? We are alive with rats. Going out to the dustbins, you take your life in your hands. I have complained and complained but no one listens. They'll listen to you. Will you—'

'I'll go out and have a look,' İkmen said.

'No! It's bad out there. Don't—'

But İkmen had ignored him. In the past, officials including police officers had been able to phone up local-authority offices and get problems dealt with. But not any more. Now municipalities wanted detailed descriptions of evidence, including photographs. He lit a cigarette and went outside to look for droppings and teeth marks.

A proud late adopter of iPhone technology, İkmen had spent a long time learning how to use his phone as a camera. But now that he could do it, he did it all the time. Photographs of grandchildren vied for space on his device with pictures of victims of assault.

Half-chewed bread crusts and what looked like large grains of brown rice had given the game away immediately. Rat droppings were so distinctive. But he went and looked behind the dustbins anyway, in case he could actually see a rat. What he found was the girl, eviscerated, coloured russet from the chest down by her own dried blood. What was that smile? Rigor? It looked serene. How could that be? Unless she'd been drugged when she died. But then her face would have sagged . . .

2

She was young, but he had seen younger. And although every-body he'd ever seen in his long years in homicide had shocked Çetin İkmen, there was a side to this girl's death that made him physically shudder.

That was because as soon as he'd seen her, he'd recognised her. And having recognised her, he marvelled at how long it had taken her to turn up dead.

'I hate her.'

'Hate is a very strong word, Silvio.'

The smoke-dried middle-aged man looked up into the priest's eyes.

'What do you know?' he said.

'About women? Not much. But I know a lot about hate. Mainly I know that it leads nowhere. I also know that we have more than enough of it in this part of the world.'

Silvio shook his head. 'She tries to make our daughter eat out of the bowl for the cat.'

'That's wrong. If it's true. Have you seen her do it?'

'No, but the girl has told me, and why would she lie? The woman is a bigot, and more seriously, she makes our other children bigots too,' Silvio said.

This wasn't the first time that Father Benito Esposito had been obliged to listen to parishioner Silvio de Mango ranting about his wife. According to Father Esposito's predecessor, Father Luigi Rossi, there had been trouble between the pair for years. But in the past few months it had escalated, which was under-standable in light of what was happening to the family.

'Whenever I leave the house, I fear I will come back and find my daughter dead,' Silvio continued.

'I think you may be overreacting . . .'

'You think?' He moved his head close to the priest's. 'You've only lived in this country for five years. You've no

3

idea what they're like. I grew up with their intolerance, their ignorance, and I've watched it grow. My in-laws are amongst the worst . . .'

The heavy front door of the Church of St Anthony of Padua creaked open. Two men, both tall and smartly dressed, walked in. Their confidence, combined with the fact that neither man crossed himself, made the priest nervous. They could be officials. After apologising to his parishioner, he stood and walked over to them.

'Can I help you?'

Mass in English was due to start in less than an hour, so the church was already bright with candles and, because it was April, heavily decorated with fresh spring tulips. Father Benito prayed that the two Turks hadn't come to tell him that the place had to close because of terrorist threats.

The taller and older of the two held up what Benito recognised as police ID.

'My name is Inspector Mehmet Süleyman,' he said. 'I'm looking for Father Benito Esposito.'

The priest bowed his head. 'You have found him. What can I do for you, Inspector?'

'I've been told by the wife of one of your parishioners that you may be with her husband.'

'Who?' Benito looked across at Silvio, who was praying.

'Silvio de Mango,' the police officer said.

Silvio, hearing his name, looked up. 'What?'

Süleyman and the other officer ignored Benito and walked towards the white-faced man.

'Silvio de Mango?'

'Yes . . .'

'My name is Inspector Süleyman,' the policeman said. 'We've just come from your apartment; we need to speak to you.'

'What about?'

4

They sat one each side of him, Süleyman and the other officer. Silvio was fragile; Benito wanted to intervene. How did he do that without giving offence?

But the policeman didn't even manage to open his mouth before Silvio put his head in his hands and wailed.

'Oh my God!' he said. 'It's about her, isn't it? You've come to tell me those bastards have killed her!'

It was said that the girl hadn't named whatever it was she saw in front of the Golden Gate of the Byzantines one frosty morning the previous December. As a newsworthy item, Maryam de Mango had long disappeared. Since her apparent recovery from leukaemia during a service known as the Night of the Miracle at the tiny Armenian Church of the Assumption in Fener the previous August, the sensation that had grown up around her had abated. In part this was because of the Turkish general election on 1 November, which had been won, in storming style, by the ruling AK Parti. Nobody cared about a girl who had apparently beaten leukaemia, even if she had done so due to divine intervention. But then the following January, rumours about an İstanbul girl and her mysterious visions began to emerge.

They came just after a terrorist attack on tourists in Sultanahmet Square. It was said that what the girl saw was the Virgin Mary. Not that she ever referred to the one she called 'the mother' in that way herself. Others did, but Maryam de Mango, apparent cancer survivor and now mystic, did not. All she said was that 'the mother' had come to earth to warn mankind that if it carried on the way it was going, disaster would follow. Throughout January, February and March, Maryam relayed messages from 'the mother' to ever-increasing crowds in front of the Golden Gate.

Harangued by this entity for their greed, their cruelty, their environmental crimes and their unthinking hatred, particularly towards women, people in the crowd were frequently reduced to tears. And in spite of official disapproval of what was seen as at best a craze and at worst blasphemy, print and Internet media became interested. Within three months, Maryam de Mango was as famous as she had been back in August. It was not something everybody liked.

'Most of the threats came from Islamist militants who said they'd either rape her and then behead her or vice versa,' İkmen told the police pathologist, Dr Arto Sarkissian, when he arrived at the crime scene in Sulukule.

Sarkissian, a portly middle-aged ethnic Armenian, just shrugged. Such extreme language was not unusual. Like his friend Çetin İkmen, he hardly felt shocked any more.

'Seeing an apparition is blasphemy now, is it?'

'I imagine so,' İkmen said. 'Just about everything else is to people of that mindset.'

'God help us!'

'If only I believed in Him, I'd second that,' İkmen said.

They walked into the tent that had been erected over the body. After he had secured the scene and then waited for the pathologist to attend, İkmen had found himself staring at Maryam de Mango's corpse. He'd noticed she had tulips threaded into her hair. He'd seen her in person at the Golden Gate on a few occasions and many times on TV, but he'd never noticed whether she wore anything in her hair. Maybe she always dressed it with flowers? He'd been too focused on the rapt expression that settled on her face every time she saw 'the mother'. It was similar to the expression on her dead face now.

The pathologist raised his eyebrows.

'Eviscerated.'

'Yes,' İkmen said. 'Given the amount of blood, I imagine she was still alive.'

'Possibly, possibly not.' Sarkissian shook his head. 'Poor child. Obviously delusional . . .'

6

'You think?'

'Just because I'm a Christian doesn't mean I'm not also rational. Even the Vatican is sceptical about things like visions, especially Marian visions. If you notice, nobody from the Holy See has been to any of the sightings, even though the girl is a Christian.'

'She isn't,' İkmen said.

The pathologist crouched down to look closely at the body.

'I thought she was.'

'No, her father is, but not her mother. Maryam de Mango was raised as a Muslim. Hence the ferocity of the threats against her. My understanding is that she went to the Church of the Assumption in Fener for the cure like lots of sick people, Christian, Jewish and Muslim. You know how it is.'

Sarkissian did. The Armenian Church of the Assumption was famous for its once-a-year miracle on the night of the nearest Sunday to 15 August. Every year, without fail, someone was apparently cured.

He frowned. 'I wonder what this smile on her face is about.'

'Rigor?'

'Possibly.'

İkmen said, 'She looks like she did when she saw her visions. In my opinion.'

Arto gave him a sceptical glance. 'No apparent defence wounds,' he said. Then he looked at her hair and murmured, 'Flowers.'

The flap of the tent opened and İkmen's sergeant, Kerim Gürsel, walked in.

'Inspector, I think you ought to know there's a rumour about the identity of the corpse,' he said.

'Accurate?'

'Yes. We're picking up reports about people piling into trams to get here. It's said both pro and anti the girl. They're just yelling at the moment . . .'

7

İkmen grimaced. 'And so the Christian bigots and the Muslim bigots unite in violence,' he said. 'I wonder if any of them realise how tiresome that is for the rest of us?' He looked at the doctor. 'I'd better get out there and leave you to it.'

He left the tent. He could hear raised voices in the distance, but he couldn't make out what they were chanting. Burhan the gypsy sat grey-faced at a table outside the back door of his coffee house, looking hopelessly at the police officers milling about around him. İkmen offered him a cigarette.

Once he'd lit up, the gypsy said, 'You know, Çetin Bey, I was going to take my niece Hatice to see the miracle girl.'

İkmen knew Burhan's niece. Now twenty, she'd been brain-damaged at birth. All she'd ever been able to do was lie down and, just occasionally, smile. Burhan and his family had taken her to every neurologist in İstanbul. When that failed, they'd tried the Church of the Assumption in Fener, then Lourdes. Now it seemed they'd been about to take her to visit Maryam de Mango in front of the Golden Gate.

İkmen put a hand on Burhan's shoulder. 'Take her somewhere beautiful, outside the city,' he said. Then, as the voices in the surrounding streets grew louder, he added, 'Get her away from this hellhole.'

# Chapter 2

That girl had said such things! He could feel his blood pressure going up just thinking about it. Or rather he imagined that was what was happening. Whenever he got angry he felt as if he was about to explode. That was blood pressure, wasn't it? Not that it mattered; with his brother and his brother-in-law at his side, and hundreds of other enraged men both behind and in front of him, Erdal felt powerful. It was said that the girl was dead, which meant God had punished her for her blasphemy. Now all that remained to do was to obliterate her filthy corpse. Some said she should be burnt, which had initially made Erdal cringe. But he was, by his own admission, a simple man, uneducated in the ways of the world and, shamefully, of God. Greater minds than his had decided that burning was permissible. Who was he to argue?

As he marched along Vatan Caddesi towards Sulukule, Erdal's righteous indignation increased as he wondered what the girl had been doing in a place that until very recently had been the haunt of gypsies. They were well known for their licentious lifestyles – or so he'd heard. Did that mean that the girl, far from being a saint, had been a whore? A moment's reflection convinced him that this was so. It also took his mind off the picture that would not leave his brain, of himself attending one of her 'visions' back when all this had first started. Everyone knew that the girl had been cured of cancer when she'd gone to the Church of the Assumption. But when she started having visions in front of the Golden Gate, did that mean she could in turn cure others? Erdal had hoped so. Unbeknown to anyone except his wife, Erdal hadn't been able to perform sexually for over a year. If the girl could cure him of that . . .

The girl had had her vision and Erdal had gone home full of hope. But nothing had happened. That, if nothing else, proved she was a fraud.

Word was that the police wouldn't stop them. Unlike the old days, when the secular military had been in charge, the authorities were on their side now. His brother-in-law had a brother in the police and he was sure they'd meet no resistance. However, there were rumours about others on the march to the site. Christians and secularists. The same scumbags who had taken over Gezi Park in 2013. Thousands of them were coming out, so Kemal the barber had said. Just thinking about it made Erdal reach shakily for the pistol in his jacket pocket.

They were coming from nearby conservative neighbourhoods like Çarşamba as well as more distant enclaves such as Kasimpaşa on the opposite side of the Golden Horn.

'They've some notion they want to destroy the girl's corpse,' İkmen said into his phone.

His superior, Commissioner Hürrem Teker, replied, 'Which is where?'

'Being loaded into an unmarked van for transportation to the path lab,' İkmen said. 'I've got to protect it. What else can I do? What I can't understand is why no one is stopping these so-called protesters. Can't you do something?'

He heard her sigh. He knew what that meant. Why had he even asked the question? Attempting to control 'righteous' mobs was becoming impossible. One got no support. He lowered his voice. 'I'll have to deal with them when they get here.'

'Make sure that van gets away with Dr Sarkissian in it,' she said.

'Already done,' İkmen said and ended the call.

He nodded to the van driver, who put his foot down. İkmen, his sergeant at his side, rallied his troops.

'Right,' he said, 'we've got protesters headed our way. Their intention, so I've been told, is to take charge of our victim's corpse and burn it. This is why I've had it moved rather more quickly than I would do normally. This, however, leaves us with a crime scene to secure. Forensic officers are due on site any minute. What I don't want is a load of incensed protesters smashing the place up and destroying vital evidence. Clear?'

He knew which of his officers had sympathy with these people. They had increased in number in the past year. But now it seemed he'd missed one.

He put a hand on the young man's wrist. 'Give me the phone, Constable,' he said.

Constable Erol was an eager new recruit who hung on İkmen's every word. Or rather, he had done. The inspector felt Erol's hand shake as he handed over the iPhone. He'd been mid-text.

İkmen put the phone in his pocket without looking at it. 'We'll talk about this later.' Then, addressing his officers en masse, he said, 'Anyone not prepared to defend this crime scene and therefore fulfil his obligation as a Turkish police officer can go now.'

He and Kerim Gürsel scanned their squad. Nobody moved. But there was a feeling of unease that bred a tension and a fear neither of them had experienced before. İkmen, who until very recently had rarely been armed, put his hand under his jacket and touched his pistol.

'Bitch! Vile, filthy daughter of a whore!'

It took both Süleyman and his sergeant, Omer Mungun, to hold Silvio de Mango down. As soon as they'd reached the family's apartment in Galata, he'd launched himself at his wife, scratching her face and even getting a blow in to her stomach.

11

'She killed my daughter!'

Pinioning de Mango to a chair, Süleyman yelled, 'Be quiet!'

The woman, Ayşegül de Mango, was crying and clutching her stomach. A teenage girl sat in a corner of the dark room with two young men. The girl cried, while the boys just stared at de Mango.

'You have both lost a child,' Süleyman said.

'She doesn't care!'

'I do!'

'No you don't!'

'Shut up! Shut up! Shut up!' The teenage girl put her hands over her ears and closed her eyes as she screamed. 'Shut up! You are killing me!'

No one went to her, but the room became momentarily silent. These three young people were the de Mangos' other children, Maryam's siblings.

According to de Mango, his wife had hated Maryam because of her apparent adherence to Christianity. Amongst the crimes she had committed against her daughter were making Maryam eat from the cat's bowl, beating her with a leather belt, pinning her headscarf to her flesh and telling her that as an apostate she deserved to die. However, by his own admission, only the verbal abuse could be ratified by de Mango himself. And although he claimed to have seen the results of the beating and the headscarf pinning, he had not seen his wife touch his daughter. Nor, it seemed, had any other member of the family.

Breathing deeply to calm his anger, de Mango said to his wife, 'You never loved her. She looked far too much like my mother for you. You always accused her of being too interested in me and my world. I didn't make you marry me. If you're such a good Muslim, why didn't you marry one of them?'

Her eyes took on a glint that made Süleyman's blood stand still in his veins. '*You* say that to *me*,' she growled.

12

De Mango looked away. White-faced now, his whole body shook.

'You think I don't mourn for our daughter?' Ayşegül said. She put her hands over her face and sobbed. 'My beautiful Maryam!'

The teenage girl got up and ran to her mother, but Ayşegül de Mango turned away. The young men continued to sit, silent and impassive.

'My wife turned our other children against Maryam,' de Mango continued. 'Ask them!'

The taller boy murmured, 'No she didn't.'

His father pointed at him. 'He lies too,' he said. 'They all lie.' He looked Süleyman up and down and shook his head. 'But then you'll believe them because you're one of them, won't you?'

Suddenly the girl turned on her father. 'We don't lie, Papa!' she said. 'You know we don't lie. But you know who does. Or did.'

They'd known the exact location. İkmen tried to look into Constable Erol's eyes, but the young man shifted his gaze.

They were surrounded. Angry eyes, many of them young, looked at İkmen, especially, with hatred. And Kerim Gürsel, for reasons of his own, looked back at them with equal venom. İkmen knew that he, as senior officer, had to speak.

'This is a crime scene,' he said. 'I'd be lying if I said I don't know why you're here. I do. And I don't approve.'

Many of the men in the crowd, and there were only men, began to murmur their own disapproval.

'You think we have the body of a person you consider an apostate here. Well, we don't,' İkmen continued. 'We have a crime scene that is none of your business.'

'Then show it to us!' someone shouted.

İkmen could have acceded to this. There was, after all, nothing to see now that the body had been moved. And some of his officers were clearly troubled by the position they found themselves in, effectively opposing men with whom they agreed. But the inspector objected to being told what to do by a mob.

'It's nothing to do with you,' he said. 'Go home.'

'We'll only go home when you show us that the whore's body isn't here!'

Had whoever had spoken not used the word 'whore', would İkmen have responded differently?

He said, 'If you're going to show such lack of respect to a person who has recently died, then no.'

A small man at the front of the crowd drew his gun. He was clearly nervous, and the weapon shook in his hands.

'Put that down.'

Kerim pointed his own gun confidently, unlike the small, shivering man. Where he couldn't match him, however, was in the look of determination on his face.

'Put it down, or I'll arrest you – if you're lucky,' the sergeant said.

İkmen could see that his officer had no backup. None of the uniformed officers had drawn their guns. In a way, that was a good thing, because it meant that there probably wouldn't be a bloodbath. But it was bad because it looked weak. And so İkmen too drew his pistol.

The de Mangos' apartment was in one of the large old Galata mansion blocks dating from the late nineteenth century. At one time the majority of the residents had been, like Silvio de Mango, Levantines, descendants of Italian, French and British merchants. Based in the lands conquered by the Ottoman Turks, the Levantines were generally astute businesspeople who had enjoyed their privileged position within Ottoman imperial society. But with the coming of the Republic, their power had waned, and many had left Turkey in the twentieth century. Those that remained, now Turkish citizens, defined their heritage mainly via their religion, which in de Mango's case was Roman Catholicism. Inspector Mehmet Süleyman, a scion of the Turkish imperial family, had grown up with tales of his ancestors' Levantine bankers.

'Are you implying that Maryam lied?' he asked the girl.

Worn out by grief and shock, the family were now, at last, quiet. Both parents held their heads in their hands, their young sons sitting motionless in the thick darkness of a heavily upholstered room that appeared to rarely see the sun.

The girl, who was called Sara, said, 'Sometimes.'

Unlike her sister, whom Süleyman had seen on television, she was a small, apparently shy creature.

'What did she lie about?'

The girl turned away.

This was not a family that had been at ease with itself before Maryam died. There was no point digging any further at this time. Süleyman had, after all, only come to inform them about the girl's death.

He said, 'At the moment, we don't know when Maryam died or indeed how.' On the face of it she'd been attacked with a knife, but that had yet to be unequivocally established.

'But she was murdered?' de Mango said.

'Unlawfully killed.'

He shook his head. 'Someone took her life.'

'We think so, yes.'

The silence washed in again. Süleyman looked at Ayşegül de Mango and wondered how a woman like her, covered, pious, had even met a person like de Mango. Some Levantines had married Turks in recent years, but generally their partners were secular, middle-class people – White Turks, as they were known. With her veiled head, her rough unmanicured hands and her alleged intolerance, Ayşegül de Mango was, Süleyman imagined, a migrant to the city from a very traditional place in Anatolia.

Silvio de Mango began to cry. Neither his children nor his wife attempted to comfort him.

Süleyman looked at his sergeant, Omer Mungun, who shrugged. Where he was from, the city of Mardin on the Syrian border, people came together when death knocked on their doors. But then in Mardin, in recent years, that had happened often.

Süleyman said, 'We will need someone to come and formally identify the body.'

Without hesitation, Ayşegül de Mango said, 'I will.'

'Thank you. I will also need to see your daughter's room.'

'Of course.'

Sergeant Kerim Gürsel cuffed the man and then pushed him into the Transit van that would take him to police headquarters. İkmen examined the man's weapon. It was an old CZ75, probably a service weapon that had belonged to Mr Erdal Çelik's father or some other older relative.

Çelik would never have fired. Just after he'd pulled out his weapon, he'd almost fainted. But then he hadn't been the problem. Having no apparent support from his uniformed team had been a far greater risk to İkmen's existence than the fumbling actions of a hysterical man from Çarşamba district. They'd finally drawn their weapons at the last possible second. Only then had the crowd moved back. Now that the forensic team had arrived on site and proper barriers had been erected, all was quiet again. The crowd, when it did finally leave, disappeared utterly.

'Tea.'

Burhan the gypsy put two glasses down on the low wall that enclosed the dustbins.

İkmen smiled. 'Thank you, Burhan Bey.'

'You boys have had a rough few hours,' the gypsy said. 'I saw it all from my place, you know. You should have words with those kids you've got working with you. When that lunatic pointed his gun at you, I thought I'd have to shoot him myself. They weren't going to!'

Kerim Gürsel said, 'I had Çetin Bey covered, Burhan Bey.'

'*You* did, yes,' he said. 'But then you're not some stupid kid.'

He walked back into his coffee house.

İkmen said nothing.

'Sir, I've put Sergeant Yıldız in charge of securing the scene for the time being,' Kerim said.

İkmen drank some tea. 'Thank you, Kerim.'

Sergeant Yıldız was one of the few uniformed officers İkmen actually knew. Since the force had been purged of those apparently supportive of what the government had described as a 'coup' in 2013, a lot of familiar faces had gone. Many of those who had replaced them had little experience and what İkmen felt were dubious standards. Yıldız was not one of those, and Kerim Gürsel knew it.

'And thank you for supporting me, Kerim.'

He shook his head. 'It's my job, Çetin Bey, and also my pleasure.'

İkmen smiled and lit up a cigarette.

'Sir, are you going to report what happened here today to the Commissioner?' Kerim asked.

İkmen didn't want to intimidate the new uniformed cohort. They were young and probably frightened working in a city that was, month by month, becoming ever more troubled. Confused by often unintelligible rhetoric on something called 'social media' – which İkmen didn't understand – the kids didn't know what to be. How did one become a good officer? Be a good Muslim? Be liberal and have a laugh? All at the same time?

İkmen didn't know. He just was.

'We'll have a conversation,' he said after a pause. 'She will need to know why, for instance, Mr Çelik is in custody. But our main job now, Kerim, is to find out who killed Maryam de Mango, and why.'

17

# Chapter 3

İkmen turned the iPhone over in his hands. 'You attempted to text your mother.'

'Yes, sir.' Constable Erol stood in front of İkmen's chaotic desk, eyes front.

'When you should have had your full attention on your job.'

'She worries,' the young man said. 'I try to tell her where I am. I haven't got any brothers.'

The text had indeed been intended for Mrs Selin Erol, who, İkmen had discovered, presided over a family consisting of three daughters and this very young son. But that was all he knew about the family. Maybe Mrs Erol, or those around her, had interests that extended beyond the safety of her son? Or perhaps she was just a traditional little housewife desperately afraid for her boy on the violent streets of İstanbul?

'As you heard me tell your colleagues after the incident with the armed man, I have to be able to trust those who work for me,' İkmen continued. 'Each one of us has to have the other's back. Do you understand?'

'Yes, sir.'

'Trust is vital. If I can't trust you, I have no need of you.'

'No, sir.'

'While we are on duty, we are required to become different people,' İkmen said. 'We are dispensers of justice, that is all. We have no preferences, no beliefs, no prejudices. Facts are our only masters. Do you understand?'

'Yes, sir.'

'I am afraid I don't care whether your mother is worried or not.'

The boy looked stunned.

'Just like I hope you don't in turn concern yourself with the anxieties experienced by my wife. I don't expect you to. Personal issues are just that, personal. They are not to be brought to work.'

'Yes, but my mother—'

'Your mother will have to accept that when you are at work, you are uncontactable,' İkmen said. 'Just be grateful that I'm not taking this matter further. I will give you the benefit of the doubt in this instance. But if you do anything like it again, I will recommend that you be formally disciplined. If neither you nor your mother can accept this, then I suggest you seek employment elsewhere. Give it some thought.' He waved a hand. 'Now go.'

The young man left.

İkmen turned to his sergeant. 'Kids,' he said.

Kerim Gürsel, who was in his early forties, shook his head. A lot of the new officers were very young. Probably too young. He changed the subject. 'Dr Sarkissian has just emailed to say he has scheduled the autopsy on Maryam de Mango for tomorrow morning at ten. He wants to know if you'll be attending.'

'Tell him yes,' İkmen said. He locked his office door, opened his window and lit a cigarette. In half an hour, he and his colleague and protégé Mehmet Süleyman had a meeting with their superior, Commissioner Teker, about the Maryam de Mango murder. Almost always in İkmen's corner, Teker would nevertheless be acutely aware of the sensitivities surrounding the de Mango case.

A Muslim girl in a mainly Muslim city had seen visions of a 'mother' some claimed was the Virgin Mary in a very emotive part of town.

Then someone had killed her.

\*　\*　\*

19

He was thirsty – again. They'd only given him another jug of water an hour ago and he was already parched. It wasn't even hot. What was wrong with him?

Before he'd been taken to police headquarters, Erdal Çelik had seen a doctor. Apparently his blood pressure hadn't been that high and the doctor had put his dizziness down to stress. But this thirst thing was a nightmare. He'd had it, on and off, for months. But now it was severe. Now he felt as if his mouth was full of sand.

Erdal sat on the bare wooden bench in his cell. The police had taken the CZ75, so he'd be in hot water with Deniz and his dad. The old man had given his eldest son his old service weapon when Deniz had gone to work in Diyarbakir. He'd said he'd need it because of the Kurds. Deniz hadn't. But when Erdal had asked to borrow it in case the supporters of that apostate girl got out of hand, his brother had given it to him. Not that Erdal had seen any of the girl's supporters on his way to or in Sulukule. All he'd found was the police, who hadn't, contrary to what his brother-in-law had said, helped the crowd to take possession of the girl's body at all. And now he was in trouble.

It was all right for his brothers and his in-laws, they were big men. But Erdal had always had to prove himself. The incident with his father's gun was just the latest manifestation.

What was he going to say when the police finally questioned him? He couldn't think. Similar things had always happened to him. Sometimes he couldn't remember them very well. Fights in the street, the time he hit Kemal the barber because he offered to give him a 'boy's' haircut . . . Why couldn't he have been big like Deniz? And why had he let that policeman just take the CZ75 without putting up a fight? If and when he got back home, everyone was going to laugh at him.

'Maryam de Mango, twenty-seven years old, was the eldest child of Silvio and Ayşegül de Mango.' Süleyman read from the notes he'd taken when he'd finally managed to get Silvio de Mango to speak to him calmly. 'They have three other children: İbrahim, twenty-five, Mevlüt, twenty, and eighteen-year-old Sara.'

There had been no decision taken to appoint two senior officers to the de Mango investigation. Süleyman and his sergeant, Omer Mungun, had volunteered to contact the victim's family when İkmen had called the incident in.

'The family's apartment, which is owned by Silvio de Mango, fifty, is situated in Büyük Hendek Caddesi in Galata. As a member of a Levantine trading family who came to this country in the eighteenth century, Silvio is apparently the first de Mango to marry outside of his Levantine heritage. His stated religion, like many Levantines, is Roman Catholicism. His wife, Ayşegül, who is fifty-five, is a Muslim Turk who was born and brought up in Fatih. It was Ayşegül de Mango who formally identified the body. With the parents' permission I removed Maryam's laptop computer and her iPhone from her bedroom.'

'The girl wasn't carrying her phone?'

'No, madam,' Süleyman said. 'It seems that she left home in a hurry.'

'Anyone under thirty is generally welded to at least one mobile phone.' Commissioner Hürrem Teker crossed her long, slim legs. 'When did Maryam get sick?'

'She first consulted a doctor in December 2014,' Süleyman said. 'According to the family, she was formally diagnosed with leukaemia at the Italian Hospital in Tophane the following March. As you know, she was supposedly cured of this condition in August 2015.'

'What did you make of the family?' İkmen asked.

'Troubled.'

'In what way?'

'There seems to have been a split,' Süleyman said. 'Between Maryam and her father on one side and Ayşegül and the rest of

21

the children on the other. Although all the children were brought up in their mother's faith, there is a belief, real or imagined, that Maryam had converted or transferred her devotion to Roman Catholicism. Each side accused the other of abuse, of lying . . .'

'What about the scene?' Teker asked.

'I found her at ten fifteen this morning behind the dustbins at the back of Burhan's Coffee House on Sulukule Caddesi,' İkmen said. 'It's one of the last Roma-owned premises in the area. I've known the owner for years.'

'Why were you there?'

'I was not due on my shift until midday. I like it up there. Burhan is a friend. He makes good coffee, we like to smoke together and sometimes I pick up useful information.'

'Is he one of your informants?' Teker asked.

'Not officially, but he's a good man to know in that part of the city,' İkmen said. 'He knows people both inside and outside the law. Like me, he had been up to the Golden Gate a few times to see Maryam de Mango. He's got a disabled niece. He was thinking about taking her when . . .' He shrugged.

'Evidence?'

'The body itself, detritus around the body, which has gone to the forensic laboratory,' he said. 'The scene has been secured. Dr Sarkissian has given us an estimated time of death; hopefully he will be able to be more accurate about it when he has completed his autopsy on the body tomorrow.'

'What time does he estimate?'

'Between ten p.m. and two a.m.'

She nodded.

'I've put out a call for witnesses, and house-to-house is being coordinated by Sergeants Yıldız and Çağlar. Both old hands, and Çağlar is local. Although not all properties in that area are currently inhabited, madam. We're looking at a considerable number of empty new-builds and some properties rented out to Syrian refugees.'

'Syrians are in the area?'

'Yes.'

'Mmm. Murder weapon?'

'Not yet,' İkmen said. 'The girl was eviscerated. Quite what was exposed we will find out tomorrow. Unfortunately Dr Sarkissian was unable to make a proper preliminary examination of the corpse *in situ* because of a risk from demonstrators.'

'Yes,' she said. 'I heard about that. Do you have any idea how they found out about Maryam de Mango's death? Your friend Burhan?'

İkmen shrugged. 'I can't be certain but I don't think Burhan would . . .' He shrugged again. 'He had no customers,' he said. 'He'd asked me to go out the back of his place to look at the rats that have been plaguing him for weeks. He wanted me to call the municipality for him. So I went out, found rat droppings and the girl. I then went back into the café to tell him to close up. The corpse was on its own for two minutes, maybe five at a stretch . . .'

Had anyone else been around when he'd found the body? Not that he could remember. But then even for someone like İkmen, the discovery of a dead body was a shocking event that would have disorientated him somewhat. Perhaps the news had been disseminated after he'd called it in. By one of his colleagues . . .

Teker, as if reading his thoughts, said, 'You had some problems with your team, Çetin Bey.'

It was a statement rather than a question. Had Kerim told her?

'No, no,' he said. 'A member of this mob who turned up to destroy the girl's body pulled a gun. He's now in custody. But we dealt with it.'

'Yes?'

'Yes.'

23

She didn't believe him, and neither, when they left Teker's office, did Süleyman.

'You know, Çetin, you shouldn't let them get away with not having your back,' he said as they walked back to their respective offices. 'These new men need to be told. And if we don't assert ourselves over them now, who knows what will happen?'

It was late. Outside, it was already dark. But Omer Mungun had heard that some of Erdal Çelik's family were gathering in front of the building, demanding his release.

Sergeant Mungun looked at his notes. 'You drew a CZ75 automatic pistol on police officers at a crime scene in Sulukule at approximately eleven thirty this morning,' he said. 'Why?'

Çelik, a small, thin man in his forties, shrugged.

'You don't know? Or you won't say?'

'I don't know.'

'I don't believe you,' Omer said. 'You must've had a reason. Threatening a police officer is a serious offence. It isn't something people do lightly. You're looking at a custodial sentence. Think about it. Why'd you do it?'

Çelik looked confused. Was he actually trying to uncover a motivation, or was he just attempting to make something up?

He said, 'We wanted the girl's body.'

'Why?'

'You know. I've said.'

'Not to me,' Omer said.

He sighed. 'She was an apostate.' Then he added the polite and respectful term, 'bey efendi.'

'And?'

'Well, the punishment for apostasy is death.'

'She was already dead. Why destroy her body?'

'Well . . . she was a . . . As one of those she . . . well, she didn't deserve a decent burial.'

'Really? And you know this because you're a qadi, are you?'

'No.'

'So did a qadi tell you this was the case?'

'No.'

'Who did?'

He put his head down.

Omer said, 'You know you're entitled to legal representation . . .'

'Don't want it.'

'Up to you. Whose idea was it to burn Maryam de Mango's body?'

Çelik returned to silence.

Omer changed tack. 'How did you know that Maryam de Mango's body had been found this morning?'

'I heard.'

'Heard from whom?'

'On the street.'

'What? From the pavement? Who told you?' Omer said. 'And think very hard before you tell me once again that you don't know. Because if I don't get names soon, then you, by default, are going to enter the frame. If you knew Maryam de Mango was dead, maybe that was because you killed her.'

Silvio de Mango stared into the fire and remembered how his father had once told him that the souls of the damned lived inside the flames. Only prayer could release them from their torment – if one was so inclined. His father, Massimo, hadn't been. In his opinion, those not inside the loving arms of Mother Church deserved everything they got. Massimo had hated Ayşegül. He'd even hated the *idea* of Ayşegül.

Silvio had screamed at him. 'There's no one of our own I can marry! Unless we are to die out, we have to marry outside!'

25

That had been true and not true. There were a few Levantine women of Silvio's age. But he didn't love them. Not that he had used that word to his father.

Massimo's response had been to die. Silvio was sure his father had willed his heart to fail.

Someone tried the door and, finding it was locked, moved away. Silvio didn't want to see anyone. What use did he have for their blank acceptance of Maryam's death? Everything that happened was because God willed it. He hated that. So God willed death and torture, and humanity wasn't supposed to do anything about it?

He heard Ayşegül's voice. 'What are you doing?'

He wanted to say something spiteful like *I'm taking my own life!*

But he didn't.

'Leave me alone.'

There was a pause, and then she said, 'She was my daughter too.'

He didn't respond.

She said, 'I've been to identify her. She looks as if she's asleep.'

Silvio clenched his eyes tight shut against tears. He heard her walk away.

The room, his study, had been created by his great-grandfather, Faustino. There were, Silvio knew, books in ten different languages on the shelves. Faustino, leather merchant by appointment to His Majesty the Sultan, had been fluent in Italian, French, Turkish, Greek and English, and had also possessed some knowledge of Latin, Armenian, Arabic, German and Ladino. He had been a Levantine gentleman, learned, rich and respected. But when the Ottoman Empire collapsed, everything changed, culminating in the hated wealth tax on non-Muslims during the course of the Second World War. The de Mango family was almost bankrupted. The only work Silvio's father could get was as a

26

language teacher, and Silvio himself had staggered from one translation job to another all his working life. The family's only remaining asset was their apartment – and that was riddled with rot and damp. Maybe, Silvio thought, he'd sell it. Ayşegül and the children could go and live with her mother in Fatih and be as religious as they liked. He was entitled to an Italian passport; he could go home. Except that Italy wasn't home . . .

He took a piece of paper from a small stack of documents by his side and threw it into the fire. He lit a cigarette, and while he smoked, he worked his way through the stack until nothing was left.

He knew that woman. Walking towards the policeman who'd come to tell Silvio de Mango the terrible news about his daughter that morning. They looked like an item. Which was odd.

She came to Mass sometimes. Her attendance was quite random. Sometimes she came to the Italian Mass, sometimes Mass in Turkish and occasionally to the English service. She didn't participate and clearly didn't know what was going on. She prayed, but who to was anyone's guess. And she lit candles. She looked like a gypsy, and indeed, people had told him that she was one. Although not young, she was what Father Benito thought some would describe as sexy. As he watched her now with Inspector Süleyman, that was how she was acting.

Wearing a dress that barely covered her breasts, the woman kissed Inspector Süleyman on the lips when they met. His hands, Father Benito observed, held her body close. The priest turned away. Of course, a liberal quarter like Cihangir was the sort of place where a gypsy and a policeman kissing would not attract attention. Only a priest would find such a sight exotic.

He crossed Sıraselviler Caddesi, thereby moving away from the couple. Sexy women were dangerous and to be avoided. As were sexy girls. Father Benito frowned.

# Chapter 4

Kemal Öneş was known to the police. In spite of keeping his head down for over thirty years and working as a barber in what had been his father's old shop in Çarşamba, back in the 1970s and 1980s Kemal had served time; mainly for petty theft, though he'd also picked up a conviction for affray in 1980 in the wake of the military coup. There were also, worryingly for İkmen, some notes from a predecessor indicating that the police at the time had thought Öneş was a member of the ultra-nationalist Grey Wolves organisation. If Erdal Çelik had been telling Omer Mungun the truth – that Öneş had been the one who had informed the men of Çarşamba about the death of Maryam de Mango – then the barber could potentially be dangerous.

'Bring him in,' İkmen said. 'For some friendly questions.'

Omer Mungun said, 'Yes, sir.'

'I'll clear it with Inspector Süleyman when I see him at the lab. Go mob-handed,' İkmen added. 'Öneş was, or might have been, a Grey Wolf.'

'Weren't they supposed to have been young . . .'

'In the eighties, Öneş was young,' İkmen said. 'An old Grey Wolf may well be more dangerous than a youngster. Take no chances.'

'Sir.' The sergeant left İkmen's office.

Erdal Çelik had held out for a long time before he'd given Kemal Öneş's name to Omer. Not that this fact alone necessarily meant anything. Districts like Çarşamba were parochial and insular, and telling on anyone, especially to the police, was frowned upon. Çelik would not have given them Öneş's name lightly. Also, İkmen doubted whether Öneş really was the original source of the news about Maryam de Mango's death. That, as far as he could see, had to be from inside the police structure, or via one who had either killed or knew the killer of the girl.

He got up and walked to his office door. Autopsy time. He felt his heart sink. İkmen was not and had never been squeamish, but the post-mortems on the young, like Maryam de Mango, were always rough. It was hard to stop himself imagining himself as that person's father – or grandfather.

'I wish you hadn't told me that,' Gonca said.

'Death is part of life.'

She sighed. Lying in his bed, she showed no signs of getting up.

'You'll need to leave,' Süleyman said as he patted cologne into his cheeks. 'I have to be at the laboratory at ten.'

'To go to the . . .'

'The autopsy.'

She sat up. 'Is it the girl who had the visions?'

'That isn't your business,' he said. He put his jacket on. 'Get up, please.'

'You know this won't end well, the murder of that girl.' She swung her legs out of bed and began to dress.

'Did you go and see her up at the Golden Gate?' he asked.

'Of course.'

'Did you believe her?'

'That she saw the Virgin Mary? I don't know. But she saw something.'

She fitted her breasts into a lacy black and red bra. It gave her an enviable cleavage. For a moment he remembered taking it off. As soon as he'd touched her naked body he'd become hard.

'I met a Greek at the Gate,' she said. 'You know the Greeks were very excited about that girl.' Then, seeing the look on his face, she laughed. 'I didn't fuck him, the Greek.'

'I didn't say you did.'

'No, but I could see that jealous Turkish thing in your eyes,' she said. She shook her head. 'We are free agents now. We fuck whoever we want. But I didn't fuck him. He wasn't my type.'

Mehmet Süleyman and Gonca Şekeroğlu had been lovers for years. At one point they'd even lived together. But he had been unfaithful to her with a colleague, and since then, they'd both decided that it was better if they pursued an open relationship. At least that was what they told themselves. They'd spent the whole of the previous night making love and it had been as fresh and exciting as it had been the first time they'd met.

'So what did this Greek tell you?'

She stepped into her tight leather skirt and pulled it up to her hips. He turned away. He wanted her again, but he couldn't have her.

'He told me that the Golden Gate is the place where the Virgin Mary appeared when you Turks were laying siege to the Byzantine city,' she said.

'Which time?'

'I don't know. But she protected the city. It's a place that's very holy to them.'

He'd heard something of the sort. His ancestors had laid siege to Byzantium several times before the conquest in 1453.

'That girl was special.'

He turned and looked at Gonca. A mature woman, twelve years his senior – if she were to be believed. Sexually satisfied, she was stunning. He kissed her.

'You know I could easily do again what we did last night . . .'

'Oh,' she laughed. 'Stud.'

'Slave,' he said. He licked her breasts.

30

She moved her hand down and reached for him. 'My prince is ready . . .'

İkmen and Kerim Gürsel sat in Dr Sarkissian's office looking through a window into his laboratory. The doctor, plus one female assistant, stood next to a trolley on which lay the body of Maryam de Mango, covered with a plastic sheet.

The doctor looked up. 'Shall we wait?'

'Five minutes,' İkmen said. 'The traffic's a nightmare.'

İstanbul traffic was always a nightmare. Where was Süleyman? He thought about ringing him but then decided against it. If he was on his way, then calling him would only make him angry. İkmen hoped he wasn't late because he was still in bed with Gonca – or some other woman. That man's sex life had always been positively byzantine.

Kerim, who was going to be taking notes for İkmen, said, 'Sir, do you want me to write a line about the mother's positive ID here?'

'Yes,' İkmen said. 'I've got a note on file, but it doesn't hurt.'

The office door swung open and Süleyman entered.

'You're late,' İkmen said.

'Traffic.'

He was slightly breathless and a little less immaculate than usual. İkmen, in spite of himself, grimaced.

Süleyman said, 'What?'

'Nothing,' İkmen said. He looked at the doctor. 'Let's make a start.'

Sarkissian read from a screen into a hand-held voice recorder. 'Body is that of a twenty-seven-year-old unmarried female weighing fifty-four kilos and measuring 1.65 metres in height. Formally identified as Maryam de Mango by her mother, Ayşegül de Mango of Büyük Hendek Sokak, Galata, in the municipality of İstanbul. Father is Silvio de Mango, a Turkish citizen of

Levantine heritage. The subject is assumed to be of joint Turco-Latin Levantine background. DNA testing will confirm.

'Circumstances of death. The body was discovered by Inspector Çetin İkmen behind Burhan's Coffee House on Sulukule Caddesi, Sulukule, İstanbul, at ten fifteen a.m. on Tuesday the twelfth of April 2016. Subject had been dead between eight and twelve hours. When discovered, primary flaccidity had passed and the body was in full rigor. This particularly affected the face, which upon discovery had the appearance of wearing a smile. While a full *in situ* examination of the body was impossible due to the threat of violent activity at the site, I was able to determine that possible cause of death was loss of blood brought about by either a puncture wound to the chest or the opening of the lower abdomen with a sharp instrument. The surface of the skin exhibited heavy bruising, which may be consistent with the diagnosis of leukaemia that the subject received in 2015. Internal organs, including intestines and uterine material, were exposed and had been placed on the left-hand side of the body.

'The body was surrounded by detritus consisting of coffee grounds, cigarette butts, discarded food material and soiled paper. All said detritus has been removed to the forensic laboratory for further examination. The subject's hair, which is black, was loose at death and threaded with cut flowers identified as tulips. Eyes are green. Subject's clothing consisted of a pair of blue denim jeans and a plain white shirt plus undergarments: white briefs and white brassiere. The subject wore no jewellery except for thin gold hoops in her ears, which are pierced. No shoes or sandals or personal effects were found at the site.'

'She was barefoot?' İkmen asked.

'Yes. And in fact I have since discovered that the subject was always barefoot when she was at the Golden Gate. Maybe it was part of her image?'

'You make her sound like an advertising executive,' İkmen said.

'Do you not think Jesus would have had a PR consultant and a social-media expert amongst his disciples had he lived now?'

'I would hope not,' İkmen said. 'But I take your point.' He turned to Kerim. 'Don't take that down.'

'No, sir.'

'What else, Doctor?'

Sarkissian cleared his throat. 'I simply wish to add that it is my belief thus far that Miss de Mango was killed unlawfully. I should also like to confirm with you, Inspector İkmen, that a full internal autopsy is required, but not a cranial examination.'

'That is correct,' İkmen said. 'I should also like to determine, if possible, whether the subject was subjected to sexual congress either pre- or post-mortem.'

The doctor inclined his head. 'Noted.'

If his own thin and straggly hair was anything to go by, Kemal Öneş was a really bad barber. But he wasn't. The hair, together with the clothes – şalvar trousers, long, rough-haired shirt – was all part of a persona that Omer Mungun decided was self-consciously mystical. Öneş was, the man himself declared, a dervish. However, when Omer asked him which order he was a member of, he said he belonged to no order but rather lived the simple life of a devout man, committed to God and brotherhood. Clearly he wanted Omer to think that he was allied to the powerful religious community that was very prominent in the district of Çarşamba. Known only as the Order, it was said that people in political high places were members. It was said they were untouchable. But Öneş wasn't.

Omer got straight to the point. 'We have received intelligence that yesterday morning you told the men in your mahalle that Maryam de Mango, otherwise known as the Miracle Girl, had been found dead in Sulukule.'

'I did not. Who says I did?'

Omer ignored his question. 'How did you know?' he continued.

'I didn't.'

'Then how did men in and around Çarşamba Mahallesi know the girl had died?'

'I've no idea.'

Omer wasn't a Muslim. But he knew how religious people thought. More significantly, he knew how those who wanted others to think they were religious thought.

'If I asked you to swear on the Holy Koran that you had no knowledge of Miss de Mango's death, could you do that?' he said.

The dead always looked ghostly. This was because, in a prone corpse, the blood sank down to the spine and the backs of the legs and arms, where it pooled, leaving the front of the body, including the face, pale and translucent. Maryam de Mango had possessed delicate features and so had the appearance of a china doll. Supported by a body block, which raised the chest and abdomen, she looked agonised. Briefly İkmen turned away.

'Externally, in addition to heavy bruising, there is one puncture wound to the chest midway between the breasts, plus a forty-five-centimetre cut running from right to left across the top of the pubic bone. Intestinal and uterine material . . .'

İkmen made himself watch. Arto Sarkissian stooped to examine the exposed organs on the left-hand side of the body. İkmen had known the pathologist all his life, but he still didn't know how his friend did this job.

'Just cursorily looking at the pubic wound, I would hazard that it was caused by a serrated or partially serrated weapon,' Sarkissian said. 'And was made with little or no skill. The flesh and subcutaneous organs have been hacked at rather than dissected.'

'And the puncture wound?' İkmen asked.

'That's the source, I would say, of the haemorrhage that probably killed her.'

'The organs were exposed post mortem?'

'I believe so.'

Omer slapped his hand over the man's fingers.

'I swear on—'

'No you don't,' Omer said as he moved the Holy Book away from Kemal Öneş. 'I know how this works, you know.'

'What? Bey efendi, I was about to swear—'

'After persuading yourself that what you are about to do comes under taqiyya, you swear upon the holiest text in existence that you did not do something that you did. You lie. But it's OK, because it's only to me, someone you believe is an atheist and therefore your enemy,' Omer said. 'So I'm not going to let you do that. You will not swear your innocence on the Holy Koran and then walk out of here as I am sure you imagined you would. You will tell me the truth and you will tell me now.'

Taqiyya, the controversial permission given, so some Muslims believed, by Islam for adherents to lie if the faith was in danger, was something Omer knew was employed by fundamentalist terrorists. He had friends in counter-terrorism who had told him about their experiences with it. It was from these friends that he'd learned the technique of getting the subject's taqiyya out into the open and then cutting off the possibility of its success.

'I can't tell you anything.'

'You won't.'

'You can beat me!'

Omer smiled. 'And give you the satisfaction of seeing yourself as some sort of martyr? How stupid do you think I am? Your faith is not in danger, my friend. This case has nothing to do with religion. The reality is that a girl has been murdered and you are obstructing the lawful apprehension of an offender. If you won't tell me then I won't press you any further. What I will do is pass you over to my superior, Inspector İkmen . . .'

'Who will beat me!'

'Who won't,' Omer said. 'It'll be much worse than that, I can assure you.'


The entire viscera was exposed. Dr Sarkissian used what was known as the 'Y' method of examination, which involved making a cut down from each shoulder, through the breasts, to a point below the sternum. A single cut then continued down the torso to the pubis. The ribs were severed and removed to fully expose the chest cavity.

The doctor continued, moving up from the pubis. He began with a vaginal examination. 'Hymen is perforated. Whether this indicates sexual activity is moot. A laxity test of the vaginal muscles will, in my opinion, be inconclusive because the subject is deceased. However, given the possibility of sexual activity, I will request a full screen for sexually transmitted infections. Do we know whether the subject was in a relationship?'

'No,' İkmen said. 'We know she wasn't married or living with anyone. What's the condition of the vagina?'

'You mean has she been raped? I'd say she hasn't. Beyond the stab wound to the chest and the cutting and partial removal of the top of the uterus, there's no sign of penetration violence. However . . .' He lowered his head to study the sexual organs more closely. 'There is some lividity around the labia and the cervix that could be consistent with a phenomenon known as Chadwick's sign.'

'What's that?'

'A very early indicator for pregnancy,' the doctor said. 'It's where blood flow to the vulva, labia and cervix increases in preparation for carrying a child.'

'So is there a foetus?'

'No. Not that I can see. There may be some remnants of it in the exposed uterine material. As I say, this is a very early pregnancy indicator, and indeed may not be that at all. I will have to perform an hCG test.'

'What's that?'

'For your purposes, Inspector, it is a blood test for pregnancy.'

Even with a glass screen between him and the body, İkmen was assaulted by the smell when the doctor removed the intestines and took samples of stomach contents for analysis. Apparently there wasn't much to test, indicating that the girl had not eaten near the time of her death.

An occasional smoker, Maryam de Mango had apparently been in good health when she died.

'What about the leukaemia?' İkmen asked.

'The liver is slightly enlarged, but I can't see anything else that might indicate the disease was active when she died, although the corpse is heavily bruised, which is an indicator for leukaemia,' the doctor said. 'I will have to compare blood and tissue results to those held by her oncologist. If she did still have the disease at death, she would appear to have been in either complete or partial remission.'

'Meaning?'

'Complete remission means that no signs or symptoms are present; partial remission involves the non-progression of the disease, which can allow subjects to take breaks from punitive treatments like chemotherapy. Remission may be facilitated by treatment or may occur spontaneously. It is the little-understood spontaneous remission that is often conflated by religious believers with miraculous intervention, and with good cause.'

İkmen frowned.

'Spontaneous remission does sometimes occur at the same time as the subject comes into contact with the "miraculous",' the doctor said. 'Whether one affects the other isn't known. Personally, I think that if the religious experience has any effect, it is psychological rather than physical. It is well known that a positive psychological state may contribute to physical well-being.'

'This is making my head hurt.'

'Greater minds than ours have pondered such things and come to no conclusion.'

When the examination was complete, the doctor thanked the three police officers for attending and then set about labelling the samples he had taken for the forensic laboratory. Outside in the thin April sunshine, İkmen and Süleyman lit cigarettes and talked briefly about what they had seen. Kerim Gürsel was unusually quiet, and so when Süleyman had gone, İkmen asked him if he was all right. Autopsies were not easy things to see and he was still relatively inexperienced.

He said, 'No, it was fine. I was just thinking about Sinem.'

'Your wife.'

İkmen was one of the few people who knew that Sinem Gürsel was Kerim's wife in name only. Homosexual men and women did sometimes marry in order to allay any suspicions their families might have about their sexuality. But Kerim genuinely loved Sinem, who suffered terribly from rheumatoid arthritis, and she loved him. They just didn't have sex.

'We thought about taking her to see Maryam de Mango at the Golden Gate,' Kerim said. 'But,' he shrugged, 'time ran out.'

When he said 'we', he meant himself and his transsexual lover Pembe, who acted as Sinem's carer.

İkmen patted his shoulder. Then his phone rang. It was Omer Mungun.

# Chapter 5

The clock, which for as long as he could remember had been at least ten minutes behind the time, had come from England. It was inscribed with the name 'Whitehurst Derby', and his father had told him that it had once belonged to the nineteenth-century British prime minister Benjamin Disraeli. But then his father had also told him that the paper knife that had belonged to his grandfather had been given to him by Garibaldi.

Nothing was ordinary. He wasn't. Ayşegül wasn't, Maryam hadn't been.

He looked at his other children and scowled. They, like him, were waiting for the car that would take them to police head-quarters. Ayşegül was in the kitchen.

Silvio addressed his second son, Mevlüt. 'Why do you have to have a beard that looks as if you never comb it?' he said.

The boy didn't answer. He didn't need to. Silvio knew the whys and wherefores of the beard.

'The police will think you're a terrorist looking like that,' he continued.

'What? Because you do?' the boy sneered.

'No! Because anyone would think it! You look a state!'

'Papa—'

'And you're not much better!' He turned on his elder son. İbrahim was more conventionally clean-shaven than his brother, but Silvio suspected that he shared many of Mevlüt's opinions. 'I've seen the kind of sick filth you look at on your phone! You like ISIS? So go and join ISIS. See how quickly they'll make you a second-class citizen when they learn that your father is a Christian.'

Ayşegül came in.

'The children need to fit in,' she said. 'Don't blame them.'

'Oh I don't blame *them*!' Silvio said. 'I blame *you*!'

She sat down next to Sara, who lowered her headscarfed head.

'It's always my fault,' Ayşegül said resignedly.

He said nothing. When they'd first met, she'd been full of life. Beautiful and fun, she'd been the antithesis of her pious mother, who was forever praying and hiding inside her scarves. But as the years passed and the country began to shift its axis away from the secular, she changed. First prayer mats began to appear alongside antique carpets from Persia, then a copy of the Koran in Arabic; then she started to cover her head . . .

'My daughter is dead,' he said. He pointed to his sons. 'Killed by people who look like them.' He looked at his wife. 'Or by you.'

This time she said nothing. When had he begun to hate her? Had it been when she decided to cover? Her brothers had said they'd disown her if she didn't. What was she supposed to do? She should have left him then, when Maryam became a thing moulded in his image. Ayşegül looked around the dark apartment and felt sick. There was nothing of her in this so-called marital home. It was all Silvio.

Her husband cried again. But no one went to him. He didn't want them. Maryam was dead and Silvio wished that he was too.


'You've not always lived in Fatih, have you?' İkmen said.

Kemal Öneş frowned. It was halfway through the afternoon, and the smells of kebab, köfte and lahmacun were wafting in from nearby lokantas. Warm, spicy and laced with grease. Mr Öneş, like İkmen, hadn't eaten. He licked his lips.

'You lived in sleazy old Karaköy before you got religion. Got yourself arrested a couple of times.' İkmen smiled. 'Back in the day, your name was associated with the Grey Wolves. Remember them?'

Öneş remained silent.

'I'm sure you can't forget all that racial purity and other fascistic fun you had with them,' İkmen said. 'However, I must say in your defence that you were only ever on the fringes of the organisation. In fact I feel that your relationship with the Wolves may well have been like your relationship with the Order . . .'

Öneş looked up.

'Not exactly one of them, but you'd like to be.'

'I—'

'I don't know how you ended up in the Çarşamba quarter of Fatih, but I can see why, even though they won't accept you, you feel as if you have to dress and behave in accordance with the standards of the Order.'

Sunni Islamic dervishes had lived in the Çarşamba district for decades. Intensely pious, the men wore long beards while the women covered completely in thick black chadors. Those who lived around them tended to dress modestly too. Alleged to have friends in high places, the Order were not people one wanted to offend.

'My father lived in Fatih,' Öneş said. 'I went home.'

İkmen said, 'Sometimes when a person is said to have information about something of a criminal nature that they deny, I go and speak to their neighbours. Sometimes this bears fruit and sometimes it doesn't. But it does alert those people to the fact that something is amiss.'

Öneş's thin face reddened slightly.

'Not that your neighbours really need telling, because a fair number of those who came to Sulukule yesterday morning were

41

members of the Order. It would, however, be interesting to know how they found out the girl was dead. Don't you think?'

'It wasn't from me.'

And that was a distinct possibility. Erdal Çelik, who had drawn a gun on İkmen and Kerim Gürsel, was hardly the brightest star in the sky, and if Öneş was indeed a bit of a square peg in Çarşamba, Çelik might well have mentioned his name in order to protect someone else. Playing the politics of the mahalle was always a delicate job.

'So, to go back to the beginning of our conversation,' İkmen said, 'where, when and from whom did you hear about the death of Maryam de Mango?'

'I heard yesterday. In my shop.'

'From . . .'

'I don't know if anyone told me. The shop was full. Men and boys getting their hair cut before work and school. Not the Order, of course. They don't use my place. None of them were around when I heard.'

İkmen felt he protested the dervishes' innocence too much.

'So who *was* around?'

'Customers.'

'Which customers? Who told you that Maryam de Mango had been found dead?'

'I don't—'

'Yes you do,' İkmen said. 'Or you know someone who does. Is that person in the Order, is that the problem? Because I can assure you it's no problem for me. I don't care who someone is. If they murder or conceal evidence of a murder then they are guilty and need to be banged up . . .'

'Bey efendi!'

He was panicking, which was good – in one way. Panic could make him tell the truth, if he indeed knew the truth. Or it could make him quickly fabricate a lie.

'It was one of you.'

İkmen frowned. 'One of who?' he said. 'A terrible atheist who will burn in hell, a member of my family . . .'

'A police officer!'


'She went to church.'

'Monday night?'

'Yes.'

'Did she tell you why?'

The girl shrugged. 'She often went,' she said. 'She knew people there.'

'Through your father?'

Sara de Mango shrugged again.

Ayşegül de Mango, her mother, said, 'She was often there.'

'At St Anthony's?' Süleyman asked.

'Yes, the priest there is my husband's confessor.'

'Father Benito Esposito.'

'Yes.'

The priest had told Süleyman he hadn't seen Maryam since Mass the previous Sunday.

'You said yesterday, Miss de Mango,' Süleyman continued, 'that your sister lied. Do you think she lied about where she was going on Monday evening?'

'I don't know.'

'I ran after her,' Ayşegül said. 'But she lost me very quickly. I've no idea where she went.'

'What sort of things did Maryam lie about?' Süleyman asked the girl.

Sara looked down at the floor. Unlike her sister, she was unexpressive. One of the things that had captured the public imagination about Maryam was her face. Always changing, it had been the face of one who could express bliss.

Still Sara said nothing.

'If you don't tell me . . .'

Ayşegül said, 'I am sorry, Mehmet Bey.'

'What for?'

'Sara.' She looked at the girl. 'Tell him,' she said.

'Tell me what?'

Sara shrugged again.

'Mehmet Bey, Sara makes things up.'

'What things?'

'All sorts. I think it began as a way of hiding who she is.'

'Which is?'

'You know.' Ayşegül de Mango retracted her head into her many scarves.

Levantines like Silvio de Mango had been an accepted group in İstanbul society for centuries. In the not-too-distant past, a Muslim woman like Ayşegül had married one, he imagined, without a thought. Then, starting with 9/11, the world had changed. Especially the world in what had once been the Ottoman Empire.

'Where did Maryam tell you she was going on Monday evening?' Omer Mungun asked.

'She didn't tell me anything,' Silvio de Mango said. 'She argued with her mother, who wanted her to stay in, and then she left.'

'Argued about what?'

'The usual thing. Her mother said that by having her visions – as if she could help having them – she was consorting with djinns. Ever since my daughter was cured of her illness at the Church of the Assumption, my wife and other children have deemed her cursed.'

'But don't Muslims go to the ceremony at the Church of the Assumption?'

Silvio de Mango snorted. 'Of course they do! They get free meat, if nothing else!'

Animals had always been sacrificed on the Night of the Miracle at the Armenian Church of the Assumption in Fener. And the meat that resulted from the sacrifice had always been distributed.

'My wife uses anything as an excuse to persecute Maryam.'

'Why?'

'Because she, of all our children, chooses her father's way of life,' he said. 'Or rather, she did.' His eyes became wet.

'To go back to Monday night . . .'

'My wife tried to lock Maryam in her room, and I let her out.'

'You didn't approve.'

'No! She is . . . was an adult. If she wanted to go out, she went out.'

'And what did your wife do when you let Maryam out?' Omer asked.

Silvio de Mango shook his head. 'The crazy bitch ran out after her,' he said. 'Headscarf flying! She was like a thing possessed.'

'What did you do?'

'Me? I went to bed,' he said. 'Such things are always happening. My wife will tell you I was drunk, but I wasn't. I'd had a brandy.'

'What happened then?'

'I slept.'

'And in the morning?'

'In the morning Ayşegül was nowhere to be seen and neither was Maryam. My other children greeted me with their usual silence. I went to St Anthony's to speak to Father Esposito. I was desperate.'

'What did you think might have happened?'

'I thought my wife had killed my daughter,' he said.

'That's a bit extreme, isn't it? Why?'

Silvio de Mango leaned forward. 'Because that's what those people do,' he said.

'What people?'

'People whose lifestyles are elevated above mine. People who belong to organisations that want to make everyone in this country behave exactly the same.'

Omer Mungun felt a shudder run through his body. He knew what de Mango was talking about. He'd felt as the Levantine did. But he never spoke of it.

'I told Father Esposito that I thought Ayşegül had killed my daughter.'

'What did he say?'

'He is a good man, he thinks the best of people. He told me I was wrong. But he doesn't understand this country.'

'So let me get this straight,' Omer said. 'You are accusing your wife Ayşegül de Mango of killing your daughter Maryam?'

'Yes.'


'I went to bed.'

'After your daughter left your apartment to go to church?'

'I ran out into the street, but she was too quick for me and I couldn't see her. I went straight back into my apartment. I don't know that she went to church. That is what Sara said, not me.'

The girl had left the room for the final phase of Süleyman's interview with her mother.

He said, 'But Sara lies.'

'Sometimes.'

'And yet when my sergeant and I came to your apartment yesterday, Sara was heard to say that it was Maryam who lied.'

She shook her head. 'My children have problems, Mehmet Bey,' she said. 'Their lives are not easy.'

'Because of their father?'

'Because of the situation. Silvio has become more and more entrenched in his identity.'

'Meaning?'

'When we first got together, he agreed that the children should be Muslims. I said that they could go to the church with him sometimes. That was fine. But in recent years he has abused that. I tell you, Mehmet Bey, he wanted to convert my children and I have had to fight to stop him.' She was almost in tears.

'Why do you think he did that?' Süleyman asked.

'I don't know!' She flung her arms in the air. She also looked away from him. 'My husband has become someone else and my children have suffered as a consequence.'

'Even Maryam?'

'Especially Maryam. Although it broke my heart, that girl was meant to suffer her illness and submit to the will of God. Silvio altered that.'

'He took her to the Church of the Assumption?'

'Yes. I was against it. Then she began to see things.' She shook her head. 'I could tell that she was being tempted by djinns. And then there is my husband, encouraging it! A snake in a basket of fruit, he has been. A snake.'

According to Kemal Öneş, a police officer had come into the barber's shop, told him that Maryam de Mango had been found dead in Sulukule and left. If İkmen hadn't possessed very good intelligence to back up the fact that this sort of thing happened sometimes, when officers had relationships and affiliations outside the service, he would have laughed. As it was, he was facing the possibility that it could be true.

Stripped of their numbers and ranks, photos of serving officers were being presented to Öneş. He had, so far, shaken his head at every one. İkmen suspected he would continue to do so. However, that didn't mean his story wasn't accurate. It might very well be. But, preferable though it was to pointing a finger at a member of the Order, accusing a police officer of misconduct was a serious step.

İkmen had identified six officers who had been in Sulukule on the morning shift, before he'd found the body. They had all submitted their records to Kerim Gürsel, who as yet had discovered nothing unusual. But then the officer that Öneş claimed to have seen had come to his shop in Çarşamba. Did this mean that he'd come from Sulukule, or that someone in that district, possibly outside the force, had told him about it? And if this meant that İkmen had not been the first person to discover the body, what implications did that have?

Katerina cried. If anything, these Levantines were even more emotional than ordinary Italians. Father Esposito put a hand on his housekeeper's shoulder. But that just made her cry even harder.

As he walked from the kitchen back into his office he heard Katerina say, 'That poor, poor girl!'

Maryam de Mango hadn't been a regular visitor to St Anthony's until she had become ill with leukaemia. Silvio was well known, and had always brought his children to church from time to time. But when the girl had got sick, it had seemed to Father Esposito that he'd brought her almost in the belief that only the intercession of the Church could make her well again. It hadn't. Maryam and her father had found that, it seemed, with the Armenian church. The annual miracle of the Church of the Assumption.

How many of those 'cures' had been discredited over the years? Benito Esposito had been pleased for Maryam, but he'd never investigated her claim. He'd spoken to the bishop about it, but he had counselled a wait-and-see approach. The girl's visions had been different. Benito had spoken to her about them – unfortunately most of the time in the presence of Silvio. Unable to conceal his excitement, Silvio had paid even less attention to the other members of his family than he usually did. Benito only knew his wife and the other children by sight, but he couldn't

48

believe they were as hostile as Silvio said. In fact they always seemed rather cowed.

The police wanted to interview him in the morning about Maryam and he wasn't looking forward to it. What and what not to tell them? Issues under the Seal of the Confessional were easy. But the rest of it was difficult. Maryam hadn't been a Catholic and so what she had told him could, strictly, be repeated. But should it?

İbrahim de Mango had broken. At first confused by Süleyman's questions, he'd cried. Then it had been as if a plug had been pulled.

'It's like living in the middle of a war,' he'd said. 'My parents always looking for ways to outwit and shame each other. I want to leave but I fear what will happen if I do. My father accuses me of being radicalised, but I'm not. I just choose to keep myself informed about those people. My parents pit us against each other. They use us to express their feelings. I feel torn in two.'

And happening in that dark, dank apartment. Süleyman imagined a weird, often silent, furious nightmare. But it was only with the younger brother, Mevlüt, that it became truly dark.

'My father touched my sister Maryam,' he said when Süleyman asked him about whether their parents favoured any of their children. 'And I do mean inappropriately,' he continued. 'My mother hasn't slept with him for years and so he took my sister.'

And possibly, if Dr Sarkissian was correct, he had made her pregnant.

# Chapter 6

The Golden Gate of the Byzantines was no longer either golden or a gate. Walled up against further incursions by the victorious Ottoman Turks, what had once been the ceremonial gateway into the city for Byzantine emperors was now just a down-at-heel marble ruin. On this particular evening, however, it glowed, lit by tea lights and perfumed candles, and the tapers in the hands of people singing 'Immaculate Mary', the Lourdes hymn.

To a Muslim copper like Sergeant Yıldız, it was all very weird and a bit spooky. But he couldn't see that those who'd come to honour Maryam de Mango were doing any harm. He'd been to see her a couple of times up at the gate himself, and although he didn't believe she was in contact with anything divine, he accepted that she thought she was. Mad.

Now his job was to make sure that everyone behaved themselves. No fighting, no selling drugs or boozing, and no converting anyone to Christianity. Not that any of that appeared to be happening. His biggest problem was keeping Syrian refugees away from the place. Some of the poor bastards, especially those who had settled in Tarlabaşı, were living in hovels with no water and no power. They looked at the Christians' candles with shining, acquisitive eyes.

'Statistically, you're more likely to be murdered by a member of your family than anyone else,' İkmen said.

Süleyman sat down. It was dark now, and after a long day of interviews, statements and an autopsy, İkmen, Süleyman, Kerim Gürsel and Omer Mungun had assembled in İkmen's office to talk. İkmen opened the window and then lit a cigarette, closely followed by Süleyman.

'Well if you come from the de Mango family, that is probably true,' Süleyman said. 'It isn't often one observes such a dysfunctional dynamic.'

'Silvio de Mango was completely open about the fact that he believes his wife killed Maryam,' Omer Mungun said.

İkmen frowned. 'A bold statement.'

'The de Mango marriage is an extremely volatile one,' Süleyman said. 'Ayşegül accuses her husband of changing, implying an increasingly anti-Muslim stance, in the wake of 9/11. She believes he was actively trying to convert their children to Catholicism, especially Maryam. I've no evidence, so far, that Maryam actually converted.'

'But she was on her way to church the night she died?'

'According to her mother and her siblings, yes.'

'Her father said he didn't know where she was going,' Omer said. 'He said that Maryam wanted to leave the apartment; her mother tried to stop her by locking her in her room, but Silvio let her out. Ayşegül then ran after her daughter while Silvio went to bed after what he described as "a brandy". I suspect it was more than that.'

'Did Ayşegül say that?'

'No, I'm just reading between the lines.'

'When did Ayşegül return?'

'Silvio says he doesn't know, Çetin Bey,' Omer said. 'He fell asleep, and in the morning neither his wife nor his daughter was at home.'

'What about the others?'

'The two boys and the other daughter said they were in all

51

night,' Süleyman said. 'But they only have each other as their alibis. They say that their mother returned almost immediately after running out in pursuit of Maryam. Ayşegül said she went shopping as soon as she woke up the following morning.'

'She didn't check whether her daughter had returned?'

'She didn't mention it and I didn't press her on it,' Süleyman said.

'Which probably means that she didn't,' İkmen said. 'Why?'

'If Ayşegül had killed Maryam, she'd know she wasn't home,' Kerim said.

'She would. But what is her motive?'

'Ayşegül is a pious woman, although I wouldn't peg her as fanatical,' Süleyman said. 'But maybe she thought that by killing Maryam, she was saving her from damnation should she convert to Catholicism. Apostates can be killed. We know this.'

'Yes, but sir, if Mrs de Mango had killed her daughter for religious reasons, wouldn't she *want* to own up to that?' Omer said. 'Isn't it like a badge of honour for some people?'

'Not always,' İkmen said. 'There are some who want the kudos *and* their freedom. I call that greedy.'

'Mevlüt de Mango, the younger of the two boys, made an allegation against his father,' Süleyman said. 'He claims that when Silvio's marriage to Ayşegül broke down, his father took Maryam as his lover.'

'Oooh.' İkmen shook his head. 'Which means that if Maryam was pregnant when she died, Silvio may be the unborn child's father. Any of the other kids talk about sexual abuse?'

'No. But we have a problem there,' Süleyman said. 'The younger daughter, Sara, apparently makes things up, according to her mother.'

'But not Mevlüt.'

'No. Sara didn't deny that she lies, but she also said that her sister lied.'

'About what?'

'I don't know.'

'Find out,' İkmen said. 'What about Maryam's personal effects? It appears she wasn't carrying anything when she left the apartment.'

'I found her laptop and her phone in her room,' Süleyman said. 'They're with the techies.'

'Anything else?'

'There were a set of house keys on a sideboard where she stored her clothes. She had a lot of books, mainly religious texts in Italian.'

'Christian, I assume.'

'Yes. Significantly, she had books about the sightings of the Virgin Mary at Lourdes and at Fatima, which is in Portugal.'

İkmen put one cigarette out and lit another. 'So, either she was investigating precedents for her experiences, or she was tutoring herself . . .'

'Or she was simply curious. All four children speak Italian, English and French. Maryam received a BA from Boğaziçi University four years ago in Teaching English as a Foreign Language. The elder brother is similarly qualified and currently works as a teacher at a private high school in Şişli. Mevlüt de Mango is unemployed, much to his father's chagrin.'

'What does Silvio de Mango do?'

'He's a freelance translator, works from home for several publishing houses, mainly English to Turkish.'

'And so he follows in the footsteps of his clever and useful Levantine ancestors,' İkmen said. 'What about the other daughter?'

'Still in high school.'

'Where?'

'Anadolu Imam Hatip in Esenler.'

'A religious school. Wonder what her father thinks of that.'

'I doubt he's happy,' Süleyman said. 'The girl, Sara, is headscarfed, quiet. I imagine such an environment suits her very well. I've a meeting with Silvio's priest in the morning; he may or may not know some more about the family.'

İkmen was due to attend the Italian Hospital with Dr Sarkissian to find out more about Maryam de Mango's leukaemia diagnosis from her oncologist. But before that, there was the matter of Kemal Öneş. The man who had brought the barber to the police's attention, Erdal Çelik, had been charged with possessing an unlicensed firearm and threatening a police officer, and was due to appear in court in two days' time. But Öneş had still not even come close to identifying the police officer who had told him that Maryam de Mango had been found dead. Omer Mungun thought he didn't exist.

'He's trying not to implicate the Order,' he said.

'So you think that one of them told him?'

'Why not?'

'Anything to do with the Order is a dangerous path to travel,' Kerim Gürsel said.

'Doesn't mean it isn't true.'

'No.'

İkmen leaned on his desk. 'People who could have found the body before I did must include the six uniforms who were in the vicinity on early shift,' he said. 'Logically we must take into account Burhan Bey, although I can't make that work in my mind, and a shifting band of refugees who inhabit some of the empty houses in the area.'

'Didn't Yıldız and Çağlar do house-to-house, sir?'

'Yes, Omer,' İkmen said. 'But only quick and dirty, and without the benefit of an Arabic speaker. So,' he looked at Süleyman, 'with Mehmet Bey's permission, I'd like you, as a fluent Arabic speaker, to go to Sulukule tomorrow and start a dialogue with these Syrians.'

Süleyman said, 'Of course.'

'And while I am at the Italian Hospital, it will fall to you, Kerim, to take statements from the six officers supposedly on duty in Sulukule on Monday night. Could be utterly fruitless, but if Kemal Öneş won't identify anyone, then we will have to see if we can find this person ourselves.'

'Yes, sir.'

'And keep it calm and friendly, Kerim, yes?'

'Yes.'

İkmen didn't go straight home at the end of the meeting. Instead he went to his favourite bar, the Mozaik, which was only a minute from his apartment. Armed with a pile of newspapers, fortified by brandy and with his faithful cat, Marlboro, on a seat beside him, he looked at what was being said about Maryam de Mango. A lot of it wasn't pretty and a lot of that was downright hostile.

When she'd been alive, the fact that she might be an apostate had only really captured the attention of the most conservative journalists. Now she was dead, however, that rather than her murder was the most significant part of the story. Why?

There had been a time when even İkmen had possessed a few friends in the Islamist press corps. But no more. Lines had formed between colleagues in almost all professions in the wake of the Gezi protests – or what the government described as 'an attempted coup' – back in December 2013. And so instead he called İdil, who was and always had been, just to the left of Karl Marx.

For a long time the phone just rang and rang and İkmen feared it might eventually ring out. But then a nervous-sounding İdil answered. When he heard it was İkmen, he audibly sighed with relief. However, when İkmen asked him about Maryam de Mango, the journalist got straight to the point.

'Don't even go there with talk about her religion, Çetin Bey,' he said. 'Find out who killed her – if they let you – and then move on.'

Who were 'they'?

\*　\*　\*

Silvio de Mango was drunk. Mourning for his daughter, he was by turns lachrymose, loud, expansive and fearful. Father Esposito tried to blank out the sound of his voice. Hidden behind a large flower display, his aim was to eat his meze and drink his wine without being spotted by either Silvio or his companion.

Now that bars were not allowed to have tables outside on the street, the only places where drinkers could imbibe alcohol and smoke were the rooftops of the meyhanes that had them. Like Silvio, Father Esposito liked to smoke. Someone else who liked cigarettes and booze was Silvio's friend Fabrizio Leon.

They'd been to school together, Silvio and Fabrizio. The posh İtalyan Lisesi. The only difference between them, according to his predecessor Father Luigi, was that while his mother had been Italian, Fabrizio's father had been a local Jew. One-time actor, author and teacher, Fabrizio, even in his fifties, was a full-time handsome man-around-town, who, since his divorce twelve years ago, was still tantalisingly unmarried. He was Silvio's best friend, and so of course he was there for him during his time of tragedy.

The two men conversed in Italian, which meant they didn't disturb the Turkish drinkers.

Silvio said, 'I want her home! I want them to let my baby come home so she can rest in her own place before they take her to the grave!'

Fabrizio put an arm around his friend. 'Of course you do,' he said. 'And you will. These Muslims don't hold on to bodies; they consider them unclean. Your Maryam will come home and we will pay for many, many Masses to be said for her.'

Father Esposito cringed. How could he say such a thing? After what he'd done?

Silvio kissed his friend on both cheeks. 'I love you,' he said.

The priest pushed his unfinished plate to one side and drank his wine. Suddenly his stomach had curdled.

56

# Chapter 7

'Maryam had a form of leukaemia known as chronic lymphocytic leukaemia, or CLL.'

The oncologist, a Dr Rizzi, was a severe-looking woman who was probably in her sixties. Her mastery of Turkish was as neat and tight as the battleship-grey bun at the back of her head.

'This is a slow-developing disease that can take some time to diagnose,' she continued. 'That is because early symptoms are diffuse. Tiredness, some weight loss, swollen lymph nodes, also tenderness around the spleen.'

'Did Maryam present with those symptoms?' Dr Sarkissian asked.

'Her main issue was fatigue,' she said. 'She was referred to me after more obvious avenues such as simple anaemia had been explored. The news came as a great shock to Maryam and her father as I remember. The treatment I advised even more so.'

'Which was?'

'We call it "watch and wait",' she said. 'We do nothing.'

İkmen said, 'Nothing?'

'Nothing. Where symptoms are not severe and blood counts are not bad, this is what we do,' she said. 'CLL is, in general, a disease of slow progression. Maryam was in the early stages and so she was able to live a normal life. It's about saving your big guns in case you have to engage in a fight later on. And it's good to avoid administering chemotherapy if you can. Some people go into remission and avoid it altogether. But I know that

Maryam wasn't happy about watch and wait. A lot of our patients find it hard. They feel as if they have a death sentence hanging over them and become anxious because nobody is doing anything about it. Hence her search for a more metaphysical cure.'

'How often did you see her?' İkmen asked.

'Once a month.'

'And when did you stop seeing her?'

'End of October last year.'

'After the miracle?'

'Yes,' Dr Rizzi said. 'She came to tell me she didn't need me any more. She didn't want me to examine her, but her father, who always came to her appointments with her, insisted.'

'To prove to himself that she was well?'

'Yes, and also, he told me, to the Holy See,' she said.

Even before her visions, or so it seemed, Silvio de Mango had possessed ambitions for his daughter. What, İkmen wondered, had that meant for Maryam?

'Of course, he didn't, to my knowledge, hear back from the Vatican,' she said. 'The Holy See is very nervous of miracles these days, and with good cause.'

'Really?'

She put her thin elbows on her desk and rested her head on her hands. 'Maryam was not ill,' she said. 'She had some symptoms and some poor blood results, but she wasn't about to die. True, when she came to me after her cure, she reported that she was symptom-free and her bloods were good. I declared her in remission and I stick to that opinion.'

'What exactly is remission?' İkmen asked. Arto Sarkissian had already told him, but he wanted to know how Dr Rizzi defined the phenomenon.

'There are two types,' she said. 'Partial remission, where treatment may safely be curtailed for a period of time; and complete remission, or no evidence of disease. This is where we can see no sign of pathology. Doesn't mean it isn't there. We just can't detect it. Complete remission may last for a week, a month, forever. It is entirely unpredictable.'

'Why does it happen?'

'We don't know. In some cases it may indicate the cumulative effect of treatment over a period of time. In Maryam's case, that wouldn't be so. Maybe a more positive mental attitude is part of the picture.'

'So if she believed she was cured . . .'

'That may have come to pass,' Dr Rizzi said. 'Don't ask me how, I'm not a psychiatrist. But we see it.'

'Often?'

'More often than Mr de Mango probably imagined,' she said.

Dr Sarkissian frowned. 'Why do you say that?'

'Because,' she said, 'he was amazed that I had ever seen anyone like his daughter before. To him she was a miracle.'

Just as İstanbul did not represent the whole of Turkey, Damascus didn't represent Syria. The people who had come to live in the new houses of Sulukule were people who had been movers and shakers. Not big businessmen and women but successful merchants, stout tradespeople and folk who had once worked in the nascent tourist industry. Omer Mungun, who had been brought up around Arabs, knew they were nobody's fools. He also knew that, like most refugee communities, they kept their heads down.

The person to go and see, according to Çetin Bey's friend Burhan the gypsy, was Sultan al-Khoury, who worked as a car mechanic. Back in Damascus he had been a lawyer. If there was such a thing as a community leader, he was it.

'I always liked to tinker with cars from when I was a small boy,' he told Omer when he eventually found him in a precarious-looking shed tacked onto the side of his new-build home. When

Omer arrived, he was looking underneath the bonnet of a Mini. 'Now my hobby makes me my living.'

A Muslim, Sultan was related to one of the first prime ministers of the Syrian Republic, Faris al-Khoury, through his Christian father, Michael. Now in his mid fifties, he had studied at Cambridge and trained as a lawyer in London. Physically he was tall and thin, and he possessed extraordinarily bright green eyes. Omer, though somewhat distracted by tiredness, found him charming.

'I know nothing of anyone finding or seeing that poor girl's body,' he said when Omer suggested that a member of his community might have chanced upon the corpse of Maryam de Mango. 'Like a lot of people, some Syrians went to see the girl at the Golden Gate. Christians particularly. I went once myself. It was odd.'

'In what way?'

They were now sitting in al-Khoury's dirt- and weed-infested garden with tiny cups of strong Arabian coffee similar to the drink known as mirra in Omer's native Mardin. Hopefully, eventually it would wake him up. A new tenant had moved into the flat above the one Omer shared with his sister Peri, and he was desperate to ask her for a date. He'd spent most of the previous night rehearsing what he might say. He still hadn't done it.

'When I was a child, we lived in Paris for a few years, and during that time, my father, a Christian himself, took us to visit the Sanctuary of Our Lady of Lourdes,' al-Khoury said. 'What struck me, even as a ten-year-old, was the singleness of purpose of everyone there. Sick or well, Catholic or not even Christian, everyone wanted something positive to happen. And it did. I didn't see anyone cured, but I did see a lot of people heartened and illuminated by the experience.'

'That didn't happen at the Golden Gate?'

'No,' he said. 'Not to say that I doubt the sincerity of the girl.

I think she saw something that she interpreted as divine. But the people who attended . . .' He shrugged. 'Many had agendas of their own.'

'Like what?'

'Like a lot of people who came were Greek. İstanbul Greek, and from Greece itself. I speak Greek and so I got talking to some of them and discovered that the Golden Gate is a sacred place for them.'

'It's Byzantine. Their ancestors built it.'

'More than that,' al-Khoury said. 'The last emperor of the Byzantines, Constantine Palaiologos, the one who defended the city against the Ottomans in 1453, was, the Greeks believe, rescued from the city walls by an angel and turned into a marble statue. This marble emperor is said to be buried underneath the Golden Gate, ready to one day retake the city for Christianity. A standard once-and-future-king myth, but in this febrile atmosphere of war and rumour of war . . .'

'You think these Greeks might have sought to use Maryam de Mango as a conduit for their ideas?'

'I don't know,' he said. 'Then you had the Salafis, the Muslims who believe wc should live as we did back in the time of the Prophet. They came to hurl abuse and make threats. Then there were the secular people and the uncertain Christians, Muslims and Jews. I got the feeling they wanted and yet at the same time didn't want something to happen. An encounter with the divine, should such a thing happen, might be frightening. Proof of faith may cause one to question the nature of free will, personal agency, democracy – all those modern things we like so much but now fear we may lose under these new religious regimes that keep arising. I have heard that some people attending were suspicious of the girl's motives. My wife even heard one woman, a Christian, say that she believed Maryam de Mango was an agent of the Turkish government. Ludicrous. But maybe not . . .'

Omer's head swam. Now was not the time to be thinking about the girl who lived on the top floor.

'Sir, what do you recall about Tuesday morning?'

'A lot of noise. We didn't know what was going on. We heard men shouting "God is great" but to be honest, that happens frequently. I have two young daughters and so I was intent upon making sure they were safe. People come here sometimes to cause trouble.'

'What people?'

'People who don't like Syrians. It wasn't until the afternoon that we heard the body of the miracle girl had been found here.'

'Who told you?'

He sighed. 'Unfortunately, it was a man called Salah, a Syrian.'

'Why unfortunately?'

'Because he is a fanatic. It made him happy.'

Two men who had been standing at the garden gate for some time now came forward and bowed. They both kissed al-Khoury's hand. They addressed him as 'sidi' – my master – and thanked him for helping their families find decent accommodation. Burhan the gypsy had been quite right about this man, or so it seemed. He got things done and he received respect. He also, if he resembled the other Arab men of power Omer had known back in Mardin, most likely had a somewhat flexible relationship with the law. And being a lawyer himself, he was in the perfect position to do that.

'In the context of the girl's death, do you think I should meet this Salah?' Omer asked.

The two men, having paid their respects, had left.

'Oh, most certainly,' Sultan al-Khoury said.

'You know him?'

He smiled. 'He is married to my sister. Would that he wasn't. I'll give you his address.'

'Thank you.' Omer took a card out of his wallet. 'And if you think of anything else in the meantime, do give me a call,' he said.

Sultan al-Khoury took the card and bowed.

'Maryam only took her shoes off when she reached the Golden Gate,' Father Esposito said. 'To walk from Galata to the walls unshod would have been an act of madness. She would have cut her feet to pieces on these pavements.'

He was right. Even in sensible shoes, a short walk to the local shop could be hazardous as one negotiated uneven paving stones, broken kerbs and poorly fitted manhole covers. There was also the issue of the summer dust turning to thick mud in the winter.

'She took her shoes off as a mark of respect, I think,' the priest said.

'I didn't know Christians did that,' Süleyman said.

'The Holy Father washes the feet of twelve priests representing the twelve apostles of Christ on the day before Good Friday in St Peter's Basilica,' he said. 'The removal of shoes is an act of humility – although I don't know whether Maryam meant it like that. The girl was uneducated in the Church.'

'She didn't become a Catholic?'

'No,' he said. 'Her father wanted her to take the faith. He spoke to me about providing instruction. But I refused.'

'Why?'

'Because that was what *he* wanted. Not her. Maryam did not once come to me and ask for instruction herself.'

'Then why do you think her visions so closely fitted the description of other Marian manifestations?'

'Maybe she read about them. But then again, look at the statues and the pictures of Our Lady just in this church. She has white skin and long brown hair, and is wearing a white dress with a blue stole covering her head, exactly as Maryam de Mango described. This is how Our Lady is perceived.'

63

Süleyman frowned. 'Maybe because . . .'

'That is how she is?' The priest smiled. 'Possibly. Anything is possible. And that includes the notion that the girl was deluded. She lived in a very stressful family situation; she had been given a life-threatening diagnosis. And she liked pretty things, like our statues, our paintings and our flower displays. Some of your mosques are sublime, but they lack the trappings of Catholicism. Maryam liked those as much as she liked her fancy shoes and handbags.'

'What kind of shoes?'

When her body had been found, Maryam had been barefoot. Now that it seemed she hadn't been habitually unshod, where were the shoes she must have been wearing?

'I don't know. I don't take account of such things. All I do know is that they came from Italy. I assume Silvio bought them for her. His only brother exercised his right to an Italian passport some years ago and lives in Milan. Silvio visits him from time to time, I believe. Maybe Maryam went with him.'

Süleyman took in the vast Gothic grandeur of the church ceiling. Familiar with the glass cabinets littered around the walls containing little silver models of body parts, he suddenly felt sad for Maryam de Mango. His second wife had been a Catholic and so he knew that some of these trinkets represented gifts to the Church from people grateful after being cured of some physical malady. Others were more in the way of requests for help. They were desperation.

'Do you know if Maryam had a boyfriend?' he said.

'Not a boyfriend, no.'

Süleyman looked up. 'A man friend?'

The priest paused. Then he said, 'I have no evidence that she had a man friend, no.'

'No evidence?'

'I never observed Maryam with a man in a romantic context,' he said.

'Did you ever hear rumours about her and men?'

'Only the spiteful things that Silvio reported to me that supposedly came from her mother and siblings.'

'Like?'

'They accused her of being a whore. According to Silvio, they even accused him of sleeping with his own daughter.'

'Do you think he did?'

'No. Although I do wonder whether it was Maryam who made that story up.'

'Why would she do that?'

'To cut her mother and siblings off from her father. That family, from what I can gather, is very competitive.'

When Süleyman left the church, he walked down İstiklal Caddesi, stopping to have a cigarette outside the shuttered remains of the old Kelebek corset shop. Until 2015, it had been the last non-Muslim-owned business on İstiklal. Süleyman's family had known the Karaite Jewish corset-makers who had run the place since 1938. When their landlord had put the rent up, due to the encroaching gentrification in the area, they had been obliged to pack up and go. Süleyman could just remember going into the Kelebek with his grandmother, Princess Naciye, when he was a small child. While she had been measured for a new corset, he and his brother had sat with the pattern cutters in a room at the back of the premises, drinking tea and being fed lokum by the owner's wife.

Father Esposito hadn't believed that Silvio de Mango had abused his daughter. He'd also been sure that she hadn't had a boyfriend. It was the issue of a man friend that had caused him problems. He'd been very careful to say he had no evidence that she had such a friend; that he'd never witnessed her with a man in a romantic context. None of what he had said, however, indicated to Süleyman that he hadn't either heard something about Maryam and a man or suspected that she had been in a relationship. Or was he reading too much into what the priest had and had not told him?

Silvio de Mango was drunk. He'd come staggering into police headquarters yelling his head off about wanting to see Süleyman. But Süleyman was out. İkmen, however, had just returned. He took de Mango to his office with instructions to Kerim to go and fetch a very strong coffee.

İkmen offered Silvio a cigarette. 'I'm glad you came in, Mr de Mango,' he said. 'I wanted to speak to you.'

'About what?'

De Mango took a cigarette and lit up. İkmen opened his office window, then he too lit up.

'That can wait,' he said. 'What did you want to see Inspector Süleyman about?'

'Maryam.'

He must have been drinking all night. The smell was oozing out of his pores.

'Do you have some more information for us?'

'No,' he said. 'I want her. I want to bring her home.'

'I'm afraid, at the moment, that isn't possible. Dr Sarkissian has yet to release her body.'

'I thought he'd cut her up already.'

His eyes were black with lack of sleep, the whites red with alcohol.

'Mr de Mango, it is up to Dr Sarkissian when he releases your daughter's body. I'm sorry. He is the expert, I have to trust his judgement. But I can assure you that he will not retain her longer than he feels necessary.'

'People want to visit, you know?' de Mango said. 'Friends. My brother from Italy. It's what we do. It's about respect.'

İkmen didn't know what to say. As far as he was aware, Maryam de Mango, as a Muslim, would be buried quickly according to Islamic custom. What her father seemed to be talking about was having a period of mourning with the corpse in the house. He knew this was what Christians did, but Maryam hadn't been a Christian.

'Have your wife and her family started contacting—'

'My wife?' De Mango shook his head. 'What's she got to do with it?'

There was no way around it. He had to address the issue. 'Sir, my understanding is that Maryam was raised a Muslim . . .'

'Oh, the Muslims who wanted to cut her head off? She was a Christian. She will be buried as a Christian. My family have a plot in Feriköy.'

'Your wife . . .'

'My wife's family, Inspector, are the sort of people who bury their dead in a dust hole and mark it with a rock. If they bury her, no one will ever know that Maryam lived! I am her next of kin. Her body will be released to me.' He was becoming agitated, knitting his fingers.

'Mrs de Mango is her mother . . .'

He raised a thin, dirty finger. 'That bitch has gone,' he said. 'That's how much she cared! Back to her parents with my children. My children!'

'They are adults.'

'Taken them to that hovel in Fatih! Maryam will come back to me,' he said. 'I am her father and she will be buried by me and my family in Feriköy.'

There was a storm brewing here and İkmen resolved to delay it for as long as he was able. He'd have to talk to Arto about the timing of the release of the body.

'All I can do is speak to Dr Sarkissian,' he said. 'Now, sir, I know that Inspector Süleyman is anxious to talk to you about an accusation that has been made against you.'

'An accusation? By whom? About what?'

'About a possible sexual relationship between you and your daughter . . .'

Silvio de Mango laughed; incongruously, İkmen felt.

'Something is funny?'

De Mango wiped his sweating brow with his hand. 'Not strictly. So who was it this time? My wife? Her parents? My children? All of them?'

'Someone has accused you of this crime before?'

He shrugged. 'How many times do you want me to tell you about? It's been happening ever since my daughter showed an interest in my culture. As a teenager, she asked to go with me to Mass. My wife did nothing but berate her, berate me. This country was relatively civilised back then. My wife, though, was ahead of the curve. Covering up to please those illiterate scumbags she calls her brothers . . .'

Bereaved and bitter, Silvio de Mango was hurtling onto dangerous ground.

'Sir . . .'

'I know you can't say anything. I know you probably don't want to,' he said. 'But this is my country too and I am sick and tired of being made to feel like a freak. I have never touched my daughter except to comfort her as a father should. My wife, who once loved me, has been taken from me by an idea that she, of her own volition, once rejected.' He put his cigarette out, took another one from İkmen's packet and lit up. 'She can go back to the thirteenth century if she likes, but she isn't taking me.'

'But isn't the world of miracles a bit, well, thirteenth century . . .'

'What do you know about it? My daughter was special. She was a pure saint. God chose her to live by curing her leukaemia, then he sent the Blessed Virgin to her. All the Muslims say she is the Devil; what can I do? And don't think the Catholics come out of this well either. You think the Bishop could be bothered to come to see her more than once? You think he ever said anything more to her than "Perhaps you need to rest, dear"? Even the Holy See . . . even they don't answer my letters!' He was sobbing. 'And now she's dead.'

Kerim returned with a cup of coffee, which he put on İkmen's desk. İkmen told him to leave again.

'Mr de Mango . . .'

Silvio banged his fist down on the desk. 'I want my daughter home!' he said. 'I want to be able to tell my brother he can come! I want people to pay their respects to my daughter.' He leaned towards İkmen. 'I want to be able to close the shutters on my windows and take my grief into my body and hold it there. Do you understand that?'

İkmen did not feel that now was the time to tell Mr de Mango that his daughter had been no virgin, and that she might have been pregnant when she died.

# Chapter 8

Kemal the barber had to be shitting himself. With his track record, he wasn't going to do well under questioning. Trying to get in with the Order when he'd been in the Grey Wolves? Everyone knew what they'd been like. Drug dealers and woman-isers. So his dad always said.

Erdal Çelik wondered who the barber had accused. Who had been at the other end of the phone when he'd picked it up on Monday morning? And would he give the police that person or just make something up? One thing he felt sure about was that Kemal would not be using his name any time soon. Erdal was no one and nothing, just a short inadequate. And Kemal had always made that very clear to him.

Marlboro the cat, though a battle-scarred and filthy street fighter, took the anchovy from his master's fingers with the utmost care.

'Good boy.'

İkmen stroked the cat's head.

'God knows how many shots I'd have to get if he bit me,' İkmen said to Süleyman. 'I imagine his mouth to be not unlike a sewer. Not that he would ever bite me.' He stroked the cat's head again. 'You're a good boy, aren't you, Marlboro? You're also completely selfish and know when you're well off.'

He gave the cat another fish.

Süleyman, who was accustomed to spending evenings with

İkmen and his cat at the Mozaik bar, called the waiter to bring more rakı.

'This place is not exactly buzzing,' he said as he looked at the empty tables around them. 'Are there more people indoors?'

'Don't think so,' İkmen said. 'Can't smoke in there.'

The waiter arrived with a bottle of rakı and another plate of fish for Marlboro.

Süleyman poured them both small measures of rakı, which he topped up with cold water. This turned the liquid white.

'Çetin,' he said. 'I know it's a bit quick, but does Dr Sarkissian have a result on the pregnancy blood test for Maryam de Mango?'

'No,' İkmen said. 'Not yet.' He lit a cigarette. 'Wonder whose it is, if she is pregnant. Don't think it's her father's. According to him, his family have accused him of incest for years. He laughed when I told him what they'd said.'

'He was drunk, wasn't he?'

They'd talked back in Süleyman's office about Silvio de Mango and his desperate need to give his Muslim daughter a Christian burial.

'Yes,' İkmen said. 'The terrible, scorching drunkenness that can accompany grief. But I really don't think he was lying.'

Süleyman sighed. 'I feel that Father Esposito is and isn't lying,' he said. 'He chose his words very carefully when he told me he has no evidence that Maryam was in a relationship with a man. What he didn't say was that he knew she wasn't. I'm afraid he may know something but be completely unable to say so.'

'This is, I take it, the Seal of the Confessional?'

'I fear so, yes.'

'My understanding is that if a priest knows that someone is guilty of something, he can recommend to them that they go to the police. Crazy but true, and one of the reasons why I don't do religion. Be interesting to know how many priests take murder confessions during the course of their careers.'

'Doesn't help us.' Süleyman shook his head. 'But Maryam was a Muslim. Why would she even go to confession?'

'I don't know,' İkmen said. 'Because she wanted to be like her father? As far as I know, anyone can go into one of those boxes and talk . . .'

'Well I think he knows something,' Süleyman said. 'But I can't prove it.'

İkmen sighed. 'So, how did Omer get on with the Syrians of Sulukule?'

'He spoke to the local godfather,' Süleyman said. 'A man called Sultan al-Khoury – a cross between a respectable London barrister and Scarface, by the sound of him. He gave Omer the name of his brother-in-law, the man who told the Syrian community on Tuesday afternoon that Maryam was dead, and did it with great glee apparently.'

'He was given to us by his brother-in-law?'

'Yes. Omer went to see this man, Salah Hadad, with al-Khoury's blessing – which he felt was odd until he got there to find that Hadad was out of his mind on bonzai. Omer was obliged to call for transport to take him to Bakırköy Psychiatric Hospital. Which is probably what the Sulukule godfather wanted all along. Troublesome relative out of the way for whom he now has no responsibility. As you can imagine, as of this moment, there is no getting any sense out of Mr Hadad about what happened on Tuesday afternoon or at any other time.'

İkmen sighed.

'However . . .' Süleyman took his tablet computer out of his jacket pocket and put it on the table. Marlboro, who had finished his fish, eyed the thing up. Süleyman pointed at the cat. 'Not for you.'

'So what is this?' İkmen asked.

Süleyman brought up a series of photographs. 'These are press pictures of Maryam de Mango at the Golden Gate,' he said. 'If you scroll through, you'll see images from January, February and March.'

He handed the computer to İkmen, who put on his reading glasses. He didn't like using them, but if he didn't, he couldn't see a thing.

'Am I looking for anything in particular?' he said. 'I mean, I know what the girl looks like . . .'

Süleyman said nothing.

'Is that Silvio?'

Süleyman leaned over his shoulder. 'Yes. And the man behind him, I should tell you, is Bishop Juan-Maria Montoya of the Apostolic Vicariate of İstanbul. He is the Pope's man here in the city.'

İkmen peered at the screen. 'He looks constipated,' he said.

'That's not what I'm asking you to look at, Çetin.'

'Ah!' İkmen looked up. 'Shoes!'

'Yes,' Süleyman said. 'In some but not all of the photos Maryam is wearing shoes. This does underline what Father Esposito said about the barefoot myth, and therefore raises the question: where are those shoes? Because as you can see, they are very distinctive.'

He enlarged the picture. The shoes had high but substantial heels. As far as İkmen could tell, they were a shiny dark blue and had gently pointed toes. On the front of each shoe was an oval panel made from pleated pink leather, held in place by rows of large pearl buttons on either side. Even İkmen could see that they were beautiful.

Süleyman said, 'Unusual, eh?'

'I'd say so,' İkmen said. 'My daughters would love them.'

'I think most women would,' Süleyman said.

'Where do they come from?'

'Italy,' he said. 'Tracked the style, which is known as "Urraca" and is made by a designer shoe company in Milan called Incorruttibile.'

İkmen looked up. 'Incorruptible. That's hopeful,' he said. 'I wonder how quickly these things fall apart?'

'Well maybe they've fallen apart and maybe they haven't,' Süleyman said. 'But I didn't see those shoes in Maryam's bedroom or anywhere else.'

'We'll circulate that image,' İkmen said. 'Important that Yıldız gets it. Maybe the little girls of Sulukule are running around in them.'

'Sure.'

He took a drink and lit another cigarette. 'What did you make of Mrs de Mango when you met her?' he asked.

'Compared to the rest of her family, she appeared almost sane,' Süleyman said. 'She identified the body without incident. I must say, I found her response to her daughter's corpse somewhat cold, but who am I to judge? Everything happened very quickly. She must have been in shock. But she didn't accuse her husband of abusing Maryam. That was the younger son, Mevlüt.'

'The one who looks a bit . . .'

'Taliban, yes. She said her younger daughter tells lies. It was her opinion that she does this because she's ashamed of her Christian father.'

'If true, that is a damning indictment of our times,' İkmen said.

'Sara, the daughter, didn't confess to lying, but she did say that her sister Maryam lied.'

İkmen shook his head. 'Oh what a tangled web we weave . . .'

'And then there are the people who came to see Maryam at the Golden Gate,' Süleyman said. 'If you look at the press coverage, you will notice that certain people are always in attendance. Her father, of course, but also two women and a man.' He pointed at three figures who were all standing near the girl. 'They're in every still and movie I've been able to find so far. We need to find out who they are. Silvio de Mango may know, he may not.'

İkmen leaned back in his chair and knitted his fingers underneath his chin. 'So many possibilities,' he said. 'Who would want a living saint dead, eh? Those who are jealous of her gift, or whatever one calls the girl's visions? Those whose God is not hers?'

'Her family?'

He nodded. 'Those whose God is hers but who cannot believe in her?'

'Those whose motives do not include the miraculous,' Süleyman said.

İkmen smiled. 'The banal. We should never forget or ignore it, my dear Mehmet.'

They'd requested his telephone records from his mobile company. They'd find the call. They'd ask him who it was from and he'd have to say he didn't know. Because he didn't.

The police would find out. Or would they? Didn't people like that have ways of disguising their footprints? But then there had been talk about the girl in the mahalle for months, and most of it had been done by men of influence. Men who made things happen, men with whom one had to get along at the very least.

The girl had threatened their way of life. Kemal Öneş couldn't see how, but he had to accept that they were right. They were learned men and he was a fool who had once upon a time dealt coke to enraged nationalists.

He'd done what they'd told him. And he'd protected them.

It was like living his youth all over again, without the physical resilience. But he'd end up OK. They'd take care of him. If they hadn't trusted him, he would never have got that call.

When her mother got into the bed beside her, Ayşegül de Mango pretended she was asleep. As soon as she'd arrived with the children, her mother had started.

'You should've got that girl married off!' she'd said. 'Then she wouldn't't've had time for evil! You killed her by neglect, and now her soul is lost.'

She was upset at Maryam's death, but not nearly as upset as she'd been when the girl had begun seeing 'the mother'. She'd even threatened to kill Maryam herself. Ayşegül had hated supporting her mother's ridiculous opinions. She'd berated herself endlessly for the times she'd humiliated the girl when her brothers came round to the apartment. What a coward she had been!

So much had changed since she'd married Silvio. When they met, she'd been so much in love with him she would have died rather than not be his wife. Rejecting her family had been easy. But when her father had decided he wanted his daughter back in his life again, Ayşegül had welcomed her family with open arms. Life in Beyoğlu with Silvio had not worked out the way she had imagined, and she had become lonely. It had been such a small thing to then cover her head to please her brothers.

Silvio had raged against it. He'd even thrown her family out a few times when they came to the apartment. But there was a limit. He didn't have possession of the moral high ground, not after what he'd done. And he knew it.

And now her mother was banging on about how she should get Sara married off immediately. Sara, of course, said nothing on the subject. Then Mevlüt had put in his opinion, which was that he thought marriage was the best thing for his sister. Silvio would go wild when he found out.

Her mother pushed her fat bottom against Ayşegül's back, shuffling her over until she was clinging on to the side of bed. Then she farted. Silvio had been Ayşegül's route out of all this, and if she'd stuck to her guns and never spoken to her family again, maybe her marriage would still be good.

But she knew that was nonsense. Her marriage had never been good. Even when she'd been in love and he'd taken her out every night. There had always been a problem and it had always been Maryam. Or rather, it had been Maryam and Silvio. As the girl had grown up, he'd favoured her more and more. Ayşegül knew he liked to delude himself that this was because Maryam showed an interest in his world, but she knew better. He had made her in his own image and then blamed his other children for noticing.

Ayşegül blamed herself. She could have explained it to them. But she hadn't. One became used to being silent, she thought.

# Chapter 9

'I'd only just learned her name.' Commissioner Hürrem Teker shook her head.

'There's no doubt the call came from her phone?' İkmen said.

'None at all. You called me directly as soon as you found the girl's body. I told Melis Hanım to call Dr Sarkissian and give him details of your whereabouts while I informed Inspector Süleyman. One doesn't expect one's secretary to betray one. Ceyda Hanım wouldn't have betrayed me.'

Ceyda Hanım, an old-fashioned Atatürkist bluestocking, had been with the commissioner for years, right from when she was an assistant commissioner in Gaziantep. Efficient and discreet, she had always got on with her work quietly and modestly. She'd retired in January and had been replaced by a woman who had come highly recommended by several of Teker's most influential superiors. She'd been in the post a month.

'Do we know what Kemal Öneş has to say about it?' İkmen asked.

'I've yet to speak to him,' Teker said. 'So much for the mythical police officer who walked into his shop and told him the girl was dead. Although it would seem that his intel did come out of this department . . .'

'What does Melis Hanım say?'

'Nothing,' she said. 'I had her picked up first thing this morning and brought straight to me. She didn't say a word.'

'Any notion that she's connected to this Kemal in some way?' İkmen said.

'No connection to anyone in Çarşamba as far as we know.'

'Where does she live?'

'In a posh flat in Şişli bought for her by her mummy and daddy, who live nearby and also have a lovely summer house in Yeniköy. I don't know whether you've noticed her clothes but they're all high-end. A thoroughly modern young woman. But it's my own fault,' Teker said. 'I should've been alerted to her unsuitability by the names of those who recommended her.'

'Who were?'

'I'd rather not say.'

He understood. There had never been a time when everyone in the department had been entirely in agreement about everything. But since the Gezi protests in 2013, things had changed. Significantly, many of those at the top of the department had changed. And some of them possessed strong opinions.

'I knew I should have chosen someone myself,' she said. 'But I wanted to appear flexible. I also wanted to trust. I was wrong.'

'Or Melis Hanım duped our superiors too?'

She said nothing.

He didn't ask her whether she knew what Melis Hanım had said to Kemal the barber. For once, he hoped this had been recorded – and not subsequently lost.

It was a beautiful day. Warm without being hot. After breakfast, Mina Amara had taken two chairs into the street so that they could sit out in what she called 'the fresh air'. But Lobna hadn't joined her. What wafted in from Tarlabaşı Bulvarı into the warren-like lanes of the quarter was neither fresh nor even probably air.

Both Lobna and her sister Mina could remember when Tarlabaşı Bulvarı didn't exist. Built in 1988, it had cut Tarlabaşı off from the rest of Beyoğlu. Isolated, the old district had rotted, making the upkeep of old Greek and Levantine houses like the one that belonged to the Amara sisters a nightmare.

Every day, or so it seemed, something broke, fell off or exploded. This morning a cornice stone had dropped from the first floor into the street, narrowly missing a kid throwing rotten fruit at a rat.

As usual, Lobna could smell sewerage. Apparently when the quarter was redeveloped the sewers would be fixed. But that was contingent upon the sisters selling their house to the property developer, and that was never going to happen. Their great-grandfather, a Sicilian tailor called Michelangelo, had bought the house as a new-build at the end of the nineteenth century. Since then the Amara family had hung on to it in spite of violence, punitive taxation, earthquakes and gang warfare. The girls' Turkish mother had died there. It was sacred ground.

Lobna switched the television on, but finding herself amid wall-to-wall chat shows, she turned it off again. She couldn't think straight. It was all right for Mina; she'd only met the girl through Lobna. She hadn't *known* her.

Maryam de Mango had been three years old when Lobna had first met her. Silvio and his family had come to Lobna's wedding, which had been held at St Anthony's. Back in those days, she remembered, Ayşegül de Mango hadn't covered her head, and at the reception afterwards, she had drunk rakı like everyone else. She even had a recollection that Ayşegül had flirted with Fabrizio. Lobna had been furious with both of them. But then Fabrizio had been very handsome in his youth. Even in middle age he was stunning. Was that why Lobna had married him? Because of his looks? Probably. It was also why she had divorced him. Men like Fabrizio got propositioned by women all the time. Not all men, however, did anything about it – at least not in the way he had.

She sat down. The tiredness was terrible again this morning. She'd slept all night but had woken up exhausted. She'd been like it for weeks. Once Mina had stopped moaning to the neighbours in the street, she'd be in again pouring fruit and vegetables into that expensive juicer she'd bought, creating vile cocktails for Lobna to take one sip from and then throw out of the window.

Suddenly she needed to go to the toilet. Incontinence again. She tried to haul herself out of her chair, but her body was slack and sack-like. She wished she still had her stick. If only she could remember where she'd put the thing! She'd have to get a new one. Not that it would ever be the same . . .

When Ayşegül had first moved into the de Mango apartment, she'd been amazed by its size. Because he'd always lived there, Silvio had never noticed. But now that he was alone, he did. Now that his father, mother, siblings, wife and children had gone, the place seemed massive.

The building had been constructed to look like a Venetian palazzo, and had originally been divided into four mansion flats. Now only the de Mangos' apartment remained in its original form. The other three properties had long ago been cut up into smaller units, inhabited by foreigners and loud Turkish families.

Silvio had already had a drink. With a bottle of rakı in one hand and a cigarette in the other, he wandered from the ostentatious entrance hall, through the dusty dining room and on through one of the two drawing rooms into the tiny chapel that nestled at the heart of the property. Had Maryam fallen in love with the Holy Virgin because of that pale wax statue of Our Lady to which Silvio's father had prayed for his soul when he'd told him he was going to marry a Muslim? Had she, so many years later, fallen under its spell?

When he was finally able to bring her home, he'd lay Maryam in the chapel so that people could come and pay their respects.

It was fitting. And with Ayşegül and the children out of the way, he could do what he liked. He could do what Maryam would have wanted.

The doorbell rang and he put his bottle down on the altar and went to the front door.

'Who is it?'

'Mr de Mango, it's Inspector Süleyman. Can I come up?'

He buzzed him in. What the fuck did he want?


'We know that Melis Bila called you at ten thirty-three on Tuesday morning.'

Kemal Öneş shrugged. 'I don't know anyone of that name,' he said.

'Well, she called you,' Teker said.

'A wrong number . . .'

'No,' she said. 'She told you that Maryam de Mango was dead. Melis Hanım is my secretary. How do you know her?'

'I don't.'

'That's not what she says.'

He looked down at the floor.

'She says that the two of you share an interest in the radical Islamist group known as ISIS,' she said. 'Although I don't believe her.'

He looked up. 'That's right!'

'No, I think that you and Melis Hanım have a connection to the Order. And before you say anything else, I must tell you that the Order is not considered a terrorist organisation or any sort of threat. In fact, they are well respected. However, there are those connected to them who were alarmed by the phenomenon that was Maryam de Mango. No one is saying they killed her, but they certainly had an interest in her death.'

He said, 'You don't know any of this.'

'How do you know I don't?'

He looked into her eyes.

'You don't know what Melis Hanım has told me,' she said.

'No,' he said. 'But if she did tell you that, she's lying. And you will find out she's lying.'

'And how will I do that?'

'Because this investigation will stop.'

There was a certainty in his eyes that Teker didn't like. It resembled the arrogant look that Melis Hanım had given her when she'd tried to get her to speak. She hadn't, and Teker knew why. There was a connection between Melis and a member of the Order. But it was not one she could ever reveal.

Did Kemal Öneş know this?

Men didn't come to the Amara sisters' house – at least not men who were clean and good-looking. Old Raşit Bey delivered their water, but he was about ninety. The rest of their male visitors consisted of the drug-addled boys that Mina insisted on giving pastries to in an effort to, as she put it, build them up. These men in the kitchen were quite different.

The taller of the two, a ragingly handsome individual probably in early middle age, announced himself as Inspector Süleyman from police headquarters. The younger man with him, also good-looking but in a darker, more ethnic sort of way, was Sergeant Mungun.

'I believe that you knew Maryam de Mango,' Süleyman said.

Mina, whose eyes had nearly been popping out of her head when she brought the two men to the kitchen, urged them to sit down and immediately went to fuss around the samovar. Lobna could see that her sister was blushing like crazy. At her age.

'Yes,' Lobna said. 'My ex-husband is best friends with Maryam's father. They've known each other all their lives.'

'Your ex-husband is Fabrizio Leon.' Süleyman pushed a photograph across the table towards her. 'This man.'

There she was, standing between Fabrizio and Mina.

'Yes,' she said. Fabrizio in his pomp, smiling. Lobna wondered how he'd react to this Süleyman person. He didn't like men more attractive than himself. 'Silvio invited me. He thought I might benefit from it. My ex wasn't too happy about it.'

'Why not? You're all Levantine Christians, aren't you?'

'My divorce was acrimonious,' she said.

'But you're still friendly with Silvio.'

'Oh yes.'

Mina chipped in. 'Who wants tea?'

The younger officer smiled. 'Thank you,' he said. 'That would be nice.'

'How do you take it?'

'Strong, no sugar.'

'So you knew Maryam?' Süleyman asked.

'Yes. Since she was a baby.' Lobna smiled. 'She was a beautiful child. The apple of her father's eye.'

'And her mother?'

'Ayşegül? Well, she loved her, just as she loved her other children.'

'No problems?'

Mina cut in. 'You mean because Ayşegül became religious? Yes,' she said.

It was pointless for Lobna to try and make her stop. Mina had always disliked Ayşegül.

Mina gave Sergeant Mungun a glass of tea and sat down.

'Those children were brought up Muslims. What more did the woman want?' she said. 'So Maryam was interested in her father's culture . . .' She shrugged. 'Ayşegül was happy enough when the Church cured Maryam of cancer!'

That wasn't strictly true, but Lobna let it pass.

'We are as entitled as anyone in this city to—'

'Have you spoken to Fabrizio?' Lobna cut across her sister before she talked herself into some sort of religious one-upmanship contest.

'No,' said Süleyman. 'Once Mr de Mango had identified those with him in press photographs of his daughter, we came here. We will speak to him. I believe he lives on Tomtom Kaptan Sokak . . .'

'He's turned his family home into a hotel,' she said.

He looked down at his phone. 'The Dondolo. Does he run it on his own?'

'Sometimes,' she said. 'Depends whether he can persuade any of his women to help him.'

God, that was bitter – and unfair. Fabrizio had not, to her knowledge, ever employed his lovers. For all his faults, he ran his business as a professional. She saw Mina look daggers at her. But it was too late.

'His women?' Süleyman said.

Mina went to the food cupboard and took out the plate of börek she usually reserved for her junkies.

'It's why we got divorced,' Lobna said.

'He was unfaithful.'

'Yes.'

'Börek?' Mina put the plate on the table and then sat down again. 'Why do you want to know about us, Inspector?'

'We're interviewing everyone who was close to Maryam de Mango,' he said. 'She has been unlawfully killed, which means we have to try and find out who did that, and why. And in order to do that, we must build up a picture of Maryam using those closest to her.'

'We weren't close . . .'

'But you knew her.'

'Oh yes.'

He turned his big brown eyes on Lobna. 'You said that Mr

de Mango thought you might benefit from attending Maryam's visions,' he said. 'What do you mean by that?'

Lobna smiled. This man had to have noticed how ghastly she looked. How gallant of him not to comment.

'I have leukaemia,' she said.

'Like Maryam.'

'Until she was cured, yes,' she said. 'Believe it or not, I am in remission at the moment.'

'Which means that you are currently free of the disease?'

'Theoretically,' Lobna said. 'Though I'm not feeling very disease-free. Not since Maryam died. Everybody said I was looking so much better when I had her in my life. I don't know . . .'

Out of the corner of her eye she saw Mina frowning.

The lovely officer smiled. 'So where were you ladies on Tuesday evening?' he asked.

'I was watching television,' Mina said.

'I was in bed.' Lobna looked down. 'I go to bed early these days. I have to.'

'Oh yes, she does,' Mina said. 'My sister goes to bed really early these days.'

Although he had only been resident in İstanbul for five years, Father Benito Esposito knew his small congregation well. The only exception to this was the girls who had come from the Philippines to work for the new rich in gleaming high-rise districts like Başakşehir. They came and then they went as their often unpredictable masters and mistresses desired. Everyone else was either of Italian or French Levantine heritage or one of the very few Turkish Muslim converts.

Even when he couldn't see them in the confessional, he knew who they were. Old Mrs Russo, for instance, always had a coughing fit before she sat down. Then she usually tried to

86

disguise her voice to make herself sound like a man. Antonio Baltazzi whispered, and Betül Darıcıoğlu always cried.

The priest knew there was one parishioner he *had* to talk to. But how?

İkmen knew he recognised the woman who had sat down next to him, pushing her face almost into his, but he couldn't place her.

'İkmen.'

She had a heavily lined, ravaged beauty at odds with her perfectly coiffured blonde hair. However, the most striking thing about her was her attire, which was so floridly and spectacularly ragged she could only, surely, be a beggar.

'Madam?' he said.

Underneath the table, Marlboro the cat, whom she had unceremoniously pushed off his usual chair outside the Bar Mozaik, growled.

'İrini,' she said.

It meant nothing to him.

'I'm sorry . . .'

'My father was Khryses Bey.'

It wasn't often that Çetin İkmen was left speechless, but this was one of those times. Khryses Bey was a name from his childhood. A Byzantine Greek, a tall, aristocratic-looking man, he had, when İkmen had known him, been a simit seller. Long ago, he had owned a fine café on İstiklal Caddesi, but like so many others, he had gone out of business after the anti-Greek riots of 1955. Left effectively destitute, he had married a Turkish woman and taken over her father's simit stall when the old man died. In time, he and the Turkish woman had produced two girls, Io and İrini. Poor even by the standards of 1960s İstanbul, the family had lived on the edge of the gypsy quarter in Sulukule.

'You arrested me three times,' the woman continued.

87

And he had. Each time for soliciting.

He took her hand. 'İrini Hanım.'

'Çetin Bey.'

Her eyes were full of tears. He bent his head and kissed her grubby fingers. As a young girl, she had possessed the kind of beauty that could make a man go mad.

'It's good to see you,' he said.

'And you.' She was crying.

'Oh, İrini Hanım, what is the matter?' he said.

He called one of the waiters over and asked him to bring the woman a brandy. He couldn't have seen her for at least twenty years. The last time, he recalled, he'd put her in a cell for the night to sober up. The intervening years had not, by the look of her, been kind.

The waiter arrived with the brandy and İkmen said, 'Here, hanım. Drink.'

She picked up the glass and threw the whole lot down her neck in one gulp. She'd always had trouble with booze. He knew he shouldn't be encouraging her, but she had the look of a person for whom only alcohol would do.

'What is the matter?' he asked. 'How can I help you?'

Apparently calmed by the alcohol, she sat back in her chair. 'Çetin Bey,' she said, 'someone has murdered my daughter.'

He didn't have time for this peacocking Turk!

'I went to support Silvio,' he said. 'We've been friends since childhood.'

Fabrizio had always enjoyed having his photograph taken, but in this instance, he wished he hadn't. He'd looked good in the Hürriyet photo, a bit spiritual even, standing next to Maryam as she saw . . . whatever it was she'd seen. At the time he'd been a bit cross about the fact that Lobna and her frowzy sister had been in the shot too. Now, however, he had other problems.

'What can you tell us about Maryam de Mango?' Inspector Mehmet Süleyman asked.

'She was my friend Silvio's kid,' he said. 'What do you want me to say?'

'What was she like? Did you believe in her visions? You are, I have been told, a Christian. I am not aware of any involvement from the Holy See. How did you feel about that?'

Yiğit was on the front desk, but there was little point. Nobody had checked in for over a week. Everybody who had taken rooms had checked out. Fucking terror attacks. Still he had to pay his staff and it pissed him off. Sitting in the bar, he would normally have offered the policemen coffee, but that would eat into his losses even further. Besides, this Süleyman and his slant-eyed sergeant were annoying.

'What do you want me to say?' he reiterated. 'Maryam was a clever kid who got sick. I was happy for her when she got better.'

'Do you believe she was cured by God?'

He shrugged. 'I don't know. I'm not heavy on religion. I was brought up a Catholic but my dad was a Jew, I've always been conflicted. Living with two religions does that to you.'

'Do you think Maryam was conflicted in a similar way?'

'Probably. Silvio never pushed Catholicism on her or any of the other kids. Can't say the same for Ayşegül in recent years.'

'She wanted the children to actively pursue Islam?'

'Didn't seem to be enough for her that they were brought up in her faith. Not that she gave too much of a shit when she and Silvio were first together.'

'What do you mean?'

'I mean she happily left her family to be with him,' he said. 'I always thought she was glad to get away. Kids were brought up nominally Muslim. But then about ten years ago she began to get, as she said, worried about how the children would be perceived in a society that was becoming more conservative. Silvio always believed Ayşegül's brothers had a hand in that decision. I don't know. Then she started covering . . .'

Süleyman looked like the type of man who would have a glamorous modern wife and a couple of sexy mistresses on the go. But who knew? Maybe his wife was a tiny covered mouse of a thing who walked ten paces behind and always looked at the pavement. Fabrizio shut up.

'It's been said that Ayşegül de Mango mistreated Maryam because of her apparent adherence to Catholicism. Do you know anything about this?'

And here was a trap. Fabrizio would have to be careful. Muslims didn't like hearing too many bad things about other Muslims, in his experience.

'No,' he said.

'I'm surprised,' the inspector said. 'Maryam complained to her father. Did he not tell you?'

'Not that I remember.'

Fabrizio had humoured Silvio. He'd had to. Maryam did tell lies. Just not all the time.

'Maryam's one fault was that she made stuff up,' he said.

'What sort of stuff?'

'Oh, trivial things. Imagining people didn't like her when they did. Fantasising about men who might or might not fancy her . . .'

'Did she have a boyfriend?'

'How should I know? Have you asked Silvio?'

'Yes.'

'And?'

'And what passed between Mr de Mango and myself is not for public consumption.'

Fabrizio shrugged. 'I'll ask him.'

'You do that, sir.'

The cop didn't like him any more than he liked the cop. With his flash Italian suit, his pointy-toed shoes and his face straight out of an Ottoman romance, Süleyman made Fabrizio want to puke. What was more, he was poking around areas that he shouldn't.

'Your ex-wife, Miss Lobna Amara, says that Mr de Mango invited her to witness Maryam's visions in front of the Golden Gate. Is that correct?' Süleyman asked.

'Yeah.'

'Not you?'

'No.'

'You know she has leukaemia?'

'Of course.'

'Do you think Mr de Mango invited your ex-wife in anticipation that contact with Maryam and her visions might cure her?'

'You'd have to ask Silvio,' he said.

The policeman's phone rang and he excused himself to answer it. While he took the call, the other cop, Sergeant Mungun, said, 'Do you live here on the premises, sir?'

'Yes,' he said. 'I've lived on Tomtom Kaptan all my life. Before I turned it into the Dondolo Hotel, this whole building was my home. I inherited it from my mother.'

'It's very beautiful.'

Was he jealous? A lot of the Turks were.

Fabrizio said, 'Nobody gave us anything, you know. We worked for it.'

The young man appeared flustered. 'Well, yes, of course . . .'

Süleyman ended his call and returned. 'I'm sorry, Fabrizio Bey, but Sergeant Mungun and myself have to go.'

The young man stood up. Fabrizio inwardly sighed with relief. 'Oh?' he said. 'Why?'

'Something has come up,' the arrogant Süleyman said.

'Oh dear,' Fabrizio replied. 'What a pity.'

# Chapter 10

Even by old Sulukule standards, İrini Mavroyeni's shack was
pitiful. Beyond a bed, all it contained was an old stove, a broken
television and a stack of empty rakı bottles.

'Look out for any women's clothing that might be clean,' Kerim
Gürsel instructed the small team of officers helping him search.

One of the young constables said, 'Not much chance of that.'

'Oi!' Kerim held up a warning finger. 'Bit of respect. İrini
Hanım is a friend of Çetin Bey. And she's lost her daughter. And
when forensics get here, I want them to be able to find something, so don't trash the place!'

The team continued the search in silence.

İrini's daughter had been due to visit her on the day she died.
But İrini had been nervous, and so, in order to make herself feel
better, had drunk herself into a stupor. Whether her daughter had
actually gained access to her property while her mother was
drunk was not something İrini could remember. Maybe she had
and maybe she hadn't. Had they met, it would have been stressful
for both of them. Maybe the daughter had chickened out.

Silvio wasn't drunk, but he'd had a few. He'd had a few all his
adult life.

'There's no point lying, because these days there are things
called DNA tests that can determine familial relationships,' Çetin
İkmen said. 'Can't say I understand why you lied, *if* you lied,
in the first place.'

92

Silvio lit a cigarette. Did he have to spell it out? Was the man a fucking idiot?

'OK. It was because we wanted all our children to be treated the same,' he said. 'We didn't want brothers and sisters to be at odds.'

'Yes, but surely your parents, your wife's family . . .'

'My mother was already dead and my father died just after I met my wife. Ayşegül left her family to be with me,' he said.

He'd felt bad only telling her not long before she'd moved in. But she'd accepted it, and later, she'd colluded.

'As far as anyone apart from my best friend Fabrizio knew, Ayşegül was pregnant when we got married,' he said. 'Two years later, she *was* pregnant.'

'But Maryam was not her daughter.'

He sipped brandy. 'No.'

'And so is İrini Mavroyeni the mother of your first child?' İkmen asked.

'She was always up for it.' Silvio smiled. Beautiful and easy, İrini would do anything for the price of a bottle. And unlike the gypsy whores up in Sulukule, she had, he always thought, a European dignity about her. 'Ayşegül was left-wing in those days, but I couldn't get her to embrace free love. Not until we married. I was a young man; what was I supposed to do?'

'İrini Mavroyeni was a prostitute,' İkmen said. 'How did you know Maryam was yours?'

'Strictly I suppose I didn't.' He'd never even considered it until now. It had always seemed absurd. 'I was in a bad way at the time. My father was dying. Both my siblings were abroad by then. I was in love with Ayşegül, but she wouldn't let me touch her. I went up to Sulukule to get drunk and I found İrini. I didn't love her, but she was the most terrific fuck. You know how these things are. I had to pay but I kept going back.'

'For how long?'

'Weeks? A month. I don't know. Then she told me she was knocked up and . . .' He shrugged.

'Did she tell you she wanted to get rid of it?'

She'd known a woman who'd do it for a small fee. Of course she had! But he'd begged her to hold off until he'd spoken to Ayşegül. Poor Ayşegül. She'd cried and cried.

'Yes, she did,' he said.

'And you?'

'I'm a Catholic,' Silvio said. 'I'm a bad one, but I am one. I said I'd keep her while she was pregnant and take the baby off her when it was born.'

'What about your girlfriend?'

'Ayşegül said she'd raise it as her own. But only if nobody knew,' he said. 'Those were her terms. When my father died, she moved in. We still didn't make love until we married. She's a good woman. She was . . .'

'And yet if, as you say, your wife wasn't happy to sleep with you, how could she consent to lying about being pregnant? Surely she'd want people to think she was still, on the face of things, a good Muslim woman?'

'I don't know what went on in her head!' Silvio said. 'Ask her! That's what happened.'

İkmen said, 'You accused your wife of abusing your daughter, Mr de Mango.'

'Maryam told me she did.'

'When did Maryam find out that Ayşegül wasn't her mother?'

He looked at the floor. 'When I thought she might die.'

'So before she was apparently cured of leukaemia?'

'Yes.'

Maryam had been bitching about Ayşegül for months. She'd started going to church with him, which hadn't helped. Ayşegül had threatened to kill her within his hearing. He'd taken her aside and had a word. Hadn't she forgotten the girl wasn't her child? It had got worse then and so he'd told Maryam. She'd sworn she'd said nothing to anyone, but whether that was true he didn't know.

'Maryam said she didn't tell her mother, but Ayşegül's verbal attacks increased,' he said. 'I became fearful for her life.'

'How did Maryam find out that İrini Mavroyeni was her mother?' İkmen asked.

'She badgered me until I told her.'

'When?'

'Last month.'

'İrini says that you went to see her and asked her whether she'd meet Maryam.'

'That's true.'

'So you knew where Maryam was going the night she died?'

'Yes.'

'Why didn't you tell us?' İkmen said. 'Didn't you think we might need to know that she was due at İrini's place? İrini herself doesn't know whether Maryam arrived or not. She was very nervous and did what she always does in such circumstances: got drunk. Or so she says.'

Was he implying that İrini had killed Maryam?

'İrini wouldn't hurt anyone,' he said.

'You think?'

Did İkmen know something he didn't?

'I thought that maybe she'd stayed over at İrini's,' Silvio said. 'I reckoned they had a lot to talk about.'

'You said at the time that you thought Ayşegül had killed her.'

'I was angry,' he said. 'Ayşegül had tried to stop Maryam going out that night. I'd had to release her from her own bedroom. Then Ayşegül had chased after her. I thought maybe she'd caught her. Neither of them was home when I got up on Tuesday morning.'

'Did Ayşegül know where she was going?'

95

'No!'

'So more secrets.' İkmen folded his arms across his chest. 'What are we to believe, eh, Mr de Mango?'

'Ask my wife,' he said. 'She'll tell you. Oh, and you should know, Inspector, that after Maryam died, Ayşegül wanted the truth to be told.'

'And you didn't?'

'I had a little bonfire . . .'

Hospital records; a witnessed certificate from İrini putting her child into the care of its father in perpetuity.

'You do know, I trust,' İkmen said, 'that İrini's lodgings and Burhan the gypsy's coffee house are in completely different parts of Sulukule?'

'Yes . . .'

'Which means that we may well have been looking in the wrong place for clues to what happened to your daughter.'

'She was found at the back of the coffee house . . .'

'Which is not necessarily where she was initially assaulted,' İkmen said. 'She died outside Burhan's but her shoes are still missing, which could mean that she was fighting for her life elsewhere.'

The Order didn't usually bother with Syrians. Sultan al-Khoury knew the old sheikh by sight, but they'd never spoken before. Now the sheikh was sitting in the garden beside the mulberry bush drinking hibiscus tea. Uncharitably, Sultan couldn't get out of his head the idea that he'd come in the wake of that policeman's visit.

'We meant the girl no harm,' the old man said. 'We feel sorry for such people because clearly they must be deluded.'

'Of course.'

'I also wanted to commiserate with you,' he continued. 'I heard that your brother-in-law was taken . . .'

'To Bakırköy, sadly,' Sultan said. 'The police wanted to speak to him, but the poor man is insane.' He didn't mention the bonzai.

'I know of him,' the old man said. 'I fear poor Salah was disturbed by that girl's visions.'

'He told us the body had been found,' Sultan said, adding a trifle slyly, 'I believe your people knew before we did . . .'

'People come in and out of our quarter.' The old man smiled. 'I myself didn't know anything until the afternoon.'

'People from Çarşamba were here in the morning.'

'I've no doubt,' he said. 'But nobody that I know.'

'I never said that,' Sultan said. 'To anyone.'

The old man smiled.

When he left, Sultan felt as if they understood one another. Nobody had seen or done anything the night the girl had died. Except maybe Salah, but he was safely tucked away in Bakırköy, which was a mercy. Sultan had been desperate to get his only sister out of Salah's orbit. Now his dear Amal was happier and calmer than she'd been for a long time. Also it was nice for Bana, his wife, to have another woman in the house. Their girls were growing fast, and fourteen-year-old Layal was proving to be a particular problem, especially around young men. Another pair of eyes was always useful.

Of course Sultan kept Layal indoors. If any young man so much as looked at her, he'd kill him. But soon he'd have to act. There were one or two Syrian families in Sulukule who still possessed good connections, and he knew one of them had sons.

His younger daughter came through the garden gate. At ten, Nour was still tied to her dolls and her soft toys. She pushed a tiny pram filled with soft monkeys and a pair of blonde Barbies.

'Where have you been, my little songbird?' Sultan said as she walked towards him.

'To the clothes shop,' Nour said.

'The clothes shop?'

She lived in a world of her own, this one.

'Where's that?'

'If I told you, the dolls would get upset and cut your head off,' she said.

'Oh no, surely—'

'They would,' she said. 'I know. It's what people do. I've seen them.'

Sultan felt his body go cold. When were any of them ever going to be normal again?

Inside the house, his elder daughter looked out of the window at her sister and scowled.

The landlord would never come. He was always making appointments and then forgetting them. The boiler had been cutting out for months and three times he'd said he'd come and fix it. Now Omer had taken a day off. If the bastard didn't do it this time, he'd have Süleyman to answer to, and he wouldn't like that.

Peri left for work at nine. Omer, already dressed and on his laptop, enmeshed in a virtual world of Byzantine myth, muttered at his sister as she closed the front door.

When he'd met the Syrian godfather, Sultan al-Khoury, in Sulukule, he'd talked about an old Greek legend concerning the city walls and the Virgin Mary. The Arab had reckoned that a lot of Greeks had gone to the Golden Gate to see Maryam de Mango experience her visions, but at the time, that hadn't seemed important. Omer had been rather more concerned with finding al-Khoury's brother-in-law, Salah Hadad. Not that he'd had anything cogent to say. A tirade of bonzai-inspired nonsense followed by a mild seizure. If he followed the pattern of most addicts, he'd probably die in Bakırköy.

But now Omer had time to follow the Greek connection. It would also help to take his mind off the young woman who had moved in upstairs. Peri said she was called Asra and she was a writer. She didn't know what she wrote. Omer didn't care. Asra was beautiful, tall and blonde, with a gentle smile, a deep, soothing voice and a figure like a curvaceous vase. It had been over six months since he'd been out with a woman, and he was becoming obsessed. He stopped staring glassily out of the window and looked back at his screen.

The first time the Virgin Mary had saved the city of Constantinople had been at Easter in the year 622, during the reign of the Byzantine emperor Heraklios. The city was under siege by both the Slavs and the Persians, and the Patriarch, Sergius I, urged all citizens to pray to the Virgin for deliverance. Shortly afterwards a female figure surrounded by angels was seen moving towards the Persian lines. From then on the Byzantine defenders could not put a foot wrong and the city was saved. This miracle was repeated twice afterwards, during the reign of the Emperor Constantine II (641–688) and then when Emperor Leo (716–750) defeated an Islamic fleet in the Sea of Marmara. According to the Greeks, the city itself was dedicated to the Virgin, a fact that later became entwined with myths surrounding the supposed immortality of the last Byzantine emperor, Constantine XI Palaiologos.

When the Ottoman Turks conquered the city in 1453, Constantine joined his men on the walls in what would be the final Byzantine push against the forces of Sultan Mehmed II. It was said by the Turks that he flung himself into the fray and was cut down by Ottoman swords. But a myth grew up amongst the Greeks that he had been saved by an angel, who turned his body to marble and placed it in a cave below the Golden Gate. There, it was said, he would rest until one day rising to take back the city for Christendom. A subversive idea that had been used by Greeks as a rallying point for centuries.

And yet as far as Omer could tell, not by Maryam de Mango. Her visions had consisted of communion with a female entity that berated mankind for its sins. It had never said anything about Greeks, good or bad. And even though it seemed that Maryam's real mother had been Greek, she hadn't been aware of that when her visions began. She may well have heard about the myth, but at that time she wouldn't have known it had anything to do with her. This was assuming she hadn't been genuine, whatever that meant.

He looked up from his screen and stared at the small super-market opposite. It was then that he saw Asra. Greeks, both ancient and modern, temporarily forgotten, he grabbed his keys and his jacket and ran out of the apartment. He'd go to the supermarket and buy something, anything.

Two odd things happened. Firstly he saw Ayşegül de Mango go into the church, and just as he'd absorbed that strange sight, he saw Gonca come out.

'What were you doing in there?' Süleyman asked her after she'd kissed him full on the lips in front of the whole of İstiklal Caddesi.

'The church? Why not?' she said.

'You're not a Christian.'

'I like to hedge my bets,' she said. 'Why are you here?'

'Work.'

He kissed her goodbye and went inside. Father Benito was expecting him, and was waiting for him in a pew at the very back of the church. He smiled when he saw Süleyman, and the two men shook hands.

'Did you see Mrs de Mango come in just now?'

The priest frowned. 'No. Why? Did you?'

'Yes,' Süleyman said. 'I thought I did . . .' Had he?

'It's possible; this church is full of nooks and crannies. Come to my office. We'll talk there.'

Father Benito's office, which was in one of the apartments

next to the church, was a small, cupboard-like space, crammed with books, paperwork and a large unplugged printer. Both men sat down.

'What can I do for you, Inspector?' the priest asked.

'Father, we have discovered that Maryam de Mango's parentage is not all it seemed,' he said. 'Basically we know that Ayşegül de Mango was not Maryam's natural mother.'

The priest's eyes widened.

'You didn't know this?'

'No,' he said.

'I thought that maybe under the Seal of the Confessional . . .'

'Not even under the Seal of the Confessional, no,' he said. 'I didn't know that.'

Süleyman drew in a breath. 'I see.'

'So do you know who her real mother is?'

'Possibly. Until we receive DNA data, we can't know for sure. But we have been approached by a woman who has a very good claim.'

'My goodness.' Father Benito steepled his fingers underneath his chin. 'I have had many, many conversations with Silvio over the years, but nothing like this has ever come up.'

'But other things have,' Süleyman said.

'Of course.'

'Some of which you are not permitted to share under the Seal of the Confessional?'

The priest leaned back in his chair. 'Inspector . . .'

'I realise it is an ethical dilemma,' Süleyman said. 'My ex-wife was a Catholic. I do understand. But, Father, this is murder . . .'

'Which under the Seal of the Confessional is irrelevant.'

Süleyman felt his heart sink. This wasn't the first time he'd come across the dictates of the Catholic Church surrounding confession. He understood, even if he didn't approve.

'However,' the priest continued, 'I can't think of anything

Silvio revealed in confession that would be of interest to you, Inspector. I can say that with one hand on my heart and the other on the Holy Bible. Silvio was not, to my knowledge, a danger to his daughter or indeed anyone else. In common with all men, he has his weaknesses. But he is basically a good soul, I believe.'

'What about other people in Maryam's life?'

'I can't speak for those I do not know.'

'And those you do?' Süleyman asked.

There was a pause. 'Inspector, you have to understand that the things people may tell me under the Seal of the Confessional are not subjects I can verify in any way. It is always possible that people lie.'

'To their God? To what purpose?'

'That I don't know. Maybe such people are delusional or mistaken; even if they are telling the truth, they are working only from one, very biased perspective.'

Süleyman shook his head. 'But if that's so, if people can basically say anything, true or false, then I fail to see the value of confession.'

The priest smiled. 'Confession can lighten a person's emotional load,' he said. 'I have elderly ladies come to me to confess to sins so small they can barely be discerned. Modern thinking on the subject is that it is the sharing of the guilt, real or perceived, and the subsequent penance and atonement that gives confession its real power. God will always forgive – in the end. It is up to human beings to do the work, if you like, that will please Him.'

'And so you . . .'

'I am simply the conduit,' he said. 'What I think about a person's sins is not important. However, if I betray the Seal of the Confessional I break the sanctity of that exclusive route to God for my parishioners, and that is unforgivable. If I did that, I would lose the trust of those I care for most.' He paused for a moment. 'You think I am holding back pertinent information, don't you?'

That put Süleyman on the spot. He wanted to lie. But he couldn't. He rather liked Father Esposito.

'Yes,' he said.

The priest smiled. 'Your honesty does you credit,' he said. 'In turn, all I can say is that I can neither confirm nor deny whether you are right.'

'Yes, and that's my problem.'

'I'm sorry.'

There was no point in pursuing the subject any further, and so Süleyman turned to the other topic he wanted to discuss.

'We understand that when Maryam was cured – went into remission or whatever – after her visit to the Armenian Church of the Assumption, her father contacted the Holy See in order to report the so-called miracle.'

'Yes. He did so unilaterally and against my advice.'

'It is your job to contact the Holy See, Father?'

'No, that's down to the Bishop.'

'And did *he* contact the Holy See?'

'No,' Father Benito said. 'The Church of the Assumption is Orthodox, not Catholic. I believe Bishop Montoya spoke to the priest, Father Kalajian, at the time. But it really wasn't our business. Maryam was a Muslim and she was cured in an Orthodox church. You can see how difficult that was for us.'

'Yes.'

'Bishop Montoya did watch Maryam receive her visions at the Golden Gate once,' he said. 'We went together.'

'And what did the Bishop think?' Süleyman asked.

'You can speak to him yourself, of course. But from what he told me, I gathered he felt that what was being experienced was too nascent to be open to proper examination.'

Details about the visions in police possession were scant. Süleyman said, 'Do you know what this "mother" actually said to Maryam?'

'Exhortations to mankind to clean up its act,' said the priest. 'Stop poisoning the seas, look after the animals, treat the world with respect.'

'Did this entity say what would happen if we didn't?'

'There was no actual prophecy, like at Fatima,' he said. 'Just what we already know, which is if we don't address these environmental issues soon, we are doomed. Obviously I don't know where you stand on this issue . . .'

'Do you think Maryam de Mango could ever be declared a saint?'

He smiled. 'Oh my goodness, there's a question! In order to be declared a saint, a person has to do more than just have a few visions. Miracles must be proven to take place due to that person's intercession. That can take decades, even millennia. And other signs may be looked for too, like incorruptibility of the saint's corpse after death. Seemingly endless commissions are required to investigate and assess such claims before the Holy Father can even consider such a thing.'

'One of your parishioners, a Lobna Amara, went to the Golden Gate with an expectation of a cure for her leukaemia.'

'Yes,' Father Benito said. 'At the suggestion of Silvio de Mango, I believe. Not with my blessing or the blessing of the Bishop. The Church does not believe in raising false hopes, and as far as Bishop Montoya and myself were concerned, Maryam's visions did not constitute, at that time, a viable source of optimism. I may be proved wrong and miracles that can be attributed to Maryam may yet occur, but I don't think so, and politically, the whole thing is problematic for us.'

'Oh?'

'Indeed. And not just because this is a predominantly Muslim country. Maryam herself was cured in an Orthodox church and the place where her visions occurred is sacred to Greek Christians, not to Catholics. Our Crusader knights sacked this city and slaughtered the local Greek Christian population in 1204 under the leadership of the Doge of Venice and with the approval of the Pope. The Golden Gate evokes nothing but shame in the hearts of Catholics – or at least it should. Maryam unwittingly stirred up divisions amongst the Christians of this city. I must admit, I was worried. The last thing we need here in this outpost of Christendom is division.'

When he left the church, Süleyman looked out for Ayşegül de Mango, but he didn't see her.

Asra bought bread, onions, eggs and sucuk. Ingredients for some sort of late lunch, Omer speculated. Hulusi Bey, who had run the tiny, and very old, İnönü Süpermarket for as long as anyone could remember, looked at Omer with suspicion. He probably wondered why the young brother of Peri Hanım was stalking the pretty new lady. When Asra had gone, Omer picked up a random object, a tin of olives, and went to the counter to pay. As usual, Hulusi Bey transacted business in silence. But before Omer left the shop he heard him call out, 'You do know that young lady you're interested in is Greek, don't you, Omer Bey?'

# Chapter 11

Çetin İkmen propped his head up on one of the shelves behind his desk.

'You're sure?' he said into his phone.

'Certain.'

Pathologist Arto Sarkissian had called him with the news that Maryam de Mango had been in the first trimester of pregnancy when she died.

'The foetus, had it been *in situ*, would have been tiny,' he said. 'But only parts of it remain, due to the violent removal of Maryam's uterus.'

'Can you DNA test what you've got?'

'I can try,' he said. 'May not get a result. I estimate she was probably eight or nine weeks pregnant. *In utero* DNA testing is usually only accurate from twelve weeks onwards. I have harvested what I can. Now I'd like to let the family have the body, if you approve.'

'You've got everything you need?'

'Yes,' he said.

'Then I'll tell the family she can be released,' İkmen said.

'Thank you. What about the pregnancy? Have you told them about that?'

'Not yet. As you know, there is a belief in some quarters that Maryam's father was also her lover. If that foetus is his, I'd like to know as soon as possible. Then I can tell them all in one hit. This is not the sort of news that can be drip-fed to anyone.'

'Agreed. I'll do my best.'

İkmen ended the call. He opened his office window and lit a cigarette. Was he doing the right thing by not telling the family? Ayşegül de Mango and her children had gone to Fatih to be with her family. He had a phone number. Maybe he should get them together with Silvio and tell them all at the same time? Although it was now beyond reasonable doubt that Ayşegül wasn't Maryam's natural mother, she still had to have a stake in what happened to her, didn't she? But then if she had mistreated Maryam, as Silvio said, did she deserve such a courtesy? He decided to leave it until the doctor came back with the DNA results.

Nothing of any interest, beyond some fingerprints that had yet to be analysed, had been found at İrini Mavroyeni's place. All the Syrians had come out to have a look when Kerim and the team had turned up, and İrini herself had got howling drunk. He had to accept that they might never know whether Maryam had met the woman her father had told her was her real mother. But Maryam's laptop was another matter.

Her Internet searches consisted almost exclusively of information about the Virgin Mary and her supposed miracles. This fascination appeared to go back at least five years. What was really interesting, however, was Maryam's lack of social-media profile. Most women in their twenties were on either Twitter, Facebook or Snapchat, but not Maryam. In addition, her email, both in and out of her account, was extremely scant. Online she barely existed. İkmen put it to her father.

'She didn't like the computer,' Silvio de Mango said. 'The other kids are forever online, but not my Maryam.'

'Sounds as if you approved of her lack of interest,' İkmen said.

'I did. Everything on those machines is fake,' he said. He was drunk again. İkmen could hear it in his voice.

'Mr de Mango, have you seen your wife today?' İkmen asked.

Süleyman had thought he had seen her at St Anthony's. Could she also have visited her husband in nearby Galata?

'No,' said Silvio. He had no interest. 'Can you tell this doctor of yours that I'm going to engage Yiannis Livadanios to organise the funeral? He's Greek, but he can't help that!' He laughed. 'He'll come with his hearse and bring Maryam home to me.' He laughed again.

Silvio de Mango ended the call. İkmen knew the undertaker, Yiannis Livadanios, so it would be easy to find out more from him. Silvio was clearly volatile. İkmen hoped he'd calm down once Maryam's body was brought home. He also hoped that he wasn't the father of his own daughter's child.

İkmen always tried not to have feelings, either negative or positive, about suspects. But almost in spite of himself, he seemed to have taken to Silvio de Mango. Perhaps it was because he'd once had problems with drink himself; or maybe, as a Levantine, Silvio brought to mind for the policeman a happier and less complicated version of his city.

They had Silvio de Mango's DNA. They'd find out what, if anything, he'd done to Maryam.

It was almost ten o'clock by the time Ayşegül de Mango got back to her parents' house in Fatih. As she walked through Çarşamba Mahallesi, she felt the eyes of the Order upon her. As a woman without a male escort, she shouldn't be out in the daytime, much less in the middle of the night. She knew they were right. But she didn't have to like it.

When she arrived home, her mother said, 'Where have you been?'

She'd left first thing in the morning because she'd had a lot to do.

Her mother grabbed her arm. 'I'm talking to you! Where have you been?'

Ayşegül saw Sara looking at her from the alcove beside the electric fire. Was the girl smirking, or was she just imagining it?

'Out,' Ayşegül said. 'My daughter has died. I have things to do.'

'Going to see that man!' her mother said.

'Silvio? No,' she said. 'But I will have to go to him soon.'

'Why?'

'Because he sent me a text to say that Maryam's body is being released and that she should be back at the apartment tomorrow.'

Her mother sat down on a cushion in front of the fire. 'She should be sent here,' she said.

Ayşegül said nothing. According to Muslim tradition, female members of a dead woman's family should wash the corpse, which should then be buried as soon as possible. But only Ayşegül knew that Maryam wasn't her flesh and blood.

Her mother shook her head. 'I suppose that man will bury her in his infidels' cemetery,' she said. She burst into tears. 'My own granddaughter!'

Ayşegül didn't attempt to comfort her. Her mother had always hated Silvio, even when Ayşegül had loved him desperately. And when she hadn't loved him desperately any more, her mother had ignored her – for years.

Sara stood up and went to the kitchen. God knew what she was doing in there, and Ayşegül didn't care. Like Maryam, Sara was a liar and an attention-seeker. All piety and headscarf, she would wait until she had an audience before rolling up her sleeves to 'unintentionally' reveal her self-harm scars. Not much more than surface cuts, they made Ayşegül sick. And that wasn't all.

Maryam had been pregnant when she died. Ayşegül wondered if the police knew. They had to. So why hadn't they said anything? She herself had picked up on it weeks ago. She'd smelt the change fermenting inside the girl.

There was a rumour that Kemal Öneş had been released. What

did that mean for him? Would he be released soon too? Erdal Çelik's whole body shook. Had someone told the police that he and Kemal the barber had issues?

Erdal's father had been 'disappeared' by the Grey Wolves back in the eighties. Everyone knew it. Back when Kemal the barber had been one of them. Why had the Order allowed Kemal to get in with them in recent years? He wasn't their type of person at all. What about Erdal's family? They had always done service for religious people. Besides, it *had* been Kemal who had told people about the girl. Erdal hadn't been lying. Of course he hoped the Order had noticed that he hadn't mentioned them at all. He also hoped that if Kemal the barber was under arrest, the Order would drop him.

But he was afraid they wouldn't.

Father Esposito was just about to blow out the remaining votive candles when he saw that the curtain in one of the confessional boxes was pulled shut. Had someone done it by mistake?

He walked over and was just about to open it when he heard a voice.

'I need to talk.'

Again?

He wanted to say that confession was over and that he was closing the church for the night, but he knew that wouldn't wash. He also knew that he had a duty to speak to this particular person whenever he could.

'Give me one minute,' he said. 'Let me just finish blowing out the candles.'

He'd been annoyed that she wouldn't answer her mobile and so he'd gone for a drink in a funky local bar and ended up with this woman. He didn't even know her name. Where had Gonca been, and why had she gone silent? Was she with someone else?

The woman, who was no more than twenty-five, had been moaning about her boyfriend. He wanted her to be a virgin when they married and so all they ever did in bed was make sure that he was satisfied. She claimed she didn't know what sexual pleasure was. After three large glasses of Rioja, Mehmet Süleyman had offered to show her.

Now he had, which had produced an explosive effect.

'You can fuck me,' she said as she massaged his penis between her breasts. 'I don't care what he thinks!'

He didn't last long enough to make that decision. She was very sexy, whoever she was, and her first exposure to oral sex had clearly been life-changing.

When he'd got his breath back, he said, 'I think you may regret losing your virginity. Best not.'

When he went down on her again, he feared that her squeaks and howls might cause his neighbours to bang on the walls. But nothing happened. Nothing bad. She had a good time and so did he. Everybody won. Except they didn't, because he felt bad. Even suspecting that Gonca saw other people didn't help. He had no proof. He was guilty and he had an overwhelming urge to confess.

The woman eventually left at three in the morning. Fearing that she might wake the kapıcı, he took her downstairs and let her out into the street himself. She had her knickers in her handbag, and as she tottered off down Sıraselviler Caddesi, it was clear that she was still drunk.

Süleyman was just about to close the front door to his apartment block when he saw a familiar figure walk wearily up the street towards Taksim. For a moment he wondered whether he should call out to her, but then he decided against it.

Whatever the current state of their relationship, Gonca wouldn't want to be exposed to him smelling of sex with another woman.

# Chapter 12

Hürrem Teker didn't cry. At heart she was a soldier, like her ancestors. Instead she got mad.

'They let him go,' she said. 'Just like that.'

Çetin İkmen, who had joined his superior at her office window for a smoke, said, 'Kemal Öneş's only previous was when he was in the nationalist camp. Since he got religion, as far as I can tell, he's been a good boy.'

'Stop making excuses!' Teker said. 'Öneş took a phone call from that bitch I was forced to employ that led to half of Fatih coming out on the street looking for a corpse to burn. I am losing. People far more powerful than me want me gone. I can only tell you this, Çetin Bey, because I know you will not betray me. I have no idea about anyone else.'

'They can't force you out . . .'

'Yes they can, and you know it!' she said. 'You know who's behind them.'

He thought he did. Those who had power in the district of Fatih. But was she also trying to tell him that she was a member of an organisation with whom the government was currently at odds? Nobody was talking about that, but everybody knew. And was she also implying she thought he was a member too? He was a member of nothing and always had been.

Her telephone rang. 'Shit!' She answered it. 'Teker.'

He couldn't hear what was being said at the other end, but

he saw her face pale. When whoever had been speaking finished she said, 'We're on our way.'

She put the phone down and looked at İkmen.

'You know,' she said, 'when you think things can't get any worse, and then they do?'

The girl's Turkish was poor and so Süleyman spoke to her in English.

'Why did you come to church this morning?'

The smell of incense mixed with the sharp tang of iron was overwhelming.

The girl, a tiny Filipino, shook her head. 'I come to pray before work,' she said.

'And the church door was open?'

'Yes.'

'Is it usually?'

'Yes.'

Out of the corner of his eye he saw Teker and İkmen enter the nave. The priest's body, sprawled on its stomach, lay directly in front of them.

'And you found Father Esposito just as he is now?'

'Yes.' She was crying. 'Why would anyone hurt him?' she said. 'He was a good man!'

'I don't know,' Süleyman said. He stood up. Now that İkmen and Teker had arrived, he needed to speak to them. He beckoned to one of the female officers. 'Constable Bulbul, I want you to take a statement from Miss Ramos.'

'Sir.'

He walked across to İkmen, who was bending over the corpse.

'Back of his head looks as if it's all but gone,' İkmen said as he straightened up. 'God help us! Did that girl find him?'

'Yes,' Süleyman said. 'She came in to pray and discovered him like that.'

'Doctor on his way?'

'Yes. I was still at home when I got the call. I ran here.'

İkmen took his arm and pulled him over to one of the large sand-filled holders for votive candles.

'You think what he was concealing under the Seal of the Confessional may have killed him?' He put a ten-lira note in a box beside a stack of candles.

'If I knew what he had been concealing I'd be able to make a judgement about that,' Süleyman said. 'The only thing he told me was that Silvio de Mango hadn't told him anything in confession that we needed to be worried about. I hope he was telling the truth.'

İkmen picked up a candle, lit it and positioned it in the sand. 'For his soul,' he said. 'We'll have to inform Bishop Montoya.'

'Miss Ramos, who found the body, called another priest, Father Colombo, in the first instance, and it was he who called us,' Süleyman said. 'Just before you arrived I sent him off to speak to the Bishop, who is, apparently, in İzmir at the moment.'

'Did you touch the body?' İkmen asked.

'To determine temperature, yes,' Süleyman said. 'Stone cold. Although in this kind of environment that wouldn't take long.'

'No. Have to see what Dr Sarkissian has to say.' İkmen looked at the candle he had just lit. 'It is tempting to think that Father Esposito's death is connected to that of Maryam de Mango, but we must keep open minds. I'll get Kerim to make an inventory of all the ecclesiastical staff connected to this place. We'll need to look at how they related to each other both personally and professionally. Just because someone is religious doesn't mean they are immune to human emotions such as envy.'

'And, being Catholics, they are celibate, which brings its own problems, I imagine.'

'Not that you'd know,' İkmen said.

Süleyman ignored the dig at his lifestyle. 'You know that St

Anthony is supposed to cure the sick? One of the physician saints, apparently. I wonder if Maryam de Mango ever came here for help when she was ill. And if not, why not?'

'What are you doing here?'

Silvio de Mango had thought that maybe it was Yiannis Livadanios the undertaker. But it wasn't. It was his daughter, Sara.

He let her into the apartment. 'Shouldn't you be at school?'

'I came to see whether Maryam had come back,' the girl said. 'She needs to be washed and I've come to do that.'

Silvio sat down in his chair, lit a cigarette and took a slug of whisky straight from the bottle. He saw the kid wince, but he didn't care.

'She'll be washed at the undertaker's,' he said. 'That's what we pay them for.'

'By a woman?' Sara said.

'How the hell should I know?'

His daughter looked down at the floor, crushed. Silvio, for once, relented.

'Look,' he said, 'I don't know whether your mother has told you, but she and I kept a secret from you and your brothers. About Maryam.'

Sara sat down. 'Mum's not said anything.'

Silvio had been sure that Ayşegül would speak to the children as soon as she knew that Maryam's real parentage was out in the public domain. She'd not want them to hear about it from strangers. After all, hadn't all the subterfuge about Maryam's birth been first and foremost to protect the children?

'What is it, Papa?'

He loved all his children, in his way. The fact that in his mind he'd been excluded by them in recent years didn't alter that.

He said, 'Listen, Sara, your mother is not to blame and you

mustn't be angry with her, because all this is my fault. The fact that your mother and I have fallen out over recent years is nothing to do with you or your brothers or even really Maryam. I am not a good man. I drink, I smoke, I'm a mess . . .'

'I love you . . .'

'I know you do, which is what makes this so hard,' he said. 'Sara, there's no easy way to say this.'

'Say what?'

'Maryam was not your mother's child. She was the result of a . . . what? A liaison between myself and a woman I used to go to for sex before your mother and I were married. Your mother is a very good Muslim woman. She always has been. When we were dating, she kept herself pure. I respected that. But I was also a young man with raging hormones.'

'Papa!' Sara looked away.

'Even more disappointed in me now? Understandable.' He took another swig from his bottle. 'The woman, a Greek, didn't want the child and so your mother agreed to raise her as her own. I sometimes think that one of the reasons I resent your mum so much is because she is so bloody fucking good in so many ways. So you see, Sara, your sister was never a Muslim.'

'She was!'

'She wasn't. She was a Levantine on my side, like you, and a Greek on her mother's. So she will be buried as a Christian.'

'She wasn't—'

'Oh, at the end of her life, she was,' he said. 'Because she knew the truth. I told her. On the night she died, she was going to see her real mother, up in Sulukule.'

'And her mother killed her?'

'No,' he said. 'I don't think so. You see, like me, Maryam's real mother is a drinker. She's barely conscious these days . . .'

Sara looked back at her father. 'And how do I know this isn't a lie?' she said. 'In this family, everybody lies!'

'Including you.'

As soon as he'd said it, he regretted it. Sara was a fantasist, but in some ways, at least, that was what she had become just by being part of her family. That was what they had all become. Then he made it worse. It just burst out of him.

'Telling people your own father and sister are having sex! You and your brothers make me sick!' he said. 'Full of shit, the lot of you!'

Crying now, Sara got up and ran out of the apartment. With a sigh, Silvio drank deeply from his bottle and then picked up his phone and called the girl's mother.

Father Colombo had an Italian accent so thick it dripped from his mouth like clotted cream.

'I don't have anything to do with the cameras,' he said.

The facade of St Anthony's was bristling with CCTV devices. They stuck out from every cornice and alcove. As well as covering the front entrance, they were also present on the apartments that lined the courtyard of the church, and on the gates that led out into İstiklal Caddesi. The control room for all this complicated-looking hardware consisted of a tiny space to the left of the entrance gates. It contained computers.

'I'm afraid I can't help you to understand all this,' the young priest said.

'Don't worry,' Süleyman said. 'We have people who know about such things. Do you know whether recordings were taken all the time?'

He sighed. Blond, with honey-coloured skin, Father Colombo was an astonishingly beautiful young priest. Süleyman wondered what his colleagues thought of him; uncharitably, he speculated about whether any of them fancied him.

'No,' the priest said.

'Why not?'

'Because of confession.'

'What do you mean?'

'Father Benito, God rest his soul, has always been very . . . er, what's the word . . . scrupulous about anonymity in the confessional. Some people will happily come to confession knowing that the priest they confess to is aware of who they are. Some are not so happy. When the cameras were installed there was much prayer seeking guidance about how to protect the identity of penitents.'

'Did you obtain guidance from us?' Süleyman asked.

'The police wanted us to record everything,' Father Colombo said.

'For your own protection.'

'I see that,' he said. 'But Father Benito, may God rest his soul, he wanted people to feel free. He hated the idea of being watched.'

'So the CCTV was not set to record during times set aside for confession?'

The young man looked down, as if ashamed. 'It was not,' he said, 'enabled in the daytime.'

Süleyman was shocked. In recent years the church had received multiple threats, mainly from people claiming to represent al-Qaeda or ISIS. Horrified, he said, 'Do you have any idea how dangerous that might have been?'

'Er . . .' The priest shrugged. 'It is important that people can feel free . . .'

'Yes, so you've said. But surely it's also important to keep people safe? In fact,' Süleyman said, 'Father Esposito may now have paid the ultimate price for his aversion to security. When did he usually switch the system on?'

'I don't know,' Father Colombo said. 'To be honest with you, Inspector, I don't know anything about how it worked.'

'And did your parishioners know that the system was switched off in the daytime?'

'I don't know,' the young man said. 'It was put in before I came here. But I suppose if Father Esposito wanted them to feel they could come and go as they pleased, they'd have to have known, wouldn't they?'

The Englishman who lived in one of the ground-floor apartments didn't say anything, but Silvio could see from the expression on his face that he didn't like what was happening. Anglo-Saxons were like that, all silent disgust and hypocrisy. He wanted to say, 'I'm bringing my dead daughter home, get over it!' But he didn't. He saved that for the Turks who lived on the floor below.

As Muslims, they believed that dead bodies were unclean and should be buried immediately. Again, they said nothing. Just stood in the stairwell, glaring at the undertaker's men hefting Maryam's black mahogany coffin. Most of the latter were Muslims too, but they showed no sympathy for Silvio's gawping neighbours.

Moved to tears by the sight of his daughter in a coffin and strained beyond endurance by his neighbours' silent disapproval, Silvio yelled, 'My daughter is coming home whether you bastards like it or not!'

They didn't speak to him anyway. None of the residents who had moved into the block in recent years did. A living anachronism, he swore and drank and he knew it was said that he was bankrupt. If only they knew. Cash poor he might be, but his apartment was worth all their little birdcages put together. And that wasn't all Silvio owned.

'Fuck you all!' he screamed down the stairwell as the coffin was brought into his apartment.

Yiannis Livadanios shook his head. 'Mr de Mango . . .'

'Well, they deserve it!' he said. 'Always peering into my business, telling my daughters to cover their heads!' He leaned over the banister one final time. 'Cunts!'

Yiannis Livadanios had seen most types of mourning behaviour during his long career; he knew that the only way forward, if and when it became antisocial, was to change the subject.

'Maryam didn't reach me until yesterday evening, but I have nevertheless embalmed her body as instructed by yourself, and my wife has set her hair and applied make-up. In the absence of clothing provided by yourself, we have dressed her in a plain white nightdress.'

The undertaker's assistants placed the coffin on a stand in the middle of Silvio's little chapel.

'I hope you approve of what we've done, Mr de Mango.'

Silvio's hands shook as he opened the coffin lid. For a moment he couldn't open his eyes. But when he did and saw how beautiful she was, he began to cry.

'Oh my Maryam,' he said, 'why have you been taken from me?'


Girls were always a problem, especially when they were teenagers. As soon as he heard Bana scream, 'What is wrong with you?' he knew she was talking to their fourteen-year-old, Layal.

Sultan al-Khoury had been in negotiation with an Iraqi who possessed a very impressive little Beretta M9 pistol that he'd be able to resell with a healthy mark-up. But then the screaming started and he had to excuse himself to go and sort it out.

'I'm doing business!' he hissed as he entered the kitchen to find his wife glaring at their elder daughter while the younger girl, Nour, cowered in a corner. 'Keep it down or I'll beat all three of you!'

Pointing at her sister, Layal said, 'She's a thief!'

'A thief? How? What did she take from you?'

Layal said nothing. Sultan was just about to go back to his Iraqi when he saw little Nour smirk.

He bent down to her. 'What's so funny?' he said.

'Nothing.'

'Oh really?' He slapped her hard across her face, and then, just so that neither of them could accuse him of favouritism in the future, he slapped her sister.

'Ow!'

'Tell me what this is about now,' he said. 'I haven't got time for this female rubbish.'

Even his wife looked ashamed.

'Eh? Well?'

Layal tipped her head at her sister. 'She stole from me,' she said.

'Stole what?'

Layal looked away. The sooner he got her married and away, the better. She was getting sulkier by the day.

'Tell your father!' Bana shook Layal by the arm. 'He's speaking to you! It's a sin to disobey your parents!'

Sultan looked at his younger daughter. 'Did you steal?' he said.

'No.' But she looked at her Barbie as she spoke.

'You did,' protested Layal.

'I didn't, you did,' Nour said.

Sultan was going to explode if this didn't stop.

'Steal what?' he roared. 'Steal—'

'Beautiful shoes,' Nour said. 'Layal took them.'

'I didn't!'

'You did,' her sister said. 'I just borrowed them from you, for my clothes shop.'

'You took them without asking, you little whore!'

'No I didn't,' Nour said. 'But you did. You took them from that dead girl. The one with her tummy hanging out.'

It was that stupid little queen, Bilal, who told him.

'There's police cars all over the place up at St Anthony's,' he said as he breezed in to do another shift at the vacant bar. 'If you ask me, there's been a murder.'

No one had asked him. No one ever asked him anything. His mouth had a life of its own. But on this occasion, Fabrizio Leon either believed or wanted to check up on his barman. He walked up onto İstiklal, past the small group of Syrian boys who seemed to now be living on the pavement at the top of Tomtom Kaptan Caddesi, and headed for St Anthony's. It didn't take him long to spot the first police car. He began to feel a bit sick. But he kept on walking until he could see the facade of the church through the wrought-iron gates.

There was a crowd, gawping. This was İstanbul; there was always a crowd.

Fabrizio stood next to a man in a suit. 'Do you know what's happened?'

'Officially, no,' the man said. 'But there's a rumour someone's been murdered in the church.'

It was then that Fabrizio saw that peacocking policeman Süleyman again. Marching around in the church courtyard, talking into his mobile phone. Unlike the last time he'd seen him, now Fabrizio had some idea about his character as well as his looks.

He liked him even less. But he feared him more.

# Chapter 13

There were four priests attached to St Anthony's, three Italians and a Pole – Father Esposito, Father Colombo, Father da Mosto and Father Wojtulewicz. Father Wojtulewicz, the Pole, was a good deal older than the others and was really in semi-retirement. Fathers Esposito and da Mosto were in their forties, while Father Colombo, at twenty-nine, was little more than a child.

They all lived, so Kerim Gürsel had discovered, in one of the larger apartments attached to the church. Looked after by an elderly live-in housekeeper called Katerina Marmara, the four priests had apparently got on well. At least that was what their superior told him.

Bishop Juan-Maria Montoya was a tall, thin Mexican who spoke English, bizarrely, with a strong British accent. As soon as he'd heard about Father Esposito's death, he had flown straight back to İstanbul from İzmir.

'We've had threats from extremists for many years,' he said when Kerim asked him whether any of his priests had been attacked before. 'But we are well known here and people accept us as members of the Beyoğlu community.'

'Did you know that Father Esposito only switched on the CCTV cameras at night?' Kerim asked.

He sighed. 'I did. You know, Sergeant, we tread a difficult line here as ministers of religion. We have to try to remain safe whilst at the same time respecting the privacy of our parishioners. We generally have a good idea who does and doesn't come to church. We even, as you can imagine, recognise familiar voices when people attend confession. But we are bound to live as if we don't. If people thought we were watching them, maybe even with a view towards offering wise counsel, we would be on the very edge of breaking the Seal of the Confessional. Counsel on issues confessed to may only be offered in the confessional. And you know, or maybe you don't, that to break the Seal of the Confessional is punishable by excommunication. We do not do these things lightly.'

'What about your parishioners?' Kerim said. 'Did they know the cameras were switched off in the day?'

'I don't believe Father Esposito ever told them so explicitly. But I do know that he did reassure them about their privacy. In spite of the many people who visit us, St Anthony's is a community,' he said. 'In this uncertain world, we try to retain an atmosphere of trust.'

Kerim shook his head.

'And also,' the Bishop said, 'an element of quiet fatalism, which you, as a Muslim, I think will appreciate. If someone is out to get you, unless you put yourself in a sealed box, you remain vulnerable whatever you do. And if you actively give up all your freedoms in order just to be safe, do you deserve to be free?'

Kerim knew exactly what the Bishop was saying. But his own feelings on the matter stemmed more from his sexuality than his religion. For a moment, he felt sad and slightly ashamed.

He said, 'We will have to interview the three remaining priests.'

'Of course. Do we yet know how Father Esposito died?' the Bishop asked.

'Repeated blows to the back of the head, according to our doctor,' Kerim said.

'Repeated blows with what?'

'We have yet to find the murder weapon, sir,' Kerim said.

'I'm afraid that while the search continues, the church will have to remain closed.'

The Bishop held his hands up in a gesture of submission. 'It is as it is.'

Being with Technical Officer Turgut Zana was difficult. He suffered from – or rather he didn't suffer so much as embody – a type of autistic behaviour that those around him could find problematic. Being in close proximity to him made it worse.

Mehmet Süleyman didn't just step outside St Anthony's small CCTV control room to take a phone call. He needed a break from Zana's deafening silence.

'I tried to call you last night,' he said into his mobile. 'But you didn't pick up.'

'I'm sorry,' Gonca said. 'Baba wasn't well.'

'Oh, I'm sorry. I hope he's better now.'

It could have been true. Her father might have been ill and she might have, subsequently, gone out. But he knew she was lying.

'He's OK,' Gonca said. 'Are you at the apartment?'

'No,' he said. 'I'm working.'

'Oh.'

'Why?'

He heard her laugh. She was going to say something glib and, possibly, crude.

'I can't stop thinking about you,' she said. 'Or rather I can't stop thinking about your cock—'

'I'm working,' he reiterated, unamused. She was fucking around. Not that he could complain.

'Where?'

The whole city had to know about the events unfolding at St Anthony's, surely. But then Gonca and her family tended not to pay too much attention to events unless they directly involved them.

'St Anthony's,' he said.

There was a pause, then, in a measured tone, she said, 'St Anthony's?'

'It's being reported,' he said. 'A priest has been killed.'

'Oh. That's terrible.'

'Isn't it.'

He ended the call and then berated himself for being so childish. They had both agreed they'd see other people. He'd picked up that girl in the bar and taken her home. They'd both had fun. What was his problem? He knew only too well.

'Inspector Süleyman?'

Ah, the unmoving face of Sergeant Zana . . .

'Yes?'

'Can you come back in?'

No 'sir' on the end of that, of course. It was a good job that Süleyman recognised it for what it was: a complete absence of social acumen.

He sat down in front of what Zana had told him was the CCTV recording device.

'The priest didn't switch the system on last night,' Zana said without preamble.

Süleyman felt his heart sink. CCTV footage always had the potential to provide short cuts.

'This is because the system switched itself on, and off, automatically,' Zana continued. 'He must have set it to do that, or maybe he got someone to do it for him.'

'Ah.' Süleyman felt a bit better now. 'So was it on last night?'

'From ten p.m. to five a.m.,' Zana said. 'Visual only, no audio, but we have one figure, a man I think, leaving the building at 22.32.'

'And?'

'And I will have to closely examine the remainder of the recording.'

'Show me this man,' Süleyman said.

126

A shaky image of a figure in dark clothes appeared on the computer screen.

'Can you do anything about the resolution?' Süleyman asked.

'I'll need some time to do that and review the rest of the recording.'

'Then you'd better get on with it,' Süleyman said.

Çetin İkmen chose not to interview any of Father Esposito's fellow priests, preferring to go to someone he felt would know more about what went on at St Anthony's.

'Father Esposito was the one that everyone trusted.'

Katerina Marmara had kept house for the priests of St Anthony's for over thirty years. A Levantine Christian in her late sixties, she had never married, preferring to give her life and service to her church.

'Why do you think that was?' İkmen asked.

'Well, I suppose it's due to how the other fathers are,' she said. 'You know that young one, Father Colombo, is really *too* young. He doesn't say a good Mass. In the future he may do, but not now. On the other hand, Father da Mosto says an excellent Mass but I wouldn't go to him for confession.'

'Why not?'

'I don't think he's really interested.'

'And Father Wojtulewicz?' İkmen asked.

'Well, he's a lovely old man, but unless he's speaking Polish, he's really hard to understand,' she said. 'He came two years ago to minister to our Polish speakers, which he does. But there's not many of those and so he doesn't really do a lot.'

'So Father Esposito was the whole package,' İkmen said. 'Good at Mass, in confession . . .'

'He was a wonderful man.' Her eyes filled with tears. 'He came from Italy, like the other two, but of all of them it was Father Esposito who understood us best.'

It was getting dark outside now. İkmen could see the lights of İstiklal Caddesi from the window of the priests' apartment. Soon the azan, the call to prayer, would begin.

'Understood who?' he asked.

'Us,' she said. 'Levantines. Not many people do. Who are we? Remnants of a world that has gone. Strangers in a country that is ours and not ours. I've heard some people say we should go back to Italy or France or Britain. But those places are not our places. Father Esposito understood that. Maybe it was because he was Sicilian. He always said he felt like a stranger in Italy.'

'The other Italian priests didn't feel like that?'

'Father Colombo is from Rome and Father da Mosto from Venice,' she said. 'Both of them from wealthy families. Father Esposito understood the ordinary person. He knew weakness and . . .'

She stopped.

'Weakness?' İkmen said. 'What do you mean?'

She shook her head. 'Nothing,' she said. 'I spoke out of turn.'

'Yes, but you did speak,' İkmen said, 'and so I can't ignore what you said. What do you mean by weakness?'

She looked as if she was about to cry.

'Hanım?'

'Some of our parishioners, you know, they commit sins that are born of weakness,' she said. 'Weakness for drink, for possessions, for women . . .'

'Father Esposito knew people's addictions and infidelities . . .'

'They told him, willingly,' she said. 'They wouldn't always tell the others, if at all.'

'And how do you know this, hanım?'

'Because,' she said, 'it was me who sent them to him.'

'Sent them to him?'

'Inspector, I know everyone in our community,' she said. 'I know every Levantine family in this city. I know their histories,

128

their problems and, sometimes, their secrets. But of course I am not in any position to help them, being just a spinster woman. When I found out how nice Father Benito was, I told people to go to him.'

'Like who?'

'Oh, that I can't tell you,' she said.

'You're not a priest yourself, you know, Katerina Hanım,' İkmen said.

'No,' she said. 'But I am true to my own kind. Isn't everyone?'

'Even when murder is involved?' İkmen asked.

But she didn't answer him.

It was nearly midnight and Süleyman was exhausted. He'd long since stopped watching Turgut Zana going backwards and forwards over the CCTV recording from the previous night. He'd interviewed Fathers da Mosto and Wojtulewicz and learned that there had been little love lost between da Mosto and Father Esposito, mainly, he felt, because the former felt the latter was beneath him.

He opened the door to his apartment and found Gonca inside. He hadn't realised she still had a key.

'Hello, baby.'

She looked amazing. Sitting by the window, dressed entirely in red leather. But all he wanted to do was go to bed – on his own.

She walked over and kissed him. 'You've had a bad day, baby?'

'I need to go to sleep,' he said.

'You don't want to talk . . .' She had her hands on his buttocks.

'I want to sleep.'

She unfastened her jacket to reveal her naked breasts. Gonca was always ready for sex; sex was what she was about. But this was excessive even for her. What was going on?

'You can sleep,' she said. She pushed him into the chair she'd vacated. 'I just want to give you something that might help.'

If she'd started using drugs, she was out of there. Three of her brothers, so far, had died from the effects of bonzai addiction. Not that she'd ever hinted that she wanted to try bonzai . . .

She unzipped his trousers and took his penis between her breasts – just like the girl he'd brought back the previous night had done. Did she know?

Her breasts were large and warm and he felt her nipples brush against his groin.

'Is that good?' she said.

It was. But was it a trick? Was she lulling him into a false sense of security prior to clawing his eyes out in a fit of jealousy? Then he remembered the guilt in her voice when she'd phoned.

In spite of himself, Süleyman groaned.

She said, 'That's it. Enjoy yourself.' She moved his penis rhythmically between her breasts and he was lost.

'Gonca . . .'

# Chapter 14

İbrahim looked smart. Dressed in a suit, his beard trimmed. Mevlüt was his usual self – looking like a terrorist.

'Where's your mother?' Silvio asked.

Mevlüt shrugged. Had the boys actually come to ask him about what he'd told Sara? If they had, they hadn't rushed over.

His sons were not the first visitors to come and see Maryam that morning.

'You remember Lobna Hanım and Mina Hanım,' he said. 'Lobna Hanım was married to your Uncle Fabrizio.'

She sat in a chair, a slim grey figure in a black dress, her head covered by a lace mantilla. Unmoving, unlike her sister, who knelt on the floor telling her rosary beads and crying. They'd brought helva, a traditional funerary gift, but no one was eating.

The boys hesitated before going to look at their sister. Silvio didn't push them. Neither of them had seen a dead body before. All he said was 'She looks beautiful.'

And she did. Before dawn, Silvio had got up, dressed in his best suit and gone to the flower shop in the Balık Pazar. Then he'd threaded tulips and roses in her hair. Not that she had needed adornment. Maryam had always looked like Silvio's mother, Chiara. A great beauty in her youth. And with the translucence of death on her face, she was, if anything, even more lovely than she had been in life.

Once they had glanced at her, the two boys sat down. Then İbrahim said, 'Dad, you know there are people outside in the street.'

'What people?'

'People who loved Maryam,' he said.

His brother muttered, 'Lunatics.'

'Keep your fucking opinions to yourself,' Silvio said.

Silence, save for Mina's whispered prayers, returned to the chapel.

Even though Mehmet Süleyman didn't speak Arabic, he had insisted upon coming to Sulukule with Omer Mungun when he got the call from Sultan al-Khoury. The Arab, however, could speak both French and English, which was the language in which they conversed.

'Here are the shoes,' al-Khoury said. He put them down on his kitchen table.

They were unmistakable. Not only were they dark blue, but they had those pink ruffled panels of leather held on by pearl buttons. Inside each shoe was the designer's logo: *Incorruttibile*.

'Where did your daughter find them?'

'You can ask her yourself,' the Arab said. He left the kitchen and disappeared into another room, returning with a heavily bruised teenage girl. She was shaking.

Omer heard him say, in Arabic, 'These are policemen. Answer their questions. We don't want any trouble.'

'Yes, Father.'

'This is my elder daughter,' al-Khoury said. 'She speaks English.'

Before the war, the al-Khourys had been the type of people who travelled, learned foreign languages, held dinner parties and were members of the professions. Omer knew such people. He'd seen others who had, of necessity, slipped into gangsterism and, out of frustration, brutalised even their own.

'What's her name?' Süleyman asked. He was clearly disgusted

by the girl's appearance. But he had an agenda that was, at present, only and exclusively about murder.

'Layal,' al-Khoury said.

Süleyman motioned for the child to sit. Then he sat on the opposite side of the table and fixed her with his eyes.

'Layal,' he said, 'I am Inspector Süleyman. I am investigating the death of a woman called Maryam de Mango. Her body was found on Tuesday morning around the back of—'

'The gypsy's coffee house on Sulukule Caddesi,' she said. 'I know.'

'You saw it?'

'Yes.'

'When?'

'Monday night. Late. I was gathering firewood.' She shook her head, her eyes filling with tears. 'I didn't plan to take her shoes. But they were so pretty . . .'

'Did you know she was dead?' Süleyman asked.

For the first time in their short conversation, she looked at him with a sulky teenage expression on her face. 'Of course,' she said. 'You think I'm stupid?'

Her father smacked her around the head. 'Be respectful!' he barked.

Süleyman held up a hand. 'There's no need for that, Mr al-Khoury.' He returned his attention to the girl. 'Didn't you think to call someone, an adult, when you found Maryam de Mango's corpse?'

'No,' she said. She looked down at the floor.

'Why not?'

She shrugged.

'And why did you take her shoes?' Süleyman asked.

For a moment she looked confused, then she said, 'They're really pretty.'

'Yes, but they're not yours.'

Omer knew what was coming. As a teenager he had, more than once, found himself on streets where the Turkish army was doing bloody battle with Kurdish separatists. War impoverished people, which meant the possessions of the dead were always fair game.

'She didn't need them, did she?' the girl said.

Her father didn't respond. But then why would he? The girl had stolen some shoes from a dead woman. So what? All he was probably worried about was the fact that this theft had meant he'd had to interact with the police. Omer knew that, in a way, the fact that he had reported it at all was a credit to what had to remain of Sultan al-Khoury's humanity.

'Did you see anyone when you stole the shoes?' Süleyman asked.

'No,' she said.

'You're sure?'

'Yes.'

'And what time was this?'

She shrugged. 'Night-time.'

'Can you be a bit more precise?'

She thought for a moment. 'I suppose about ten.'

'On Monday night?'

'Yes.'

'What did you do with the shoes once you'd taken them?'

'I put them in my bag,' she said.

'What bag?'

'I'll get it. It's in my room.' She walked, with some difficulty, out of the kitchen.

When she'd gone, Süleyman said to al-Khoury, 'How did you find out about this? Apart from clearly beating the information out of her?'

Omer flashed his boss a warning glance. Süleyman ignored him. 'Well?'

'Layal's younger sister Nour stole the shoes from her,'

al-Khoury said. 'She'd made some phoney dolls' clothes shop over by the rubbish tip. Stuff she'd found, I don't know . . .'

'These are adult shoes.'

'Did I say any of this was logical?' al-Khoury said. 'In the space of five years, my children have gone from living in the Damascus mansion my family have owned for two centuries and having every advantage that life can provide, to being shot at, bombed and subjected to horror and death. Now they are refugees in a country that doesn't want them. And you expect them to behave like normal children?'

Süleyman sighed impatiently. 'I take your point,' he said. 'But how did you—'

'They fought,' he said. 'I had to break them up. Then I found out. I called Sergeant Mungun this morning because he had spoken of the dead girl's shoes and Layal admitted she had taken them from a body.'

The girl returned with a large leather tote bag. On one side were the letters GG. Süleyman knew that was Gucci.

'Where did you get the bag from?' he asked.

'Not from that woman behind the coffee house,' she said. 'I brought it from home. It was my auntie's.'

Süleyman didn't ask why her auntie no longer needed the bag, because he knew.

Çetin İkmen was determined to keep things low-key even if some of the uniforms who accompanied him didn't.

By five o'clock that morning, Technical Officer Turgut Zana had finally managed to increase the size and sharpen the resolution of the CCTV image of the man leaving St Anthony's at 22.32 on the night Father Esposito was murdered. His first call had been to Süleyman, who had identified the man but had then been called away to Sulukule with Omer Mungun. It was therefore now left to İkmen to bring this man in for questioning.

He made what he called the hit squad wait outside while he entered the building with Kerim Gürsel. When he caught the eye of the young, exquisitely dressed man on the reception desk, he held up his badge and watched the receptionist's smile fall.

'Inspector İkmen,' he said softly. 'I need to speak to Mr Leon.'

Mina Hanım and Auntie Lobna, whom he only just remembered, stayed for ages. Mina, disgustingly, kept on touching his sister's corpse, which made İbrahim shudder. Mevlüt had wanted to go almost as soon they arrived, but their father wouldn't let him. When the women did leave, he heard his father tell Auntie Lobna, 'I'll speak to him, my dear. He'll listen to me.'

He had to mean his Uncle Fabrizio, Lobna's ex. His mum always said that Fabrizio was a crook.

Once the women had left, Mevlüt got up.

'Where are you going?'

'Home,' he told his father. He wasn't. He was going to buy bonzai and get off his face.

'No you're not.'

Their father made Mevlüt sit down. Then he told them that Maryam wasn't their real sister, and for İbrahim, a lot of things fell into place. His father had always favoured Maryam. Mevlüt had railed against it for years. That was why İbrahim had always sort of believed his brother's mad ravings about his dad and Maryam being lovers. Actually his love for her was just guilt, which was almost as creepy.

Of course Mevlüt went mad and lost his shit. Ranting about how their father disgusted him and how he never wanted to see him again. İbrahim, if he was honest with himself, was more upset about the fact that his father had told Sara first. Not that she'd said anything. She never did. If anyone was truly damaged by their parents' bizarre marriage it had to be her. Sara was so overlooked she was almost invisible. And she knew it.

Mevlüt stomped out, leaving İbrahim alone in that chapel with his father and his dead sister. Was it any wonder they were all fucking crazy? Why did his dad even bother to question why they adhered so closely to Islam? Being the same as most people was a comfort. Their mother understood that, even though İbrahim was angry with her too. She had known about Maryam and said nothing.

'We didn't want you to feel as if any one of you was different in any way,' his father said.

'Yeah, but Maryam *was* different,' İbrahim said. 'You loved her!'

'Oh. Not this again!' Their father put his head in his hands. 'İbrahim, I didn't sleep with Maryam, how—'

'I didn't think you did,' İbrahim said. 'That's always been *him*.' He meant his brother. 'I just thought she was your favourite. And you know, Dad, Maryam used to rub our faces in it.'

'In what?'

'In the way you indulged her,' he said. 'All the trips you took her on.'

'When she was ill, yes,' his father said. 'To hospitals, churches . . .'

'And the Pera Palas for tea, trips out to the islands . . .'

He shook his head. 'I never took her to any of those places! I took you all to the islands a few times, and once to Bebek for ice cream. I've never set foot in the Pera Palas since any of you were born!'

They both stopped and stared at the open casket. Maryam looked so peaceful.

'She lied . . .'

'A lot,' İbrahim said.

'So why did you take any notice of what she said?'

'Because it was possible. Because you favoured her.'

His father reached for a bottle of rakı. İbrahim didn't say anything. His old man was an alcoholic.

'She always showed an interest in me, in where I came from, in my religion.'

'Maybe she knew . . .'

'I only told her when she became ill,' his father said. 'The night she was murdered, she was going to see her real mother for the first time. I organised it.'

'The night she died?'

'Yes. The night your mother tried to stop her going out and I had to unlock her room.'

'Then Mum ran out after her.'

'She wasn't quick enough.'

'No . . .' İbrahim had tried to push what he was about to say from his mind ever since Maryam's death. He was sure it meant nothing, or so he told himself.

'Sara left too,' he said.

'No, Sara was in bed. She came out of her room in the morning. I saw her.'

'Yes. But she did go out. When Mum came back, she was out.'

'She can't have been!'

'She was,' İbrahim said. 'I saw her leave.'

'Where did she go?' his father asked. The old man's face looked grey now. He took a swig of rakı.

'I don't know.'

'When did she come home?'

'I don't know that either.'

His father shook his head. 'Does Mevlüt—'

'He was listening to hip hop on his headphones.' He'd also been stoned out of his gourd, but İbrahim didn't mention that. 'Sara was in her room in the morning. I don't know when she got in, but it must have been after Mum went to bed. Mum would have said something.'

'Mmm.' His father drank. Then he turned suddenly. 'Did you tell the police this?'

'No,' İbrahim said.

His father said, 'Mmm,' again, and his fingers tapped the neck of his bottle.

Fabrizio Leon was the type of man Çetin İkmen had wanted to be when he was young. Back in the 1960s, when Europe had been in love with the Fellini film *La Dolce Vita*, he'd thought he might grow up to be Marcello Mastroianni, or indeed any man who looked vaguely Italian. But of course he hadn't. Fabrizio Leon, however, had given it a shot.

'I went to church and then I left,' he said.

'Why did you go to church at such a late hour?' İkmen asked.

'I had . . . have, whatever, a problem. I wanted to talk to my priest.'

'You are a religious man?'

'Not really. But I liked Father Benito. He was a good man if you had a problem.'

'In what way?'

The only interview room available had been one that had blood on the floor. İkmen managed to get it cleaned up before he brought Leon in. But the image of that redness on the lino wouldn't leave his mind. There had been a time, not long ago, when the brutality had all but stopped. When Turkey had been pushing forward towards European Union accession.

'He was my confessor,' Leon said. 'He was good. He didn't just go through the motions.'

'You talked.'

'Yes.' He ran his hand through his thick greying hair. The gesture made him look boyish.

Süleyman had told İkmen that Fabrizio Leon was divorced. İkmen was not surprised. For a man like that, even in middle age, life had to be one long carnal temptation.

'What about?'

139

'It's private.'

'Maybe,' İkmen said. 'But you're not a priest and so you can tell me what your confessions were about – or so I understand.'

'Theoretically.'

'So . . .'

'So, it's private,' Leon said. 'I'd been to confession earlier in the day as well. It was a continuation of that conversation. That happens sometimes. I thought you wanted to know who killed Father Benito. Not what problems I might be having.'

'You were the last person to leave St Anthony's either before or after the death of Father Esposito,' İkmen said. 'According to our doctor, rigor mortis, which sets in one to two hours after death and may last for five to six hours, had almost completely subsided when he examined the body at seven o'clock on the morning following his death. Therefore Father Esposito probably died between ten and eleven at night, which means that you, Mr Leon, could have killed him.'

'Why?' Fabrizio Leon held his arms wide and shrugged.

'I don't know,' İkmen said. 'Did you go to St Anthony's to see Father Esposito the night he died?'

'Yes,' Leon said. 'I've not denied that.'

'Why?'

'I told you, I wanted to continue my confession from that morning. When I entered the church, I knew he might have gone to his apartment. It wasn't a time set aside for confession. But then I saw him, snuffing out candles.'

'Did you speak to him?'

'No. One doesn't at confession, not outside the box.'

'What did you do?'

'I entered the confessional and waited until he came to extinguish the candles in front of the cabinet.'

'Then you spoke to him.'

'No,' he said. 'He could see that the curtain across the front

140

of the box was closed. That means it's occupied. He asked if anyone was inside, and I said I wanted to talk.'

'How long did you talk for?'

'I don't know. Twenty minutes maybe.'

'Was anyone else in the church?'

'Not as far as I know. I didn't see or hear anyone.'

'You do know,' İkmen said, 'that I am going to have to ask you what you were talking to Father Esposito about?'

Leon said nothing.

'I didn't know,' Ayşegül said. 'When I lost Maryam out in the street, I just came home.'

'You didn't see Sara leave?'

'No.'

They both looked down at Maryam's pale, half-smiling face. Ayşegül squeezed her husband's hand. İbrahim had asked her to come. He and his brother now knew about Maryam. In a way, it was good that they had one secret fewer in their lives.

'She may not have been my flesh, but she was special to me,' she said. 'I loved her. You have to believe me, Silvio. Those things she said I did to her never happened.'

He shook his head.

'Maybe she sensed she was only your child long before she knew the truth,' she said. 'Even as an infant she hung on your every word.'

'She needed to know who she was,' Silvio said. 'My world has been so completely subsumed by everything that is Muslim and Turkish . . .'

'This is Turkey.'

'Yes, and I am part of it!' he said. 'I belong here just as much as you. Maryam wanted to know that side of herself.'

'And it caused chaos. *She* caused chaos. She lied.' Ayşegül shrugged. 'And I don't know why. Do you think she just wanted to be on her own with you?'

'I don't know,' he said. 'We'll never know now. But in the meantime, what do we do about Sara? Do we confront her?'

'We have to,' Ayşegül said. 'I don't believe she would have hurt Maryam, but she may have seen something.'

'And not told us?'

'What does she tell us, Silvio?' she said. 'She's so quiet, there have been times I have wondered whether she has slipped out of this world. What does she do in that head of hers?'

'She makes up lies,' Silvio said. 'Maybe she learned to do it from Maryam.'

'Or maybe she creates her own version of reality for a different reason,' Ayşegül said.

Silvio looked down into the coffin. 'We should tell the police.'

Ayşegül didn't reply.

'Shouldn't we?'

She walked out of the chapel and stood by the window in the hallway.

'There are people outside,' she said.

'I know.'

'People for Maryam.'

'Well they can do whatever they like,' Silvio said. 'She's staying in here, with me.'


'When I left St Anthony's, I went back to the Dondolo,' Leon said.

'To work?' İkmen asked.

'Yes, but I met up with a woman.'

'Your girlfriend?'

'A woman I sometimes see.'

'A casual . . .'

'I've known her for years,' Leon said.

142

'Yes, but this woman can't provide you with an alibi unless she accompanied you to the church,' İkmen pointed out.

'I met her at the hotel directly after.'

'And yet you still won't tell me what you talked to Father Esposito about,' İkmen said. 'You may think it's not relevant, but believe me, everything is relevant.'

Leon bowed his head. 'I know it's relevant.'

'Then I must insist you tell me,' İkmen said.

Fabrizio Leon breathed in and then out slowly, as if preparing to take part in some sort of sport. Then he said, 'I spoke to Father Benito about whether I should come and talk to you.'

'To me?' İkmen said.

'You, the police.' He breathed in deeply again, and continued on his outward breath, 'I haven't and wouldn't kill anyone, least of all those I care about. I have to preface what I'm about to say with this.'

'Why?'

'For the last ten years,' he said, 'I've been having an affair with my best friend's daughter. Neither Maryam de Mango nor I wanted it to happen, but it did. When she was murdered, she was pregnant with my child. We didn't want that to happen either. Or rather she didn't.'

İkmen wasn't shocked, but this information had subdued him. What sort of man had an affair with his best friend's daughter? What sort of girl went willingly with such a man? If she'd gone willingly . . .

'I didn't know what I wanted,' Leon said. 'But I didn't want her dead. I swear I didn't.' His eyes glistened. 'She was always a strange girl. Right from when she was very young, she used to say that one day she was going to do something marvellous.'

'Like what?'

'She never said.'

'As you can appreciate, Mr Leon,' İkmen said, 'my next

143

question to you has to be about where you were the night Maryam died.'

'I know,' Leon said. 'I was with the same woman I spent time with the night Father Benito died.'

'And who is she?'

He shook his head. 'Father Benito said you'd ask me that.'

'Father Benito was, I'm beginning to see,' İkmen said, 'very often right. Give me her name.'

# Chapter 15

Maryam de Mango's shoes safely deposited at the forensic insti-
tute, Omer Mungun returned to headquarters, where he found
his superior, Mehmet Süleyman, gone. In his place was Kerim
Gürsel, who said, 'Mehmet Bey is in Çetin Bey's office. They
need, it seems, to be alone.'

'Do you know why?'

'Çetin Bey brought Silvio de Mango's friend in for questioning.'

'Fabrizio Leon? Did he say what he was doing at the church
the night the priest died?'

'I don't know,' Kerim said.

Süleyman's phone rang. Omer picked it up.

'Where's Inspector Süleyman?' Commissioner Teker asked.

'In a meeting with Inspector İkmen,' Omer replied. 'Can I do
anything for you, madam?'

'You can get him and İkmen out and over to Galata,' she said.
'There's a crowd gathering outside the de Mango apartment.'

'Do you know—'

'They want to see their saint,' Teker said. 'Mrs de Mango has
just called. She and her husband are extremely agitated.'

Mina had been shopping. She'd walked up to the Balık Pazar,
where, as usual, she had been both bewildered and entranced by
the sheer volume and variety of produce on offer. Although she'd
lived in the city all her life, she had never ceased to be bewitched

by its food. Not that she was an organised shopper. She bought jars of pickles because she liked their colours – scarlet peppers, dark green cucumbers like vast ancient emeralds, and creamy clotted kaymak that went so well with the preserved quinces she'd bought from Ismail Bey at the Tarlabaşı Pazar the previous Sunday.

She bought a lot of fruit, mainly to make juices for Lobna. Everyone with cancer was drinking juice these days. She'd also bought flowers. The back wall of the bathroom was damp again and had started to smell. Mina had bought roses and carnations from Abdülkadir Bey the florist, both to brighten the bathroom and to help disguise the smell.

It was while she was choosing her flowers that she heard the old florist telling two women about Maryam de Mango.

'Her father has her body in his apartment,' he said in low tones to a woman Mina recognised as a local Atatürkist grand dame.

The woman shook her head. 'Pure superstition,' she said. 'Such practices should be illegal.'

'Oh, but Ayşe, don't you think the girl had something?' said her friend, a small, heavily made-up woman who was probably in her seventies.

'No, I do not!' Ayşe said.

'He came in this morning, the father,' Abdülkadir Bey said. 'Bought tulips mainly. He said they were for *her*.'

'What a waste of money!'

'Be that as it may,' the old man said, 'a lot of people who have come in here today have bought extra flowers to take to Galata for the girl.'

'Oh, and I wonder who gave them that idea?' the grand dame said.

The florist looked away.

As soon as she'd unloaded her shopping, Mina went to see

her sister, who was sitting out in the tiny mud-baked patch that passed for their back garden.

'Lobna,' she said, 'I've put some roses in the bathroom. It won't entirely kill the bad smell, but it should help. You won't believe what I just heard at Abdülkadir the florist's . . .'

'What?'

'Apparently lots of people are buying flowers to take to Silvio's apartment for Maryam.'

'What people?'

'I don't know,' she said. 'I wonder how they found out she had come home?'

'Did you see the size of that coffin?' Lobna said. 'Three flights of stairs that had to be pulled and pushed up.'

'Yes, but even so . . .'

'Muslims don't make such elaborate gestures to the dead,' Lobna said. 'Silvio said people were watching.'

'And he went to the florist's to buy tulips and roses this morning,' Mina said.

'Well, there's your answer.'

Mina sat down next to her sister.

'Lobna,' she said, 'do you think Maryam will perform miracles?'

Like Lobna, Mina had been married. She even had a daughter, a lawyer who lived in Florida. But unlike her sister, she was, and had always been, a little unworldly. Mina was a good Catholic. She liked to believe everything the Church told her. The only time she'd ever openly disobeyed its dictates was when she had been briefly married to a Muslim. She was, in her head if not in reality, still doing penance for that twenty years on.

'I don't know,' Lobna said.

'If she does, she could become a saint,' Mina said. 'In death, her life will have great meaning. Imagine that.'

\* \* \*

There was a gunshot. It was unmistakable. Silvio had done his national service; he knew what guns sounded like. He put his head in his hands. Ayşegül had left the apartment to go and speak to the neighbours. She'd called the police when the first people came into the building. A girl, apparently, carrying a posy. But she'd been followed by a man screaming about infidels. That was when Silvio felt the fear. Now it was all over him.

When Maryam's body had been found, it had taken no time at all for the news to get out and for religious fanatics from places like Çarşamba to make their way to her with bad intent, calling her an abomination and a whore, wanting to burn her corpse. And although İkmen and his officers had protected her, Silvio suspected there were also elements in the police who agreed with the radical Islamist agenda. How else could word of her death have got out so quickly?

Maybe his brother was right and he should have moved the whole family to Italy when the children were little. Ayşegül would have gone in those days. And the kids would have got Italian passports because of him. Instead of mourning Maryam in his damp apartment, they'd all be sipping grappa in Amalfi. Well, maybe not . . .

A voice outside muscled its way through the general uproar. He heard it scream, 'Blaspheming whore!'

Had she been? Not a whore – he knew Maryam hadn't been one of those – but had what she had done constituted an act of blasphemy? Was that why the Holy See had not responded to his letter?

Another gunshot. Now he could hear sirens, and people screaming. The police must have arrived. In one way, he was relieved, but in another way he was more frightened than ever. If the protesters and the people who had come to mourn Maryam got into fights with the police, things could turn ugly very quickly. But then even if the crowd was dispersed peacefully, they would be back, especially those who hated his daughter. They'd come back and try to take her. Now everyone knew where she was, she wasn't safe. Silvio began to shake. What was he going to do?

It was worse than İkmen had imagined. The loose collection of ISIS supporters, self-styled al-Qaeda followers and every religious fanatic who felt in any way aggrieved about anything had come armed with sticks, knives and, in a couple of cases, guns. Ranged against them were mainly women who had come to lay flowers on the steps of the de Mangos' apartment building.

But still his superiors had, to İkmen's way of thinking, overreacted. Tear-gas canisters, even a fucking riot-control vehicle waiting in a side street. The crowd, which was probably at most two hundred strong, had gathered in Büyük Hendek Caddesi. He wondered what the Genoese architects who had built the Galata Tower would think of what was happening. Levantine traders interested only in commerce, they would have been horrified.

He looked at Süleyman's grey face. Not only was he having to deal with this, but he was also in pain. To discover that Gonca had been having an affair had come as a bitter blow. He'd fooled around with other women and had assumed that she had only fooled around with other men. But what she'd had with Fabrizio Leon had been more than that – according to Leon.

The women who had come to lay flowers got out of the way once the police arrived, scattering into side streets, many of them crying with fear. İkmen had always hoped that one day the inhabitants of İstanbul and the police could be allies. Now he felt foolish. That was never going to happen.

A group of men had unfurled the ISIS flag over the entrance to the apartment block. Whether any of them had gone inside, he didn't know. He called Ayşegül de Mango's mobile.

'Are you in your apartment, Mrs de Mango?' he said.

'I'm just going back in,' she said. 'I went to see our neighbours.'

'Well go inside and stay there,' he said.

'Are they coming into the building?'

'I don't know. Just get in and stay put.'

He ended the call. Then he put the megaphone he'd brought with him to his lips and yelled, 'Move away from the entrance to the Kuleisi Apartments! Leave the area now!'

His men were at his back, all in full riot gear. İkmen didn't want to deploy them, but he knew he'd have to if this mob didn't do as it was told. He saw some of the crowd laughing. Provoking bastards. But they were the opportunists, men who didn't give a shit about blasphemy or anything else that wasn't fighting or shagging. The ones to be feared were of a different order. They never laughed, or at least they could never be seen laughing because they had their faces covered. There were four of them holding up the ISIS flag. Then there were three . . .

İkmen looked at his men. 'Fuck it, they're in. On my signal . . .'

Someone was shouting in the corridor. Ayşegül ran to the front door of the apartment and locked it. Then she ran to one of the windows that looked out into the street.

The men, some in şalvar trousers, some dressed in funky T-shirts and tight jeans, their faces covered by black scarves, were fighting the police. Armed with sticks and knives, they stood no chance against men dressed in stab vests and riot helmets. But some of the men had guns; she'd heard them. Of course the police had firearms. Would there be a gun battle? Should she even be looking out of the window?

Silvio had collapsed into a shaking heap of fear. She could hear him crying. But she didn't want to be with him. Someone needed to be alert in case whoever was in the corridor tried to get into the apartment. The English family on the ground floor were probably going mad. She doubted they'd seen anything like this before.

There was a crack as something ricocheted off the front of the building. Ayşegül ducked. One of the police shouted into a megaphone, 'Put your weapon down! Now!'

Ayşegül scampered across the floor of the living room and made for the hall. It hadn't been a good idea to be close to a window. But then she saw that the front door was shaking.

İkmen pushed the man's arm so far up his back it made him scream. Then he called to Kerim Gürsel. 'Cuffs! Now!'

Kerim already had a boy in a headlock, but he handed a set of handcuffs to İkmen and then took both men with him to the prison van. Someone had fired a shot and İkmen knew it wasn't one of his men.

Although a lot of the demonstrators, men as well as the women, had left the scene, a hard core remained around the front of the apartment building. Ahead of him, İkmen could see Süleyman cutting a furious swathe through a group of middle-aged men who looked like the type that could be armed. He hoped he didn't do anything stupid, like kill someone.

Then suddenly İkmen's face was wet.

'Fucking atheist!'

The man who'd spat at him stood his ground and waved a knife.

'Put that away!' İkmen said.

The man raised his arm. İkmen drew his pistol. He didn't usually have it with him; he hated it. Was he, after all these years, going to have to kill someone?

'Put it down,' he said. 'Or I'll shoot you.'

'Then I will die . . .'

Suddenly the man was on the floor, his legs kicked away from underneath him by Omer Mungun, who cuffed him and took him away.

Shaking and relieved, İkmen put his pistol back in its holster.

151

He'd never shot anyone in his life and he didn't want to start now. He looked up to see where Süleyman had gone. But he'd disappeared.

The door shook on its hinges. Whoever was outside wanted to get in.

Ayşegül called out, 'Go away!'

But the door just kept on shuddering. He was kicking it in. She'd told Silvio to get it replaced years ago.

'Silvio!' she called. 'Someone's trying to get in!'

Whether he'd been lost in his thoughts of Maryam or actually asleep, she didn't know. But he came.

'What's going on?'

'Look!' she said.

The lower panel of the door splintered and a foot appeared.

Silvio looked at her, and then, as if in a dream, he said, 'I'll get the pistol.'

'No!'

But he'd gone. Ayşegül started to go after him. 'We don't want—'

A huge crashing sound stopped her, and she saw a man in the doorway, surrounded by what remained of the front door. Dressed in camouflage trousers, his mouth and nose covered by a black scarf, he had a gun.

Ayşegül screamed.

The man raised his weapon.

'Silvio!'

The man walked towards her.

'Silvio!'

And then he dropped to the floor.

# Chapter 16

'He's lucky just to be in hospital,' İkmen said to Süleyman as they walked into the older man's office and sat down.

'If he hadn't been making such a terrible production of kicking the door in, he would have heard me behind him,' Süleyman said. 'I saw him follow Mrs de Mango. Just hope he hasn't got brain damage.'

'We'll see.'

Süleyman had followed the man, whom they had found out was called Erol Hasefe, to the top floor of the de Mangos' apartment building and waited until he could land a blow on his head with the stock of his pistol. Hasefe had collapsed immediately, leaving Süleyman with a hysterical Ayşegül de Mango, plus her husband who was armed with some antique pistol. Kerim Gürsel had stayed with the family while İkmen, Süleyman and the rest of the riot detachment had returned to headquarters with those they had arrested. Erol Hasefe had been taken to the Cerrahpaşa Hospital for treatment for a head wound.

They both lit cigarettes and İkmen opened his office window.

'Do you know,' he said, 'when Maryam's funeral is taking place?'

'No.'

'We need to find out as soon as possible. We'll have to make sure we've got boots on the ground. Wouldn't put it past some of those we saw today to dig her up.'

'You think?'

'Between the delusional flower carriers and the men who think it's a sin to do anything but pray and fight, anything is possible,' he said. 'I want to get the de Mango family here tomorrow so that we can discuss the funeral, amongst other issues.'

They sat in silence. İkmen knew they had to report to Commissioner Teker once she was out of her meeting with the chief of police. If she'd been meeting anyone else, it would have been possible to interrupt her.

Süleyman said, 'What about Fabrizio Leon's alibi?'

In spite of his protestations, İkmen had arrested Leon on suspicion of murder and had him placed in a cell. He still needed to check out the man's alibi, but it was clear that he had a credible motive. Maryam's pregnancy couldn't have been allowed to continue, not least because her father would, he imagined, have ripped her lover's head off once he knew he was responsible. But İkmen had needed to speak to Süleyman about it, and then events around the de Mango apartment had exploded.

'I'll ring her now,' İkmen said.

Süleyman stood.

'You can stay.' İkmen picked up the phone. 'You know . . .'

'I'd rather not,' Süleyman said. And with a tight smile, he put his cigarette out and left the room.

İkmen waited for an answer for a long time. Not unusual in her case. When at last she picked up, he said, 'Hello, Gonca, it's Çetin İkmen.'

The policeman was nice and Ayşegül was happy to make him tea. That Silvio kept giving him venomous looks was his business. As far as Ayşegül was concerned, the police had saved their lives.

She put the tea glass on the chair beside the officer and said, 'Sugar?'

'No thank you.' He smiled and carried on looking at the

room he was in, probably unable to believe his eyes. It had been Silvio's great-grandfather's idea to have a personal chapel installed in their apartment. He had, it was said, been profoundly affected by a trip he had made to a Venetian palazzo, where such chapels were common. The de Mango version, however, was more Neapolitan than Venetian. The room was dark and stuffy, while the pictures on the walls, painted by renowned Levantine artist Fausto Zonaro, were ornate and clearly influenced by Orientalism, and the statues and crucifixes that crowded every niche and surface were heavily detailed and visceral.

Ayşegül had always felt creeped out by the chapel. If Maryam had been her daughter, she would not have wanted to have her displayed in there. But she wasn't her daughter. Ayşegül thought about Sara and felt a twinge of disgust. Maryam hadn't always lied, but there had never been a time when Sara didn't play one parent or sibling off against another.

'We will leave an officer at the front door of the apartments,' the policeman, Sergeant Gürsel, said. 'And of course I will stay until the kapıcı has repaired your front door.'

'Thank you.'

'What for?' Silvio asked. 'What good will one policeman do against all these madmen who want to destroy what remains of my child?'

'It's all—'

'You can spare for someone like me?' He laughed bitterly. 'Don't bother.'

'Silvio!'

'Maryam is nothing to do with you!' he snapped.

He looked into the open coffin again and put his hand on the dead girl's forehead. Ayşegül saw the policeman cringe.

'Do you have a date for the funeral, sir?' the officer asked.

'What's that to you?'

He was being even more offensive than usual. And he wasn't even particularly drunk.

'We will need to provide security . . .'

'No you won't,' Silvio said. 'I will look after my daughter on my own. I don't need you. Any of you.'

The officer breathed in deeply, then said, 'Sir, Inspector İkmen has told me he will need to speak to your family when things have quietened down tomorrow.'

'Has he?' Silvio shook his head. 'Well he can fuck off, can't he!'


The street was a mess. Why did people leave so much litter wherever they went? Of course a lot of this consisted of cut flowers, which at least were inoffensive. Lobna bent down to pick some up.

'Miss Amara?'

She looked up into the face of the young priest from St Anthony's.

'Father Colombo,' she said. 'What are you doing here?'

He helped her to stand up. Life wasn't easy without her stick.

'When I heard about the trouble outside the de Mangos' apartment, I thought I'd better come over and see them,' he said.

'I just came to look,' Lobna told him.

He shook his head. 'Terrible scenes, apparently. I don't understand why people can't let the dead rest in peace.'

Apart from the flowers on the ground, the Galata seemed almost normal again. A few people sat outside one of the cafés, and there were even tourists looking up at the tower.

'I assume you've heard about Father Esposito?' he said.

She looked away, distracted by a patch of rare sunshine gleaming on the side of a van. 'Yes,' she said. 'My sister, Mina, is organising flowers for him. Do you know—'

'No,' he said. 'The police are investigating. The church remains closed.'

She turned to him and smiled. 'Won't be for long,' she said. 'Let's pray not.'

He always felt relieved when a test that might or might not work came back with a definite result. The child that Maryam de Mango had been carrying when she died had not been fathered by Silvio. That didn't mean he hadn't abused her, but at least he hadn't made her pregnant.

Arto Sarkissian put the result slip from the lab down on his desk and pulled on a pair of plastic gloves. Apparently there'd been some sort of riot outside the de Mangos' apartment building, which meant that İkmen was unable to attend the autopsy on Father Benito Esposito. Mehmet Süleyman was on his way but had been held up for the same reason. Arto looked through the window into his laboratory. The body of the priest, underneath a sheet, looked small and pathetic. Preliminary examination of the corpse had shown that the blow that had almost certainly killed him had been delivered with great force. Who had hated him that much? Arto wondered. Who, amongst all the thousands of angry people who seemed to be everywhere in recent years?

A knock on his door made him jump. That was probably Süleyman. Now they could begin.

'You know why you're here?'

Gonca Şekeroğlu tipped her head to one side. 'Yeah.'

'A man called Fabrizio Leon has said that he was with you last Monday night, when Maryam de Mango died,' İkmen said.

She sighed. 'He was.'

'At what time and where?'

'In his hotel, the Dondolo,' she said. 'I must've got there at about eight. What's Fabrizio got to do with the Miracle Girl anyway?'

He didn't answer. 'And when did you leave?' he said.

'In the morning.'

There was an awkward pause.

'Miss Şekeroğlu . . .'

'I fucked him,' she said. 'It's what he and I do. I've known him for years.'

'So how long have you been . . . in a . . .'

'Since last year,' she said. 'My partner at the time had been unfaithful to me. I'd thrown him out. But Fabrizio, Mr Leon, didn't know about that. He's bought various pieces of my work over the years and he called me to make an appointment to look at my latest stuff.'

İkmen knew that Fabrizio Leon's hotel was not doing well and wondered how he could even consider buying expensive artwork.

'One thing led to another,' she said.

'And you've been seeing him periodically ever since?'

'Yeah.'

'And your partner?'

She looked into his eyes. They both knew she'd taken Süleyman back. Even though they no longer lived together, they had resumed their affair.

'I see him too,' she said. 'He doesn't know about Fabrizio. Or rather, he didn't.'

Neither of them wanted to use Süleyman's name. He had nothing at all to do with what she did when she wasn't with him, and it was important for İkmen not to compromise his colleague in any way.

'Did Mr Leon leave you at any point during the time you spent with him at the Dondolo Hotel last Monday night?'

'No,' she said. 'Not that I know of.'

'What do you mean?'

'I went to sleep,' she said. 'Don't know when exactly. Fabrizio cooked and we had a couple of bottles of wine. Then we went

158

to bed and . . .' She shrugged. 'I guess I probably dropped off in the early hours of Tuesday morning. All I do know is that Fabrizio fell asleep before I did.'

'How do you know?'

'He was snoring,' she said.

It was difficult for İkmen to imagine someone as elegant and poised as Fabrizio Leon snoring, but he was a man of a certain age and so he probably couldn't help himself.

'What about the night before last?' he asked. 'The night Father Esposito was murdered.'

'I got to the Dondolo at about eleven,' she said.

'Why so late?'

'I'd been working all day,' she said. 'I was very focused. That's how it goes sometimes. People think that when you work in collage you just glue things to a canvas. But all my works are carefully planned. I'm a storyteller.'

'Did Mr Leon phone you that day?'

'No,' she said. 'I phoned him when I'd finished working.'

'Which was when?'

'Around nine in the evening. He didn't pick up.'

'How come you went to the Dondolo at eleven?'

'I went to Beyoğlu to have a drink,' she said. 'My daughter Arsena works in the Azeri meyhane on Nevizade Sokak.'

Arsena Şekeroğlu was, if İkmen recalled correctly, a very clever girl who was also wild.

'She's at the university,' Gonca said. 'But she works in the bar when she can. I'll be honest, I go to keep an eye on her from time to time. You know how men can be around beautiful young girls.'

And İkmen knew how Arsena could be around young men. Süleyman had told him many stories about how Gonca trawled the beds of İstanbul men looking for her daughter.

'When did you get to the bar?'

159

'I didn't,' she said.

'Why not?'

'I met a friend.'

'Who?'

'Madam Edith.'

İkmen knew her. Madam Edith was an elderly transsexual who made her living performing impressions of French chanteuse Edith Piaf in gay clubs.

'Edith likes to hang out around Fransız Sokağı,' Gonca said. 'She feels safe there. We went to a bar that played non-stop Piaf. The only reason I agreed to it was because when we met, Edith was crying.'

'Why?'

'Oh, some heterosexual bear she'd been seeing had beaten her up and then dropped her,' she said. 'I've been telling her for years she needs to give up on straight men. Anyway, we drank some wine, Edith felt better and I went off to go to Nevizade Sokak.'

'But you didn't get there.'

'No,' she said. 'Because I saw Fabrizio.'

'Where?'

'On Tomtom Kaptan.' She waved a hand in front of her face. 'Ah, so you have me,' she said. 'I wandered down there to see if he was around. I felt a bit . . .'

'Yes.' If he'd let her go on, he would have been given some details about her needs that he didn't want to know.

'He didn't see me. He'd been standing outside having a cigarette. I followed him in, as a surprise.'

'At eleven.'

'Or so,' she said.

'How was he?'

'Subdued at first,' she said.

'At first?'

'Later he was horny.'

160

'When you say subdued . . .'

'Thoughtful,' she said. 'As if he was puzzling over something. No idea what.'

'How did he look?'

'Look? Hot.'

'I mean, was he dishevelled? Did he look as if he might have done something strenuous?'

'Like kill a priest? No.' She shook her head. 'Fabrizio likes to behave as if he doesn't give a shit about religion, but he does. He'd never kill a priest. If he did that, he'd go to hell, and you know how Catholics are about all that eternal fire and endless damnation stuff.'

İkmen leaned forward on his desk. 'Miss Şekeroğlu, did you know that Fabrizio Leon had been having an affair with Maryam de Mango?'

He watched her go white. 'No . . .'

'For the last ten years,' İkmen said.

He did two hairstyles – short and neat, and crew cut. Nothing fancy, nothing modern. And that was just as well, because Kemal Öneş was on automatic. Deep in thought, he couldn't remember whose hair he had cut, whether he'd also performed a shave or what time of day it might be. The only things he could concentrate on were the memory of how a sheikh from the Order had bowed to him early that morning, and the abuse one of Erdal Çelik's brothers had thrown at him.

Çelik was still in a police cell. His family blamed Kemal. But it wasn't his fault! They forgot, it had been Erdal who had given the police his name, not the other way around. It had been Erdal who had threatened the police with a gun.

Erdal had been in the shop when he'd got the call. But Kemal hadn't just blurted out that the girl was dead. He'd tried to find out who the woman on the end of the phone might be. Apparently she was a secretary at police headquarters. He'd never heard of her. How had she known him? Or was the key to that in the smile he'd received from the sheikh?

If, say, they had instructed the woman to call him, then it had to mean that they trusted him. For a moment Kemal felt his chest puff out with pride. But then it struck him: that implied the call was prearranged. How did the Order know the girl was going to die unless . . .

Kemal stopped thinking and just cut hair.

'Obviously I didn't know we were going to find *that*,' the doctor said.

'No . . .'

Mehmet Süleyman breathed in deeply. But even outside the laboratory, the smell lingered in his nostrils. As soon as Dr Sarkissian had cut into the priest's chest cavity, they'd both realised that something was wrong. Where his lungs should have been was just a mass of brown matter.

'Do you know how long he'd had it?' Süleyman asked.

'I'm not an oncologist, so no,' the doctor said. 'Some time, I imagine. Although lung cancer can be rapid-growing.'

Süleyman lit a cigarette.

'Something you should think on maybe, Inspector.'

He waved a hand. 'Not now, Doctor,' he said.

The news about Gonca and Fabrizio Leon had hit him hard. They'd both *said* they could and would see other people, but he'd never expected her to actually do it.

'Anyway, that's not what killed him.'

'No, he died because someone hit him repeatedly over the back of the head with a blunt object,' the doctor said. 'What, I don't know.'

'Neither do we. There's nothing so far in terms of blood or tissue on any of the candlesticks, statues, collection boxes . . .'

İkmen had sent him a text to tell him that he had applied for a warrant to search Fabrizio Leon's hotel, which meant that Gonca must have given him some reason to believe Leon could be guilty. He'd seen her that night, walking up Sıraselviler Caddesi towards Taksim at three in the morning. He'd wondered where she'd been.

The doctor interrupted his thoughts. 'The assailant could have taken it with him.'

'Indeed.'

Had Leon had anything in his hands when he'd come out of the church after his confession? He couldn't remember. His mind was clogged with Gonca and the fact that she'd only done what he'd done. But he couldn't forgive her. He wouldn't.

Çetin İkmen looked at the tiny old man sitting in front of him and felt ashamed. Father Mesrob Kalajian had travelled, on the busiest day of his week, all the way from Fener on public transport to come and see him. How had he managed to overlook the man in whose church Maryam de Mango had supposedly been cured?

'I am so sorry to hear about the death of Father Esposito,' the Armenian said.

'You knew him?'

'We all know each other in this city.' He smiled. 'You know how it is.'

Fifteen million people or thereabouts now lived in the greater İstanbul area, and yet it was still like a village.

'And we had a connection through Maryam,' he continued.

'Did you go and see her up at the Golden Gate?'

'Yes. Although I can't tell you what I made of it.'

İkmen said, 'What do you mean?'

'I mean that you will not find many priests these days who will automatically cry "miracle" as soon as someone starts seeing or hearing things or a cure is effected. I can't tell you without any doubt whatsoever that it was God who cured Maryam when she came to our Church of the Assumption.'

'And yet it is known that one miracle is granted every year . . .'

'So the story goes,' said the priest.

'You don't believe that?'

He put his head on one side. 'Inspector,' he said, 'the human race knows so much more about the mechanics of life than it did even fifty years ago. To find the origin of my religion, you have to go back two thousand years. In that time Christianity has experienced much change and also, it must be said, some stagnation. How one explains so-called miracle cures in the twenty-first century is more than a challenge; it is almost impossible. Maryam was sick and then she wasn't. A girl who was officially a Muslim came to my church and was touched by the power of God over and above parishioners of mine who had been ill for decades. How do I explain that?'

'I don't know.'

'Nor do I. But apparently it happened.' He shook his head. 'And then of course she began to have visions. I had a long discussion with Bishop Montoya when it first started. Mr de Mango was, apparently, expecting a visit from the Holy See at any moment. But the Bishop didn't support such a move.'

'Do you know why?'

'There are many reasons, Inspector,' the old man said. 'Not least of which is that as Christians living on the edge of the Middle East, we do not want to draw attention to ourselves.'

Çetin İkmen had always been one of those Turks who had believed that the chaos of the Middle East could never take root in his homeland. But now it had. It was a hard rock to swallow.

'At the same time, as men of faith it falls to us to recognise the signs that God puts in our way from time to time.'

'Miracles.'

'If you like,' said the priest. 'Had Maryam's experiences continued, and had a miracle occurred, I am sure Bishop Montoya would have requested a visit from the Holy See. But this thing, whatever it was, was nascent. It was also a picture that was confused.'

'In what way?'

'The girl, as I have said, was a Muslim. Her father is a practising Catholic. Maryam was cured in an Armenian Orthodox church and yet her visions occurred at a site most holy to the Greeks. You know that the Church of the Holy Sepulchre in Jerusalem is shared by multiple Christian sects.'

'I do,' İkmen said. 'And it's a Muslim family who possess the key to the front door.'

'Absolutely. You probably also know that fights between the various sects break out all the time. A war over Maryam de Mango is something we didn't and still don't need.'

'So . . . she was a problem?'

'For all of us, yes,' said the old man. 'Not least because of the jealousy of the people who attended my church.'

İkmen hadn't thought of that. Or rather he had but he'd glossed over it. Had he been so keen to blame the jihadi boys for Maryam's death that he'd turned a blind eye to those with other religious affiliations?

# Chapter 17

'Do you have any children, Mr Leon?'

'No,' he said. 'Well, maybe somewhere, I don't know. Not that I know of.'

'Did you not want any?' İkmen asked.

'Yes,' said Leon. 'But my ex-wife couldn't conceive.'

'So were you pleased when Maryam de Mango became pregnant?'

'In a way,' he said. 'Of course.'

'But in a way not.'

'Telling Silvio and Ayşegül was going to be difficult. I've known Silvio all my life; he is my best friend . . .'

'Whose daughter you defiled when she was seventeen.'

Leon looked away for a moment and then stared İkmen in the eyes.

'You're a man; you must know what it's like to want a woman,' he said.

'Yes, I also know what it's like to shrug my shoulders and accept that said woman is actually a girl.'

'I can't help being who I am!' He flung his arms in the air. 'It took real guts for me to confess to Father Esposito! He told me I had to come to you. I have, and now you arrest me!'

'Yes, but you didn't come to me, did you?' İkmen said. 'I came and got you.'

'Yes, but . . .'

'Who else besides Father Esposito knew about Maryam's pregnancy?' İkmen asked.

166

'No one.'

'Are you sure?'

'I told no one!'

'What about Maryam? Did she tell anyone?'

Leon shook his head. 'Why would she? We were going to tell her parents together.'

'When? She was already three months pregnant.'

'I don't know.' He put his head down.

İkmen glanced at the case file in front of him. 'All right, let's look at what you did on the day Father Esposito died.'

Silvio had fallen asleep in his chair. It had taken the policeman forever to leave, but when he had finally gone, Silvio had crashed out. Now, however, he was awake.

The first thing he did, even before he took a drink, was to look at Maryam. So peaceful in death. Maybe, in some strange way, it had been for the best. Tormented by illness, conflicted by her own family, she'd been a solitary girl, close to no one except Silvio. And because of that, the family had decided that his relationship with her had to be unnatural. Or rather Mevlüt had come to that conclusion. Playing the good Muslim, that boy had dreamed up sins no one else had ever heard of. Silvio wondered how much all the bonzai he took had to do with his fucked-up state of mind. İbrahim and, probably, the rest of the family thought Silvio didn't know about the drugs. But he too was an addict, an alcoholic, and it was obvious to him what Mevlüt was doing.

Ayşegül had been kind. She had raised Maryam as her own, with no prejudice against her for years. Until, that was, she decided to reconcile with her parents and, more significantly, her fucking awful brothers. That had all started twelve years ago, when Maryam had been a teenager. God alone knew what the effect of her mother covering herself and then taking her to

167

see those superstitious morons in Fatih had been! They'd turned Mevlüt into a sly, bigoted hypocrite, Sara into a snivelling little liar, and who the hell knew what İbrahim was.

He wondered if Ayşegül's mother knew yet that Maryam wasn't really her granddaughter. Part of him hoped she did, so that the old bitch hurt, while part of him hoped she didn't. She and her sons were quite capable of giving Ayşegül and the kids real grief over it. And whatever had happened in the past, he didn't want that for them.

But more seriously, would his in-laws join in with the next mob to attack his home, trying to get at Maryam? He took a swig of rakı and lit a cigarette. His father had always smoked in the chapel on the basis that it was *his* chapel. Also, if God saw everything everywhere, what did it matter?

He needed to arrange the funeral. His brother, Angelo, was arriving from Milan on Tuesday, so ideally it would be sometime soon after that. He'd have to speak to Livadanios. But then would that turn into a circus? Everyone, it seemed, knew where he lived, and when that coffin was moved, they would all be able to see where it was going. Would the crazies try and dig her up and then burn her? He'd have to have one of those metal cages around her grave that people had erected in the past to prevent grave robbery. Either that, or he'd have to sit on her grave holding a gun.

He looked at her again. They'd saved her this time, but what about the next time?

'In the morning we actually had some guests, so I got them booked in,' Fabrizio said. 'Japanese. They'd never been to the city before, so I spent some time doing the gracious host thing – talking about transport, places to eat, sights. We need all the help we can get these days, and you put the effort in hoping they'll tell their friends about the place. In the afternoon, I went to see Lobna in Tarlabaşı.'

'Your ex-wife,' İkmen said.

'That terrible old house where she lives with her mad sister is practically falling down. Not strictly my problem, but Silvio had seen her and he'd guilt-tripped me into it.'

'Into what?'

'Going to visit her holding my wallet.'

'To pay for repairs.'

'Or so I thought,' Leon said. 'But I wasn't in a good frame of mind. Wrestling with myself about my involvement with Maryam. I knew I needed to speak to someone, get some advice, but I also knew I'd messed up my confession. I was in a state. Lobna and I rowed.'

'What about?'

'She wanted to have a conversation and I didn't,' he said. 'I wanted to give her some money and go. She, on the other hand, wanted to make tea and small talk, and get me to eat one of her sister's cakes. I tried, but I had to tell her I was too agitated for all that.'

'Did she ask you why you were agitated?'

'Yes.'

'And did you tell her?'

'About my need to explain to someone that I'd got Maryam pregnant? No!' he said.

'So what *did* you say?'

'I said I had something to confess, something I was ashamed of, and that I needed advice. She laughed.'

'Laughed?'

'Yes. She thought I wanted to own up to an affair. I've had a few. I told her it was more than that. She got serious then and told me I could talk to her if I wanted. We'd parted on bad terms, Inspector,' he said. 'I gave Lobna a bad time, I admit it. I humiliated her. But in recent years we've been civil at least, and so I think her offer was genuine. I didn't take her up on it, though.

169

She's a Catholic, and so she understood when I told her I had to speak to a priest.'

'Did you say you intended to see Father Esposito?'

'No, but she'd know that.'

'Because he was your confessor?'

'Yes.'

'So your ex-wife knew you'd be at church,' İkmen said.

'She didn't know when. Going to St Anthony's that evening was a spur-of-the-moment decision on my part.'

'How did it come about?'

'I left Lobna at about four, after finally getting her to take some money,' Leon said.

'Did you leave her at her house?'

'I took her to the bakkal at the end of her street so she could get some chicken. I took her home, then I left.'

'Why did you escort her?' İkmen said. 'Is Tarlabaşı so dangerous these days?'

'Well it is, but she's used to it,' Fabrizio said. 'Mina, her sister, feeds all the junkies and street kids, so she and Lobna are unlikely to get attacked. No, she's not good on her feet since she got ill, and her road is full of potholes. She had a walking stick some time ago but she doesn't use it any more.'

'Why?'

He shrugged. 'Vanity, knowing her.'

'What happened then?'

'I went back to the hotel. By which time our Japanese guests had returned, so I talked to them in the bar for a couple of hours. I did some paperwork, then I went out for a walk.'

'Why?'

'To think, to smoke. I wandered up onto İstiklal, as one does if one lives in Beyoğlu, and it was then that I decided to go into St Anthony's and see if Father Esposito was around.'

'Talk me through from when you arrived at the church until you left.'

Leon sighed.

İkmen said, 'We make you repeat yourself for good reasons, Mr Leon. Please do as I ask. For your own sake.'

'I went to church.'

'Did you see anyone?'

'No. The church was empty.'

'What about outside? On the piazza in front of the building?'

'There was no one about,' Fabrizio said. 'Ditto when I went inside. As I told you, I saw Father Esposito snuffing out candles. He didn't see me. I went into the confessional, pulled the curtain and waited. There was a small gap between the curtain and the box and so I saw him come to the bank of candles before the confessional. He said he'd be with me shortly, which he was. I made my confession. Then I left.'

'Did Father Esposito speak to you after you'd left the confessional?'

'No.'

'You left him in there?'

'Yes. I left the church.'

'You saw and heard no one?'

He put a hand to his mouth and paused. Then he said, 'I saw nothing and no one, but . . .'

'But?'

'There was a noise.'

'What noise? When?'

'While I was in the confessional. I stopped speaking, just for a moment. But it was nothing. I think it must have been, I don't know, the pews creaking . . .'

'Did you look?'

'No. I wanted to get my confession over. I wanted, I don't

171

know, guidance . . . Maybe I wanted Father Esposito to say that I didn't need to tell you about Maryam. He didn't.'

'But you heard the sound of creaking wood?' İkmen said.

'Maybe. It was just once. Anyway, how could anyone have been in there without being picked up by the security cameras?'

How indeed?

When he left to finally go home, İkmen called Silvio de Mango to tell him he wanted to see his family at the apartment in Galata first thing the next morning.

# Chapter 18

'I could've killed you!'

'Since when do you sleep with your gun?' Gonca said.

Sprawled across Süleyman's bed, she pushed the pistol away from her temple and stood up.

'Since I've been living here,' he said.

He put the pistol back into its holster on his night table and ran his fingers through his tangled hair.

'What were you doing coming here?' he asked. 'I've hardly slept!'

'We need to talk,' she said.

He sat up and picked up a shirt that had been on the floor. 'No we don't.'

'We do. I know you know,' she said, 'about—'

'We're free agents. We can do what we want.' He lit a cigarette without offering one to her. It was petty and he knew it.

'I've known Fabrizio Leon all my life,' she said. 'He's nothing to me.'

He shrugged.

'I want you to know that, that's all!'

She'd obviously dressed and made herself up with great care. It was only just after eight, which was usually akin to the middle of the night for Gonca. Maybe she hadn't slept.

'So now you've told me,' he said.

It took a moment for the chilliness in his voice to filter through. When it did, he saw her face fall.

'Ah,' she said.

He didn't respond. Not to her. But inside, to himself, he wondered. Was he actually punishing her for doing what he had always done? And if he was, why did he feel so clinical about it?

'I have to go to work,' he said.

When her face dropped, she looked old. She was still beautiful, though . . .

She looked down at the floor. 'I might have guessed.'

He said nothing; just smoked and waited.

'You're not European enough for this, are you?' she said. 'You're even less European than I am.'

'If by European you mean—'

'You know what I mean, Mehmet,' she said. 'I mean able to rise above your male pride. Not that I think even European men can do that. They just aren't capable.'

'You cheated on me,' he said.

'Yes, I did. And you cheat on me, all the time. But I still love you.'

She waited for him to say something, but he didn't. And that was just as much a surprise to him as it was to her.

The younger of the two de Mango boys was on something. İkmen knew the look, hostile and shaking. Probably bonzai. The rest of the family just looked tired.

When they'd arrived at the de Mangos' apartment, İkmen had noticed how relieved Kerim Gürsel had looked when Ayşegül de Mango had not shown them into her husband's chapel. Irreligious he might be, but even Kerim had the Muslim horror of dead bodies.

Silvio de Mango was already drunk. When İkmen and Gürsel entered the living room, he didn't even say hello.

'So what's this farce for?' he said. 'You can't imagine the

174

grief I've had from my family, getting them over here from the wilds of Fatih for nine. I had to pay for a fucking taxi!'

'Mr de Mango,' İkmen said. 'I have some news from our pathologist that I thought you should all hear as a family.'

Ayşegül de Mango asked if they would like tea. İkmen said they would, and the whole company sat in silence until she returned with their drinks.

In the intervening time, Silvio de Mango's face had turned from white to grey. Did that mean he was anxious about what he was about to be told? And if he was, what was in his mind that was so terrible?

Eventually he said, 'Well?'

İkmen took a deep breath. 'There's no easy way to tell you . . .'

'Then spit it out.'

'Maryam was pregnant when she died,' he said.

He scanned the faces around him. There wasn't a flicker. Just silence.

'Three months,' he added.

Ayşegül de Mango turned her face away. Mevlüt mumbled something and his father told him to 'Shut the fuck up!' Then he turned on İkmen. 'Who was it?'

İkmen had known the question would come and that he would have to answer it honestly.

'At the moment we are awaiting DNA comparisons on a sample from an individual who claims to be the father,' he said. 'Until we have a positive result, I am not prepared to give any more details. I hope you can understand why.'

The older boy, İbrahim, said, 'Is it someone we know?'

'I can't say,' İkmen said. 'Believe me, as soon as we know, we will tell you.'

'Which means it *is* someone we know,' Silvio said.

'Mr de Mango . . .'

'Of course it fucking is!' he roared. 'Why conceal the identity of someone we don't know? Someone raped my daughter and you won't tell me! I'll fucking kill him!'

'Which is precisely why I am not going to give you a name,' İkmen said.

'A crime has been committed against my daughter and you won't tell me who committed it?'

'Mr de Mango . . .'

'She wasn't raped.'

They all turned to look at the skinny teenage girl who sat separately from her family in a dark, distant corner of the room.

'Sara?'

Her father went to her and pulled her off her chair.

'Dad!'

'Come and explain yourself!' Silvio said. He smacked the girl around the face. 'Explain yourself!'

'Mr de Mango . . .'

'Shut up!' he said. Then he turned back to the girl. 'Well?'

Standing in the middle of the room, Sara de Mango said, 'She had a lover.'


The Bishop wasn't happy.

'Is this strictly necessary?' he asked Süleyman.

'I'm afraid so. Inspector İkmen received intelligence yesterday that there may have been someone else in the church while Mr Leon was making his confession to Father Esposito.'

'Really?' The Bishop had slipped into English again. Apparently he'd studied at Oxford when he was a young man. He hadn't been back for decades, but he found English much more comfortable than Turkish. 'Wouldn't our cameras have picked that person up as he left?'

'Unless he left by some other route,' Süleyman said.

'What route?'

'I don't know. That's what we have to investigate.'

Bishop Montoya sighed. St Anthony's wasn't full, and no service was scheduled, but people had come in to pray and the woman who organised the flowers was gathering up dead blooms for composting.

'All right,' he said. 'Just give me five minutes to ask people to leave.'

'Thank you.'

Süleyman wiped his brow. Still sweating from his angry altercation with Gonca, he walked over to the pews and sat down. The gypsy had followed him from his apartment to the church, and had only backed off when she'd seen Omer Mungun coming towards them. Then, at least, she'd had the sense to make herself scarce.

Süleyman had felt that another search of St Anthony's was probably pointless, but he had to accept that İkmen could be right. Maybe those noises Fabrizio Leon claimed to have heard during his confession did mean that someone else had been in the church. But then maybe it had just been the wind. Whatever it was, he now had a squad of uniforms waiting outside the church with Sergeant Mungun.

He watched as Bishop Montoya and the Polish priest went around the church asking people to leave. They did it so gently. Why hadn't he been gentle with Gonca? The way he'd treated her had been inexcusable. After putting up with his infidelity for years, she'd finally cracked and found someone else of her own. That was understandable, wasn't it? Of course it was. And yet his pride told him it was beyond the pale. His pride had told him, just that morning, that he didn't love her any more.

'You are a lying little shit!' Silvio de Mango went to hit his daughter again, but İkmen stopped him by taking the girl to one side.

'Sara,' he said, 'you said that Maryam had a lover. It's very important you tell me everything you know about that.'

'That's all,' the girl said. 'Maryam told me she'd had sex. That's it.'

'Did you know she was pregnant?'

'No.'

'I did.' Ayşegül de Mango showed no emotion when she spoke. 'I could smell it on her,' she said.

İkmen watched, horribly fascinated, as Silvio de Mango's face crumpled into an expression of utter hatred.

'You knew that *my* daughter was pregnant and you didn't tell me?'

Suddenly Ayşegül looked frail. 'It's something my mother can do,' she said. 'It must be to do with chemical changes in the body . . .'

'Did you ask her—'

'No.'

Silvio de Mango made to move towards her, but Kerim Gürsel stopped him.

'Enough violence, sir,' he said. 'Please.'

İkmen said, 'Mrs de Mango, do you know who made Maryam pregnant?'

'Not for certain, no,' she said.

'But you have a notion?'

'She met him at St Anthony's,' she said. 'Or rather that was where they could go and meet legitimately.' She looked at her husband. 'I don't know whether Maryam really did take to your religion after she got ill, but in the early days—'

'Who the fuck is he, woman?'

She went over to her husband and took his hand. İkmen noticed that Kerim Gürsel was still holding de Mango's arms.

'I've been to St Anthony's many times to speak to him,'

Ayşegül said. 'But my courage has always failed me. I am ashamed of myself . . .' She began to cry.

'For Christ's sake!'

'It's Fabrizio,' she said. 'It's always been Fabrizio.'

Father da Mosto was, now that Father Esposito had been murdered, the longest-serving priest in residence at St Anthony's. And he claimed not to know about any key.

'As far as I know, there isn't one,' he told Süleyman.

The church had only one proper entrance, which was through the basilica leading off from İstiklal Caddesi. The only other direct way in from outside was via a battered door hidden behind a tapestry to the left of the altar. Süleyman touched the lock with one plastic-gloved hand.

'You've never seen this door open?'

'No.'

Father da Mosto was a Venetian aristocrat, and he made sure that everyone knew about it. Omer Mungun found himself quietly amused as he watched the clash of Ottoman and Venetian civilisations enacted once again via the medium of Süleyman and da Mosto's egos.

'I believe it was used by cleaners and workmen at one time,' da Mosto continued.

'Do you know where it leads?'

'No. Why should I?'

Bishop Montoya interjected. 'It leads to an alleyway that connects to Yeni Çarşı Caddesi, Inspector,' he said. 'I know you think our security measures here at St Anthony's are rather lax, but I can tell you that one of the reasons this door isn't used now is so that we only have one entrance to worry about in the event of attack.'

'Yes, that's wise.'

Father da Mosto snorted. 'Christians shouldn't be—'

'Nobody should ever be under attack for their beliefs, Father,' the Bishop said. 'But sadly we live in an imperfect world. Inspector Süleyman, as Father da Mosto says, any key for this door has long since disappeared. However, if you'd like to follow me out onto Yeni Çarşı Caddesi, I can show you it from the other side.'

'That would be useful, Bishop, thank you.'

They walked through the church, across the basilica and out onto İstiklal, then turned right into Yeni Çarşı Caddesi. The alleyway, which was squeezed between a bookshop and a café, was narrow, dirty and choked with litter. And as they walked towards the back of the church, it just got worse. It was obvious that some local people used it as a dumping ground for almost anything. As well as the ubiquitous cigarette ends, the ground was covered in food waste, plant stems, paper, plastic bags and even the carcass of a dead dog. Some of it was scattered across the cobblestones, while a significant proportion, driven by the wind, was piled up against the church. Strangely, however, the door without a key was clear.

The two de Mango boys said nothing. Their father was an emotional man; they'd probably seen him cry many times before. İkmen concentrated on the girl.

'Sara,' he said, 'I know your parents have said that you are in the habit of lying. I have no evidence of that myself, but I must urge you to tell me the truth now. It's very important.'

'Yes, sir.'

Although she was eighteen, Sara de Mango seemed a lot younger. A combination of slight sullenness, extreme thinness and a truly huge and elaborate headscarf made her look like a little girl wearing her mother's clothes.

'Did you really have no idea who Maryam was seeing?'

'No, sir,' she said.

'Your sister didn't confide in you?'

'No.'

'Why would she?' Ayşegül de Mango interjected.

'Mrs de Mango?'

'Sara lies.'

'So did Maryam,' the girl mumbled. 'So does Mevlüt.'

'No I don't.'

'You do.'

İkmen looked at the boy. 'I'm almost certain that most people are aware you're on bonzai, Mevlüt. You can't live in this city and not know the signs.'

The boy jumped out of his chair. 'I—'

'Oh sit down, you stupid bastard!' yelled his father, now roused from his weeping. 'Of course you're on drugs. Nobody behaves the way you do otherwise! Inspector, I must see Fabrizio. He is my oldest friend. I must see him and ask him face to face.'

'And then what?' İkmen said.

'Then . . .'

'Then I have yet another murder to deal with? No,' he said. 'Mr Leon is currently in custody.'

'So he killed my daughter too? Is that what you're saying? I can't believe it!'

'There's no evidence so far to suggest that,' İkmen said. 'We don't even know for sure whether he was in fact the father of Maryam's child.'

'So why is he in custody?'

'In connection with another matter,' İkmen said.

'You think he killed the priest?' Silvio shook his head. 'Fabrizio likes people to think he's cool about religion, but he isn't. He believes everything the Church says. In spite of the fact that he had a Jewish father, the Church is his whole identity. It is the same for many of us. He may have abused my daughter, but he didn't kill her, if for no other reason than that she carried unborn life.'

'He said as much himself,' İkmen said.

'I'm sure.'

Now that the atmosphere in the room had become less fraught, İkmen sat down again.

'I am sorry you had to know this,' he said. 'But you did, and I must now ask you not to share this information with anyone else. I must also ask you all to think hard about any details, however trivial, that may help me find who killed Maryam. Think carefully about that night again and—'

'Sara followed Maryam out,' İbrahim said. 'She got back sometime after Mum did.'

# Chapter 19

'You've checked the database?'

'Yes, sir,' Omer said. 'Including Fabrizio Leon's. There's nothing. Well, only the Syrian girls' prints.'

'No matches to anyone in the family?'

'No, sir.'

Süleyman sat down at his desk. 'So Maryam's shoes get us no further.'

'Seems not.'

He sighed. He'd only just returned from St Anthony's with rather more questions than answers.

'Did you find anything new at the church?'

'Not really.' He told Omer about the door at the back of the building.

'Do you think someone has been using it?' the sergeant asked.

'Apart from the fact that the doorway was the only place where litter hadn't collected, no. Maybe the wind was in the wrong direction? I don't know.'

'But?'

'But I feel it's possible that someone else was in St Anthony's when Leon made his confession. I've watched the images of him leaving the church that night over and over again and I can't make myself believe that he'd just killed a man. I may be wrong. He may be the coolest customer alive, but I don't think so. Why would he do that?'

'If the priest told him something he didn't want to hear? If he told him he had to come and tell us about his relationship with Maryam? Which he did.'

'Yes, but Leon had almost made his mind up to come to us anyway. Why kill the priest for simply confirming what he already had in mind?' Süleyman said.

'Perhaps he lost his temper?'

He shrugged. 'There is no physical evidence. And no murder weapon. And if you recall, Omer, when Leon left the church that night, he was empty-handed.'


Yiannis Bey had seen most things during the course of his long career as an undertaker.

'But people don't usually nail up a loved one's coffin,' he told Silvio de Mango. 'That's my job.'

Silvio waved a dismissive hand. 'I couldn't look at her any more,' he said.

'Isn't your brother, Angelo Bey, due to arrive today?' the undertaker said. 'Surely he'll want to see Maryam. I know it's short notice, but now we have the Wednesday slot at the cemetery . . .'

'Angelo won't mind,' Silvio said.

Yiannis Livadanios doubted this. In his experience, Levantine families like the de Mangos were very keen on open coffins. But Silvio was the customer and so he had to do what he wanted. Also he had to accept that he'd come at a very bad time. The police had just taken the younger de Mango girl away for questioning in connection with her sister's death. Silvio's wife and two sons had gone with her. Yiannis Bey wondered whether things could get any worse for this family.


'It's a long way from Galata to Sulukule,' Çetin İkmen said. 'You have to cross the Golden Horn. How did you do that? Did you get a tram from Karaköy? Did Maryam get a tram from Karaköy?'

184

Sara said nothing. Ayşegül shook her.

'Answer the inspector!' she said. 'Do you want to spend the rest of your life in prison?'

Sara lowered her head. Then she said, 'She got a tram.'

'From Karaköy?'

'Yes.'

'How do you know that, Sara?' İkmen asked. 'Your mother lost sight of your sister very quickly when she left your apartment. Did you know where she was going?'

'No.'

'So?'

'I saw her,' she said. 'Mum went the wrong way. But I can see better than she can. I spotted Maryam. She disappeared down Midilli Sokak. Mum went up towards İstiklal.'

İkmen looked at Ayşegül de Mango. 'Did you?'

'Yes,' she said.

'Where did Maryam pick up the tram?'

'Karaköy.'

'And you got on the same tram?'

'Yes.'

'Didn't she see you?'

'I thought she didn't,' Sara said. 'But when she got off at Sultanahmet, she turned on me.'

'Turned on you? How?'

'I got off when she got off and then suddenly she was behind me. She pulled my arm tight behind my back and told me to go home.'

'Did anyone see this?'

She shrugged. 'Don't know.'

'What happened next?' İkmen asked.

'Maryam got in a taxi, and that was the last I saw of her.'

'You didn't try and follow her?'

'I only had my İstanbul Kart,' she said. 'I didn't have any money.'

İkmen leaned forward and looked her in the eyes.

'Why did you follow her?' he said. 'And why didn't you call out to your mother when you saw she was going the wrong way?'

The girl put her head down.

'Well, Sara?'

'Tell him,' her mother said. 'Now.'

İkmen raised his hand. 'Just a minute, Sara,' he said. 'Mrs de Mango, I can't help noticing how harsh you and your husband are with your children.'

'I'm not . . .'

'Maybe not with the boys, but with Sara you exhibit absolutely no tenderness,' he said. 'Why?'

'Why?'

'Why. Please. I have been around your family for over a week now. Indulge me.'

He saw the girl look furtively at her mother, who said, 'We knew they would have to be tough, the kids. Both Silvio and I were left-wing students when we met. We were going to change the world. I gave up my family for it! Until the world changed us.'

'And you returned to your family and their religion.'

'Yes.'

'But you continued treating your children—'

'Harshly? Unfairly? In this world, Inspector, you have to be able to adapt or you won't survive. When Maryam was a baby, I used to carry her around in a blanket embroidered with the hammer and sickle. Now Sara covers her head and attends an Imam Hatip school. We do things we don't like so our children can survive. Life is hard and the sooner children know this the better.'

The de Mangos were not the only thwarted leftists İkmen had met. But they were probably the most pragmatic, and the saddest.

Maybe the children lied to escape into their own, gentler worlds. Maybe that was why Mevlüt poisoned himself with bonzai.

İkmen looked back at Sara. 'Did you know where Maryam was going?' he asked.

'No.'

'So why did you follow her?'

'Because I saw she left her phone behind,' Sara said. 'She did it deliberately. I saw her look at it and then leave it. She'd never do that, not unless she was doing something really secret.'

'And you knew she was having sex with a man and wanted to know who?'

'Yes,' she said.

'Why? What was it to you, Sara?'

She looked at her mother when she spoke. 'I wanted to tell you and Dad,' she said. 'I didn't know that you already knew.'

'How could you? I could barely acknowledge it myself.'

'Why did you want to tell your parents?' İkmen asked.

She turned to look at him. 'Because I wanted to get her into trouble,' she said. 'Because I hated her.'

'Why?'

'Because my dad made her his favourite,' she said. 'I didn't kill her, but I'm not sorry she's dead. Like my granny says, she should have died when she had leukaemia, because that was her fate.'

There were only a few places where a sheikh of a dervish order and a senior police officer could meet. One of them was a small house in the pretty Bosphorus village of Yeniköy.

'When Uncle Osman lived here, there were pictures on the walls,' Hürrem Teker said to the small elderly man sitting in an armchair in front of her.

'My brother took those,' the man said.

'But you still own the house.' She sat down.

'I am the eldest son,' he said. 'Now, Hürrem, my dear, I am short of time and so I would like it if you would get straight to the point.'

'OK.' She clenched her hands in her lap. Her knuckles were white. 'Melis Bila,' she said.

'Your secretary.'

'Ex.'

'Ex,' he repeated. 'What about her?'

'Why did your people put her in my office?'

'I don't know what you're talking about.'

'No? My superiors, who I know are very close to you, foisted her on me and then she betrayed me. Kemal Öneş received a phone call from her about the death of Maryam de Mango. I wanted to question Öneş for much longer than I was allowed. Melis was your creature, wasn't she?'

He said nothing.

She shook her head. 'Oh Abdullah, what happened to you, eh? When I was a little girl, I looked up to you. You looked so handsome in your Marine Brigade dress uniform. I think I was probably a little in love with you. A sin, I admit.'

'A small sin.' He smiled. 'Hürrem, dear cousin, you know I can't talk to you about my life as it is now.'

'Because I am the enemy.'

'Because you are the past. You are passing to give way to a new reality, just as the Ottoman Empire passed in order to give birth to the Republic.'

'The Ottoman Empire, which you seek to revive.'

'Some do,' he said. 'Not me. I care only that this country regains its religious heritage. Unfortunately, people like my father, and yours, disenchanted this nation and turned its soul to stone. That's wrong.'

'Enforced secularism is as twisted as enforced religion,' she said. 'I admit we went too far, but what you're doing now isn't going to make that right. What you're doing is revenge.'

'For all the years our people suffered at the hands of the military, yes,' he said. 'In part. But you know, Hürrem, we have nothing to do with the murder of the so-called Miracle Girl. I give you my word.'

'Do you? So why did that awful woman call your creature in the barber's shop?'

'I've no idea,' he said.

'Really? You expect me to believe that? You people always have an agenda. Nothing ever happens just by chance. You're planning all the time. Seeing what you can do next to gain the advantage. As if you need it . . .'

'Indeed. People like me are in the ascendant,' he said. 'People like you . . .' He shrugged. 'But we're not here to discuss your future, are we?'

'I don't have a future,' Hürrem said.

He didn't reply.

'Hordes of people, men, came on to the streets when Öneş got the word out about Maryam,' Hürrem said.

'But not our people.'

'Those you live amongst, who listen to you,' she said.

'We can't control those around us and wouldn't seek to do so.'

She laughed. 'Oh, please . . .'

'Hürrem . . .'

'I know my career is as good as over and that my replacement has probably already been chosen, but I tell you this, cousin,' she said. 'If I find you and your people had anything to do with Maryam de Mango's death, then I will end you.'

He just smiled.

'Oh, smile away all you like,' Hürrem continued. 'But if you've been lying to me, I will make it my personal mission to put a stop to you.'

189

Did his face whiten a little? His smile fall just a tad? She didn't know, but she liked to think so.

'And you know that I can do it, don't you, Abdullah? Inside the police or out. Because you know that I know where the bodies, metaphorically speaking, are hidden.'

'I've hurt no one,' he said. 'Although I may be about to hurt you.'

'Go ahead,' she said.


'They shut the church again this morning.'

Lobna had been asleep in her chair. Her sister's voice woke her.

'Mina?'

'Oh and you haven't drunk the juice I left you!' Mina said. She put her bag down on the floor. 'What is the point?'

Lobna sat up. She wasn't prepared to talk about her sister's anti-cancer juices. Not now, not ever really. 'Who's shut the church?' she said.

'The police. Looking for something, I don't know.'

'To do with Father Esposito's death?'

'I imagine. Although I was rather more disturbed by something Father Colombo told me.'

Lobna looked around. 'I wish I knew where I'd left—'

'Fabrizio has been arrested,' Mina said.

'Fabrizio Leon?'

'Yes.'

'Are you sure? What for?'

Mina shrugged.

'Not for anything to do with Father Esposito's death?' Lobna said. 'He had nothing to do with that. I can tell them.'

'But you don't know, do you?'

'Of course I do. Fabrizio may be many things, but he isn't a violent person.'

190

'How do you know? You've not lived with him for years.'

Lobna became silent. She still loved her ex-husband, and it broke Mina's heart.

Mina squatted down beside her sister's chair and took her hand. 'I'm sorry,' she said. 'I shouldn't have said anything. But I thought you should know from me before you heard about it elsewhere.'

'I know.' Lobna squeezed Mina's hand.

'If I were you, I'd stay out of it and let the police do their job. Fabrizio had no need to hurt Father Esposito.'

'I can't think of anyone who would harm him . . .'

'No. No.' Mina smiled. 'I went to Paşabahçe when I came out of church and they had a sale on. I bought a couple of new vases. Would you like to see them?'


Silvio de Mango put his phone down and turned to his brother and sister-in-law. 'Sara has been released.' He flopped down into his chair and lit a cigarette.

His brother, Angelo, a thickset man in his early sixties, sighed. 'Well that's a relief. Are they on their way home now?'

Silvio shook his head. 'They're staying with Ayşegül's parents in Fatih.'

'Why?'

He took a drink and waved a hand. 'You know how Muslims are about the dead. Can't bear to be around them even when they belong to their own family. Not that I'm saying that's . . .'

His sister-in-law, Francesca, had insisted that she and her husband stay in a hotel, as opposed to Silvio's apartment, for just that reason.

'No, no.' Angelo reached out a hand to his brother, which Silvio took.

'They'll all be here tomorrow,' Silvio said, 'provided the police don't come and get one of us again. I'm sorry to bring you here for such a thing, Angelo.'

'Maryam was a lovely girl,' Angelo said. 'It's the least I can do.'

'Did you speak to . . .'

'Yes, briefly. But you know how she is.'

Silvio and Angelo had a sister, Maria, who lived in Turin. She had fallen out with Silvio many years ago and had refused to speak to him ever since. No one, including Silvio and Maria themselves, could even remember what the dispute had been about.

Francesca said, 'So, Silvio, the funeral is on Wednesday.'

'Yes,' he said. 'In Feriköy.'

'Which is?'

'North of here,' Angelo said. 'A short drive.'

'Oh.'

She'd never been comfortable with İstanbul. The first time she'd visited the city, she'd become hysterical when a shoe-shine boy had pursued her across Taksim Square.

Angelo said, 'Shall we go to the chapel?'

Silvio shrugged. 'If you want to.'

'To see . . .'

'Oh, I've had the coffin sealed.'

Visibly relieved, Francesca said, 'Oh, that's unusual.'

'I have seen my daughter,' Silvio said. 'My daughter is dead.'

'Yes, but . . .'

'If you want to see her, Angelo, then I can arrange for the undertaker to unscrew the coffin lid when he comes on Wednesday.'

'Yes, but that's the day of the funeral.'

He shrugged. 'It won't take long to remove some screws.'

'No. No, it won't.' Angelo smiled.

'But that said, I do feel it is probably for the best that you remember her as she was,' Silvio said.

'Didn't you have her embalmed?'

'Of course! But . . .' he sighed, 'what can I say? She is dead, Angelo. I have seen her for the last time and I just can't do it any more. Not again. She was so, so beautiful . . .'

He began to sob. His brother squeezed his hand again, while Francesca de Mango looked at the dark paintings on the walls.


'Where's Marlboro?'

'I don't know,' Çetin İkmen said. 'Probably working on increasing the size of his family. He's his own cat.'

Süleyman sat down. 'You really should get him neutered,' he said. 'His children are probably already in triple figures.'

'I have to catch the bastard first,' İkmen said. 'Drink?'

'Thanks. Vodka and tonic, please.'

İkmen called the waiter over and ordered for both of them. He was already on his second brandy courtesy of the Mozaik, and looked as if he was settling in for the evening.

'I've had a call from Mungun's sister, Peri,' Süleyman said. 'It's his birthday next week and she wants to have a dinner party for him.'

'Yes, I know,' İkmen said. 'She invited me too, and Kerim. They don't know too many people in the city so I will attend. Don't know about Kerim.'

'I told her I'll try and come, but of course, I will be on my own. Will you take Fatma Hanım?'

'I'll ask her,' İkmen said. 'But you know how uncomfortable she is around alcohol.'

Their drinks arrived. Süleyman wondered whether İkmen might ask him about Gonca, but he didn't and he was grateful. His feelings for her were too confused for him to articulate.

'So where are we?' İkmen said.

Süleyman told him about the door at the back of the church and the results of the fingerprint analysis on Maryam de Mango's shoes.

İkmen leaned back in his chair and lit a cigarette. 'Do you think Father Esposito's connection with Maryam de Mango is relevant?' he said.

'Yes and no,' Süleyman said. 'With no evidence from Fabrizio Leon beyond some vague allusion to creaking noises in the church when he was at confession, I nevertheless can't get out of my mind the notion that he and the priest were not alone the night Father Esposito was killed. The discovery of that back door beside the altar was, I thought, a breakthrough. But not only does no one, apparently, have a key, but there was no sign that anyone had even attempted to open it. On the inside there was a line of undisturbed dust piled up against the bottom of the door, though outside it was clear, which was odd.'

'Prints?'

'No,' he said.

'So if we assume the door wasn't involved but someone was inside the church, that means that whoever that was must have stayed in there all night,' İkmen said.

'With a dead body.'

'With no choice because of the security cameras trained on the front entrance.'

'Assuming that whoever was in the church knew about the cameras.'

'Which may mean an inside job.'

'Possibly . . .'

'I'm going to have another friendly chat with the priest's housekeeper,' İkmen said. 'In my limited experience, house-keepers often know more than they will tell on a first meeting.'

'Her loyalty will be with the Church, Çetin.'

'Yes. But she also liked Father Esposito.' He sipped from his glass. 'Mr Livadanios has been in contact. Maryam's funeral will take place on Wednesday at eleven a.m. I've requested manpower from Teker. Provided no one decides to blow up the Topkapı Palace in the meantime, we're good to go. She's even indicated that she might come.'

'Why?'

'She says it's so she can make sure the event goes smoothly,' he said. 'And I think that is part of her motivation, but I also believe she has a fixed idea about who, if anyone, might try to disrupt the proceedings.'

Süleyman narrowed his eyes. 'You mean . . .'

'That secretary of hers.'

'Melis Hanım?'

İkmen nodded. 'When it was discovered that she'd let Kemal Öneş know that Maryam de Mango had been found dead, Teker as you know, went ballistic. She told me she hadn't even wanted the woman. She was foisted on her by those above.'

'Ah . . .'

'And because Maryam was murdered on the edge of the district some would say is controlled by the Order . . .'

'Yes, well, de Mango's apartment was attacked.'

'But not by them.' İkmen smiled.

'The few members known to us have thrown up no fingerprint or DNA matches for anything connected to Maryam,' Süleyman said. 'The others . . .'

'No one saw anyone in the area where she was found.'

'So how do we bring them in with no evidence?'

'Exactly. Personally I don't think that anyone of interest, shall we say, will turn up at Maryam's funeral,' İkmen said. 'I think any attack will happen a good while after she has been interred. But Teker, for some reason, is rather more interested in the Order than might be wise.'

'But if they are guilty . . .'

'Oh, indeed, I would be the last to defend anyone who has killed,' İkmen said. 'But we must also face certain realities here too. One of which is that some people in this country have the power to make themselves untouchable. Who those people are changes over time. But at the moment it is these particular men. If they are behind Maryam's murder, we will have to tread carefully.'

'We've done that right from the start,' Süleyman said.

'Yes,' İkmen said. 'Galling, isn't it?'

# Chapter 20

Omer knew that Peri had something planned for his birthday, he just didn't know what. She'd made him promise to make sure he wasn't working that evening and so he assumed she must be planning to take him somewhere to eat.

His sister was far more concerned with his birthday than Omer was. He was going to be thirty. Thirty and alone. What was there to celebrate?

Quite by chance, he left his apartment just as the woman he fancied, Asra, was walking down the stairs. She didn't even look at him. But then he remembered something that Hulusi Bey, the owner of the İnönü Süpermarket, had told him about her. He ran to catch her up.

'Er, hanım . . .'

She had amazingly blue eyes.

'Yes?' she said. 'Can I help you?'

'Um, maybe. My name is Omer Mungun, I'm a police sergeant . . .'

'Oh, yes,' she said. 'I've spoken to your sister, I think. She's a nurse?'

'Yes,' he said. He didn't know what else to say. Hulusi Bey had told him that Asra was Greek, but he didn't *know* that she was, although the name on her buzzer down in the entrance hall was certainly Greek. Katsoulis.

'Er . . .'

'Yes?'

'Look, I know you might think this is very rude, but I have noticed that you have a Greek name.'

'Yes . . .' Suddenly she looked uneasy.

'Oh, it's not a problem,' he said. 'No! No, I er . . . Look, I'm working on something at the moment that involves a Greek legend. The Marble King?'

'Oh yes.'

Now she looked even more suspicious, as well she might. The subject of the Greek legends surrounding the Golden Gate location of Maryam's visions had barely arisen in relation to the girl's murder. But then that wasn't why Omer was approaching this woman.

'What do you want to know?' she asked.

'Well, everything really . . .'

'Mmm. It's a big subject,' she said. 'I can probably recommend some books, if you like. But I'm just on my way out.'

'Oh, yes, so am I,' he said.

They reached the front door of the building. Omer pressed the remote control to open his car.

'Can I offer you a lift?' he said. 'Anywhere?'

She smiled. 'No thanks. I'm fine. You're in number seven, aren't you?'

'Yes,' he replied.

'I'll drop you a list of books sometime,' she said. Then, more to herself than to him, she murmured, 'The Marble King, eh?' and began to jog up the road towards the bus stop.

St Anthony's was open again, and so Katerina Marmara had gone to make her private devotions before she began work on spring cleaning the fathers' apartment. As she was leaving the church, she saw a familiar figure walking towards her.

'Inspector İkmen,' she said. 'I do hope you're not going to close the church again.'

'No,' he said. 'But I would like to take you for coffee if I may, Katerina Hanım.'

'Coffee? I can make you coffee,' she said.

'Ah, but the establishment I have in mind is rumoured to make the best Turkish coffee in town,' he said. 'I really think we should test that hypothesis, don't you?'

His phone rang. He looked at the screen.

'Excuse me,' he said. 'I have to take this.'

He turned away from her.

Of course he needed something. Katerina was under no illusion that he just wanted the pleasure of her company. She didn't particularly want the pleasure of his. He was small and raddled and probably a Muslim. She was accustomed to better – at least in her mind.


Only Sara and Ayşegül came to the apartment.

'İbrahim had to work and I don't know where Mevlüt is,' Ayşegül told her husband. 'He left before I got up.'

'He's gone to score,' Silvio said.

She ignored him. She knew as well as he did that Mevlüt was on bonzai. She didn't want it pushed in her face.

Sara went to her bedroom, leaving her parents alone in the kitchen. Silvio made his wife tea and poured himself a glass of sambuca. He didn't really like it, but he'd drunk everything else.

Ayşegül, who had already looked at the dire state of the fridge, said, 'When I go and get food, I'll buy a couple of bottles of rakı.'

'Sure you can bring yourself to touch booze?' he said.

She ignored him a second time.

'Silvio, about Fabrizio . . .'

'If he did it, I will kill him. If he didn't and the police are just making it up so that no Muslims are involved, I'll kiss his feet,' he said. His eyes filled with tears. 'Fabrizio has always been my brother. More than my brother! He wouldn't do such a thing. Not to me!'

'Yes, but this isn't about you, is it?' Ayşegül said. 'It's about Maryam. About how Fabrizio and Maryam felt about each other.'

'No.' He shook his head. 'No, I've thought about it. It isn't true.'

'And I've thought about it and concluded that it is,' Ayşegül said.

He waved a dismissive hand at her. 'Ah, you were always jealous of him!' he said. 'You hated it when Fabrizio and me went out together.'

'Hated him?' she laughed. 'I knew him before I knew you and I fancied him like crazy!'

'You did not!'

'I did,' she said. 'Ask Lobna. When he was going out with her, just before I met you, I was *so* jealous of her. And she knew it. Even at her wedding, she still didn't trust me. She made sure I didn't get near Fabrizio all evening.'

'I don't remember that,' Silvio said.

'You were drunk.'

'Oh.'

'But the point is,' Ayşegül said, 'I had an instinct that Maryam was seeing someone connected to the church a long time ago. I know I wasn't her real mother, but I loved her and . . .' She held back tears. 'Silvio, I never hurt her, I swear to you! I don't know why she made those things up!'

'The girl is dead, we'll never know,' he said. He shook his head again. 'Was she a saint or was she a . . . a . . .'

'Silvio, Fabrizio was the only other person we told about Maryam, wasn't he?'

'What, about her real mother? Yes, of course. I haven't told Angelo even now. Don't know if I will . . .'

'Well, so she wasn't ever my child, and until these DNA tests the police did, there was always a small doubt about whether she was really your child too, wasn't there?'

'She looked like my mother,' he said.

'Yes, but that could have been a coincidence,' Ayşegül said. 'I remember when you told Fabrizio what we were going to do and you said there was some doubt you were the child's father. You told him.'

He shrugged. 'So I told him. How is that relevant to anything?'

'If you told Fabrizio that you thought Maryam might not be yours, maybe he convinced himself she wasn't. Maybe that was why he felt able to start a relationship with her. We don't know,' she said. 'But I want you to be prepared for it. And I don't want you to harm Fabrizio.'

'So, is it the best Turkish coffee in the city?' İkmen asked.

'I don't know about the best . . .'

'Ah, you make better, do you, Katerina Hanım?' He smiled.

'The fathers like it,' she said. 'They are very complimentary.'

'Including Father Esposito?'

She looked down into her cup. 'Especially him,' she said.

'Katerina Hanım, do you know anything about a key for the door at the back of the church, beside the altar?' he asked.

She sighed. The little café on Asmalı Mescit wasn't full, but a lot of people were getting takeaways and the noise was loud enough to cover their conversation.

'Yes,' she said. 'We sometimes used it in the eighties. But then as the security situation deteriorated we closed it up. It was too much of a risk to have more than one entrance. There used to be a couple of keys, if I recall correctly.'

'Who had them?'

'Well, back then it was Father Rossi and old Belkis Hanım. She was our cleaner for years. What they did with the keys once

201

the door was put beyond use, I don't know. Father Rossi left us in ninety-five and Belkis died a few years ago.'

'Who cleans the church now?'

'Ah, well there's a sign of the times,' she said. 'The fathers and myself take turns. To save money.'

'Heavy work,' he said.

'God's work,' she replied. 'I wouldn't that it was any other way. I don't know what happened to those keys. I haven't seen them for decades.' She looked into her cup again.

He said, 'Do you read the coffee grounds, Katerina Hanım?'

She smiled. 'Oh, no,' she said. 'That's sorcery, Çetin Bey. I know your mother did good trade in the future . . .'

Old İstanbul residents like Katerina Marmara had all known İkmen's mother, Ayşe İkmen, the witch of Üsküdar.

'She did,' he said. 'She did.'

'Although around here she'd have competition these days,' Katerina said. She pointed to the street outside. 'Every apartment has its witch now, every coffee shop its falcı, and they're all doing good business.'

He smiled. 'The world is a dangerous place; people are anxious,' he said.

'In this year more than most,' she said. She looked up at him. 'I know you want me to tell you some scandalous things about the fathers. I know you need to solve this murder so that you can say you are protecting minorities. But you have to face up to the fact that the majority in this country do not like us. I can tell you, my hand on the Bible, that none of my fathers killed Father Esposito. They are men of God and I will not tell you what, if anything, they do when they are not in public.'

'And if I take you in, hanım? What then?' İkmen said.

She shrugged. 'The same. Get the bastinado out, it will change nothing.'

'We don't use such methods of interrogation . . .'

'I don't care if you do,' she said. 'I'm saying nothing.'

'I need a cigarette,' he said.

They went outside into the street. There was a queue of people outside a doorway on the other side of the pavement. No doubt, İkmen surmised, lining up to see a witch.

He turned to Katerina. 'You do want to find out who killed Father Esposito, don't you?'

'Of course,' she said. 'And I've told you who I think did it. St Anthony's has been attacked before. You know who by.'

He sighed. 'I take your point. But if that is the case, then what harm is there in telling me more about the fathers?'

'What, when there's nothing to tell?'

'No, but . . .' Something occurred to him. 'But think on this, if you will, hanım.'

'What?'

'Both you and I know that Muslims have a problem being in close proximity to dead bodies.'

'Yes. Doesn't mean they don't kill, though.'

'No,' he said. 'But no Muslim will linger where the dead reside. One theory we are currently exploring is that whoever killed Father Esposito also spent the night in the church with his corpse. Only when the security cameras went off the next morning would he have been able to leave.'

She frowned.

'So just tell me one thing and I will leave you alone,' he said. 'Hanım, were all the fathers that you look after in their apartment the night Father Esposito died?'


People bandied about terms like 'iconic' far too much for Mehmet Süleyman's taste. But sometimes such trite terms were appropriate. There was something biblical in the sights and sounds that surrounded Süleyman's car when he and Omer Mungun entered the Çarşamba quarter of Fatih district. Most of the women wore thick black chadors reminiscent of Iran, while a considerable number of the men sported şalvar trousers and turbans.

But there were exceptions. Not all the men, the young ones particularly, wore what Çetin İkmen chose to call 'the gear' – religiously delineated clothing – and in fact many of the boys were quite stylish. In contrast, however, it was difficult to find a woman whose head was uncovered.

Süleyman hadn't actually wanted to bring his sergeant with him on this excursion into one of İstanbul's most religious districts. He'd wanted to contemplate this place on his own. But Omer, too, appeared to want to disappear into his own thoughts.

The narrow streets were punctuated by small groups of men sitting on stools, rosaries in their hands, talking or staring into space. Half-drunk glasses of tea were abandoned on low tables while small bands of older, secularly dressed men stood in doorways, smoking furtively. The turbans of the Order were not everywhere, but they were prominent.

What was not prominent, however, was their reputed wealth. It was said, admittedly mainly in secular circles, that the Order was, as an organisation, extremely rich. But there was no sign of even moderate means on these streets. Shabby and neglected, the apartment blocks constructed in the 1960s looked dirty, while the few wooden Ottoman houses that remained looked as if they were about to collapse. The quarter's mosques were, however, another matter. Like the church Süleyman had spent so much time in recently, these buildings were magnificent, clean and expensive.

Would people like this kill or arrange the murder of a young woman they deemed sinful? Pregnant or not, Maryam de Mango was not what Süleyman would have called a loose woman. He knew plenty of those and they were nothing like her. But then that wasn't the point. Her sin had been in her visions and in her perceived apostasy from Islam.

What, if anything, had Maryam de Mango seen when she stood in front of the Golden Gate of the Byzantines? The Virgin Mary? Some long-dead Byzantine empress? A lot of Greeks had gone to see the Miracle Girl hoping, it was said, that she might provide them with a conduit to the world of the once-and-future Marble King, who resided in a cave beneath the gate, waiting to bring Christianity back to Constantinople. Unwittingly, this flawed girl had brought multiple competing groups into conflict with each other at a time of heightened political sensitivity. No wonder Bishop Montoya hadn't wanted to refer her case to the Holy See. Nobody needed that kind of trouble, and that could be said to apply to the Order too.

Why would one of their number kill Maryam out of the blue? Beyond some possible twisted religious fervour, there was, as far as he could tell, no motive.

'I'm not exactly sober, but I'm not drunk either,' İrini Mavroyeni said.

She poured herself another glass of rakı and offered the bottle to İkmen.

'No thanks,' he said.

'It's lunchtime.'

'Yes, and I have an issue with drink, as you know.'

She sat down on her tangled, filthy bed.

'What can I do for you?' she said.

'Well, first I've come to ask whether you're going to Maryam's funeral tomorrow,' he said.

He didn't sit down. There was only the floor or that dreadful bed, and neither was a viable option.

'Silvio has invited me,' she said. 'I don't know. I don't want to upset his wife. She was the mother to Maryam that I never was. I never even met the girl.'

'You're sure about that?'

She shook her head. 'Listen, I was fucked,' she said. 'I was nervous about meeting her. I didn't know what she'd say to me. I don't need any more guilt in my life. I drank a bottle of rakı and then I had a dream about the old days.'

'Oh yes?'

'It meant nothing,' she said. 'I know you might disagree. I remember your mother used to interpret dreams. But in my opinion they're all just brain-shit.'

'Tell me about it anyway,' he said.

She lit a cigarette. 'If I must.'

'So?'

'Before I started fucking Silvio, years ago, we went to the same school,' she said.

'The Italian lycée? I didn't know you went there? Why?'

'Listen, I know my mother was an illiterate peasant, but my dad was a Greek gentleman down on his luck.'

'I know. Why didn't you go to one of the Greek schools?'

'Because the Greeks didn't like my dad. You should know that! He married a Turk. The Italians, on the other hand, didn't give a screw. As long as Dad paid them, they were happy. He broke his back to send me there.'

'That's a good school,' İkmen said. 'Why—'

'Didn't I go on to become a respectable schoolteacher? I'd like to say that it was because people were prejudiced against me, but that's not true. You and I both know it was because I liked a drink from a very early age and I could never keep my knickers on. But anyway . . .' She drank some more rakı. 'I was best friends with Valentina Leon, sister of Fabrizio. She's been dead for years. Fabrizio's best friend was Silvio de Mango, who used to hang about with the Amara sisters, Lobna and Mina. Fabrizio ended up marrying Lobna for some reason. He could've had anyone he wanted. But that didn't last. He couldn't keep it in his pants.'

'Did you ever sleep with Fabrizio?'

She pulled a face. 'Not my type,' she said. 'Too good-looking and he knows it.'

İkmen smiled. He'd heard people say the same thing about Süleyman over the years.

'No, I always fancied Silvio,' she said. 'But at school he only had eyes for Mina Amara, who in turn only had eyes for that Muslim doctor's son who went to Galatasaray Lisesi. She married him, but it didn't work out. Why am I telling you all this shit?'

'Dream,' he said.

'Oh, yeah.' She coughed. 'So I dreamed about Silvio that night. Looking at me, you'll be disgusted to know that he and I were getting intimate.'

İkmen said nothing.

'It was good. He did good sex. And of course, in my dream we were both in our twenties again. But then suddenly there's Lobna looking at us. She looked old and disgusted and I think I probably woke up for a bit, but no one was with me. Of course. Then I remembered I was supposed to meet my daughter . . .'

She looked down at her bedcovers and shook her head. 'What a fuck-up, eh?'

İkmen took the integrity of his overcoat in his hands and sat down beside her.

'I can't bring Maryam back,' he said. 'But I can and will come and get you tomorrow morning and take you to her funeral.'

She smiled. 'You've always been kind,' she said. 'I appreciate that.'

'And in return, you tell me the truth.'

'I try,' she said. 'The booze doesn't help. I wish I could say I saw someone hanging around the night Maryam died. I wish I could say that I met her . . .' She began to cry.

He put an arm around her shoulders and she rested her head in his neck.

'But I didn't,' she said. 'It was just me and the bottle, the way it's always been.'

İkmen had given him this poisoned chalice and now Kerim was nervous. What if the inspector was wrong?

The young priest was about Omer Mungun's age; he wore stylish clothes, as one might expect of a young Italian, and he had perfect skin.

'I don't know what Katerina Hanım thinks . . .' He batted his eyelashes, which Kerim was sure he hadn't intended to.

'All she told Inspector İkmen was that you were out the night Father Esposito died,' Kerim said. 'She didn't speculate about where you'd gone, only that she'd seen you turn right when you exited the basilica. There is no record on the security cameras of you returning to St Anthony's, and so we have to assume that you were out all night.'

Kerim let that information hang there for a moment. Father Colombo didn't strike him as a fool; he'd know what that meant. He hoped. But the priest didn't respond.

Kerim cleared his throat. 'To put this in context for you,' he said. 'We are, at the moment, working with the idea that whoever killed Father Esposito may have stayed in the church all night until the security system shut off in the morning. We need to know where you were.'

The priest looked at him. He had large, doleful brown eyes, dark blond hair and skin the colour of pale honey. To Kerim he was the image of a beautiful suffering saint. He was also a suspect in a murder investigation.

'Father Colombo?'

'I only go to look,' he said.

'Look at what?'

He turned his head away. 'There is a club, on Taksim . . .'

Kerim wondered which one. He also wondered whether he'd been there at the same time as this priest.

'Which club?'

'It's called the No-Name,' Father Colombo said.

That was a trans club. It was where Kerim's lover Pembe went whenever she needed to be with other trans girls. It was, in Kerim's experience, nothing much more than a pick-up joint.

'Do you know people at the No-Name?' he asked.

'God, no!'

'So . . .'

'I just go to watch,' the priest repeated. 'I've never broken my vow of celibacy.'

'You go as yourself? A priest?'

There was a pause.

'Father Colombo?'

'No,' he said.

'You see, if you are citing the No-Name as the place you were when Father Esposito was murdered, then we are going to have to speak to people at the club in order to confirm your alibi. Think carefully: does anyone know you at the No-Name?'

He put his head in his hands. 'Oh God.'

'Father Colombo, please.'

He looked up reluctantly. 'I don't give myself a stupid name or anything, but I do dress up.'

'So nobody knows your identity?'

'No, but some of the men call me Sophia. After Sophia Loren.' He put his head down again. 'Because I'm Italian . . .'

# Chapter 21

The lawyer, a Mr Demirköz, looked İkmen straight in the eye. 'You have no murder weapon, no forensic evidence, and in fact you have CCTV footage showing that my client left the church before the priest, Father Esposito, was killed.'

'You are incorrect,' İkmen said. 'Time of death in this case can only be approximate. Father Esposito was murdered around the time your client left St Anthony's.'

'Around the time . . .' The lawyer smiled. 'And what was my client's motive for killing a man he had just opened his heart to? A trusted confessor?'

Although he didn't advertise the fact, Fabrizio Leon was a devout Catholic, hence his absolute opposition to even the idea of Maryam having an abortion. And now that İkmen knew from Arto Sarkissian that Leon was beyond doubt the father of her unborn foetus, he was inclined to believe that he had turned to the Church for help more fervently than ever before.

'My client was, further, nowhere near Sulukule district when Maryam de Mango was murdered. He has multiple alibis for that night, and so I believe, in common with the Public Prosecutor, that you should release Mr Leon now.'

İkmen had known it was coming. He said, 'Well, I have no choice.'

'And yet you have doubts?' Mr Demirköz said.

'I'd be a foolish man if I didn't have doubts,' İkmen replied. 'And I'd be even more of a fool if I did not advise your client

not to go to Maryam de Mango's funeral tomorrow morning.'
He looked at Fabrizio. 'You hear me, Mr Leon?'

Ever since he had closed Maryam's coffin, Silvio had stopped
sitting with her in the chapel. Angelo was worried he would also
omit to keep vigil for her.

'I will sit with you,' he told his brother.

Silvio lit candles at the head and foot of the coffin.

'I'd rather be alone,' he said.

'What about Ayşegül?'

'What about her? She's a Muslim.'

'So was Maryam,' Angelo said.

Silvio sat down. 'Don't interfere,' he said. 'The funeral is
tomorrow and then you can go back to Milan. Your wife will
be wondering what's taking you so long. I suggest you go to
her.'

'Silvio . . .'

'Listen,' he said, 'when I die, which I sincerely hope will be
sooner rather than later, you and our sister will inherit all the
artwork and everything of value in this apartment. If you don't
get at least half a million euros, I will be very surprised. But
I'm not leaving you the property. That will go to Ayşegül and
the children.'

'Your wife who has thrown you over for God and the children
you don't like?'

'We've had this conversation a million times! Papa left
everything to me,' Silvio said.

'Including land you don't even want.'

'Oh go away, will you, Angelo! What is happening now isn't
about you . . .'

'Or you! It's about Maryam!'

'Yes,' he said. 'My daughter. Mine! I know you don't have
children, Angelo, but have some empathy. My daughter has been

211

murdered and tomorrow I will have to bury her body. Go away and leave me to grieve for her in peace.'

Madam Edith was going to be singing her Piaf tribute later. If Sinem didn't mind being left alone for a while, Kerim and Pembe could go and watch her. But then he saw a familiar face at the bar and thought better of it.

'Gonca Hanım,' he said.

She looked at him through heavy, slitted eyes. 'Kerim Bey?'

'Yes.'

She was drunk, which in Kerim's experience was unusual. Gonca liked a drink, but he'd never seen her like this.

'What are you doing here?' she asked. 'I wasn't aware that you had interests like this.'

'I'm here to see the manager,' he said. 'On business.'

'Oh. What's that about then?' she asked. 'Somebody here blackmailing some politician?'

'No.'

She put an arm around his shoulders. 'You can tell me . . .'

'Sergeant Gürsel?'

Fortunately for Kerim, the manager of the No-Name Club arrived just at that moment. An extremely straight man in his forties, Atalay Bey took Kerim to his office, gave him coffee and offered him a cigar.

Kerim refused.

'I'm here to check out an alibi given to us by a suspect in an ongoing investigation,' he said.

'Oh, what? A robbery? A murder?'

Although he'd been to the No-Name in the past, Kerim didn't know it well and had never met the manager before.

'I can't tell you, I'm afraid, sir,' he said. 'What I need from you is information regarding a person who claims he was on these premises last Friday night.'

'Friday nights are always busy for us,' Atalay Bey said. 'The place is packed. Do you have a name? A photograph?'

'No. But I can tell you that this man, by his own admission, likes to wear very tight 1950s-style women's clothes. Sheath dresses with nipped-in waists, very dark bobbed wigs . . .'

'Oh, you mean Sophia Loren!' Atalay laughed. 'The priest.'

The dress swamped her. She'd told her sister she'd been losing weight again. Now this confirmed it.

'Is that the watered silk costume you had made by Elif Hanım?' Mina asked. She stood in front of the open door of Lobna's bedroom. She'd never had a sense of privacy, even as a child.

Lobna said, 'Yes. But it's too big now. I look ridiculous.'

'No you don't.'

'I do.'

She took the dress off and put on her final choice, the one she'd worn for her father's funeral.

'Lobna!'

'Yes, I wore it for Daddy,' she said. She shook her head. 'But it's too big now.'

'No! No!' Mina rushed over to her and stopped her taking the dress off. 'No, you must wear it! I will take it in for you. It'll be fine!'

'No it won't.' Lobna shook her head. 'Why am I even thinking about going anyway? I can't go to a funeral feeling as if I'm about to fall asleep all the time. I can't go looking like . . . this.'

'Like what?'

'Like death,' she said. 'Haven't you noticed, Mina? There's a clue in the prominent collarbones and the skin the colour of porridge. I know that flies in the face of all the health-food nonsense you've been persisting with, but the fact is that I'm not well. I'm not well and so I'm not going to anyone's funeral, saint or no saint.'

'Oh Lobna!'

'No!' She pushed her sister away. 'I'm not going and that's that.'

'You have to!'

'Why? Fabrizio is still in a cell somewhere and I'm worried about him. I've phoned the police and told them he's innocent. But do they get back to me? No! I can't stand it! I just can't stand it!'

She was becoming hysterical. Mina fought to put her arms around her in order to calm her down.

'Lobna, you have to go. If you don't, it will look strange, and we can't afford for anyone to think we're strange, now can we?'

Lobna looked into her sister's eyes and she knew. Horrified, she simply said, 'No.'

There was nothing else to say.

There was being casual about mess and there was the short drop into health hazard. The Kervansaray Coffee Shop behind Tünel Square at the end of İstiklal Caddesi had fallen all that short distance and more. Strangely, for a man who enjoyed the unusual and the dangerous, Çetin İkmen hadn't been to it before. But when he opened the door, he recognised its type. When he'd been a child there had been thousands of dives like this all over the city. In those days many of them had been illuminated by hurricane lamps.

He ordered coffee from a tobacco-scented individual behind the counter and said he'd like a reading.

The coffee, when it came, was good. Thick, sweet and granular. There weren't any *No Smoking* signs anywhere and so he lit up. The man at the counter said nothing.

When he'd finished his coffee, İkmen sat back and waited. İrini Mavroyeni had told him about this place. Apparently you could get a decent coffee and your fortune told for under eight lira, which was a bargain by anybody's standards, especially if your falcı, your fortune-teller, was good.

On the face of it, Büket Teyze didn't seem like a good bet at all. Of unknowable vintage and massively overweight, she plonked herself down in front of İkmen with a grunt. He pushed his coffee cup and saucer across the table towards her, and wordlessly she turned the cup over.

Once she'd caught her breath, she said, 'What do you want to know?'

With her many scarves and cheap tin jewellery, she looked like a fairground gypsy from the 1960s. İkmen briefly thought about Gonca and wondered how she was managing. Ever since her affair with Fabrizio Leon had come to light, Süleyman had stopped talking about her.

'Am I doing the right thing?' he asked.

Büket Teyze lifted the cup and looked inside. He knew that the right-hand side represented the present, the left the future.

Her voice, which was scratched and toneless, came out in a bark. 'No,' she said. 'Not yet.'

'When will this change?' he said.

She peered at the left side of the cup. 'Soon.'

So far, so standard. Changes requested always came 'soon', in his experience.

'Can you see what I need to do to help this to happen?'

She took her time, peering closely into the tiny cup, her many chins wobbling as she muttered to herself. İkmen knew not to rush her. He'd always been warned not to disturb his mother when she'd been doing a card reading for a client. But time ticked on and he had to resist the urge to say *Well?*

She put the cup down and then riffled about in a large patchwork bag at her side. Careful not to reveal what was within, she shielded it from him with one meaty, glittery arm. When eventually she withdrew her hand, she was holding what İkmen could see was a tarot card.

'This is your card,' she said, laying it on the table in front of him. The picture was of a hand holding an upright sword. 'The Ace of Swords. I saw it in your coffee grounds.'

'What does it mean?' he asked.

'It means clarity, power, a breakthrough. But it's also a cold card, so care must be taken.'

'In what way?'

'To employ coldness, or logic, you'll have to be ruthless, and that won't be easy.'

He knew that ruthlessness wasn't his greatest skill, and so he nodded.

'You won't want to use the cold,' she said. 'But that's because your adversary is hot.'

'Hot?'

'Hot, jealous, emotional, vulnerable,' she said. 'You won't want to do it. But you have to.'

He thought about those under suspicion of murdering Maryam and the priest. Fabrizio Leon was hot in many senses of that word. But was he also vulnerable? Silvio certainly was. His whole family were, especially the girl, Sara. Could the Order be described as hot? There was no way they were vulnerable, but a group of Catholic priests on İstiklal Caddesi might be . . .

He got up to leave. Why was he even doing this? Some fat old bag in a shop full of scarves did not in any way resemble his mother, in spite of what İrini Mavroyeni had said. İrini, the woman who dreamed . . .

'You paid?' Büket Teyze asked as İkmen made his way to the door.

'Yes,' he said. 'Thank you.'

'Oh, and don't forget to look out for a real sword, İkmen,' the falcı said.

This made him turn and look at her.

She smiled. 'Of course I know who you are,' she said. 'We all recognise the faces of the law. You should know that. But anyway, a sword, all right? Look for one. You'll thank me. Trust me.'

# Chapter 22

'So you're going, are you? And taking the children?'

Ayşegül turned to her mother. 'Maryam was my daughter. The children were her siblings.'

The old woman sat down beside her fireplace. 'She wasn't your child. She was a bastard. And she lied.'

'Yes, well, we lied to her too,' Ayşegül said. 'Not because we wanted to but because of some twisted notion of morality that was imposed upon us.'

'You did as you pleased,' her mother said. 'You went off and you married that man.'

'And when you and my father and my brothers threatened me, I did what you wanted me to do. I covered, I brought my children up as Muslims . . .'

'Not the girl.'

'Maryam, Mother. Her name was Maryam. And she lied because she was confused. She knew she was different but she didn't know how or why. When she became a teenager, I didn't know what to do with her and so I ignored her. I admit it! And of course she went to her father for affection.'

'And elsewhere.'

It hadn't been easy for Ayşegül to tell her parents the truth about Maryam. She hadn't wanted to. But in the end it had been the only way to get them to give up trying to have her buried in Fatih.

'Will there be a Catholic priest?'

218

'Yes,' Ayşegül said. 'But there will be no Mass, just a committal at the graveside.'

The old woman shifted uneasily in her seat. 'If your father wasn't confined to his bed, he'd stop you,' she said. 'I should call Erkan and Binali.'

'Then call them,' Ayşegül said. 'I'm sure my brothers will be delighted to have to leave their shop and come and fight with me.'

'Where honour is at stake . . .'

'Oh, they're honourable, are they?' she said. 'Erkan who beats his wife so hard she ends up in hospital, and Binali who needs the money from the shop to fund his gambling habit. Maryam may well have for a while cheated her own death, when she went to the Armenian Church, something of which I did not approve, but she wasn't a beast like Erkan or a weak moron like Binali. Don't you dare hold those mindless thugs up as paragons of honour, Mother. Don't you dare!'

One armoured vehicle and two transport vans full of armed men in riot gear wasn't what İkmen would have deemed entirely appropriate for security at a funeral, but he appreciated the gesture.

'Sometimes one has to show force,' Commissioner Teker said.

Teker, İkmen and Süleyman were in the former's office, looking down at preparations for the security operation for Maryam de Mango's funeral.

'I've no intelligence that we are going to come up against any trouble,' she said. 'But why take the risk?'

'I'd like to suggest that we deploy one van and the Skorpion vehicle to the cemetery and allocate vehicle number two to follow the cortège from Galata,' İkmen said.

'If you think that's best.'

'Maryam's mother, İrini Mavroyeni, may be attending,

provided she's not drunk. I offered to take her myself, but she will call a taxi.'

'Inspector İkmen and myself will follow the cortège in my car,' Süleyman said.

'The undertaker, Yiannis Bey, has a Western-style hearse in which the body will be transported plus a limousine for the immediate family,' İkmen said. 'Other mourners have been asked to assemble at Feriköy Latin Catholic Cemetery.'

'It's going to be a tough day,' Teker said.

'Yes, madam.'

'I'd like to see you both as close to eighteen hundred hours as you can, please,' she said. She had decided not to attend the funeral.

'For debrief?'

She smiled. 'Sort of.'


The last time the Amara sisters had visited Feriköy Latin Catholic Cemetery had been when their father was buried back in 1998. They'd come early today so that they could visit his memorial. On the edge of the western sector, where all the great Levantine families had their huge and expensive mausoleums, the grave of Isidore Amara consisted of just a plain stone cross.

Lobna squatted down and touched it. 'I wish I could find Papa's stick,' she said to her sister. 'My memory is so bad now . . .'

'Don't worry about it,' Mina said. 'How are you feeling, dear?'

'Not good.'

'Do you want to get up?'

'I think maybe I should.'

Mina helped her to her feet.

'You didn't eat or drink anything this morning,' she said.

'I felt too sick,' Lobna confessed. She looked down at her father's gravestone again. 'What would he make of what we've done with our lives, I wonder?'

Mina didn't answer.

Lobna looked around at the mature trees that lined every pathway, and at the spring flowers that grew wild in the grass between the gravestones.

'This is such a beautiful place,' she said.

Mina nodded. 'It's where we'll both end up.'

'Our bodies will,' her sister said.

'That's what I meant.'

'Yes, but what about our souls, Mina? Where will they go once we're dead?'

Mina watched a tiny bird land on her father's grave and begin to sing.

'To heaven,' she said flatly. 'Of course.'

Her sister turned to stare at her. 'You don't believe that fairy story, do you?'

Father da Mosto had left to go and perform the committal ceremony for Maryam de Mango when Kerim Gürsel arrived at St Anthony's. He found Father Colombo alone, sitting in a pew at the back of the church.

'I pray so hard for all this horror to be over,' he said as Kerim sat down beside him. 'Father Esposito's family want his body to be repatriated to Sicily. But while we still don't know who killed him, is that the right thing to do?'

'Our doctor will release the body soon,' Kerim said. 'I checked out your alibi at the club. You're well known there. You should be careful. On Friday night you were seen leaving with someone.'

'Not for sex.'

'Maybe not, but I'll need to know a name.'

The priest sighed. 'She calls herself Scheherazade. I don't know her male name. Comes from a religious family somewhere over in Fatih. She lives in an apartment in Tarlabaşı with another trans girl. They're always getting beaten up. I'm not sure I could live like that. I went there to talk.'

'About what? Being a priest with—'

'No! I just . . . I need to know other people like me,' he said. 'I can't be completely alone. I can't.'

'Did you ever tell anyone here about your desire to dress?' Kerim asked.

'Father Esposito,' he said. 'He was my confessor. He was most people's confessor. Poor man. None of us reciprocated in anything like the same way. He was probably the most compassionate and understanding man I've ever known.'

'What did he say about your dressing?'

'He told me that provided I didn't break my vow of celibacy, he thought God would understand.'

'So he approved . . .'

'He gave me permission,' Father Colombo said. 'He didn't approve. He was a very moral man. He was so kind!' His eyes filled with tears. 'I knew he found what I did . . . distasteful, but still he was anxious on my behalf in case I got found out. He told me to only change when I got to the club and to always leave dressed as a man. When Father Wojtulewicz had pneumonia last year, he tended to him day and night . . .'

'I am sorry you've lost such a good friend.'

'And mentor,' the priest said. 'Father Esposito was the modern face of the Church, Sergeant. He understood weakness.'

'Your weakness.'

'Yes!' He frowned. 'Mind you, he did have some rather old-fashioned opinions about women.'

'Like what?'

'He thought they tempted men,' he said. 'I think he felt they had some kind of genetic fault . . .'

Had Father Esposito maybe expressed this view to Fabrizio

Leon in relation to Maryam, and in the process infuriated him?

The black coffin was lowered into the ground by Mr Livadanios himself, his three sons and his two drivers. As soon as the funeral started, the cemetery had been closed to the public and the gravesite ringed by armed officers. The armoured car covered the main entrance on Teyyareci Fehmi Sokak.

İkmen and Süleyman stood away from the main group of mourners. Silvio, Ayşegül and their three children were joined by Angelo de Mango and his wife. Süleyman pointed out the two Amara sisters, but apart from the priest, Father da Mosto, the other fifteen or so attendees were unknown to İkmen. Most of them were old, and he assumed they were members of the dwindling Levantine community. Given the way they crossed themselves all the time, they clearly weren't Muslims.

The process of leaving the de Mango apartment with Maryam's coffin had been easier than İkmen had imagined it would be. All the other residents of the building had stayed inside while the undertaker and his men removed the coffin, and while it was being loaded into the hearse, only one person, a young boy, hurled any sort of abuse. But then in spite of his pathological cynicism, Çetin İkmen did still believe that his fellow countrymen were basically good. Turks respected other people and their points of view. He clung onto that. Sadly, Süleyman broke that particular spell.

'What do we do if some lunatic digs her up and burns her?' he asked.

İkmen closed his eyes. 'God help us!' Then he opened them again. 'We can't guard this place around the clock,' he said. 'We don't have the resources.'

'I know.'

'Just have to hope that the surrounding walls and the fact that there's always a custodian on the site will discourage anything like that.'

Süleyman shook his head. 'I remember when I was a kid, a group of men stole some stone angels and advertised them for sale.'

'Stupid bastards!'

'They'd be straight on eBay these days.'

'Ssshh.'

The mourners were praying. Ayşegül de Mango and her children stood with their heads unbowed, but İkmen could see that the woman and her sons were crying. Only her daughter was apparently emotionless. But then maybe that was Sara's way of dealing with her grief. Had she loved or hated Maryam? Had she killed her? İkmen was still unsure.

The door to Commissioner Teker's office was shut. This wasn't unusual except in its duration. She always shut her door when she was smoking. But ever since İkmen and Süleyman had left for Maryam de Mango's funeral that morning, she hadn't budged and her door had remained closed except for once. That had been when the chief of police and his retinue had turned up. They'd only stayed for ten minutes at the most, and ever since their departure, her office had been characterised by silence. Something was going on.

Omer returned to the office he shared with İkmen and continued his researches. He was confused about the religious community known as the Order. Not being a Muslim was a disadvantage. There were so many sects and societies, he didn't understand where one finished and another began. He knew that the Order was a spiritual organisation and that its teachings were based upon respect and acceptance. They were Sunnis, and unlike their Alevi counterparts, who were Shias, they believed in strict segregation of the sexes. They were involved with a lot of charitable organisations, to which they donated considerable sums of money. But there was also, it was said, a political dimension to the Order.

Depending upon who one spoke to, the organisation was either a group of community-minded people who wanted to make the world a better place, or a threat to democracy. When he'd driven through their quarter the previous day with Süleyman, he had observed a place peopled by individuals who seemed closed off and secretive. Received wisdom on the subject stated that they were suspicious of outsiders due to the many years of prejudice they had suffered at the hands of the secular state. And Omer knew from his own experience as a member of a persecuted religious community that secrecy was often the only way to remain safe. But in spite of this, the Order made him feel uneasy. Maybe it was because when they had left Çarşamba and driven up into Sulukule, he and Süleyman had seen members of the Order on the streets there too. He had no evidence to back it up, but he wondered whether local Syrian godfather Sultan al-Khoury was familiar with these people. And if he was, did they do each other favours? Like not telling the police when one of them had committed a crime?

When Maryam de Mango had been having her visions in front of the Golden Gate, many of those attending had been Greek. According to anecdotal evidence, they had managed to connect Maryam's visions with their own legends about their Christian emperor, the Marble King. For them, as for the city's Catholics, the Virgin Mary, Maryam's supposed confidante, was the patron saint of the golden city on the Bosphorus. The entity to whom Maryam had spoken was, apparently, very disappointed in the recent actions of mankind. But did that mean she intended to revive Constantine XI Palaiologos, the Marble King, in some way?

Omer knew that some people would simply dismiss the whole thing as a fairy tale. But not the Order, he suspected. They, like him, lived alongside things that were outside what could be called normal experiences. Through prayer and contemplation, they attempted to close in upon the divine. Omer and his family did the same thing by going out onto the Mesopotamian plain, below their city of Mardin, and dreaming of their mistress the Şahmeran, the ancient snake goddess of the land between the Tigris and the Euphrates.

Unlike the Order, however, Omer and his people did not have Swiss bank accounts.

'I'd like to be on my own tonight,' Silvio de Mango said to his wife.

Ayşegül said, 'I understand. I'll take the children to my parents' place.' She led him to one side, away from the mourners drinking rakı in the living room. 'We have to talk, Silvio. We still love each other.' She looked at him and he nodded. She smiled. 'I don't want to live my old life again. I've realised that since Maryam died. All the resentments of the past, we have to put them behind us. I mean, we both gave up so much to be together . . .'

'Your brothers will have to be persuaded not to kill you, then,' he said.

Suddenly she felt deflated.

'I love you too, I always have,' he went on. 'But I can't go through you rejecting me again because of your family. They threatened you and me and our children. Oh, and the drinking's non-negotiable.'

Ayşegül felt her world collapse around her again.

In the living room, people wept for Maryam, but nobody ever wept for Ayşegül. Not even her husband, who she knew loved her.

# Chapter 23

İkmen and Süleyman caught up with Kerim Gürsel as they were walking back from the de Mango apartment to Süleyman's car. He told them about Father Colombo.

'I'm led to believe that gay priests aren't that unusual these days,' Süleyman said.

'They are in Italy, and anyway he's not gay,' Kerim said. 'He likes to dress as a woman and look at other men dressed as women.'

'And that isn't sexual how?'

'The point is,' İkmen said, 'does Father Colombo have an alibi for last Friday night?'

'Yes, sir,' Kerim said.

'You have a statement?'

'Yes.'

'Good.' İkmen lit a cigarette. Süleyman didn't smoke in his car any more and he didn't allow his passengers to do so either. He had to get one in while he could.

'How was the funeral?' Kerim asked.

'Full of sound and fury signifying I don't know what,' İkmen said. 'To paraphrase Shakespeare.'

'Nothing unusual?'

'No,' he said. 'Although I felt that Silvio de Mango was calmer than he's been for the last few days.'

'Maybe now his daughter is buried he feels he can start to put his life back together.'

Süleyman looked at his watch. 'Çetin, we need to see the Commissioner in less than half an hour,' he said.

'True.' İkmen looked at Kerim. 'We'll see you tomorrow, Sergeant.'

'Yes, sir.'

Kerim lived just off Tarlabaşı Bulvarı at the Taksim end. As he headed off up towards İstiklal Caddesi, İkmen said, 'At the risk of disagreeing with my sergeant, I don't think Silvio is at peace with Maryam's death at all. I really don't believe he killed her, but I do think he may have some other secret he's hiding from us. I just don't know what it is.'

'Çetin Bey, Mehmet Bey.'

The familiar voice caught them both by surprise.

'Madam?'

'I wondered whether I'd find you gentlemen here in Galata,' Commissioner Teker said. 'Thought I'd come and meet you. You know, I really fancy a drink . . .'

Mina slipped into the church behind a group of Japanese tourists. She'd seen Fabrizio walking along İstiklal and had only just managed to avoid him. She didn't want to talk to anyone she knew. Especially not him or, even more so, any of the fathers.

Carrying a black dustbin bag, she walked up to the floral display in front of the statue of St Anthony and began clearing away dead flowers. She'd removed some just before the church had been closed by the police, but there were still a lot more to get out of the way. As far as she could tell, only the old Polish priest was in the church. She didn't know him very well and he was never sure who anyone was these days. He nodded and smiled and she did the same.

Lobna had thankfully been too tired to come here after the funeral, as Mina had known she would be. She'd coped with it well under the circumstances. But then she'd had to. Much as she loved her sister, Mina knew there was no point feeling any more sorry for her than she had to. At least she hadn't had to deal with her ex-husband, who, Mina imagined, had been warned off by the police.

Now things just needed to return to normal, with no further discussion. That was the only thing to do. She and Lobna had suffered shock after shock and now it was time to be calm.

He'd taken her to the nameless bar in Tarlabaşı once a couple of years ago. But she'd remembered it.

'I would never have come here on my own,' she said. 'But when my brother visited last year I brought him here. He liked it.'

Süleyman looked at İkmen. 'You . . .'

'I brought Commissioner Teker here when she, well . . .'

'I asked Çetin Bey to take me somewhere outside the usual middle-class drinking establishments and the tourist haunts,' she said.

'I've never been here with you,' Süleyman said to İkmen, clearly slightly aggrieved.

İkmen laughed. 'My dear boy, there's only one thing on the menu here, and that is rakı.'

'I like rakı.'

'You also like clean water with your rakı, a few sour plums to sharpen your palate and a lack of bonzai addicts,' İkmen said.

They sat down at a table as far away as possible from every other table in the place. Although not exactly crawling with bonzai addicts, the bar, which was on the ground floor of an old Greek house, did provide alcoholic succour to a selection of İstanbul's less privileged residents. Bonzai addicts mixed with trans girls down on their luck, men of a certain age who couldn't get work, prostitutes and illegal migrants.

'Çetin Bey . . .'

İkmen looked up at the waiter and smiled.

'You've not come to cause problems?'

'Rifat, have I ever caused problems here?' İkmen said.

'Well, no . . .'

'No. And that will not change now,' he said. 'I'd like a bottle of rakı, please, a jug of what passes for water round here and three glasses that haven't been spat in.'

'Yeah . . .' The waiter sloped away.

İkmen offered cigarettes to his companions and they all lit up. 'As attendees at a private party, we are perfectly entitled to smoke with the permission of the householder,' he said.

'And who is that?'

'God knows. But look around you.'

Everyone was smoking, and not just tobacco.

Süleyman said, 'Madam, why are we here?'

'Because I want to talk to you both,' she said, 'without worrying about unwelcome ears listening in.'

Some of the patrons had to recognise them; Süleyman could see at least one woman he'd arrested multiple times for soliciting. But nobody seemed worried by that and no one was leaving. Drunk, stoned or simply depressed, they had other things on their minds.

Teker turned to İkmen. 'Did İrini Mavroyeni turn up at Maryam's funeral?'

'No,' he said. 'And I don't blame her. She was never part of Maryam's life. The only reason she had any involvement was because Maryam asked to meet her.'

The waiter slammed a bottle of rakı, a jug of brackish-looking water and three glasses down on the table.

'Thank you, Rifat,' İkmen said. 'Very gracious of you.'

The man scowled.

'Shall I charge everyone's glasses?' İkmen said.

'Only a few millimetres for me,' Süleyman said. 'Remember I'm on call.'

Once the viscous spirit had turned white with the addition of water, they all clinked glasses.

'Şerefe.'

They drank, İkmen closing his eyes blissfully as the rakı, or 'lion's milk', hit the back of his throat. Süleyman, who sat with his iPhone on the table in front of him, put his weak drink very obviously to one side.

Commissioner Teker smiled, then said, 'I had the pleasure of hosting the chief of police and three members of his team today.'

'Oh? Why?'

'I asked him to come,' she said. Whether she paused for effect at this point or whether it just seemed that way, İkmen would never know. She said, 'I've resigned.'

İkmen felt as if he'd been punched.

'Madam?'

'Hürrem,' she said. 'That's what you call me from now on.' She laughed.

Süleyman looked at her as if she'd just gone mad. Teker was usually a stickler for titles.


He saw Fabrizio as he walked over the Galata Bridge towards the Old City. He was talking to one of the few fishermen who continued to hunt for their food late into the night. As kids, Silvio and Fabrizio had both fished from the bridge. Fabrizio had been rather good at it.

Silvio hurried past, hoping that the man who had defiled his daughter hadn't seen him. There was no evidence that Fabrizio had killed Maryam, but Silvio's relationship with him was over. One day, when he least expected it, he'd kill him for what he'd done to that girl. Had he done it to spite him? After all these years?

He walked quickly towards the Eminönü end of the bridge and joined the crowds walking over the road bridge towards

Sirkeci. The old railway station, from where the Orient Express had once left for Paris, was now just a commuter station as well as a stop on the Marmary Metro line that went underneath the Bosphorus. But fiddle with the facade as modern developers might do, Silvio could still see the Ottoman-style grandeur of the old station beneath its modern concrete clothing. Designed by Germans in the nineteenth century, it was hardly a thing of beauty, but it was part of the fabric of Silvio's life. As a child, he'd taken the shabby Orient Express to visit distant relatives in Venice.

As he walked up the hill towards Sultanahmet, Silvio had to keep flattening himself against shops and hotels so that he didn't get pushed over by trams. Pavements could be very narrow in the Old City. But still, it was good to be out. Now that all the mourners had gone, he could do as he pleased. He wanted to walk.

One bottle of rakı had met its end and they were now on to their second. But İkmen wasn't what anyone, including Süleyman, would have called drunk. Commissioner Teker – Hürrem – was more obviously intoxicated, but even she was managing to remain comprehensible and serious.

'My replacement will arrive tomorrow,' she said.

'Tomorrow!'

'I don't know who, I wasn't told,' she continued. 'All I know is that he's from Trabzon. I could speculate, but I'm not going to.'

The city of Trabzon, on the far eastern end of the Black Sea coast, had become a troubled place in recent times. Once the last seat of the Byzantine Empire, the modern city was plagued by unemployment, drug addiction and an uneasy relationship with nearby Russia.

Hürrem Teker looked into Çetin İkmen's eyes. 'I jumped and

232

so I am able to convince myself that I got out with my honour intact. I didn't, but at least I don't lose too much materially.'

Süleyman's phone rang.

In spite of being surrounded by apartment blocks, Feriköy Latin Catholic Cemetery retained the dark and haunted quality it had possessed since its creation back in the nineteenth century. A city of the dead, rotting in their ornate mausoleums amongst closely planted trees and thick, unkempt undergrowth. Somewhere amongst the stone crosses, angels and agonised saints, his great-grandfather's banker was buried.

Süleyman glanced down into the empty casket that lay beside the recently excavated hole in the ground, and then looked at the terrified boy who stared up at him. His right leg was very obviously broken. His foot, which hung limply from his upraised leg, was twisted so that it pointed backwards. At the graveside, as well as a squad of uniformed constables, was a tiny head-scarfed woman holding a pistol in one hand and a mobile phone in the other.

'Could someone please take that weapon away from that woman,' Süleyman said.

An officer stepped forward and removed the gun from the woman's hand. When it had gone, she visibly slumped.

'I heard something long before I came out and found this idiot, Inspector Bey,' she said to Süleyman. 'I took my husband's gun because I was scared. It went off once but I don't think I shot anyone.'

According to Sevgin Hanım, who was the wife of the caretaker of the cemetery, she'd heard noises in the graveyard fifteen or so minutes before she actually went outside to see what was happening.

'Where is your husband, hanım?' Süleyman asked.

'Out,' she said.

He knew there was no point asking where. Sevgin Hanım was a disappointed-looking woman of a certain age, and Süleyman imagined her husband was out of the same mould. He was probably getting drunk somewhere. Either that or he was with a load of men whose idea of a good night out was to go to an old-fashioned coffee house and talk about the glory days of the Ottoman Empire.

'How many men did you see?' he said.

'As well as this one, two,' she said. 'When they saw me first of all, they laughed. Then they spotted the gun and somehow it went off.'

'What did they do?'

'They ran,' she said. 'Except for the boy. I think they were trying to get him out of the hole when I disturbed them.'

'Well, we have you to thank for bringing at least this one to us, hanım,' Süleyman said. He turned to one of his officers. 'Take Sevgin Hanım back to her house. I will come and see you later, hanım.'

The constable escorted her towards the small house she shared with her husband in the middle of the graveyard.

Süleyman crouched down and looked into the pained and terrified eyes of the young man down in the hole.

'You,' he said, 'are in a world of shit.'


He'd had to finally call a halt to the drinking. He hadn't wanted to, and ex-Commissioner Teker had clearly been keen to keep the session going. But İkmen knew he had to work the following day. He also knew that he'd need to speak to Süleyman before too long. The call he'd received in the bar had concerned an incident at Feriköy Latin Catholic Cemetery.

Cabs didn't often come this deeply into Tarlabaşı, and so he was walking towards the Bulvarı, where he'd be able to flag one down without too much trouble. In spite of the fact that it was almost 2 a.m., the quarter was alive with kids playing in the street, prostitutes escorting customers into dark alleys for cheap bunk-ups and gypsies playing fiddles in basements. Hürrem Teker had left the bar with a man İkmen recognised as one of Gonca Şekeroğlu's many brothers. He'd told the man to take care of her and had given him a very generous incentive to keep her safe. Now she was probably dancing what remained of the night away in a basement somewhere, probably in tandem with Gonca's ancient father. He found himself hoping fervently that somehow Süleyman and the gypsy would be able to get beyond her affair with Fabrizio Leon.

Teker hadn't said exactly why she'd resigned. But İkmen knew. She had no autonomy left. Who did? But she'd also cited family reasons, something he hadn't understood. She had no close family as far as İkmen knew.

Walking up to Tarlabaşı Bulvarı was no mean feat for a man whose lungs had been pickled by over forty years' worth of cigarette smoke. Then to add insult to injury he had to climb a small staircase to get to the dual carriageway. As he paused to catch his breath before mounting the stairs, İkmen saw that on one side of the dirt road there was a shop selling raunchy under-wear, while on the other was what had once been an elegant Greek house. Stone steps led up to a battered double front door, where a boy sat smoking a cigarette.

'What are you doing?' İkmen asked.

'None of your fucking business,' the kid said.

İkmen wearily took his ID out of his pocket and waved it in front of the boy's face. 'Police,' he said.

The boy shrugged. 'I'm getting in line for my breakfast.'

'What do you mean?'

'The ladies who live here hand out börek and tea in the morn-ings,' he said. 'But if you don't get here early, they run out. I don't want to be beaten by some fucking bonzai head.'

'What ladies?' İkmen asked.

'I dunno. Couple of old biddies.'

Süleyman had told him that the Amara sisters lived somewhere near the Bulvarı. He wondered whether this was their house. But he didn't dwell on that idea. He wished the kid good luck and went and got a taxi. He had troubles of his own now.

'Where's the body?' Süleyman asked.

The boy, who was now on the ground beside the empty coffin, winced with pain.

'Man, this isn't funny,' he said. 'If I don't get my leg fixed soon, they'll cut it off. It happened to Ismail Bey when he fell down the cellar steps.'

'I'm not interested,' Süleyman said. 'You know what I want to hear, Ata.'

'Bey efendi!'

Some of the officers with Süleyman looked at each other. Their superior had called for an ambulance, but it was being held at the cemetery gates.

'I don't care if they have to cut your fucking head off,' Süleyman said to the boy. 'Tell me who you were with and what you were doing. And if you say "nothing" again, I will not be responsible for my actions. Do you understand me?'

'Yes . . .'

He was in a lot of pain and had to be in shock. The officers who had lifted him out of the hole had not been as gentle as he would have liked, but still the boy held on to what he knew and just groaned.

'Grave robbing is a serious offence,' Süleyman said. 'Why'd you do it, eh? Can't get a living girlfriend?'

'No!'

One of the officers, alarmed by the colour of the boy's face, said, 'Sir . . .'

'Shut up.' Süleyman turned back to the boy. 'So tell me, Ata,' he said. 'I want to know who you were with and why you were digging up this particular grave. Come on, it's easy. Tell me.'

The boy's breath was coming harshly now. Eventually he said, 'The girl had offended against God.'

'Maryam de Mango? The girl in the grave?'

'Yeah.'

'And what were you going to do with her once you'd dug her up, given that she'd offended God?' Süleyman asked.

He was shaking. 'B-burn her.'

'Because you're such a good religious boy, such a patriot . . .'

'I . . .'

The boy's eyes had rolled up inside his head, which now lolled onto the ground at an unnatural angle.

'Sir . . .'

'Yes, all right, Feyzioğlu!' Süleyman shouted at the young officer at his side. 'Get the ambulance here now.'

# Chapter 24

Fatma İkmen knew better than to ask her husband for details when he'd been out drinking. She got out of bed at five, as usual, washed the bathroom down, put the samovar on to boil and fed Marlboro, worn out from some all-night cat orgy. At six she returned to the bedroom she shared with her husband and said, 'Get up, Çetin.'

He smelt like a rakı distillery. She was glad she hadn't seen him come in. He'd probably looked even more appalling than he did now.

'Çetin!'

He opened his eyes, which were mostly red.

'You look like Dracula,' she said. 'Get up and get washed. I can't stand the smell of you any longer.'

In spite of a hammering at the back of his skull that made him wonder whether he'd been hit on the head at some point, he swung his legs out of bed and then sat for a moment before rising shakily to his feet. He hadn't thought he'd been *that* drunk. But clearly he'd been mistaken.

He toddled to the bathroom like one of his smaller grandchildren and locked the door behind him. He'd fallen into bed in his clothes, but luckily Fatma had put a dressing gown on the back of the bathroom door. He removed his stinking clothes and switched on the shower.

The water was cold. He screamed. He heard his wife laugh.

But as the water gradually heated up, the pain in every part of his body began to ease. He had to have put away over half a bottle of rakı. Teker had probably drunk even more. But then he knew her drinking of old. She had a fearsome capacity. He hoped she'd had a good time with Gonca's brother Rambo. Yes, that was his name!

And then he remembered some other details about the previous night too.

Teker was leaving, had left, the department. Pushed out to make way for someone from . . . was it Zonguldak, or Trabzon? Somewhere on the Black Sea coast. More significant than that, though, was what she'd said to him just before they'd parted outside the Tarlabaşı bar.

'You must retire,' she'd told him. 'The knives are being sharpened and I can no longer protect you. I spent much of today looking at your employment record. Go now and they won't be able to touch you.'

He'd said, 'But I still don't know who killed Maryam de Mango. Or the priest.'

Her reply, he felt now, would live with him for a very long time: 'This is the last order I will ever give you. Go. Immediately.'

Rambo Şekeroğlu had reeled her off into the night then. Had he wandered for long before getting that cab home? He didn't know. He knew he'd tried to call Süleyman at some point but he couldn't remember why. He couldn't retire! What would he do with himself? And why should he? Just because they had come after Teker didn't mean they'd come after him, did it? He knew the answer to that, but he ignored it.

He heard his wife yell out from the kitchen. 'Çetin! Mehmet Bey is here to see you!'

Then what little he remembered about Süleyman's call-out came back to him, and he began to hurry.

Not Silvio's snake hips but her mother's fat bottom pushed

239

against Ayşegül's back, while her father, on his mattress over by the fire, snored like a beast. This was not the home she'd shared with her husband for almost thirty years. This was the hell she had been born into.

She got up and walked into the dusty, antiquated scullery that constituted her mother's kitchen. Sara, already dressed for school, was making herself a cheese sandwich.

'How are you?' Ayşegül said as she filled up the samovar and put it on to boil.

The girl shrugged.

'You don't have to go to school today,' Ayşegül said. 'Your teachers would understand, given what has happened.'

'I want to go,' Sara said. 'At school, no one judges me.'

Ayşegül frowned. 'What do you mean by that?' she said.

'I know you all think I killed Maryam because I was jealous of her,' Sara said. 'But I didn't and I wasn't.'

She left without another word. Stunned into silence, Ayşegül sat down at the kitchen table and stared into space. She didn't think Sara had killed her sister, but something wasn't right.

'Can we go home today?'

İbrahim, who she knew had taken the day off work, wandered in wearing pyjamas.

'Where's your brother?' Ayşegül asked. Mevlüt had left his father's apartment before the wake for his sister had finished. He'd taken the tie his mother had made him wear and thrown it down the stairwell.

'I don't know,' İbrahim said.

He was out getting stoned. They both knew it.

İbrahim sat down. 'So are we going home today?' he said.

Ayşegül sighed. 'Not today.'

'Why not?'

Did she tell her son that his father had rejected her in spite of the fact that he still loved her – or so he said? Silvio wanted

240

to be alone for the foreseeable future. That was what he'd told her and that was what she had to accept. She had no right of ownership to the apartment, unlike her children. But he didn't want them around either. At least not for a while.

'Your father needs some time on his own,' she said.

'That's not normal.'

Turks, it was said, didn't do being alone. Ayşegül would have begged to differ, but she had to admit her elder son found it hard.

'That's how he is,' she said.

Silvio had always been pandered to. By his parents, especially his mother; by his previous girlfriends and by her. Except for his mother, he'd always treated women badly. He'd never been violent and he'd worked hard to support his family, but in the deepest part of his soul, and in spite of his left-wing allegiances, he had always been a misogynist. There was his way and nothing else, and he always got his way because he was, even now, beautiful. Not as fabulous as Fabrizio, but then Fabrizio was too pretty in Ayşegül's opinion. Vain and faithless, he had humiliated Lobna with his endless affairs. Until she came to her senses and left him. Poor Lobna. Ayşegül didn't think of her often. When she did, she imagined she felt her pain. It was just a mercy she hadn't still been married to Fabrizio when he had his affair with Maryam.

What had possessed the girl? Had he seduced her? She knew she should ask him, but how to do that without Silvio finding out?

'Mum?'

She looked up. 'Sorry,' she said. 'I was just thinking.'

'About Maryam?'

'In part,' she said.

'You know, Mum,' her son said, 'in spite of everything, I do think there was something special about her.'

\* \* \*

241

It was a lovely morning and so the two men took their tea out onto İkmen's balcony. It overlooked Sultanahmet Square, with its Blue Mosque and a sneak peek, to the left, of Ayasofya. Should İkmen and his wife ever wish to move, it was a view a prospective buyer would be prepared to pay a lot of money for.

'We have,' Süleyman said, 'a delicate situation.'

'Tell me,' İkmen said. His colleague looked, if anything, even worse than he did.

'Well, you may or may not remember that I had a call from the Feriköy cemetery,' Süleyman said.

'Yes.'

'A grave had been defiled and one of the culprits was still inside the empty hole with a broken leg. The wife of the care-taker, who at the time was in one of the fleshpots of Karaköy, was holding her husband's gun on him.'

İkmen shook his head. 'Licensed?'

'Of course not. Anyway, the culprit was a teenage boy, Ata Goner. He and two accomplices had decided to advance the cause of godliness by digging up Maryam de Mango and burning her corpse.'

İkmen felt his face turn white. 'Oh my . . .'

'Don't worry,' Süleyman said, 'they didn't succeed. They did dig up the casket and open it, but by the time I got there, two of them had run away.'

'And Maryam?'

He held up a finger. 'I'll get to her,' he said. 'First, Çetin, I'd like to tell you about my recent travels, because, you know, I have done a lot of that in the past few hours.' He took a deep breath. 'Firstly I arranged for Ata Goner to be taken to hospital, then I went to Etiler to inform his parents.'

'Etiler.'

'Yes, amazing, isn't it?' Süleyman said. 'One of the most prosperous districts of the city, also one of the most secular.

Goner's parents conformed to that stereotype. But not, sadly for them, their three sons. Because when Ata Goner finally decided to tell me who had been with him on his grave-desecration mission, it turned out that the other people involved were his older brothers, Aydın and Ege.'

'So you got them all?'

'They are all in custody, yes. Although of course Ata is in hospital having surgery on his leg.'

İkmen sighed. 'What did the parents say?'

'They were appalled. They asked their sons what desecrating a grave had to do with religion and were told in no uncertain terms that they were filthy sinners and should follow the example the boys were in thrall to, which turned out to be some TV preacher whose name escapes me. But significantly for me, Aydın and Ege confirmed what Ata had told me, as did a search of their parents' apartment. Which then led me to a very lovely house in Tarabya.'

'Why?' İkmen asked.

'Because that is where Mr Livadanios, the undertaker who arranged Maryam's funeral, lives,' Süleyman said. 'He has a fabulous yalı. Death clearly pays well amongst the Christians . . .'

'And the Jews,' İkmen said. 'He organises Jewish funerals too. Ask my son-in-law, Berekiah. Livadanios organised his uncle's funeral last year.'

Süleyman nodded. 'So I got the poor man up,' he said, 'and his charming daughter made coffee. That is where I have just come from.'

'And Maryam?' İkmen asked.

'According to Mr Livadanios, Silvio de Mango insisted on sealing up his daughter's coffin himself two days before her funeral. His brother, Angelo de Mango, hadn't then arrived from Italy, which meant, as Mr Livadanios made clear to Silvio, that he would be unable to see his niece's body. But Silvio was adamant that he didn't want to look at his daughter any more. It was too painful for him.'

İkmen held up a hand. 'Oh no,' he said. 'Don't tell me . . .'

'When the Goner boys opened up Maryam's coffin, it was empty,' Süleyman said. 'They may be lying, and we still have uniforms searching the cemetery and nearby streets. All I will say is that the coffin was clean inside. There appeared to be no detritus from a body or its clothes, which one would expect in what was a smash-and-grab situation.'

'Oh God.' İkmen put his head in his hands.

'So we need to see Mr de Mango and ask him for his comments,' Süleyman said. 'And we need to do it in such a way that he sees sense.'

Their meeting happened quite by chance.

'Lobna.'

'Fabrizio.'

He'd gone to Tarlabaşı to visit his cousin and was now on his way back to his hotel. She was sitting outside her house in the sunshine.

'I'm assuming you know . . .'

'About you and Maryam? Yes,' she said.

'I'm sorry.'

She shrugged. 'Nothing to do with me. We were divorced when you took up with her. You should apologise to Silvio.'

'I can't face him. How was the funeral?'

'Peculiar,' she said. 'Maryam wasn't a Christian and so there was no Mass. Or rather, she was a Christian but she didn't know that until recently. İrini Mavroyeni didn't come.'

'That's a shame.'

'Why? She didn't know her. It was Ayşegül who brought her up,' Lobna said. 'She was there, with the children. Why didn't you tell me she wasn't Maryam's real mother?'

'Because Silvio asked me not to,' he said.

'Since when did you do as you're told?'

'He's my best friend!'

'Who you shared with İrini Mavroyeni,' she said. 'How did you know Maryam wasn't yours?'

'Oh for God's sake, Lobna! I went with İrini when we were kids! I'd lost touch with her long before Maryam was born. And if you must know, I was shocked when Silvio told me he'd knocked her up.'

'Why? You were both out of the same mould when it came to women.' She shook her head. 'How Ayşegül could have married him after that I don't know. What kind of man goes with another woman while he's engaged to be married?'

'Ayşegül wouldn't—'

'She wouldn't sleep with him until they were married, yes, I know,' she said. 'He knew that. It was his choice to accept her terms. He could've said no and moved on.'

'He was in love with her.'

She laughed. 'Oh please. Love? Him?'

'I thought you liked Silvio,' Fabrizio said. 'You've always got on with him. He asked you to come and witness Maryam's visions because he thought it might help you.'

'He asked me to assuage his guilt,' she said.

'Guilt? For what? Take your anger out on me, by all means, but don't bring Silvio into this. He's done nothing to hurt you. Quite the reverse.'


'When I nailed down Maryam's casket, she was inside,' he said.

İkmen shook his head. 'She wasn't.'

'Those boys who robbed her grave took her somewhere and burnt her,' he said.

'Only if they did it at the speed of light,' Süleyman said. 'When Mrs Balcı, the caretaker's wife, saw the two boys running away, she didn't say anything about them carrying a body. We've searched the graveyard, the surrounding streets and the apartment where the boys live and have found nothing.'

'Caretaker's wife must be lying.'

'Why would she?'

'I don't know,' Silvio said.

Was the implication that she was lying because she was a Muslim? Neither İkmen nor Süleyman wanted to pursue that point.

'Where is she, Mr de Mango?' İkmen asked.

'I don't know.' He lit a cigarette and leaned back into his chair. He appeared relaxed, almost casual about the matter.

'Mr Livadanios has told us he didn't look inside Maryam's coffin after you sealed it,' Süleyman said. 'This was, he said, entirely your idea.'

For a moment, Silvio de Mango said nothing. When he did speak, it was with a growling intensity that came as a shock.

'Then you'd better go out and look for my daughter, hadn't you?' he said. 'Because if those boys didn't take her body, and neither myself nor Livadanios has her, then someone else does.'

'Who? Your daughter had been buried less than a day,' İkmen said. 'Who in that short time—'

'I don't know!' Agitated now, Silvio de Mango stood up and paced the floor. 'You're the police, not me! Do your job! Maybe the caretaker's wife knows? Maybe Maryam is in her house. Have you searched it?'

'Of course we have.'

'Well her garden then,' he said. 'They have a well, look there!'

'We have,' Süleyman said through clenched teeth. İkmen put a hand on his arm in an attempt to calm him. It didn't work. 'And anyway, why would Mrs Balcı call us if she and her husband had already taken the body? It doesn't make sense,' he said. 'It's my belief, Mr de Mango, that Maryam's coffin was already empty when it was buried yesterday.'

Silvio de Mango shook his head. 'No.'

'No? Then how do you account for the fact that her body is missing?' Süleyman said. 'And gone without apparently leaving any sort of trace.'

She didn't want any more trouble. She had managed, through judicious use of alcohol, to miss her daughter's funeral, and now she just wanted to do what she had to do and make everything else go away.

'You were wrongly informed,' she said to the young girl standing in her doorway. 'You need to go elsewhere.'

'Where?'

Her eyes were large with fear, her foreign-accented voice trembling.

'I don't know,' İrini said. 'Don't you have women who do this amongst your own people?'

'No,' she said. 'It's a sin.'

İrini wanted to say, *So you get a foreigner to risk their soul and that doesn't matter.* But she didn't. All she said was 'I can't help you.'

The girl walked away and İrini shut her door. Fucking Syrians. When the Roma had still lived in Sulukule en masse, they'd been much easier to deal with. If their men wanted sex, they just paid for it and got on. Ditto their women who wanted the occasional abortion. Even if they'd felt it, they'd never hit her with the 'sin' business. Women consumed with fear were no good to work on. All they did was cry, scream and call attention to themselves. She'd only ever done that willingly once. Whenever she thought about it, she shuddered. That had been bad. She poured herself a glass of rakı and drank it neat.

It was strange that a girl should come to her after so many years of having nothing to do with terminations. How had she known about her? And why now, when not so many days ago, out of the blue, she'd dreamed about that poor woman?

# Chapter 25

For a while, neither of them said anything. Then Kerim Gürsel locked the door to İkmen's office and sat down. Omer Mungun sat too, close to Kerim, so they could whisper.

Both their superiors were out. Maryam de Mango's body had apparently disappeared from Feriköy cemetery and İkmen had applied for a warrant to search Silvio de Mango's apartment. That was bad, but what was worse was that Kerim and Omer had just come back from Commissioner Teker's office. There they'd been told by a man they'd never seen before that Teker had gone and he was her replacement.

'What did he say his name was?' Omer asked Kerim. 'I didn't take it in.'

Kerim typed something into his laptop. 'Selahattin Ozer. I'm looking him up now.'

Commissioner Ozer hadn't told them anything. Not why Teker had gone, or where, or anything at all about himself. To make matters even stranger, Ozer's secretary was the disgraced Melis Bila, who had apparently betrayed Commissioner Teker and broken her trust.

Kerim peered at the screen. 'He's fifty-nine and from Trabzon. Was commissioner in Bingöl until two years ago, when he retired.'

'So why's he doing this now?' Omer said. 'Why come out of retirement?'

'Maybe he thought İstanbul was too big a job to turn down?'

'Or maybe someone made him an offer he couldn't refuse,'

Omer said. 'And where's Teker? All I managed to get out of Mehmet Bey was that she's gone.'

'Perhaps he can't say any more than that?' Kerim said. 'Maybe that's all he knows?'

'Mehmet Bey won't like him,' Omer said.

'You think?' Kerim laughed. 'Çetin Bey will run rings around someone like him. Did you see those pictures on Teker's desk?'

'Yeah.'

There had been two photographs placed prominently on what had become Ozer's desk: one of him with a covered woman, possibly his wife, and the other of him again with a prominent conservative politician.

'Did you notice,' Omer said, 'that his face was like stone? Not once did it express anything beyond what I interpreted as disapproval.'


Father Marek Wojtulewicz had never wanted to leave his native Poland. He'd never been good at languages. As a child, he'd wrestled with Latin; he had made the best of a bad job studying English as a young man, and now he struggled constantly with the torment that was Turkish. God could be a cruel master. But who was Father Wojtulewicz to argue? Obedience to the Almighty was just something one did, like cleaning the church, which wasn't easy for a man who was nearer eighty than seventy. But it was his turn, and now that Father Esposito was dead, there were the same number of chores to do but fewer people to do them.

He swept behind the altar and picked up the dust using a piece of cardboard. Father Esposito had been the only Italian he'd really been able to get on with. He'd been a nice man. He'd nursed the elderly priest, all but alone, when he'd had pneumonia. None of the others had given a damn. Now that Father Esposito was dead, he had no one to talk to. Father Colombo wasn't a bad boy, although all that dressing up he did wasn't exactly healthy. Everyone dismissed Father Wojtulewicz because of his less than perfect language skills, but he didn't miss much. He'd known about Father Colombo for months. And Father da Mosto's problem with gambling.

When the police had come to search the church, twice, he'd not said very much to them but he had made sure they did a thorough job. That was why, now, he knew he wasn't wrong about what he found underneath the altar. A familiar item, it had not featured in either of the searches.

İkmen left Süleyman in charge of the search at the de Mango apartment while he went over to Fatih to visit Silvio's wife.

Ayşegül's parents lived right in the centre of the Çarşamba quarter, deep in amongst the Order. When İkmen knocked at their door, he felt many eyes on him. Was it just his imagination that they were hostile?

Ayşegül de Mango was alone except for her ailing father, who was asleep. She took the policeman through into the kitchen and shut the door.

It wasn't easy telling her that her daughter's body was missing. She sat down and put a hand over her mouth.

'We don't think she was in the casket when it was buried,' he said.

'But my husband sealed it himself . . . Oh.'

'Mrs de Mango, there's no easy way to say this, but can you think of any reason why your husband may have hidden Maryam's body?'

She paused for a moment, marshalling her thoughts. 'He was worried that her grave might be desecrated,' she said. 'I was too. He told me he was going to order one of those metal cages to go over the grave site. But of course it's not been made yet. Do you really think that Silvio has hidden Maryam?'

'I don't know,' İkmen said. 'But at the moment it is the only feasible explanation we have. Officers are searching your apartment now.'

'Our apartment?' She shook her head. 'Where could he put her there?'

'I don't know.'

She sighed. 'You won't find anything.'

'Maybe not, but we have to look,' he said. 'Unburied dead bodies are a public health issue. Can you think of anyone who might have helped him secrete her body?'

'No!'

'Mr Leon?'

'No,' she said. 'Silvio is furious with Fabrizio because of what he did to Maryam. If he'd come to her funeral, I think he would have killed him. He's the last one Silvio would have gone to.'

'Anyone else?'

She shook her head. 'He doesn't talk to people,' she said. 'Just his priest, the Amara sisters . . . None of them would have condoned that. It's impossible!'

'Nothing is impossible, Ayşegül Hanım . . .'

'Yes, well, you know what I mean,' she said.

They sat in silence for a moment. İkmen lit a cigarette.

'Mrs de Mango, do you or your husband have any other properties besides your apartment in Galata?' he said.

'You mean houses or apartments? No,' she said.

'Anything? Garages?'

She put her chin in her hands. 'All I can think of are some plots of land.'

'Plots of land?'

'I don't know where they are,' she said. 'All I know is that they're old things that have belonged to the de Mangos for a very long time.'

\* \* \*

'Who are you?'

'I may well ask you the same question,' the man said.

Silvio was infuriated. 'This is my fucking home!'

'And I am Police Commissioner Ozer . . .'

'More policemen, eh?' Silvio said. 'Just what I need.' He sat down and poured himself yet another drink.

'You're drunk.'

'Yes, my daughter's been murdered and now her body has disappeared and you people haven't been able to do a thing about it. So excuse me but I think I need a drink, don't you?'

Mehmet Süleyman walked into the de Mango chapel and found himself looking at a tall, thin man with an almond-shaped moustache wearing a dusty suit and tie. Omer Mungun, at his side, said, 'Oh, Mehmet Bey . . .'

'Commissioner Ozer,' the man said without extending his hand.

Süleyman, who recognised this type of person as one who didn't shake hands, bowed slightly. 'Sir.'

'You're in charge of this search?'

'Yes, sir.'

'What about Inspector İkmen?'

'He's gone to Fatih to interrogate my wife,' Silvio de Mango said.

'This man is drunk . . .'

'With respect, sir,' Süleyman said, 'this is his property.'

Ozer looked confused. 'And?'

Silvio de Mango looked at him with undisguised contempt.

Süleyman felt his hackles rise. Teker had been pushed out for this?

'Well?' Ozer said.

Did he want Süleyman to take Silvio de Mango's bottle away from him? Not only was he unsure whether he could do that; he was pretty convinced that he shouldn't. He smiled and said,

'Commissioner, if you'd like to accompany me to Mr de Mango's kitchen, I will tell you about some developments in this case.'

'Found out who murdered this man's daughter, have you?' Ozer said.

Silvio de Mango laughed. 'Oh no, I doubt it,' he said. 'Unless, of course, you think it's me, Inspector?'

Çetin İkmen's phone rang. He thought about not answering it but then decided to.

'I need to see you,' İrini Mavroyeni said. Her voice was only a little bit slurred, so she wasn't actually drunk.

'I'm in the middle of something at the moment, İrini Hanım,' İkmen said. He watched Kerim Gürsel squat down and look inside a hole in the ground. 'Is it urgent?'

'I don't know.'

'I'll come when I've finished here,' he promised.

'Where's here?'

'Physically, Sultanahmet,' he said. 'Culturally, who knows?'

He ended the call.

He and Kerim Gürsel were in the area of Sultanahmet behind the Blue Mosque known as Cankurtaran. Specifically they were walking around a piece of wasteland at the bottom of a stretch of the outer wall of the Topkapı Palace.

İkmen looked at his sergeant. 'Anything?'

Using the torch on his phone, Kerim peered into a crack in the earth. 'It could be one of those small cisterns. Or it could just be a load of stones down there.'

'The story of the modern city's constant battle with archaeology,' İkmen said.

'This close to the wall . . .'

'Absolutely. We'll need help,' İkmen said.

Kerim stood up. 'How many of these bits of property do the de Mangos own?'

'Mrs de Mango only knows of three,' İkmen said. 'But that doesn't mean a thing. There could be a lot more. Some of the old Levantine and Greek families have property they don't even know about. Who owns what here is a vexed question, as I'm sure you know, Kerim.'

He did. And it wasn't just the Greek and Levantine families who still owned property all over town. There were many buildings that even had multiple owners: the real owners, those who thought they were the owners, and those who believed they should be the owners. Many İstanbul law firms made a lot of money out of people making property claims, particularly relatives of people who had emigrated.

'Where's the next site?' Kerim asked.

'On Küçük Ayasofya Caddesi,' İkmen said. 'Mrs de Mango described it as a rubbish dump.'

'Sir, if all these sites are basically abandoned ruins, how would it be possible for Mr de Mango to bring his dead daughter to such a place without provoking comment? He doesn't have a car,' Kerim said.

İkmen nodded. It was a good point. But that still didn't mean these plots of land didn't require investigation. They would need extra manpower.

'I don't know what you want to say to me, Mehmet Bey, but I want to say a few things to you,' Ozer said.

The de Mango kitchen was a mess. Dirty plates and glasses were scattered across every surface. The oven was open, with a tray of cold, congealing börek still inside.

'I understand this change of administration has been very sudden,' Ozer continued. 'But I want to make it as smooth and easy as I can. None of us knew that Commissioner Teker was going to resign when she did, or that she would be required to go immediately. I have been brought in, at the moment, on an interim basis. I know very little about the department's ongoing investigations and so I will, on this occasion, allow those involved to conduct this case as they see fit. My understanding is that two people have been unlawfully killed – this man's daughter and a priest.'

'Yes, sir,' Süleyman said. 'Plus there's the missing body.'

'Right.' Ozer looked around and shook his head. 'You're working with Inspector İkmen?'

'Yes. I expect you've heard of him.'

'I am aware of both of you.' He smiled. 'You come from an illustrious family, Mehmet Bey.'

Süleyman said nothing. He knew that there were people these days who had an entirely different take on the Ottoman Empire than had prevailed in the past. Now it was fine to be an Ottoman again. In some cases it was an asset.

'I have been led to understand that the murder of this clearly delusional young woman has been connected in some people's minds with certain religious people. Is that correct?'

'With some justification,' Süleyman said. 'When her body was found, by Inspector İkmen, there was a breach of confidentiality that was traced to Commissioner Teker's former secretary . . .'

'Now my secretary,' Ozer said.

Süleyman felt the blood leave his face.

'Melis Hanım made a mistake,' Ozer said. 'This has now been corrected. Where are you with the involvement of these religious people?'

'We have no evidence,' Süleyman said. 'This doesn't mean that we are entirely convinced . . .'

'Of course not,' Ozer said. 'You must be seen to do your job. What about other suspects?'

'At the moment we remain concentrated on Maryam's family and known contacts,' Süleyman said.

'Well most murders occur within family and friendship groups, don't they? What about the girl's followers at the Golden Gate?'

'We've identified the regulars. Most were casual, curious . . .'

'And the priest?'

'Ongoing again, sir,' he said. 'Both these cases are complex. Father Esposito was a foreign national, and the fact that Maryam's body has gone missing further complicates the case.'

'But no religious community is involved?'

'I will never say never, sir, but it is not at the forefront of our minds at the moment.'

Ozer smiled. 'So do you think that this Mr de Mango has secreted his daughter's body somewhere, Inspector?'

Süleyman felt that this new commissioner wanted him to say yes. He said, 'I don't know.'

'You don't know?'

'After the funeral, the grave was filled in and then left. So there is a time lapse between the burial and the known attempted robbery of the grave. What may have happened during that time, we don't know.'

'And yet this man, as I understand it, considers his late daughter to be some sort of saint.'

'I don't know about that,' Süleyman said.

Did Ozer know that de Mango had contacted the Holy See? And if he did, what did he think about it?

The Commissioner smiled. 'So what did you want to speak to me about, Mehmet Bey?'

'I only wanted to say that although Mr de Mango is a suspect in the apparent abduction of his daughter's corpse, we have no reason to believe that he killed her. I wanted to make that clear.'

'And you have,' Ozer said. 'So who *do* you think killed Maryam de Mango?'

'What I think is not important,' Süleyman replied. 'Only the facts have relevance to what we do. At the moment, the facts are not pointing with any certainty anywhere.'

'Really?'

'No.'

'And yet we do need a result, don't we.'

'It's—'

'That wasn't a question,' Ozer said.

Süleyman went back to the de Mango chapel, where Silvio was watching his officers search behind heavy baroque furniture. He must have noticed the policeman's expression, because he said, 'I'm sorry I can't offer you a drink, Inspector.'

Süleyman smiled. Then, once he was certain that Ozer wasn't coming back, he called İkmen.

# Chapter 26

Although she rarely had contact with her officers' partners, Hürrem Teker knew Gonca Şekeroğlu. After the previous night's activities, she also knew her brother, Rambo. However, he wasn't with her when she turned up at Gonca's house in Balat in the early evening.

As usual, as soon as spring was in the air, the gypsies came out into the large garden that went all the way around Gonca's large detached Ottoman house. Children of all ages ran and screamed around groups of adults, mainly women, who sat on the ground eating, drinking and smoking nargile. In the middle of all this, and the only one sitting on a chair, was an old man who was fast asleep.

'Commissioner Teker?'

Gonca appeared not in front of her, but behind. Of all the people Hürrem had met in İstanbul, the gypsy was the only one who was capable of unnerving her.

'Oh, Gonca Hanım, you, er, you . . .'

'You wanted to see me?'

'Yes.'

'I hope it's not about Rambo,' Gonca said. 'Did he behave himself last night?'

'He was a perfect gentleman,' Teker said. And he had been. She had no idea where he'd taken her or who the other people involved in what had been a sort of house party with live music and dancing might have been. But she'd had a marvellous time.

Even when she'd finally woken up that morning, safely in her own apartment, courtesy of Rambo, she'd still had a smile on her face.

Until she'd looked at her computer and seen the email.

'Gonca Hanım,' Teker said, 'I am in trouble.'

Çetin İkmen was exhausted. Usually he drove himself everywhere, but this time he couldn't face it and let Kerim Gürsel take him to Sulukule. The sad little patches of de Mango land he'd explored had convinced him that Maryam's body was not hidden in any of them. Nothing had been disturbed, in any significant way, and he had quickly tired of sifting through used hypodermic needles and discarded condoms. Kerim had made a good point when he'd raised the question of how de Mango could have got Maryam's body so far without his own transport. Then Süleyman had called. The only development at the de Mango apartment was, apparently, the appearance of their new commissioner, Ozer. Rather poetically, İkmen thought, his colleague had described him as 'a threat inside the body of a pious uncle who just wants you to do well at school'. He was also a neo-Ottoman, which was worrying. But then İkmen had expected nothing less. Teker wasn't the first officer to leave suddenly only to be replaced by someone with deeply conservative views.

Kerim drove up to İrini Mavroyeni's shack. 'Do you want me to come in with you, sir?'

'No.'

'OK, I'll wait here.'

İkmen knocked on the door and was told that it was open.

'Sorry, I'm a bit disorganised,' İrini said.

She was wearing a thin slip and a pair of fluffy slippers. İkmen had the strong impression she'd just finished with a customer.

'You want to sit down?'

'Thanks.'

He sat on the only chair in the room – a recent addition, still covered in brick dust probably from a demolition site. He declined her offer of a drink and then watched her fill a glass with neat rakı for herself and sit down on the bed.

'So? You've something to tell me, hanım?'

She shrugged. 'I think so, yes. I had a young girl, one of the Syrians, come and knock on my door today. She wanted a termination.'

'But you don't do that any more, do you?'

'Course not,' she said. 'That's why it came as a shock. Who told this girl I still did? But anyway, that's not the point. You know I told you about a dream I had the night Maryam was supposed to visit me?'

'About Silvio and Lobna Amara, wasn't it?'

'Yeah. Well this visit from the Syrian girl, it made me think about Lobna and her sister again.'

'Oh?'

'When we were at school together, I think I told you, Lobna was sweet on Silvio de Mango.'

'Yes.'

'Well, I don't know if this had anything to do with him or not, because I don't know that the two of them ever went out, but when she was fifteen, Lobna got pregnant.'

'How do you know that?' İkmen asked.

'She told me,' İrini said.

'Why you?'

'Because I lived here. Tarlabaşı, where Lobna lived, was almost respectable back then. You had to go to the Sulukule gypsy women if you wanted an abortion. She thought I knew them. I didn't, not then, but I found her one and she was grateful.'

'Who else knows about this?' İkmen asked.

'No one as far as I know.'

'Not her sister?'

'Not at the time,' İrini said. 'Mina was always such a good girl, it would have been impossible.'

'What do you mean?'

'Ah, she was always at her prayers,' she said. 'I was amazed when I learned that she'd married and even more shocked when she had a baby. I thought she'd die a virgin. What didn't surprise me was that her marriage failed. As a child she was about as much fun as a rain storm. Which brings me back to my dream.'

'In what way?' İkmen said.

'Well, when I was thinking about it today, I realised that it wasn't Lobna who was in the dream, it was Mina,' she said. 'And if it was Mina, then why? Of all the people I went to school with, I knew her the least.'

No wonder Sara hated her family so much, thought Ayşegül. Mevlüt had arrived just after the girl had got home from school and told her that in future he wasn't going to let her go out without a male escort. Ayşegül's mother had thought this was a good idea and had agreed with him. The old woman either didn't know or wouldn't accept that her favourite grandson was on bonzai. Ayşegül had thrown him out. But then Sara had clung to her, which had been irritating because Ayşegül had wanted to phone Silvio to ask him what the hell he was doing. She'd sent the girl to her room, and as Sara left, she'd given her a look of such hatred that Ayşegül had gasped.

It was a miracle Silvio had picked up his phone. He usually just let it ring out.

'What's this about Maryam?' Ayşegül asked him. 'Where is she?'

'I don't know,' he said. 'Why do you think I would?'

'I've had the police here.'

'Me too.'

'Silvio, Maryam wasn't a saint. She was a confused young

262

woman who was having an affair with a much older man. She became very ill . . .'

'And was cured.'

'She went into remission, yes,' Ayşegül said. 'You know her doctor said that was possible right at the start.'

'I don't want to hear this!'

'I know,' she said. 'But you must. Because you have to give her up. I know you're frightened that people will harm her—'

He cut the line. Ayşegül put her head in her hands. People had always assumed because she now covered that she was the superstitious one. But that had always been Silvio. Even as a young man he'd had rosaries hidden behind his posters of Che Guevara; he'd used the holy pictures they gave out as prizes at school as bookmarks in his copy of Marx.

Maryam had been pregnant when her visions began. Her body raging with hormones, her mind consumed by the need to protect her unborn child. And then there was Fabrizio. Ayşegül knew how he was with women. Had he been unfaithful to Maryam once he knew she was going to lose her figure? She wouldn't put it past him. No wonder the Virgin Mary had told Maryam that the world was falling apart because of man's wickedness.

'I've been accused of corruption,' Hürrem said.

Gonca poured her guest another glass of rakı and then shouted at a child who was trying to get into her bedroom.

'I am supposed to have taken money in return for turning a blind eye to the illegal practices of a media organisation.' Teker shook her head. 'I don't even know the company. When I got the email, I had to go on Google to find out what it does. Or did. It was closed down last week.'

Gonca put a hand on her arm. 'Why?'

'Officially, for accounting errors. But they made an unwise documentary . . .'

'Ah.'

'It suggested that some people who are held up as role models in certain quarters are as flawed as the rest of us. If not more so. You know?'

Gonca smiled.

'I have relatives amongst such people,' Teker said. 'I know them.'

'They won't help you?'

She laughed. 'God, no!'

Gonca offered Teker a cigarette, which she took.

'So why are you here?'

'Because İkmen and Süleyman are engaged in an investigation that may involve people like . . . people who are being protected,' she said. 'Now I've gone, I can't look out for them. But I had to go when I did, or at least I thought I did. Now I'm not so sure.'

'Why?'

'Because I thought that if I resigned I'd be allowed to walk away. I thought that was what was required. I was wrong. I'm here, Gonca Hanım, because I want you to tell Mehmet Bey what has happened to me and to be careful. And I want you to tell Çetin Bey that if he does as I begged him to now, it may already be too late. Please also say that I am very, very sorry for that.'


It was in the very small hours of the morning that the car pulled up across the road. Even the dealers were in bed, so if whoever it was happened to be looking for bonzai, crack or heroin, they'd be out of luck.

Why were they there? Mina tried to peer into the car but it was too dark. Maybe it was just one person? A man looking for a good time with one of the trans girls? If it was, he was late even by their standards.

A fog had come to shore from the Bosphorus and the street

lamps that hadn't been shot out were shrouded in small clouds of greying yellow light. The road outside was still the same dirt track it had been in her grandfather's time. If she half closed her eyes, Mina could be back eighty years with ease. Except for that car.

She walked away from the window and sat down in a chair in front of the silent TV. She could hear Lobna groaning in her sleep. Sometimes she said things, but Mina made a point of never listening. Not really. Of course her words were bitter and sad. They would be. But Mina still didn't want to know what she said.

In the morning, when the sun came up and burnt away the sea mist, everything would be all right.

Later, Mina got up to go back to bed. But she couldn't resist looking out of the window again first. The car was still there.

# Chapter 27

New flowers had come, delivered to the church. Katerina had been obliged to run down and help stack them inside. Father da Mosto looked out of the dining-room window for a moment and then went back to his newspaper. Father Colombo was nowhere to be seen. Father Wojtulewicz hoped the young man wasn't out and about with the lady boys again. It wasn't very dignified for a priest to wear women's clothes. But he kept his own counsel on the matter. Ever since he'd arrived at St Anthony's, he'd pursued a policy of non-intervention. He didn't like confrontation, and his language skills weren't really up to an argument.

Now, however, that could change. New flowers had arrived, which meant that new arrangements would be created. This would take time and so there would be ample opportunity for him to build up his courage.

Unless she looked immediately for what she'd left behind when she'd taken the dead flowers away.

Gonca got out of bed naked and put her clothes on.

Süleyman, still half asleep, sat up. 'Are you going?'

'I've done as Hürrem Hanım asked. Now I need to check and see that she's OK,' she said.

'You're going to her apartment?'

Gonca didn't reply. She'd arrived at Süleyman's apartment around midnight, passed on Teker's message and then slept with

266

him. As their sexual repertoire went, it had been dirty but perfunctory.

'Well tell her I appreciate her concern,' he said. 'At the moment, Commissioner Ozer seems keen to keep me on side. He's a neo-Ottoman and so he finds my provenance impressive.' He lit a cigarette. 'But I take her fears about Çetin Bey seriously. I have no doubt they will clash and I've equally no doubt that Ozer's main task is to shield significant people from the full force of the law. That won't play with İkmen.' He shook his head.

Gonca thought about saying something else, something about the two of them, but then stopped herself. What was the point? She had to accept that her fling with Fabrizio Leon had damaged Süleyman's pride too seriously for there to be a way back. The fact that he'd been serially unfaithful to her didn't figure. But then that was men. She'd find another one, and even if she didn't, he'd have her back for sex. She could still make him come just by licking his balls.

'Goodbye, Mehmet,' she said.

He didn't even look at her.


Sitting up in his car all night wasn't something Kerim Gürsel did lightly. Usually he only undertook such a course of action when someone else instructed him to. This, however, had been all his own idea. It had come about after İkmen had told him what İrini Mavroyeni had said about the Amara sisters. At first he'd only driven over to see where they lived. Then he'd stayed.

Pembe had called him at about three, shaking him out of something that was almost sleep.

'Where are you?' she'd said. 'Sinem has been in terrible pain and has only just got to sleep. She wanted you here.'

Sinem, the wife who wasn't a wife but was his best friend, had suffered from rheumatoid arthritis all her adult life. In the early days she'd been well enough for Kerim to both work and care for her. But now that was impossible, and Pembe Hanım, Kerim's transsexual lover, was her carer. The three of them lived in knowing harmony, except when Kerim's job occasionally put his life at risk.

'I'm sorry,' he'd whispered into his phone. The streets of Tarlabaşı had been eerily quiet. A thick mist had rolled in from the Bosphorus and had given the whole city a feeling of isolation. A misty island drifting towards a morning that might or might not bring leaden, threatening rain.

'Yes, but where are you?' she'd asked.

He'd told her he was in the car, but he hadn't said where.

'Çetin Bey has some new information about the Maryam de Mango case,' he'd said. 'I can't get it out of my head.'

'So why don't you think about it at home?' Pembe had asked.

That was of course very reasonable. But it wasn't practical if what one wanted to do was think about a notion that was very alien without being questioned by one's nearest and dearest. Kerim didn't go home to ponder the nature of reality. He went home to love and be loved.

He sat up and looked at his watch. It was 8.30, and he could already see a drug deal going down outside the bakkal at the end of the street. A man wearing only shorts and a filthy vest peered at him through the windscreen, and then flopped down on a doorstep with a bottle of Efes. Anywhere else in the city, drinking at such a time in the morning would be unheard of. But this was Tarlabaşı.

Kerim looked up at the Amara house and saw that the curtains were still closed. He reversed the car through a crowd of kids, who scattered, swearing, and parked at the end of the road.

Silvio de Mango had been on the phone when Süleyman and Omer Mungun arrived at his apartment. Clearly the call was important, as he made no attempt to curtail it. He put them in

268

the kitchen while he continued his conversation, walking around the rest of the apartment. Conducted in Italian, Silvio's end of it sounded furious.

For a while Süleyman tried, using his knowledge of French, to work out what de Mango was saying. But it was hard work and inexact. All he could really make out was that it was something about his daughter. Which one, he couldn't tell. He gave up.

He attempted to speak to Omer Mungun, but the sergeant seemed very far away from some reason and so he gave that up too.

Not for the first time that morning he wished he'd not just fallen into bed with Gonca the previous evening. He couldn't forgive her. Since when had he ever forgiven any woman who had betrayed his trust? But the sex had been good even if what she'd come to tell him hadn't.

According to Gonca, Teker had told her that she was under investigation for corruption. Süleyman had been stunned. Teker had always, to his knowledge, been scrupulously honest. Like her predecessor, Commissioner Ardıç, she'd sometimes had to play a somewhat clever game with higher authorities to get what she needed for the department, but she'd never taken bribes.

And then there had been the revelation about İkmen. Teker had told him he needed to resign before he was forced out. But Çetin had said nothing about it to him. Süleyman had to fight with himself not to feel hurt. It had almost made him phone İkmen, but then Gonca had made him see sense.

'If Teker is under investigation, they could be recording your conversations,' she'd said.

He would have to wait until he saw İkmen in person and alone.

Fabrizio Leon ended the call he'd been engaged in. 'What now?'

İkmen insisted they go somewhere private, so Leon took him to his office.

As he sat down, İkmen said, 'Now, Mr Leon, I want you to think hard before you answer my question.'

'Why, because you'll put me back in one of your cells?'

'No,' he said. 'This isn't really to do with you.'

'Makes a change!'

İkmen ignored him. 'I know you told me that you kept your affair with Maryam a secret from everyone, including your ex-wife, but—'

'I didn't want Lobna to know!' he said.

'You were divorced by that time.'

'Yes, but I still didn't want to tell her,' he said. 'Why cause unnecessary upset? Lobna is a very sensitive woman, Inspector. She would have taken it badly.'

'Why?'

'It's just what she's like.'

'She would have had to know sometime.'

'I know. I know.'

Should he bring up the abortion Lobna had got İrini Mavroyeni to organise for her all those years ago? İkmen wondered. There was a possibility the child had actually been Fabrizio's. But he decided not to.

'What about her sister?' he asked.

'Old maid Mina?'

'She was married at one time, wasn't she?' İkmen said.

'Yes,' he said. 'She has a daughter in America. Strange but true.'

'What do you mean?'

'Mina was always a frigid cow,' Fabrizio said. 'I was amazed when she got married; we all were.'

'Including Lobna?'

'Lobna especially,' he said. 'I think she always expected Mina to stay at home with their parents. Now they've both ended up in that old house in Tarlabaşı, with Mina driving Lobna out of her mind.'

İkmen frowned.

'Since Lobna got ill, Mina has found the meaning her life has always lacked, in my opinion,' Fabrizio said. 'She organises her medication, her food, her exercise. That, and the good works she does for the Church, mean she'll definitely go to heaven.' He laughed. 'She's always been a stupid bitch.'

İkmen said, 'What works does she do for the Church?'

'Who do you think I am?'

'Just answer the question,' Süleyman said. 'Do you have any other pieces of property apart from these?'

The list, provided by Ayşegül de Mango, was short and the locations had already been visited. But nothing had been found.

'I haven't been to any of these places for years,' Silvio de Mango said. 'I don't even know this İshak Paşa Caddesi one. There's our family burial plot in Feriköy, which of course you know about, but that is it. And by the way, do you have any more information on where my daughter's body may have gone after we buried her? There was about eight hours when she was entirely alone.'

'No, sir.'

He looked up at Omer Mungun.

'What do you think, young man?'

Omer took a moment to answer. Only the previous evening he'd found out that his sister had organised a dinner party for his birthday at the end of the week. She'd invited their new neighbour, Asra. The one he liked. She'd also invited his colleagues. Omer felt that he was going to be hideously embarrassed. It was hard to think of anything else.

'Well pardon me for interrupting your thoughts!' Silvio said.

Süleyman shot Omer a filthy look.

'Mr de Mango,' he said, 'if you tell me where Maryam's body is now—'

271

'I don't fucking know! Can you find her in this apartment? No!'

'Sir, you had some fears about the security around Maryam . . .'

'Of course!' Silvio said. 'But what could I do, eh? No one at St Anthony's took her seriously; the Holy See didn't have any interest in a woman who was chosen by God to be cured of cancer, who was chosen again by the Blessed Virgin Mary to give her message to the world. In years to come, all these people will be proved wrong. All of them.'

His passion temporarily spent, he sat down at his kitchen table.

'First, according to you, I was a murderer; now I am a grave robber. What I really am is a grieving father,' he said. 'You forget that.'

'We don't,' Süleyman said. 'But try as we might, Mr de Mango, we cannot find any evidence that your daughter's body was removed from her grave after her coffin was buried. If I look at the probabilities that surround this situation, and putting your pain to one side, I have to conclude that the most likely scenario is that her body never actually left this apartment.'

'So where is it?' de Mango said.

'I don't know.'

For a moment the two men looked into each other's eyes. Then Süleyman said, 'But I should tell you, Mr de Mango, that I have put in a request to Beyoğlu municipality for a copy of the original architectural drawings of this building.'

Silvio de Mango said nothing.

'Which were,' Süleyman continued, 'drawn up under instruction from your great-grandfather, I believe.'

De Mango shrugged. 'Well I hope you can read Ottoman, Inspector. Because those plans will not be in Roman script; they're too old.'

'We have that organised,' Süleyman said. 'Although we don't have to go that far if you—'

'I've told you,' de Mango said. 'She's not here. Don't you

think that if she was, you'd be able to smell something by this time?'

And for once, Süleyman had to admit that he had a point.

God had provided and that strange car had gone. Mina had thrown stale bread out into the garden for the stray cats and had then opened the front door to see who was waiting for börek and tea. It had been misty overnight and so most of her regulars had stayed wrapped up in their rags, intoxicated against the spring cold. But that didn't include Abubekir. As ever, this heroin addict, who could have been forty or seventy or anywhere in between, was waiting on her doorstep, smoking discarded cigarette ends. Mina gave him tea in a paper cup and a large portion of börek made with creamy tulum cheese, straight from the oven.

Lobna was still in bed, but if the day was going to go as planned, Mina needed her to get up. She walked up the stairs to her sister's bedroom and knocked on the door.

'Lobna, dear, I should be at the church soon. The new flowers are arriving today. We need to talk about shopping before I go.'

Her sister made a noise that sounded like a grunt.

Mina said, 'I'll bring you some tea.'

The shopping list wasn't long, but it did include two books that Mina had ordered from the Homer Bookshop on Yeni Çarşı Caddesi. One of them was a novel by an Icelandic writer, while the other was about homeopathic treatments for cancer. Lobna didn't comment.

'You'll have to pick up the vegetables too, so it will be a lot to carry,' Mina said. 'Which is why you must bring it to me at the church. That way I can come home with it all when I've finished.'

'I wasn't planning on going to church,' Lobna said. 'It . . . Well, I'm not ready. Not since Father Esposito was killed.'

'You don't have to stay. Just give me the bags. Then you can come home,' Mina said. 'I'd like to do the shopping myself, Lobna, but I can't do everything. If you do it, it will really help me.'

Mina had been creating flower arrangements for St Anthony's for twenty years. It was a lot of work and sometimes it took her more than one day. But she'd never let anyone help her.

Lobna sat up in bed. 'Of course I'll do it,' she said. 'Just give me an hour or so to wake up and get myself ready.'

Mina smiled. 'I'll go once I've washed up,' she said. 'I'll see you there.' She kissed her. 'And thank you, Lobna. I do so love you, you know.'

'You again?'

İkmen turned and found himself looking into the face of Father da Mosto.

When he'd left Fabrizio Leon's hotel, he'd received two phone calls, one from Kerim Gürsel and the other from Süleyman.

Kerim was supposed to be off, but had apparently spent the previous night in his car, parked outside the Amara sisters' house. He'd taken what İkmen had told him outside İrini Mavroyeni's place, which had been pure speculation, rather seriously. Apparently now Mina Amara had gone out. İkmen had told Kerim to go home and get some sleep. Then Süleyman had called demanding he speak to him immediately and in person. He'd sounded angry, which made İkmen wonder what he'd done wrong. But he'd told him he'd meet him, although why Süleyman wanted to see him amid the vast concrete wastes of Taksim Square he couldn't imagine. Maybe he wanted to talk about their new commissioner. And in the meantime, here was this arsey priest . . .

'Yes, sir,' he said. 'Me again.'

'What do you want?' the priest said.

Knowing that Father da Mosto was Venetian made İkmen

smile inside. With his haughty attitude and long, thin face, he looked like a caricature of one of that great city's doges.

But it was a fair question.

'Just killing a bit of time,' he said. Süleyman had called him from the offices of Beyoğlu Municipality, which wasn't far away, but he'd needed to finish something.

'Well, if you'd refrain from smoking . . .'

'Oh, sorry. Sorry.' İkmen had been smoking without thought. One wasn't supposed to light up in front of the church. He put his cigarette out on the ground and Father da Mosto tutted, then walked away.

İkmen was about to leave himself when he saw someone looking at him from the front door of the church. It was the old priest, who was, if he remembered correctly, Polish.

'Can I help you?' İkmen said.

The elderly priest smiled. He either hadn't heard or he didn't understand.

İkmen walked towards him. 'Do you want to speak to me?' he said in English.

'Oh?' The priest shook a finger at him. 'Oh, no, thank you,' he said. 'I am . . . I hear Father da Mosto. I come to see . . .' He laughed nervously.

'Well if you want to speak to me, then do feel that you can,' İkmen said.

The old priest began to back up into the church. 'That won't be necessary,' he said. 'No . . .'

As İkmen walked out onto the street, Kerim Gürsel called.

There were no guests. The hotel was finally entirely empty. Even the Japanese had finally succumbed to fear of terrorist attack. Fabrizio Leon helped himself to a large glass of whisky from his own bar and tossed it down his throat. Then he had another. As he poured a third glass, he comforted himself with the thought that he wasn't like Silvio, who needed to drink all the time.

Silvio! How were things ever going to be right with him again? They weren't. In reality, even if Maryam had lived, his relationship with Silvio was over. Maryam had been pregnant, by him. And in fairness, Fabrizio had to admit that had he been in Silvio's position, he would have felt exactly the same. Silvio had threatened to kill him. It was possible he'd make good on that.

Fabrizio had tried to explain himself, but he knew he'd made a mess of it. Maryam had been an extraordinary child. Bright and funny, she'd been like a favourite niece. Then she'd become a beautiful woman and he hadn't been able to stop himself. That was his fault.

And yet she hadn't been what Silvio had said she was. She hadn't been a saint. In the early days she'd gone to church to meet Fabrizio. That her attendance made her father happy was a by-product of her love for *him*. And it had been love. They hadn't slept together for three years. He'd waited until she was ready. When did he ever do that for any other woman? Silvio had waited for Ayşegül, but he'd also gone off with İrini Mavroyeni when he became frustrated. Fabrizio himself hadn't lived as a monk during that three-year period, but . . .

That Maryam should be İrini's daughter was farcical. All the time they'd been at school together, none of them had taken much notice of İrini because she was a Greek slut. Fabrizio had had her once, but then he'd had a lot of the girls. Only Mina and Lobna Amara had escaped him, mainly because he had always felt they were too good for him. Poor sad Mina had mooned after Silvio for a while, but he'd never been interested in her. He'd never been interested in anyone back at school. And as Lobna was beautiful, so her sister was plain. A plain frustrated bitch. She'd never liked him and the feeling had always been mutual.

Another thing he'd never done was have a child – as far as he knew. Only Maryam's child, and that was dead, murdered along with its mother. His heart had broken when he'd first been told. But he'd kept his emotions in check because he'd had to. It had hurt him, of course it had. But what to do about it, eh?

Fabrizio finished his drink, put his coat on and left the Dondolo. When all else failed, and although he didn't always believe it to be true, there was always prayer. Or sometimes there was only prayer.

# Chapter 28

Marek Wojtulewicz had never been able to speak to the woman. His lack of facility with languages had always held him back. His English was adequate, but she didn't speak that, as far as he knew, and his Italian was poor, while his Turkish was basic at best. He sometimes wondered why God had chosen to send him to a place where he could barely communicate.

Luckily Katerina Hanım was very patient with him. Father Colombo and the now sadly late Father Esposito were unfailingly kind. Only Father da Mosto was difficult. He'd even been scolded by the Bishop for his behaviour, but nothing made him change. Apparently he believed himself some sort of aristocrat. Silly man.

The woman made beautiful floral arrangements. Out of respect for Father Esposito, these new ones were more muted than usual. Lilies, evergreens, white carnations and dark blue irises. There were also white tulips and even a few very rare black ones. So many wonderful flowers!

As he sat, apparently deep in thought, Father Wojtulewicz wondered whether she knew he was watching her. Was that why she hadn't attempted to retrieve what she had hidden? In order to reassure himself that he hadn't forgotten, he felt for the silver top of the thing as it leaned against his leg.

The young priest would surely have been aware that Kerim Gürsel had passed on what he had told him to İkmen, but he said nothing about it. Then again, İkmen thought, how did anyone, much less a priest, open a conversation about cross-dressing?

İkmen had turned up in the concrete wasteland of Taksim to find that Süleyman hadn't yet arrived. He'd been sitting on one of the barriers at the top of the stairs leading down to Taksim Metro station when Father Colombo had come along.

'On Saturday I will go with Father Esposito's body to Sicily,' the young man said. 'It is sad, but it is an honour.'

'He was well liked,' İkmen said.

'Is that why his death is such a . . . a puzzle?'

İkmen smiled. He had a point. Finding the killer of someone who was apparently a friend to everyone was difficult.

'Yes,' he said. 'That's certainly part of the problem.'

Father Colombo sat down. 'Why do you come here?' he asked.

'Taksim? To meet a colleague,' İkmen said. 'I wouldn't come here for pleasure.'

The young man frowned.

'I find it depressing these days,' İkmen said. 'Too much concrete.'

'We too have too much in Italy.'

'It is a worldwide scourge,' İkmen said.

Father Colombo laughed. 'I know. But we must be happy sometimes with small things.'

İkmen looked around the bleak, weakly sunlit square and shrugged. Why did religious people always do the grateful-for-small-mercies thing? To his way of thinking that just made for false contentment, which led, ultimately, to a sheep-like acceptance of the unacceptable. But he didn't say anything.

'Today we have new flowers in St Anthony's,' Father Colombo said. 'For Father Esposito. Normally the flowers change every two weeks. But this time we do it to honour a dead brother. It is a small thing but it brings a lot of comfort, you know?'

İkmen said nothing.

'In the spring, we have very bright flowers. But because of Father Esposito's death, this time they will be pale,' the priest continued. 'The lady who arranges them—'

'Mina Amara.'

'Yes,' he said. 'How do you know that?'

But İkmen didn't answer him. Instead he took his phone out of his pocket and called Süleyman. 'Don't meet me in Taksim, meet me at St Anthony's.'

Süleyman, who had just walked past the church, said, 'Why?'

But İkmen cut the connection. He stood up.

The priest, who had been rather confused by his actions said, 'Is there something wrong, Inspector?'

İkmen didn't know, and so he only said, 'Maybe.'

But what İrini Mavroyeni had told him about her dream, as well as his latest conversation with Fabrizio Leon, was at the front of his mind again – as was the fact that Kerim Gürsel was still agitated by İkmen's late-night theorising. He, it seemed, was now following Lobna Amara.

Mina saw him, but she ignored him. Fabrizio was used to that. He didn't care. She was doing her flower-arranging; he'd come to pray. There was room for both of them.

Before he sat down, he nodded to the old Polish priest, who was apparently contemplating the vaulted church ceiling. There was no point trying to speak to him, even if he'd wanted to. His Italian was bad and his Turkish laughable. Fabrizio knelt and bowed his head. Praying didn't come easily to him. But what else could he do? If God couldn't help him save his hotel, he didn't know who could. He closed his eyes and began to silently beseech, like a pathetic supplicant who wanted to win the lottery so he could have a new car. He made himself cringe.

Unable to concentrate, he became aware of noises behind him, but he didn't look up until he heard Mina speak.

'Oh Lobna,' he heard her say. 'Put those heavy bags down!'

Now that made sense. The stick belonged to her sister, so if she had taken it for some reason, maybe she now wanted her sister to think she'd found it in the church.

But she wasn't doing anything. The two women were talking, quietly, in front of the altar. That was where she'd hidden the stick, pushing it underneath the altar with her foot when she'd come to take out the dead flowers. Had she seen him? He didn't know. He thought not.

Father Wojtulewicz looked around the church. Not many people were in. The man who had nodded to him was praying in the last row of pews. The priest had recognised him as the man who had been taken away by the police because he'd had an affair with that poor girl who had died. Maryam had been a true visionary. He didn't know what the Blessed Virgin had said to her or what she had said to the Blessed Virgin, but he felt in his marrow that it was true. He'd seen the girl up at the Golden Gate. He'd watched her eyes light up with the power of God.

When he turned his gaze back to the women, the flower-arranger had indeed started to pull up the altar cloth and look beneath. As soon as he saw confusion cross her face, he stood up and walked over to her.

'A dream.'

'Or maybe reality,' İkmen said. 'I don't know and neither did İrini, and that's the point.'

'İrini said she thought it might be a dream or it might be reality?' Süleyman said.

'No, she thought it was a dream.'

'So . . .'

'Yes, that's my interpretation,' İkmen said. He was becoming agitated now. Hadn't Süleyman worked alongside him long enough to know he didn't say these things lightly?

'And yet according to you,' Süleyman said, 'it wasn't Lobna Amara that İrini saw in her dream, but her sister Mina.'

'She thought it was Lobna, then that it was Mina.'

'Who are very different women,' Süleyman said. 'Çetin, this is rakı talking. Maybe, *maybe* Lobna Amara was in Sulukule the night Maryam de Mango died, but we have no evidence of that. And Mina – why?'

'I don't know,' İkmen said.

'From what you've told me about İrini, she went to school with the Amara sisters and procured an abortion for Lobna. No other involvement with Mina. See what I mean?'

He realised too late that Father Colombo was still by İkmen's side. Why had he mentioned Lobna Amara's abortion?

There was an awkward silence, which fortunately the priest ended.

'Women have abortions even though we may find it a sin,' he said. 'It is life.'

'Father . . .'

But he looked away, his face shadowed by a frown.

They stopped outside the gates of the basilica of St Anthony. İkmen said, 'Sergeant Gürsel is inside.'

Süleyman shook his head. Kerim Gürsel had apparently been so struck by İkmen's theories about İrini Mavroyeni and the Amara sisters that he'd sat up all night in his car watching their house. And yet there was no evidence against either of them. There wasn't even, as far as Süleyman was concerned, a motive. No one had known about Maryam's affair with Fabrizio Leon, except possibly the man's confessor, who was dead.

'Çetin, I need to speak to you about something really important,' Süleyman said. 'I need to speak to you alone and—'

'I can't tell you why,' Father Colombo interrupted, 'but I think that maybe Mina Hanım knows more than she says.'

Completely focused on the priest, İkmen said, 'What does she know?'

The priest ushered them off the street, through the church gates and into the basilica.

'I can't say . . .'

Süleyman shook his head. 'Confession.'

'She came to me once only,' the priest said.

'Mehmet Bey,' İkmen said, 'the penalty for breaking the Seal of the Confessional is excommunication. What do you want Father Colombo to do?'

'Mina Amara knew things she shouldn't have known,' the priest said. 'And that is all I can tell you. I have already said too much.'

Mina snatched the silver-topped cane out of the old priest's hands.

'Oh, so I left it here in church!' Lobna said. She smiled.

'Yes, dear.'

'No,' the priest said.

Mina couldn't remember his name. All she knew about him was that he was Polish and hardly ever spoke. Until now.

'You put it to underneath the altar when you come to take out dead flowers,' he said in very poor Turkish.

'No I didn't.'

'I saw you.'

Lobna's smile faded. 'Mina, what's he saying?'

'Nothing.'

'You lose your stick before Father Esposito is murdered I think,' Father Wojtulewicz said to Lobna.

'About two weeks ago, yes . . .'

'Lobna, I think you should go home now,' Mina said. 'You have your stick now.'

'Two times the police have searched this church now and still they don't find your stick,' he said.

'They're incompetent. Lobna, here . . .'

She tried to hand the stick over, but Lobna wouldn't take it. Had she realised? Mina looked down from the altar into the nave. The church was quiet. She said to the priest, 'You don't know anything.'

'I know you put the stick under the altar,' he said. 'I do not know why you do that. But I know a wrong thing when I see it.'

Lobna saw Mina twist the stick's silver handle. 'No!' she hissed.

Mina looked into her sister's eyes. Only the two of them and their father had known that this cane had a dual purpose.

'We have to stay together,' she said.


The old priest and the Amara women were having a conversation in front of the altar. Kerim couldn't hear what it was about. It seemed a bit emotional, but that was understandable given the fact that they'd all been through some bad experiences in recent days.

Why had what İrini Mavroyeni had said, as well as how Çetin Bey had interpreted it, affected him so deeply? Çetin Bey's mother had been a witch, but Kerim had never been convinced by sorcery in the past, in spite of Pembe Hanım's addiction to fortune-tellers.

Had it been because İrini had been confused by her dream, or vision?

Alcoholics often blacked out after they'd been drinking, but sometimes they regained consciousness in the middle of a blackout. Only for a second, maybe even less. But Çetin Bey had experienced such a thing himself, and so it was his contention that maybe İrini did see a woman when she came round briefly on the night Maryam died. A woman who would have been in Sulukule at the right time to put her in the frame for the girl's death.

A grunting sound from in front of the altar captured Kerim's attention. He looked up and saw that the old priest was now bent double. He looked as if he was in pain.

Kerim stood up and began to make his way forward.

Çetin İkmen stopped just inside the church doorway. He couldn't feel anything, but he could see some of the small votive offerings in front of the statue of St Anthony shaking ever so slightly.

Süleyman was impatient to get inside. 'What is it?'

İkmen waited until it had stopped and then said, 'Tremor.'

'Oh.'

But it wasn't just a tremor. As he looked down the nave towards the altar, everything seemed normal. Kerim Gürsel standing up from his seat in one of the pews, people praying with their heads bowed, a girl looking up at the statue of St Anthony, the two women with their flowers at the altar and the old priest bent at the waist.

But there was a charge in the air.

Was it because the tiny tremor had thankfully not developed into an earthquake?

İkmen knew that was possible.

But he also knew what blood smelled like.

And then he saw it.

The other sister, the one who didn't arrange the flowers, tried to catch him but she couldn't. He looked up into the face of his attacker and found that he could only speak in Polish.

'You killed him,' he said. 'It was you . . .'

She didn't understand. She kicked him.

Kerim threw himself across the priest's body while Süleyman kicked the weapon down into the nave.

For a moment İkmen couldn't take his eyes off it. A sword. It was a *sword*.

'Call an ambulance!'

He saw a face he recognised: Fabrizio Leon. He saw him take his phone out of his pocket.

Kerim said, 'Better be quick.'

He had both hands on the wound in the priest's abdomen, providing compression. But blood was pouring out from between his fingers.

'He'll go into shock.'

İkmen bent down and looked into the priest's eyes. 'Stay awake, Father,' he said. 'Look at me and stay with me.'

He wasn't aware of the women any more. Had they run? He didn't know. Sounds were happening around him but they didn't mean anything. Only this old man's blue eyes. And his blood. Kerim's hands were deep red.

İkmen took his jacket off and folded it into a pad. He pushed Kerim out of the way and placed the pad on the priest's abdomen. Then he leaned down on it with all his weight. The old man groaned.

'Look at me!' İkmen repeated. Then, remembering that the man didn't speak Turkish, he reiterated it in English.

The blue eyes gazed up into his and he could tell that there was still light behind them.

'That's it! That's it!'

If he could engage his attention, he stood a chance.

'You're going to be all right,' he said. 'Look into my eyes and keep with me. I know you can't talk, but say something, in your head. A piece of poetry, film titles, a prayer . . .'

Keeping the mind active.

The eyes moved slightly and İkmen smiled. 'That's it.'

It was as if, for as long as he pushed down on his jacket and looked into the old man's eyes, a bubble sealed them both in. İkmen felt his breathing even out and his heart rate subside. Time became irrelevant. If he just kept the compression on . . .

He was only slightly aware of something or someone touching him. But he was completely unaware of the moment his jacket could absorb no more liquid.

Eventually, just as the ambulance arrived, Kerim Gürsel pulled İkmen's bloodied hands and arms away from the dead priest. He didn't think any of them could bear to watch him trying to bring a man back from the dead any longer.

When İkmen finally got to his feet, he felt the priest's blood drip down his fingers and onto the floor. He looked at the two women. Lobna Amara was crying, while her sister, handcuffed to Süleyman, looked up into the great vaulted ceiling of the church of St Anthony and screamed.

# Chapter 29

'She had nothing to do with it. All she did was lie,' Lobna said.

'All?' Süleyman raised an eyebrow.

'She knew I left the house the night Maryam . . .' She put her head down. 'She saw me go. But she didn't know where. I didn't tell her anything.'

'So when I asked you both where you were . . .'

'She covered for me.'

'Did you ask her to?'

'No.'

'So how did you know that she would?'

Lobna didn't answer.

'Did you discuss it?' he asked.

'No.'

She'd refused legal representation, and so the only other person in the room was Omer Mungun, who, detained at Beyoğlu Municipality obtaining documents that had proved unintelligible, had missed the incident at St Anthony's.

'I killed Maryam,' Lobna said. 'I did it deliberately and in the full knowledge that what I was doing was wrong.'

They helped each other wash the blood from their hands and arms. İkmen's jacket, which was beyond salvation anyway, had been bagged up by forensic investigators. Kerim produced a nail brush and handed it to the inspector, who scrubbed his hands until they were red.

'You've met Commissioner Ozer,' İkmen said. 'What's he like?'

Before they could begin interviewing Mina Amara, İkmen had to go and report to his new superior. Lobna Amara was already being interrogated by Süleyman, but her sister had yet to be examined by a doctor to determine whether she was fit for questioning. Lobna, according to Süleyman, had come through her medical examination with no problems. And she was the one who was ill.

'I've not met him,' Kerim said. 'I've only seen him.'

'And?'

Kerim was still shaking. İkmen wasn't sure the sergeant would be up to supporting him when he interviewed Mina.

'Conventional,' Kerim said.

İkmen knew that for Kerim that was an insult.

'I see.' He ran his hands underneath the tap one last time and then dried them on a paper towel.

'Do you think he'll appreciate seeing me in this state?' İkmen's shirt was stiff with blood.

'Can you change?' Kerim said.

İkmen put his hand in his pocket and took out his wallet.

'Go and ask Sergeant Yıldız to pick us up a couple of shirts,' he said. 'He's down in the squad room.'

'Sir.'

Kerim left. İkmen looked at himself in the mirror over the sink and wondered whether he'd ever be able to get the mark of sadness and fear out of his eyes. The old priest had died from a single wound inflicted by a woman who, from İkmen's vantage point, had simply reacted. To what, he didn't know. If Mina Amara chose not to speak, or she lied, would he ever know?

And then there was the weapon that had killed the priest. A sword. A short one, but a sword. Just as the fortune-teller had warned him.

\* \* \*

'I left the house, crossed Tarlabaşı Bulvarı and walked down İstiklal,' she said. 'I took the Tünel to Karaköy, crossed to Eminönü and then got the number 34 bus to Topkapı. I met Maryam in front of the Mihrimah Mosque.'

'At what time was this?' Süleyman asked.

'She was supposed to meet her mother somewhere between eight and nine,' she said. 'I got to the Mihrimah at eight, but she didn't arrive until nearly nine. She'd had difficulty getting away. She had a big bunch of flowers with her that she'd bought at the bus station. They were for her mother.'

'Did you have her mobile phone number?'

Lobna shook her head. 'She didn't give it to me. I didn't think.'

'So you waited.'

'Yes. I thought she might be late if Ayşegül wanted to know where she was going. I didn't know whether Silvio was at home, but if he wasn't, there was a chance she'd be unable to explain herself sufficiently well for Ayşegül to let her go easily.'

'For which you feigned sympathy.'

'I *was* sympathetic,' she said.

'You went out with the intention of killing her,' Süleyman said.

'Yes, I did.'

'And yet you had sympathy for her too.'

'Yes.'

'How does that work?'

She shook her head. 'I didn't hate Maryam. It was what she represented that I hated. I still do.'

'And what does she represent to you, Miss Amara?'

'My own failure,' she said.

The new shirt was too big. Most clothes were. But at least Kerim looked fairly decent. By contrast, the man sitting in front of them was smartly, if plainly, dressed.

'I don't intend to keep you for long,' Commissioner Ozer said. 'I know you have much to do.'

Neither of them spoke.

'But I felt I needed to introduce myself to you,' Ozer continued. 'Especially given that my predecessor left so suddenly.'

Teker had been pushed and they all knew it. İkmen could see it in Ozer's face. He'd have to learn to lie better if he wanted to stay in his new job for any length of time.

'I appreciate how distressing this must be.'

'Yes, sir.'

Ozer looked down at the paperwork on his desk. Was he afraid to make eye contact?

'Sadly, there is more,' he said. 'I'm afraid I have to tell you that ex-Commissioner Teker is now under investigation for corrupt practice.'

İkmen looked at Kerim Gürsel, who widened his eyes. Was this what Süleyman had been trying to tell him before the incident at St Anthony's?

'This must be disappointing for you, and I imagine you may also feel duped . . .'

'I never witnessed anything that even so much as hinted at corruption during Commissioner Teker's tenure,' İkmen said. 'And I'll stand up and say that in front of anyone.'

'You may well have to,' the Commissioner said.

He paused for a moment. 'I applaud your enthusiasm. And let us all pray for a fair and just outcome.'

'You do what you please,' İkmen said.

The Commissioner looked up. 'Excuse me?'

'You can pray if you want to,' İkmen said. 'I'll just get my evidence in order.'

Ozer had to know what İkmen was about. Everyone knew he was an atheist. Everyone also knew that he wouldn't pretend to be religious in order to advance himself. And Teker had told him that knives were out for him. This was no surprise. Even if the sudden urge to slip his head into a career-killing noose had come as a shock. But it was out now. This Ozer looked as if he might die from the sadness that the idea of a soul without God had brought to mind, while Kerim, aghast, was a strange shade of white.

'But in the meantime,' İkmen said, 'Sergeant Gürsel and I have to go and conduct an interview.' He smiled. 'Very nice to meet you, sir.'

He left the room, pulling Kerim Gürsel after him.

Uniformed police had set up a temporary incident room in the priests' apartment, where they took statements from anyone who had been inside the church when Father Wojtulewicz had been killed. The only person admitted into the area who had not been in the church when the incident took place was the Bishop.

Juan-Maria Montoya, as a good son of Mexico, made vast amounts of hot chocolate, which he distributed to everyone and anyone who wanted it. The housekeeper, Katerina, cuddled her cup to her chest after she had given her statement. Father Colombo cried.

But the person the Bishop felt most sorry for had chosen to sit alone in the basilica. Fabrizio Leon had answered the police officers' questions in a reasoned and organised manner. But then he'd gone and sat outside, where he remained. Not talking to anyone, crying or even blinking very often, he just sat on the steps leading up to the church and stared straight ahead.

Bishop Montoya didn't know exactly what had happened, except that poor Father Wojtulewicz had been killed, apparently by the woman who arranged St Anthony's flowers. Katerina had told him that she was Mr Leon's ex-wife's sister. First his lover had died, then his confessor, now an in-law . . . Montoya looked at Leon again before going back to the kitchen to make more hot chocolate.

'Why did Maryam ask you to accompany her to İrini Mavroyeni's house?' Süleyman asked. 'Did you know her well?'

'No,' she said. 'But when Maryam's visions began, and knowing that I was ill, Silvio invited me to come and see her at the Golden Gate.'

'And your sister, Mina?'

'Only I was invited,' she said. 'Mina just came too. She does that.'

'She follows what you do?'

She turned her head away for a moment, then said, 'I didn't know that this mother Maryam was going to see was İrini Mavroyeni. I'd been to school with her and hadn't thought about her for years. It came as a shock.'

'Because she'd helped you to procure an abortion when you were fifteen?'

She looked up. 'Who told you that?'

'Is it true?'

He was brutal. How had she ever found him in the least attractive?

'Yes.'

'And so you saw İrini . . .'

'No,' she said. 'Maryam knocked on the door – a wretched shack, and not the one I remembered – but no one answered. We tried for about fifteen minutes until Maryam decided that İrini must've changed her mind. She was sad. But it was a warm evening and so I said I'd take her somewhere for a drink.'

'Surely you were thinking of old Sulukule . . .'

'I was thinking that she was carrying my ex-husband's child,' she said. 'And that it wasn't fair.'

'Sir . . .'

'We think about the job in hand, Kerim Bey,' İkmen said as they stood outside the interview room. Mina Amara was already inside. They were waiting for the custody officer to come and open up.

'Sir, what you said . . .'

İkmen took his arm and led him away from the door, in the opposite direction to the custody officer's post.

'Kerim,' he said, 'Teker warned me. I've a target on my back. Now I have plans to deal with that. Leave it to me. I will do everything I can to protect you.'

'That's not what's worrying me!'

'It should,' he said. 'You have your two ladies to think about. Provided they don't somehow work out a way to take away the benefits I have accrued over so many years, I'll be all right. But now that Teker has gone, I can't carry on. This has been coming for a long time. I think you know that.'

Kerim looked crushed.

İkmen put a hand on his shoulder. 'Come on,' he said, 'Miss Mina awaits with a story that I feel will be both tragic and riveting.'

'I cleaned the knife and put it back in the block beside the fridge,' Lobna said.

'You took a knife from your kitchen with the specific intention of killing Maryam de Mango.'

'I did.'

'Did your sister know—'

'My sister knew nothing!' she said. 'I went out, I killed another human being and then I came home.'

'Where was your sister?'

'I don't know. I went to bed. I was tired. I went to sleep.'

She'd slept after killing someone. How was that possible? Süleyman had killed, in the line of duty. He hadn't been able to eat or sleep for such a long time he thought he might go mad. He still had nightmares. He suspected he always would. Taking a life was like that. It marked you. Forever.

'Tell me how you knew Maryam was pregnant. She and your ex-husband, Mr Leon, had been very careful not to allow anyone to know about their affair.'

'Oh, I knew about it,' she said.

'The affair?'

'Years ago,' she said. 'When Maryam started coming to church. I could see them looking at each other. I knew. I also knew that he'd never be faithful to her.'

'Didn't you want to tell the girl's father?'

'Silvio is as bad as Fabrizio,' she said.

'For Maryam's sake.'

'She was a little fool.'

'And what about when she got sick?' Süleyman said. 'What did you think about Maryam then?'

'I was sorry for her,' she said.

'And when she recovered?'

'I didn't believe she was a saint. Especially when she began thinking she was one.'

'So why did you go to the Golden Gate?'

'Silvio asked me, and I thought it might be interesting to see whether Maryam and my husband were still together now that she was all but beatified. Of course Silvio had told the saint that I too had leukaemia, and so we bonded over cancer. I noticed she still looked at Fabrizio like she was a bitch on heat, so I assumed it was still going on. Then she told me she was pregnant.'

'Why?'

'I don't think she could stop herself,' she said. 'I think she saw it as proof that she was cured. Proof of her sainthood. She told me to keep it a secret, and I did.'

'Did she tell you who the baby's father was?'

'No, but she didn't need to.'

'How did her pregnancy make you feel?' Süleyman asked.

'Feel? A failure,' she said. 'As I told you. I couldn't have children after that abortion I had at fifteen. I didn't know that until I'd been married to Fabrizio for a few years. It was one of the reasons he divorced me. Or so he said. Between them, my husband and Silvio de Mango wrecked my life.'

'Silvio . . .'

'If you know I had an abortion, then you surely have to know that he was the father of my aborted child,' she said.

'Did he know?'

'No! Nice girls don't tell,' she said. 'Only İrini knew, and she wasn't saying.'

'How do you know?'

'Because I told her that if she did, I'd cut her. She knew I meant it.'

And so did Süleyman. Here was a woman who had, admittedly, suffered, but who also had an unusual amount of ice in her veins.

'Women in this country keep their honour or they're lost,' Lobna said. 'Silvio never knew and still doesn't. He's been spared that pain.'

'I think he is suffering now,' Süleyman said.

'His saint is dead, yes. Although now he can worship her without the vision of her pregnant belly forever in his mind. I think it will work out well for him. Silvio de Mango always wanted a perfect woman, and now he's got one.'

'What do you mean?'

'I mean he had a perfect woman in Ayşegül but he didn't

recognise it,' she said. 'When they were first together, she did everything he wanted except sleep with him until they were married. But the fool couldn't be content with that and so he screwed İrini and got her pregnant and complicated everybody's lives. If I'd had a child with Fabrizio I could have put up with anything. Even his infidelity. But I wasn't even given that.'

Her bitterness hurt. It soured everything around it, making even her crime pale into insignificance.

'Did you kill Father Esposito?' Süleyman asked.

'No, I did not,' she said. 'What kind of monster kills a priest?'

'I didn't know what else to do.'

İkmen saw real distress on Mina Amara's face. 'I didn't mean to kill him,' she said. 'I just wanted him to stop talking about it.'

'Stop talking about what, Miss Mina?' İkmen asked. 'I'm sorry, I'm going to have to ask you to be as precise as you can.'

'Yes. Yes,' she said, 'of course. The Polish father had found Lobna's walking stick underneath the altar.'

'Where you put it?'

'Yes,' she said. 'I wanted everything to go back to normal, and I thought that if I "found" Lobna's stick for her, that would happen.'

'Why would that happen?' İkmen asked. 'Can you clarify it for us?'

'Do I have to?'

Kerim Gürsel said, 'I beg your pardon?'

Although she had been deemed physically fit enough to withstand interrogation, İkmen had wondered about her mental state as soon as he'd seen her in the interview room. As she'd watched the two officers come in, she'd laughed. But then people often did laugh inappropriately when they were nervous. Now he wondered whether it had signalled something more profound than just anxiety.

'Miss Mina, a man has died today,' İkmen said. 'We have to find out why.'

'Oh.'

'You do see that, don't you?'

'Oh yes,' she said. 'Yes, I see that.'

But she didn't offer any more information. Her mouth set in a straight line, she didn't even look as if she was going to speak again.

# Chapter 30

Fabrizio Leon's salvation, when it came, arrived in the form of Ayşegül de Mango. She'd been in the Balık Pazar when she'd heard that a priest had been attacked in St Anthony's. She'd finished her shopping and then had a cup of coffee in Nevizade Sokak before she'd gone up onto İstiklal Caddesi and walked past the church, where she'd seen Fabrizio sitting on the steps, staring into space.

They didn't speak to each other once as Ayşegül led Fabrizio back to his hotel. The place was entirely empty, which was shocking even when the obvious lack of tourists in town was taken into account.

Fabrizio poured himself a drink from the bar and then told her about Father Wojtulewicz.

'Mina?'

'Yes,' he said. 'I've no idea why she did it. I didn't know that that stick Lobna uses can turn into a sword. All I knew about it was that it had belonged to her father. Why did you take me away from the church?'

'Because you looked ill,' Ayşegül said.

'Aren't you furious with me for defiling your daughter?'

'Yes,' she said. 'But I'm also sorry for you. I've been sorry for you for years.'

'Why?'

'Because you've always been a slave to your libido,' she said. 'When you came on to me all those years ago at your own

299

wedding, I knew it was not because you loved me but because you were driven. I was young then and, I guess, desirable. You had to try.'

He shrugged. He knew it was true.

'And I knew that Maryam was pregnant probably before she did,' Ayşegül said. 'Don't ask me how, but I'd thought she'd been seeing someone for a long time. Silvio was so happy when she began going to church such a lot, but I knew there was another reason.'

'Did you suspect me?'

'Not until recently,' she said. 'I went to St Anthony's a couple of times to see if I could spot the object of Maryam's affections. I saw a few young men but I never saw her with any of them in church or on the street. I didn't become obsessive about it, but that was how I missed you. Maybe I should have tried harder.'

'You've been a brilliant mother, you know,' Fabrizio said.

'Really?' She laughed. 'So why did Maryam try to drive a wedge between her father and me by telling lies? Why is my younger son a bonzai addict? My daughter a repressed bigot?'

'You've had a hard life, Ayşegül,' Fabrizio said. 'I say this with love for the man, but Silvio is difficult. Your family rejected you when you fell for him; his father hated you.'

'So much he made himself die,' she said.

Fabrizio smiled. 'He was a terrible old man. I remember him well. Mad.'

'Like his son.'

They looked at each other for a moment, then Fabrizio said, 'Mina and Lobna have been taken in for questioning.'

'Mina, yes, but Lobna?'

He shook his head. 'I don't know why,' he said. 'I swear to you that Lobna never heard about my affair with Maryam from me. But seeing her with Mina in the church, I had this feeling she was involved.'

'In Maryam's death? How?'

'I don't know,' he said.

'I saw them talking when I went to see Maryam once or twice at the Golden Gate.'

'About leukaemia, yes.'

'Do you know that for certain?' Ayşegül said. 'Did you listen in?'

'No.'

'Then you don't know,' she said.

They lapsed into silence again for a while until Ayşegül broke it with 'You know I can never forgive you for what you did to Maryam, don't you?'

He put his head down.

'But I still love you as a friend and I always will. You know, Fabrizio, Silvio has hidden Maryam's body somewhere . . .'

He looked up. 'God!'

She shook her head. 'I don't know what to do.'


'I followed Lobna,' Mina said.

'The night Maryam de Mango died?'

'Yes.'

'Why did you follow her? She's a grown woman,' İkmen said.

'Yes, but she's ill,' Mina replied. 'Also when she left the house she told me not to wait up for her. That's not like my sister. I was worried.'

'Tell me how you followed her?'

'She walked to Tünel and so did I. She got into the first carriage of the funicular and I got into the second. She walked across the Galata Bridge, which surprised me. Then she got a number 34 bus to Topkapı bus station.'

'Did you get on the same bus?'

'No, I grabbed a taxi and asked the driver to follow the bus. When she got off at Topkapı, she stood and waited at the entrance to the Mihrimah Mosque. She waited a long time and kept looking at her watch. At nearly nine o'clock, Maryam appeared.'

İkmen said, 'Why did you think they were meeting?'

'I had no idea. To be honest, I was confused as to why she hadn't told me about the meeting. I almost approached them. But then I thought that Lobna might be cross if she thought I'd been spying on her.'

She looked sad.

'She's always there,' Lobna said. 'I suspected she listened in to my conversation with my ex-husband when he came to see me. He was being pathetic, as I thought. Talking about wanting to confess to something he wouldn't tell me about. I told him to either do it or not do it, but he insisted on agonising about it. I don't go in for confession. He left. But then Mina was on my case immediately.'

'What do you mean, on your case?' Süleyman asked.

'Telling me what to do,' she said. 'What to eat, when to rest, when to go out, come back . . . I could go on.'

'She clearly worries about you.'

'Oh yes,' she said. 'I'm not saying her devotion isn't sincere. It is. But it's also desperate. When I went back home after my divorce, Mina was delighted. We were both at home again as we'd been as children. Her marriage had been unhappy. Her ex-husband had taken their daughter to America and Mina was lonely. She knew nothing about Maryam, I swear to you.'

'Lobna and Maryam went to this shack in Sulukule,' Mina said. 'Like an old gecekondu, you know? Barely standing. I thought maybe they were visiting a gypsy for some sort of occult healing. But then I heard Maryam calling İrini's name through the door. They called for a long time before they gave up and left. Of course I remembered that İrini Mavroyeni had lived in Sulukule.

302

I had to find out whether the person they'd come to see was the İrini I remembered from school.'

'What did you do?' İkmen said.

'What they didn't. I forced the door and went inside. At first I thought the place was empty, but then I saw her underneath a pile of rubbish on her bed. She was drunk, but I recognised her immediately.'

'Did she recognise you?'

'I don't know. She opened her eyes once. But she was out of it. She just made noises, she couldn't talk. So I left.'

'What did you do then?'

'I couldn't see Maryam and Lobna. I was confused. Why had they come to see İrini? She'd been a bad girl at school, and later I heard she'd become a prostitute. What did they want with her? I felt bad about it, and confused. I wondered why Lobna hadn't told me what she was doing. When I left İrini, I just walked. I came across the two of them in an alleyway behind Sulukule Caddesi.'

'What were they doing?'

'Talking. Laughing. Everything seemed fine.'

'Did you approach them?' Süleyman asked.

'No.'

'Why not?'

She shrugged. 'I didn't want Lobna to know I'd followed her, I guess. I know she doesn't always like the attention I give her.'

'What did you talk about?' Süleyman said.

'About İrini mainly,' Lobna said. 'Maryam wanted to know about her. This was natural; she was her mother. I told her İrini had always been a bit wild.' She paused. 'Then I told her about the abortion.'

She closed her eyes for a moment. 'She was horrified, of course she was! I don't know whether she believed me when I told her that her father had been the cause of my pain.'

303

'How did she respond?'

'She didn't,' she said. 'Because I stabbed her in the chest. I'd come to do just that and so I did it. I think she died almost immediately.'

There were no tears and not even a suggestion of remorse in her voice.

'Why did you cut her open?' Süleyman asked. 'Surely you must have been afraid that someone would come and find you with her?'

'No,' she said. 'I didn't really care. I put some of the flowers she'd brought for İrini in her hair at first. I was going to just walk away. But then, as I looked at her lying there, I wanted to see her child and make sure that it too was dead. I didn't hate her.'

'You didn't behave as if you didn't hate her.'

'I opened her up but I couldn't see anything. I cut the uterus but there was just . . . mess. I began to wonder whether she had lied . . . She did lie, you know . . .'

'Yes. But she wasn't lying about her pregnancy,' Süleyman said.

'No . . .' Her eyes began to mist over. 'I went home then,' she said.

'Covered in blood?'

'I don't know. I don't remember. I put my coat on and I walked home. Who even sees a middle-aged woman in this city? Then I went to bed.'


'Maryam collapsed. I couldn't see why because Lobna was obstructing my view.'

'If she collapsed, why didn't you go and help her?' Kerim Gürsel asked. 'And your sister?'

'I saw the blood,' she said. 'My sister had done something terrible. She put flowers in Maryam's hair but then she cut her

304

open. I was so confused. I felt sick. Why would she do something like that? She had to have a reason, which I know about now. She must have been so hurt! But at the time . . .'

'And at no point did you reveal yourself to your sister?'

'No,' she said. 'She was . . . involved. Cutting and looking . . .' She shook her head. 'It was dreadful! I didn't recognise her.' She put a hand up to her mouth.

'What happened then?'

'She left.'

'And what did you do?'

'I left too. I walked back to Topkapı and got the 34. When I arrived home, she was already asleep.'

'You didn't look at Maryam?'

'No!' she said. 'I couldn't! I went home.'

'And in the morning you said nothing to your sister about what you'd witnessed?' İkmen asked.

'No,' she said.

'Why not?'

'Because she's ill. Because she must've had a good reason. Because I love her.'

It was getting late. İkmen needed a break for a cigarette. He decided to suspend the interview for twenty minutes.


'Didn't you ever think to ask Mina why she covered for you?' Süleyman said. 'When we asked you and your sister where you had been that night, you said you'd been at home and she confirmed it.'

'No,' she said.

'You never talked about it? Not once?'

'No. She loves me. She wouldn't want trouble.'

'So she would, theoretically, let you get away with murder?'

Lobna shrugged. 'But I didn't kill Father Esposito. That's got nothing to do with me.'

305

'And Father Wojtulewicz?'

'You were there!' she said. 'You saw what happened!'

'Yes, but I don't understand it,' Süleyman said.

'Nor me. Mina had found my stick. I lost it a couple of weeks ago. It was my father's old sword stick. I was so pleased to see it again. But Father Wojtulewicz had it for some reason, and he was implying things that made Mina anxious. I don't know why she attacked him, but she looked desperate. She was trying to get him to be quiet.'

'Why?'

'I don't know!' she said. 'But she was upset. Very upset.'

She looked down at her hands and then closed her eyes.


Fortified by coffee and nicotine, İkmen began the next phase of his interview with Mina Amara with 'Tell me about Father Esposito. Your sister's walking stick is going to be forensically examined. Bear this in mind.'

He had an idea about that item that Mina Amara quickly confirmed.

'I hit Father Esposito with it.' She began to cry. 'I didn't mean to!'

İkmen let her cry. Now that he was no longer desperate for a cigarette, he felt able to give her, and himself, as much time as necessary. This story was more complicated than even he had envisaged.

He handed her a packet of tissues and waited while she gathered her thoughts.

'My ex-brother-in-law Fabrizio had come to the house in the afternoon,' she said. 'He wanted to talk to Lobna and so I left them alone. But I couldn't help hearing some of their conversation. I didn't listen at the door or anything!'

Which meant that she probably had.

'Carry on,' İkmen said.

'Fabrizio hurt Lobna when he asked for that divorce, and so I've never trusted him.'

'You don't have to justify why you listened, Miss—'

'I didn't listen. I didn't!'

İkmen gave up. If that was how she wanted to remember those events . . .

'All I did hear was that he was guilty about something,' she said.

'Something concerning your sister?'

'I didn't know. Not then,' she said. 'Fabrizio left and I didn't ask Lobna. I didn't want to bother her.'

Or, İkmen thought, let her know that she'd been listening to her conversation.

'Tell me how you came to be in St Anthony's.'

'I went to do some cleaning,' Mina said. 'I arrange the flowers and have done so for years. But the cleaning is a problem. The fathers and Miss Marmara, the housekeeper, are supposed to do it. But men don't clean well and Katerina Hanım has too much to do with the apartment, so it's always a bit dusty and dirty. I like to help out.'

'That's very good of you,' İkmen said. 'So tell me, Miss Mina, do your cleaning duties also involve having a key to the back door of St Anthony's?'

'No,' she said. 'That's lost, as far as I know. Why?'

'We thought for a while that the back door might have been the route Father Esposito's killer took when he or she entered the building, but clearly not.'

'No,' she said.

'Please continue.'

She cleared her throat. How was she, a Christian, going to justify killing two priests?

'No one knows about the cleaning,' she said. 'I don't want the fathers to feel bad. So I just do it. I was aware that the church was closing when Father Esposito came in.'

'Did he know you were there?'

'No,' she said. 'I was about to tell him I was going to leave when Fabrizio came in and walked into the confessional. Father Esposito was snuffing candles out, but when he realised someone wanted confession, he went into the box to do that.'

'What did you do?'

'I'd found Lobna's stick,' Mina said. 'She'd left it somewhere about a week before. I found it in the church, underneath a pew. So I had that and my cleaning materials and I was leaving quietly . . .' She stopped, put her head down and then raised it again. 'I listened, because it was Fabrizio. I wanted to know what guilty thing he'd spoken about to Lobna.'

'And did you find out?' İkmen asked.

'He was Maryam de Mango's lover,' she said. 'I was horrified.'

'Did you think then that that was why your sister had killed Maryam?' Kerim asked.

'I feared it was,' she said. She began to cry. 'I felt so sorry for Lobna! But then as Fabrizio went on cataloguing his crimes, which included making the girl pregnant, I became more and more angry. I found it hard not to scream, especially when Fabrizio asked Father if he should go to the police and Father told him he should.'

'Why did that anger you particularly?'

'Because then a connection would exist between my sister and Maryam through Fabrizio,' she said. 'I was afraid that Lobna would become a suspect.'

'You knew she'd killed Maryam,' İkmen said.

'Yes, but I didn't want her punished! What she did was understandable, but I knew you people wouldn't see it that way!'

Also, İkmen inferred, she wanted her sister all to herself.

'Fabrizio left, and it was then that I confronted Father Esposito,' Mina said. 'I asked him why he'd told Fabrizio to go to the police. I said it would do no good in terms of finding out who killed Maryam.'

'But Father Esposito disagreed.'

'I asked him to call Fabrizio and tell him he'd made a mistake,' she said. 'But he said it was Fabrizio's duty to report what he knew. I begged him. And it was then that I saw his face change. As if he'd suddenly seen why I was asking him to do this. He took my hand, saying he wanted to talk to me, that he'd do me no harm but I had to speak honestly to him. I was already angry, and I had Lobna's stick in my hand . . .'

'You hit him?'

'A lot,' she said. 'I didn't know at the time. I just wanted him to shut up and do what I asked. It was only when I'd finished that I saw . . .'

'He didn't put up a fight?'

'No!' she said. 'He was the kindest and gentlest of men. And I killed him.'

'And Father Wojtulewicz?' İkmen said.

'He wouldn't shut up. I didn't want Lobna to know what I'd done with our father's stick, and he just went on and on and I could see she was confused.' She looked up into İkmen's eyes. 'If he'd just left the stick where he found it . . .'

'Where you'd put it?'

'Everything would have been all right,' she said. 'But I think he must have realised something. He must have seen or heard . . .' She shrugged. 'Nobody noticed him a lot of the time. Old men and middle-aged women, we're invisible, you know.'

# Chapter 31

'Papa?'

It was only İbrahim, but Silvio was annoyed that any of his family still had keys.

'What do you want?' he said.

The young man walked into the de Mango chapel and frowned. His father wasn't drunk, but he looked unkempt. His beard was full of . . . stuff. Food, maybe? But then he was thinner than ever, so probably not. He wore the same clothes he'd worn at Maryam's funeral.

'Mum says that you want to be on your own,' İbrahim said.

'I do. Which is why I'm wondering why you're here.'

İbrahim sat down. He'd never felt comfortable in this ornate and floridly Italian room.

'Because we miss you,' he said. 'Mum especially.'

'Your mother's happier with her own people and her own family,' Silvio said.

'No she's not! Grandma is driving her crazy, talking about getting Sara married off.'

'Sara'll be up for that.'

'Dad!'

'Sara's a religious bigot. She hates me,' Silvio said.

'No she doesn't!'

'And you and your brother!'

'That's not true!' İbrahim said.

'Oh no? So why'd you all gang up on me then, eh?' Silvio

310

said. 'It was always you lot against me – and Maryam in recent years. You, all of you, over to see your grandparents and your toxic uncles in Fatih. Praying and fasting, and then your mother covered her head . . .'

'We're Muslims, Dad,' İbrahim said. 'It's what we do. It's what you agreed to when you married Mum. Now that we know the truth, I can understand about you and Maryam.'

'You don't need me, boy,' Silvio said.

'Yes we do! We all know that Mevlüt is on bonzai, we know that Sara is turning into . . . something.'

'Ask your uncles about that,' Silvio said.

'Our uncles mean nothing to us! They're tossers, the pair of them. Going on about jihad. All they ever do is talk and sneer and try to be what they're not. You accused me of looking at jihadi websites, but that was only because I was trying to inform myself about this nonsense. You and Mum always taught us to question . . .'

'I can't do anything about Mevlüt,' Silvio said. 'He hates me.'

'No he doesn't. He's trying to get your attention,' İbrahim said. 'We all are. You turned away from us, Dad. When Mum covered her head and started seeing our uncles again, you should have told those bastards to fuck off and mind their own business. But you didn't; you dug yourself into your past and you took Maryam with you.'

'Only because you rejected us.'

'And here you go again, not taking any responsibility for anything!' İbrahim stood up. 'You think I want to live in Fatih with my grandparents? You think any of us feel at home there? Mevlüt's bonzai habit has got worse since Mum took us there because he's so unhappy. If you don't do something about it, Sara will be married off to some cretin who will beat her!'

İbrahim may have been wrong, but for a moment he thought he saw a flicker of regret or even a change of heart on his father's face. But then Silvio dashed his hopes.

'Well, maybe I don't want you,' he said. 'Maybe I'm happier and better off with my own company. Had you thought of that? Because that is the reality, İbrahim. I want to be alone and I don't want any of you to visit me from now on. I wish you no ill-will, but this family is finished. It is at an end. We will take different roads now and that is as it should be.'

Çetin İkmen managed to make it down to the car park before he had to sit down on the low wall behind the canteen.

Süleyman said, 'Are you all right?'

İkmen lit a cigarette and dragged a hand down the side of his face. They'd just spent an hour with Commissioner Ozer. He'd been pleased that between them they had solved both the Maryam de Mango murder and that of Father Esposito. But after a day characterised by yet another killing, as well as some disturbing results from their respective interrogations, they were both exhausted. Especially İkmen.

'I'm just tired,' he said.

'I'll drive you home,' Süleyman said.

'I can't leave the car . . .'

'I'll pick you up in the morning too.'

İkmen looked up at him and smiled.

'Come on,' Süleyman said. 'Fatma Hanım won't be able to sleep until you're safely at home.'

İkmen stood up and walked slowly towards Süleyman's car.

When they were both inside, Süleyman started the engine and turned to the older man. 'Can I ask why you requested a meeting with the Commissioner tomorrow? Processing the Amara sisters is now up to us and the Public Prosecutor. Ozer is out of the picture.'

He thought he knew. If what Gonca had told him about what Teker had said was true.

As he began to manoeuvre out of the car park, he heard İkmen sigh.

'Çetin?'

He sighed again. Then he said, 'I can tell you, but only if you promise not to tell my wife I told you first. Or Dr Sarkissian.'

Süleyman toyed with the idea of feigning complete ignorance, but then decided he was just too tired.

'I promise,' he said. 'But I think I know what it is anyway. Teker spoke to Gonca . . .'

'Tomorrow I will resign,' İkmen said. 'I don't want to join poor Teker in the hell she's going through at the moment.'

'You know?'

He nodded. 'What I'm doing is a gamble. I know that my resignation is what is wanted, but whether they'll let me get away with my pension and my liberty, I don't know.'

'They have to give you your pension!'

He laughed. 'Mehmet, they don't have to do anything.' His face dropped. 'But even if they do take it, I can work. And if they lock me up, the apartment is paid for and the kids won't see Fatma starve. What is happening in our police force isn't right. People are interfering with what we do.'

'I don't think it's right either.'

'Yes, but at the moment, you're the golden Ottoman boy. They won't do anything to you.'

'I know,' Süleyman said. 'And that's hateful too. I'm not an Ottoman. They're all dead and gone. I'm not a neo-Ottoman either, because to revive all that is also to revive the mistakes the Empire made, and they were legion.'

'You mustn't say that,' İkmen said. 'I'm lucky, I don't have either young children or elderly parents, but you have both.'

'I know.'

They drove past the darkened Grand Bazaar. Silent and deserted, the world's greatest market played host only to street cats, the odd dog and a few homeless men drinking, probably,

313

moonshine vodka. A lot of people had stills now that the government had hiked up the tax on alcohol.

'I will miss you badly,' Süleyman said.

'And I you. But we're friends,' İkmen said. 'We always will be. And I'll need you to look after Kerim Bey for me. I am going to recommend his promotion, but . . .'

'He's not quite the modern type?' Süleyman said.

'You could put it that way.'

'I could also put it to you, Çetin, whether you think it's a good idea to raise Kerim's profile,' Süleyman said.

İkmen frowned. 'What do you mean?'

'I mean, so far, his homosexuality has been kept a secret . . .'

'You know?' İkmen said. As far as he was concerned, he was the only person on the force who knew about Kerim.

'I'm a detective, Çetin,' Süleyman said. 'You taught me, remember?'

They smiled at each other. Then Süleyman said, 'I will take care of Kerim Bey.'

When they arrived outside İkmen's apartment, they sat together in silence for a moment. Before İkmen got out, he said, 'I'm seeing Ozer at eleven. Can we get together with our two boys in my office at nine? I think we all need to talk about what happened today.'

'Of course,' Süleyman said.

He drove home with tears in his eyes. İkmen had always been there for him. İkmen, in many ways, was İstanbul policing. What was he going to do without him? And how was he going to manage a future that seemed so very precarious?

İkmen walked into his kitchen and went to take his one bottle of brandy out of the cupboard underneath the sink, but then stopped. His wife was a good Muslim woman; he owed it to her to be sober when he told her. He shut the cupboard door.

'Çetin?'

She was behind him, her long grey hair loose down her back, wearing the thickest nightdress known to man. He went to her, took her in his arms and kissed her. She, like he, was old. She had varicose veins and operation scars and she was overweight, but she was still the most beautiful woman in the world. She was the woman with whom he'd shared a life, a home and a passion that had produced nine children.

As he held her, he said, 'Tomorrow I'm going to resign.'

He felt her sigh as if with relief, and then she said, 'Thank God.'

Arto Sarkissian laid a sheet over the body and took off his plastic gloves. The old priest had died from a single stab wound to the gut. He'd bled out, a process that had been assisted by the fact that he had been taking warfarin for a heart condition. There had been nothing Çetin İkmen could have done to save him.

He looked at the paperwork on his bench that had accompanied the corpse. Father Wojtulewicz was a Polish citizen and so, he imagined, his body would have to be repatriated to Warsaw. The Polish consul had been informed, but as far as Dr Sarkissian was concerned, the body could be retrieved immediately. There was no mystery here. A woman had stabbed him in full view of many people, including police officers, and he had died.

Arto removed his lab coat and threw it into the laundry basket. He wondered how Çetin İkmen was getting on. The inspector had witnessed a murder and he was having to deal with Teker's resignation. It was said that her replacement was pleasant. But that didn't mean much. Pleasant to whom? And if Teker had been arrested, had that been on this new man's orders?

Arto, though a man of science and rationality, was experiencing a feeling that he knew his friend İkmen had often. Cold, irrational dread. When İkmen had those feelings, it usually presaged some sort of disaster. But then he was the son of a witch; he felt such movements in the universe. But what did it mean when felt by an overweight Armenian scientist?

# Chapter 32

'So Mina Amara killed Father Esposito because she lost her temper with him?' Omer Mungun said.

'Yes.'

'And then she stayed in the church with his body all night?'

'She knew about the security cameras,' Kerim Gürsel said. 'She had to; she was in and out of St Anthony's all the time. She says her sister didn't know she was out all night because she'd gone to bed. But I don't know . . .'

The two men had, as instructed by Süleyman, arrived at İkmen's office with cardboard cups of posh coffee and a bag of börek provided by Kerim's wife, Sinem. Their superiors had yet to appear and so they were using the time to plug the gaps in each other's knowledge about their recent investigations.

'The two of them knew so much about each other and also so little,' Omer said. 'Lobna Amara never told her sister about the abortion she had when she was a teenager. She didn't tell anyone, including her ex-husband. Or the father of the child.'

'Silvio de Mango, right?'

'Yes.'

'What probably appals me more than anything else is that Mina saw her sister kill Maryam de Mango and did nothing,' Kerim said. 'She didn't know why she'd killed her and, it seems, didn't want to know. How can you let even a relative get away with murder? How can you not want to know why it happened?'

Omer shrugged. 'Lobna planned it,' he said. 'She set out to kill Maryam to punish the two men she felt had used and abused her. Maryam's pregnancy was the last straw. I don't think she really hated her; it was those men she hated.'

'And Mina loves her sister,' Kerim said. 'Her own married life was something of a car crash, as far as I can tell, and so when Lobna came home to her, she became her whole life. Then Lobna fell ill, and for Mina her role became even more prominent.'

'Lobna found it stifling.'

'I'm sure she did,' Kerim said.

Omer sat down. 'You must've felt terrible when the old priest died.'

'I did.' Kerim shook his head. 'Even with both of us pushing down on the wound, he just bled out. It was as if his blood was made of water. Çetin Bey bought us new shirts so we could go in to see the Commissioner without looking as if we'd just been shot.'

'How was he? The Commissioner?'

Kerim shrugged. 'I don't know,' he said. 'Very sympathetic on the face of it, but . . . I don't know how to put it really except to say that I think he's the sort of man who will either dismiss you or promote you. I get the impression his opinions do not have shades of grey.'

'Unlike Teker.'

'Right.' Kerim lowered his voice. 'Do you know whether it's true that she's been arrested?'

'Corruption, they say,' Omer said. 'I don't believe it.'

'Nor me.' Kerim paused. 'Do you think it will involve us?'

'I don't know,' Omer said. 'Who knows anything these days?'

The door to İkmen's office opened and he and Süleyman came in.

'Good morning, gentlemen,' İkmen said. He smiled. But

Süleyman looked grey and red-eyed and stressed. As if he hadn't slept.

The Bishop took Father Colombo's hands in his.

'Would you like to be assigned another parish, Father?' he said. 'Given the circumstances, it can be arranged.'

They were at Atatürk airport, where Father Colombo was waiting to board a flight to Sicily along with the body of Father Esposito.

'I don't know at the moment,' the young man said. 'I need to think.'

'Which is why I think you should go on to Rome for a few days after the funeral,' Bishop Montoya said. 'Spend some time with your family.'

'Thank you, Your Grace.'

'I will assist Father da Mosto in the interim,' the Bishop said. 'And we have also been assigned a priest from Argentina who will help us out for a few weeks. Sadly, he doesn't speak Turkish, but he does speak Italian and so we must be grateful.'

When his flight was called, Father Colombo kissed the Bishop's hand and left. Alone with his thoughts at last, Bishop Montoya wondered whether he'd ever see the young priest again. He'd realised some time ago that old Father Wojtulewicz was the sort of man who saw everything and said little. That was, tragically, what had eventually got him killed. But Montoya himself was no slouch when it came to knowing what was happening around him.

Young Father Colombo was a good lad. But at some point he'd have to choose between the Church and his sexuality. The Bishop hoped he would make the right choice.

Kerim and Omer had been stunned. Süleyman had looked, if İkmen didn't know him better, as if he'd been crying all night.

Now the only significant person left to tell was this man to whom he'd just handed his resignation letter.

Ozer read it without comment while İkmen stood. Eventually he said, 'Please sit down, Inspector.'

İkmen sat.

'This is something of a shock,' Ozer said as he pointed to the letter. 'I do hope it has nothing to do with the resignation of my predecessor?'

'Not directly, no, sir,' İkmen said. 'I had a good working relationship with Commissioner Teker, but . . .'

'You feel you can't work with me?'

He did, but he couldn't say so. 'No,' he said. 'It's just that at this point in my career, to learn a whole new way of working.'

'You would not be required to work any differently to how you have worked before, Inspector,' Ozer said.

They both knew he was lying. İkmen could see it on his face. He smiled.

'I could and maybe should have retired some years ago.'

'Oh no!'

İkmen had seen men in turbans and robes crowding into Ozer's office that morning. He'd once seen them trying to book an appointment with Teker. But she'd always instructed the front desk to tell such people she was out.

'I anticipate there will be no problem with my pension . . .'

'Of course not! You have been a very valuable member of the force, Çetin Bey. Now you must, quite rightly, get your reward.'

Ozer had done the 'sorry you're going' expression, but now he looked relaxed, as if a weight had been lifted from his shoulders. Inside, İkmen knew he was gleeful. He was, with no bother at all, getting rid of someone who was a dinosaur.

'And when would you like to leave?' Ozer said.

İkmen had thought about this. He'd talked to both his wife and, first thing that morning, Arto Sarkissian about it.

320

'Immediately,' he said.

'Oh.'

Now *that* had caught him off guard. Although İkmen had thought it might elicit more delight. Why hadn't it?

'Sir?'

'Oh well, I thought you—'

'Sergeant Gürsel is a very capable officer,' İkmen said. 'He can certainly take over my duties on an interim basis. And as you know, we have no outstanding cases. Not as of yesterday.'

'No . . .'

'I will complete any remaining paperwork today and—'

'Çetin Bey, you may be required to give evidence in the upcoming investigation into my predecessor,' Ozer said.

'Why?'

The Commissioner looked up. 'Why? You worked with her for many years.'

'Yes,' İkmen said. 'And not once did I ever have reason to believe that Commissioner Teker was corrupt. I can make a statement to that effect for you today.'

'Well, that's very . . .' Clearly this had taken him by surprise too.

'I can do it now.'

Ozer waved a hand to dismiss his suggestion. 'That won't be necessary,' he said. 'We will contact you when we need your input.'

'And in the meantime you will arrange with personnel for my pension to be forthcoming?'

He bowed his head in agreement, but he didn't say anything.

When İkmen left Ozer's office, he wondered how long it would take for his pension to become contingent upon his saying what they wanted him to about Teker.

Silvio knew he had to eat something, but he really couldn't be bothered. Ayşegül had phoned him that afternoon, three times, but he'd ignored her. She wouldn't come round; neither would the kids and neither would Fabrizio, if he valued his life. It was still very strange to think that Lobna had killed Maryam. It was awful.

He turned her face so that she was looking at him and said, 'I am so sorry that you had to die for my sins. But that does mean you are truly a saint. Like Christ, you die for the filthy lives of others. I am so proud of you.'

If he'd known all those years ago that Lobna was pregnant, would he have asked her to keep the baby? He knew the answer to that and it made him cringe. What had he ever done to deserve a saint like Maryam in his life?

Not that she hadn't suffered; she had. Saints did. Or rather the great ones did. She had sacrificed, she had suffered and now she was also exhibiting another saintly trait, one he had known she would. She was incorruptible. He stroked her face gently with his finger. Her skin was as soft and supple as it had been in life. The idiotic policeman İkmen had tried to find her by smell. But she would never smell. He would never have found her either.

His great-grandfather, who had constructed the building, had always said that Levantine or not, a man born of a Venetian was always a Venetian. And the de Mangos had once been a very powerful family of Venice. They had been the sort of family who knew how their powerful republic worked, which was why they had ventured outside it to trade and make it richer. But they had also known that to preserve its strength, Venice had to keep its secrets. Only when those started to emerge did the republic fall.

Maintained via oaths and punishments, secret courts in secret rooms and arcane ceremonies performed in distant cemeteries, the Republic of Venice, ruled by the doges, was a lesson in both concealment and suspicion that Silvio's grandfather had taken very seriously.

322

'Never trust the Turks' had been one of his mantras. And to that end he had built a small hidden room behind the altar in the family chapel, designed to sound solid when tapped. Not even the Turks' expensive heat-seeking and scanning equipment had been able to find it. Or her.

And now that he was alone with her, to hell with the Holy See and whatever they thought. She was his saint and he was going to be with her forever.

## One week later

Kerim Gürsel handed Omer Mungun a small box.

'Now that you're thirty and a proper grown-up, you really should have this,' he said.

Omer opened the box and found a gold tie pin. It was in the shape of a snake. For a moment he felt a bit alarmed. Did Kerim know that he and his sister were adherents of the ancient religion of the snake goddess?

But then Kerim said, 'I hope you like the snake motif. I think it looks stylish. The others they had were golf clubs and tennis racquets and things that were just not you. Oh, and it's gold.'

Omer hugged his colleague. 'Thank you, Inspector Kerim Bey,' he said.

The rest of the people around the Munguns' table clapped their hands. Peri, Omer's sister, had got her way and he was having a birthday party with Çetin İkmen, Mehmet Süleyman, Kerim Gürsel, the Munguns' cousin Beril, who also lived in İstanbul, and their new neighbour Asra.

Of course the whole thing was Peri's way of getting her brother in contact with Asra. Some boys, as Peri had told Çetin İkmen, were far too nervous around girls for their own good. Some boys had to have birthday parties to get them out of their shells.

Peri and cousin Beril had spent all day cooking, and even as the first guest had arrived, the dining table had already been groaning with kebab, hamsi, fasulye, pide, fruit, salad and many different varieties of rice, bulgur wheat and potato. They had even brewed up a cauldron of the thick, viscous mirra coffee native to their eastern Turkish city of Mardin. And of course there was alcohol.

As İkmen helped himself to a glass of rakı, he said to Kerim, 'How does it feel to be in charge, Kerim Bey?'

Kerim smiled. 'It's an honour, sir,' he said.

'Çetin.'

'Sir?'

'Call me Çetin. I'm the public now, and your friend,' İkmen said.

Kerim winced slightly. 'Çetin. Well, yours are big shoes to fill. And of course I miss you. We all do.'

'I will second that,' Süleyman said. And for a few seconds the room went silent until Beril, unaware of the significance of the moment, put on Tarkan's latest CD. The slightly maudlin spell broken, people began to speak of other things again. Much of the conversation revolved around what İkmen was doing with himself now he was no longer employed. Omer wondered whether he spent all day in old-fashioned coffee houses, while Kerim claimed to have seen him walking beside the Bosphorus. Only İkmen and Süleyman knew that neither of these things reflected the truth.

Ozer had pressed for a statement about Teker, and İkmen was having some problems putting him off. He had not yet received any sort of notification about his pension.

Peri Mungun came in with yet another plate of hot food and put it down on the table.

'Please sit down, everyone!' she said. 'Food that is hot must be eaten hot.'

People began to sit. But Peri pulled İkmen away. 'Not you,' she said. 'I need you in the kitchen for a moment, please.'

'Ah!'

He suspected that he, as guest of honour, would be required to bring out a special present or cake for Omer.

But he was wrong.

Peri Mungun, her face suddenly set and serious, lowered her voice.

'Çetin Bey,' she said, 'you know you've always had to fight for justice for some people the law chooses to ignore? Well, I have a colleague at the hospital who has a problem with her ex-husband. She thinks he may be planning to have her killed. He's tried to strangle her himself many times. But no one listens. As far as I can see, you are her only hope . . .'